Praise for Michael Ennis's

THE MALICE OF FORTUNE

"A stunning work of historical fiction, and equally a page-turning murder mystery. The depth of research, the compelling characterizations, and the addictively readable storytelling all combine to produce a novel of the highest accomplishment." —Vincent Lam,
Scotiabank Giller Prize–winning author of
Bloodletting and Miraculous Cures and *The Headmaster's Wager*

"Machiavelli and [Da Vinci] aren't just another Holmes and Watson. What Ennis has created is a scenario with two Sherlock Holmeses, each applying his unique approach to crime-solving in an age when even the most fundamental forensics techniques would be regarded as heresy."
—*The Dallas Morning News*

"A thrilling whodunit." —*Entertainment Weekly*

"*The Malice of Fortune* captures the glorious and gritty details of Renaissance Italy in a propulsive story. Ennis has achieved a great accomplishment: historical fiction that places us right into the characters' present." —Matthew Pearl,
author of *The Dante Club* and *The Technologists*

"Ennis brilliantly re-creates the complex politics of early-sixteenth-century Italy in this absorbing and intelligent thriller that teams Leonardo da Vinci with Niccolò Machiavelli." —*Publishers Weekly* (starred review)

"Ranks among the best. . . . Firmly rooted in history, as recorded in Machiavelli's writings."
—*San Antonio Express-News*

MICHAEL ENNIS

THE MALICE OF FORTUNE

♦ ——————————————————————————————— ♦

Michael Ennis studied history at the University of California, Berkeley; taught art history at the University of Texas, Austin; and developed museum programs as a Rockefeller Foundation Fellow. He is the author of two historical novels, *Duchess of Milan* and *Byzantium*. He has written for *Esquire* and *Architectural Digest* and is a regular contributor to *Texas Monthly*. He lives in Dallas with his television producer wife, Ellen, and their daughter, Arielle.

Also by Michael Ennis

Milan

DUCHY OF MILAN

REPUBLIC
OF
VENICE

Genoa

Mantua

Po

Venice

Ferrara

River

LIGURIAN SEA

Bologna

Imola

Ravenna

ROMAGNA

Pisa

REPUBLIC

Cesena

Florence

OF FLORENCE

Rimini

ADRIATIC SEA

Siena

Pesaro

Sinigaglia

PAPAL

STATES

TYRRHENIAN SEA

Rome

ITALY

KINGDOM

IN 1502

Capua

Naples

OF

NAPLES

N

THE
MALICE OF FORTUNE

A Novel of the Renaissance

MICHAEL ENNIS

EMBLEM

McCLELLAND & STEWART

Cloth edition published 2012
Emblem edition published 2013

Published simultaneously in the United States by Anchor Books,
a division of Random House, Inc., New York.

Emblem is an imprint of McClelland & Stewart,
a division of Random House of Canada Limited
Emblem and colophon are registered trademarks of McClelland & Stewart,
a division of Random House of Canada Limited

Library and Archives Canada Cataloguing in Publication

Ennis, Michael (Michael B.)
The malice of fortune / Michael Ennis.

ISBN 978-0-7710-3079-6

I. Title.
PS3555.N63M35 2013   813'.54   C2012-906083-6

Illustrations by Michael Ennis
Book design by Maria Carella
Cover design by Kelly Hill
Cover Image: © Bettmann / CORBIS

Printed in the United States of America

McClelland & Stewart,
a division of Random House of Canada Limited
One Toronto Street, Suite 300
Toronto, Ontario
M5C 2V6
www.mcclelland.com

1 2 3 4 5   17 16 15 14 13

In memory of
Charles Livingstone Ennis

ITALY IN 1502

Excerpted from *Cesare Borgia: A Study of the Renaissance*
William Harrison Addington
London, 1903

istory seldom presents a paradox more striking than
Italy at the outset of the sixteenth century. As the
Renaissance reached new heights of splendor and
innovation—Leonardo, Michelangelo, and Machiavelli
now shared the stage—Italy foundered in a morass of
political treachery and chaos. Fragmented into dozens of autonomous
entities, varying from such formidable nation-states as the Republic
of Venice to myriad small city-states, the Italian peninsula became a
battleground contested by powerful family dynasties, mercenary warlords
known as *condottieri*, and the armies of foreign monarchs.

Amidst this endemic turmoil, the Italian people despaired of finding a
remedy in God and the Church, and instead regarded themselves as subject
to the goddess Fortune (a revival of the ancient Roman cult of *Fortuna*),
personified in both literature and daily discourse as the capricious and
ill-intentioned governess of all human affairs. Even the most enlightened
intellects of the age were not immune to this belief in the tyranny of
Fortune. Leonardo da Vinci opposed her anarchy with a new vision of the
natural world, where order was established by mathematics and common
principles. To similar purpose, Niccolò Machiavelli examined ancient
and modern history, bent on deriving fundamental principles of human
behavior, in the hope that this new science would allow Italy's hapless
leaders to anticipate crises and prepare for Fortune's onslaughts . . .

The year 1502 represented the historic moment when the intellect
of man began to strike back against Fortune's malice and might. This

insurrection of human will and reason, which would alter the subsequent course of civilization, did not find its spark in the familiar capitals of the Renaissance but rather in a neglected region of Italy known as the Romagna, an elongated, fertile plain bounded by the Adriatic Sea and Apennine mountains. For generations only nominally a possession of the Roman Catholic Church (as one of the so-called Papal States), the Romagna had remained a collection of lawless fiefdoms, ceded to the rapacious local nobility by a succession of weak popes, until Rodrigo Borgia purchased the papacy in 1492. Assuming the name Pope Alexander VI, and declaring his intention to restore and expand the Church's worldly domains with deeds worthy of Alexander the Great, the Borgia pope filled his war chest by peddling Church offices and indulgences with unprecedented industry. Inexplicably, however, this shrewd and conniving judge of men vested his martial ambitions in a woefully inept illegitimate son, Juan Borgia, the Duke of Gandia, who led the armies of the Church to a series of humiliating defeats. Only when Juan of Gandia was murdered in 1497, in mysterious circumstances, did Pope Alexander find a suitable instrument in yet another papal bastard: Juan of Gandia's previously overlooked older brother, Cesare Borgia, transformed himself from an obscure cardinal into the celebrated "Duke Valentino" and reconquered the Romagna with extraordinary ingenuity and audacity. By 1502, no man in Europe inspired more hope among oppressed peoples or caused greater trepidation among tyrants . . .

Even as Valentino's conquests presaged a new Italy, he was compelled to achieve them with the assistance of a long-established evil, the *condottieri*. These mercenary generals well deserved their vile reputation, as they cynically contrived and perpetuated conflicts solely to finance lives of luxury and wanton pleasure; although such campaigns posed little risk to the "soldiers of fortune," they were exceedingly onerous for the peasantry in their paths, and the helpless populations of cities subject to bombardment, starvation, and pillage . . . Pope Alexander, however, disregarded a long history of personal enmity and employed the detested *condottieri* to hasten his own ambitions . . . The *condottieri*, observing firsthand Valentino's swift and unsparing consolidation of power in the Romagna, as well as his efforts to conscript and train his own citizen soldiers, apprehended an increasingly grave threat to their livelihoods, and their lives . . . In October

1502, the *condottieri* commenced large-scale armed assaults against papal strongholds in the Romagna.

Among Italy's many sovereign states, this blood feud imperiled none more imminently than the fledgling Republic of Florence. The Florentines had invested their civic genius in culture and commerce, and were all but indifferent to their own defense, even as the most capable of the *condottieri*, Vitellozzo Vitelli, declared a personal vendetta against them, his *casus belli* the Florentines' execution of his brother for treason in 1499 . . . Duke Valentino, better cognizant of the common enemy, offered Florence a mutual defense agreement . . .

Florence's leaders, notorious for vacillation and indecision, were reluctant to bind their fate to the Borgia. Refusing to send a full ambassador to Valentino's redoubt at the fortress city of Imola, in the heart of the Romagna, they instead dispatched a junior chancellery secretary, from whom they withheld any authority to negotiate terms, and who was instead instructed to delay the ever more impatient duke with glib promises and clever repartee. This Florentine envoy arrived in Imola on October 6, 1502, and he would place the events of the subsequent three months at the center of one of the signal works in the history of Western thought: Niccolò Machiavelli's *The Prince*. ◆

DRAMATIS PERSONAE

Pope Alexander VI (Rodrigo Borgia) History's most worldly and venal pope, Rodrigo Borgia bought the papacy in 1492, promising deeds and conquests worthy of Alexander the Great. As Pope Alexander, he ambitiously expanded the Church's temporal power under the aegis of his son Cesare (see Valentino), the most gifted of his seven acknowledged illegitimate children.

Agapito da Amelia Valentino's confidential secretary and official spokesman.

Antonio Benivieni The prominent Florentine physician who documented his many postmortem examinations in a collection, *De abditis nonnullis ac mirandis morborum et sanationum causis* (*The Hidden Causes of Disease*), regarded as the foundational work of scientific pathology.

Juan Borgia, Duke of Gandia (deceased) The murder of Pope Alexander's favorite son on June 14, 1497, was the most notorious crime of the Renaissance—and remained conspicuously unsolved as of the autumn of 1502.

Camilla Maid and attendant to the courtesan Damiata.

Damiata A cultured, highly desirable Roman courtesan of the class known as *cortigiana onesta*, or "honest courtesan," often interpreted more colloquially as "honest whore." Her relationship with the Duke of Gandia and her suspected role in his murder are matters of historical record. "Damiata," however, was almost certainly an alias.

OLIVEROTTO DA FERMO An orphan trained for the soldier's profession by Vitellozzo Vitelli, Oliverotto became lord of the city of Fermo after brutally usurping his uncle. He first served Valentino as a *condottiero* (mercenary general), then became instrumental in the conspiracy against him.

GIACOMO (GIAN GIACOMO CAPROTTI) Leonardo da Vinci's servant, apprentice, and companion. Adopted by Leonardo when he was ten years old, Giacomo was in his early twenties in 1502. His nickname "Salaì" meant "little devil."

GIOVANNI Damiata's young son, born in 1498.

FRANCESCO GUICCIARDINI The close friend and frequent correspondent to whom Machiavelli addresses his narrative. At the time of Machiavelli's writing (1527), he was lieutenant general of the armies of Pope Clement VII. Guicciardini would later become a pioneer of modern historical method as author of the classic *History of Italy*.

LEONARDO DA VINCI Officially designated as Duke Valentino's engineer general and architect, Leonardo was fifty years old in 1502. His map of Imola, drawn that year, is regarded as one of his most revolutionary works; presently in the collection of the Royal Library at Windsor Castle, it was the first map to have been made with precise measurements and the use of a magnetic compass, anticipating by centuries the advent of modern cartography.

RAMIRO DA LORCA A Borgia family retainer of long standing, Ramiro earned both respect and notoriety as the harsh military governor of the Romagna, before being assigned to less politically sensitive duties in the autumn of 1502.

NICCOLÒ MACHIAVELLI Machiavelli's official titles in 1502 were second chancellor of the Republic of Florence (a second-tier civil service position) and secretary to the Ten of War. Although he was the ranking Florentine diplomat at the court of Duke Valentino, Machiavelli had no authority to conduct direct negotiations and was regarded as nothing more than a mouthpiece for his government. He was thirty-three years old at the time, and would not write *The Prince* for another eleven years (1513).

MICHELOTTO (MICHELE DE COREGLIA) Valentino's most trusted intimate.

PAOLO ORSINI Scion of one of Italy's most powerful and ruthless families, Orsini became a leader of the *condottieri* who first worked for and then conspired against Valentino in 1502.

TOMMASO (TOMMASO DI GIOVANNI MASINI) A student of alchemy and other occult arts who frequently went by the alias Zoroastre, Tommaso joined Leonardo's entourage during the latter's long tenure (1482–99) at the court of Lodovico Sforza in Milan.

VALENTINO (CESARE BORGIA) Duke of the Romagna and captain general of the armies of the Holy Roman Church. Designated Duke of Valentinois by the French king in 1498 (in a deal that bought Louis XII a divorce), Pope Alexander's gifted bastard son was commonly known as Duke Valentino or, in a shorthand that spoke to his celebrity throughout Europe, simply Valentino.

VITELLOZZO VITELLI One of Italy's most experienced *condottieri* and maestro of a new technology—artillery—Vitellozzo essentially invented the modern infantry rifleman. He was Valentino's most effective subordinate prior to leading the conspiracy against him.

THE MALICE OF FORTUNE

The following narrative is based entirely on actual events.
All of the major characters are historical figures, and all of them
do exactly what the archival evidence tells us they did, exactly where and when
they did it. What history fails to tell us is how and why they did it.
And thereby hangs a tale. . . .

To Messer Francesco Guicciardini
Lieutenant general, statesman, and historian
9 January 1527

*M*agnificent One. I have sent you this great pile of pages in order to
provide a more faithful account of the final weeks of the year 1502, when the
condottieri violently conspired against Duke Valentino and his father, Pope
Alexander VI. As you know, my intimate witness of those events inspired
my little pamphlet, The Prince; what you do not know is that there was
considerably more to the entire matter than I have ever allowed. Hence I
submit to you this lengthy "confession," with the hope that you will not judge
me—or attempt to write your own history—until you have read these pages
entirely. Only then can you begin to grasp the terrifying nature of the secret I
deliberately buried, let us say, between the lines of The Prince.

You will find here a narrative divided into four parts, all but one in my
own hand. The exception is the account that precedes my own, authored
twenty-four years ago by a lady I knew as Damiata. Over the span of scarcely
a fortnight, this learned woman recorded in every particular a number of
conversations and occurrences that I am certain will intrigue you. She wrote
not only to indemnify herself against the accusations that were made against
her but also to provide a last testament to her boy, Giovanni, although she
intended that it be withheld from him until he was a young man of sufficient
maturity to understand both the truth and the lies.

My dear Francesco, I should remind you that Fortune achieves her worst
ends by relying on our own willful blindness, as we proceed upon her twisting
and obscure paths. When you read these pages, you will marvel at how cleverly
Fortune led us on a perilous road to the Devil's doorstep. And you will see how
blind we remained, even as we stared into the face of evil.

Your
Niccolò Machiavelli
Author of histories, comedies, and tragedies

PART ONE

BE CAREFUL OF
THE TRUTH YOU SEEK

Rome and Imola: November 19 – December 8, 1502

I

My dearest, most darling Giovanni,

We lived in two rooms in the Trastevere. This district of Rome lies across the Tiber from the old Capitol Hill, on the same side of the river as the Vatican and the Castel Sant'Angelo. Gathered around the Santa Maria church, the Trastevere was a village unto itself, a labyrinth of wineshops, inns, tanneries, dyers' vats, and falling-down houses that were probably old when Titus Flavius returned in triumph after conquering Judea; many of the Jews who lived there claimed to be descended from his captives. But our neighbors came from everywhere: Seville, Corsica, Burgundy, Lombardy, even Arabia. It was a village where everyone was different, so no one stood out.

Our rooms were on the ground floor of an ancient brick house off a narrow, muddy alley, with little shops and other houses crowding in on every side, their balconies and galleries so close overhead that we always seemed to go out into the night, even at noon. I kept my books and antique cameos hidden, displaying nothing that might tempt a thief—or reveal who I had formerly been. But we whitewashed the walls once a year and always swept the tiles, and you never slept on a straw mattress but always on good cotton stuffing; there was never a day we didn't have flowers or fresh greens on our tiny table—or wanted for bacon in our beans.

In the evening, before you slept and I went out, I would read Petrarch to you or tell you stories. That was what we were doing on our last night together—19 November, *anno Domini* 1502. I showed you this bronze medallion stamped with a portrait of Nero Claudius Caesar, about whom I recited tales I had read in Tacitus when I was little more than a girl. Hearing of his crimes, you gave Signor Nero a very stern look and wagged your finger at his engraved visage, telling him, "Even an emperor does not have lice . . . lice . . ."

"An emperor does not have lice?" I asked, which made you frown like a German banker, so I said, "I think the word you are reaching for is license."

"*Sì*, Mama, license. Even an emperor does not have license to be so evil." Your sweet cricket voice was so grave. "Therefore, we shall punish Signor Nero. No dessert! His sugared almond will be given to Ermes."

Do you remember Ermes, my eternal love? He was our darling Tenerife, who adored you as much as you adored him. When you said his name he wiggled his woolly rump and lapped at your precious hand with his little pink tongue.

Camilla sat on the bed with us, sewing patches on her skirt. She was my dearest friend and most devoted servant, who took you on a journey to the piazza in front of Santa Maria every day, when I could not go out, and slept next to you every night, when darkness freed me to do my business. Your *zia* Camilla was not your real auntie, but she was my sister in everything but blood, and if one day I did not come home, I trusted her to keep you safe and see that you became a man. Thin as a birch and taller than I am, our sweet Camilla had a pale, grave face, her eyes and mouth dark smudges, which made her seem like a lovely ghost, though she was as strong as a Turk wrestler. She was born in Naples, and nature made her hair as raven-hued as I dye mine now.

I could describe every detail of that tiny room in the Trastevere, my most adored and most precious son, yet I could never describe the love that surrounded you there. And now I have no greater fear than that we will become separated by an ocean of time, which no words can cross.

Perhaps all you will remember of me is that I did not come back for you.

An old Jew named Obadiah lived next door to us, above a noisy wineshop. He was a divine man, scarcely tall enough to look through a keyhole, who loved to discuss the works of Flavius Josephus and often arranged for me to purchase antiquities from dealers and *cavatori*—diggers—of his acquaintance. So when I heard the pounding on our ancient oak door, it was not at all remarkable to find Obadiah there, although I was surprised at his urgency. His face was always like a marvelous drawing on old parchment, all the lines carefully marked in sepia ink. Yet as I looked down at him peering around the side of our door, that yellowed parchment seemed to bleach out in an instant.

The three men were in our house even before poor Obadiah could sag and fall to the ground; they made certain we saw their saber and stilettos. But you weren't frightened, nor was Ermes, who rushed at them even before you did, barking like a woman screaming until the man with the saber swatted him with his blade and our precious dog flew against the wall like a bundle of wool. A heartbeat later you collided with this man's legs and at once he clapped his hand to your mouth and directed the tip of his blade at your little belly. The invaders had entered without a word, but now this man, who had only one seeing eye—the other was like a poached egg—said with a coarse Neapolitan accent, "We'll slit the boy like a November hog."

I wanted to say, "I don't believe the man who sent you will permit you to kill his grandson." But if your grandfather had sent these men, he was very shrewd, because they sufficiently resembled common thieves that I could not be certain they weren't. So I had to say, "I'll show you where my things are."

The second man came around behind me and shoved the wooden gag in my mouth; it is a miracle he did not knock out my teeth. He tied the leather cord behind my head so tight that the knot felt like the butt of a knife jammed into my skull. The wood sucked all the moisture from my tongue and I could only watch as the third man gagged Camilla. I will never forget the look in her eyes just before he pushed her down on the mattress.

The one-eyed man had started out the door with you, clutching you to his breast, you kicking and flailing until he said, "Do you want me to kill your mama?" Though you were not even five years old, you were clever enough to at once cease your protest. And by then you could see the body of dear old Obadiah lying outside our door, his shirt sopping with blood as red as a cardinal's hat. He had died trying to warn us.

For my part, I bolted to the door, preferring to perish in pursuit of you than share our beloved Camilla's fate. I was not forced back into the room; after the second man grabbed me by the hair, he proceeded to drag me alongside you and his accomplice, pricking his knife into my ribs whenever I struggled. The flock of chickens that roosted on the balcony next door clucked and chortled as we passed beneath them.

♦

It did not take us long to arrive at your grandfather's residence, even though we circled around the back. As we came up through the garden mazes, the basilica and palazzo rose like mountains above us, lamps flickering in dozens of windows. Within moments we were inside that great edifice, glimpses of gilded furniture and new frescoes rushing past, the brightly colored patterns of the tapestries and Oriental rugs flying at me like confetti at Carnival. The entire establishment reeked of pleasure: smoldering censers, fresh orange and rose water, roasted meats, musk, wax candles, and spilled wine.

Halfway through our passage two more men, hooded like monks, took you from your one-eyed captor. I could say nothing to you in farewell, merely issuing terrible, strangled sounds that nearly choked me, until I thought a merciful God would take me away. But of all the dwellings in this sinful world, our Immaculate Lord is least present in the house where you and I had just become captives.

Light from an open doorway burst before me, as brilliant as fireworks. Laughter leapt out at me as mercilessly as Caesar's assassins when he entered the senate. The room I was shoved into was the big *sala reale*, most of the floor transformed into a forest of brass lampstands. In a scene our Dante never thought to invent, two dozen or so women, on their hands and knees, crawled like pigs rooting for acorns, bare breasts swaying and naked white bottoms quivering, some squatting in an effort to retrieve the prizes—chestnuts—strewn upon the Turkish carpets. In accordance with the rules of the house, they were not allowed to use their hands or mouths—or even their toes.

The master of that evening's quaint ceremony was your grandfather, Rodrigo Borgia, though the rest of Christendom calls him *il papa*: Pope Alexander VI. His Holiness was seated upon the raised wooden dais, behind a table covered with cloth of gold, the saltcellars arrayed atop it in a symposium of miniature gold and silver gods and goddesses. The silvered sugar desserts, in the shapes of deer, dolphins, unicorns, and lions, crawled among the little deities like the disgorged cargo of some confectionary ark.

As I was dragged toward the master of the house, the men at the table stared with eyes reddened from the smoke, not a jacket remaining on anyone—they were down to shirts and hose, or breeches, all those bald or tonsured heads glistening. Your grandfather's white silk shirt was so wet that it had become a milky membrane, clinging to his great chest and sagging old-man's breasts. His skull gleamed like a brass bowl, the rim of this vessel a fringe of gray-tipped chestnut hair that fell over his ears. I had not seen him in five years, but it was as if that time had been only an illusion.

Leaning back in his immense gilt chair, he offered me his scrutiny, his pupils as black and empty as the holes drilled in a marble bust. He tilted his head slightly, his magnificent predator's beak pointing the way back out.

◆

I did not have to be carried far, just around two corners. Once we entered your grandfather's apartments, I even knew precisely which of these lavishly frescoed rooms would witness my travail. Called the Hall of Saints, it was empty save for a few chairs and sideboards; in the center remained a brazier, a small intarsia table, and a single armchair, upholstered in scarlet velvet embroidered with little gold bulls, the symbol of your family.

Once I was tied upon this throne, I quickly received my first visitor, your grandfather's master of artillery, Lorenzo Beheim—he of the treatises on dark magic and procedures to summon Satan. Beheim carried a wooden box such as physicians haul about. Placing this item on the table beside me, he opened it so that I could admire instruments that indeed looked like those used to explore the womb and extract a reluctant infant—tongs, hooks, picks, and pliers. As he brought the brazier closer, no doubt for his convenience when heating these devices, the reek of burning charcoal invaded my nostrils.

Having completed these preparations, he left.

Yet I was not entirely alone. The upper walls all around me were framed by massive gilded arches, and the painter Pinturicchio had filled each of the half-moon-shaped lunettes with tales of saints, their legends portrayed as extravagant ceremonies teeming with spectators. My chair had been placed so that I could look up at the lunette opposite the window, upon which the enormous *Disputation of Saint Catherine of Alexandria* had been painted in gorgeous peacock hues.

This view allowed me to renew my acquaintance with some of your grandfather's bastards. You see, Pinturicchio used all sorts of people at your grandfather's court as models for the characters in this tale, though in the short years since he finished his labor, time and Fortune had altered so much about them. At the center of this glorious pageant was Saint Catherine, presenting her defense of the Christian faith to the Emperor Maximinus and his colloquy of scholars. Saint Catherine was a perfect likeness of your aunt Lucrezia, the present Duchess of Ferrara, her hair falling in flaxen waves, her puckered mouth as red as a cherry, her cerulean gaze fixed on a dream. This portrait was more real than life, because when I knew Lucrezia, if ever she was caught in a momentary thought, she would at once show her perfect teeth, a smile intended to draw one's attention from the desperate hope in her eyes.

In my worst fears, my darling, you have come to know Lucrezia's expression; but if this is so, then perhaps you have an image in an imperfect mirror of your mama. Because it was often said, in those years when I was familiar with your family, that I looked enough like Madonna Lucrezia to be her older sister. I never thought so; your aunt's nose was smaller, her forehead less broad, her eyes a lighter tint. But perhaps now I share with your aunt Lucrezia the same sorrowful hope.

No less real than Lucrezia's portrait were the two figures at opposite sides of the scene. Your grandfather had intended his most cherished son, Juan Borgia, the Duke of Gandia, to serve as the model for the Emperor Maximinus. But Pinturicchio's vision had been less clouded by sentiment and he instead made another bastard son, Cesare Borgia, the face of this all-powerful sovereign. At the time the painting was done, Cesare had been twenty years old; he was still a cardinal of the Holy Roman Church and he still had his sister Lucrezia's delicate beauty. Yet Pinturicchio had given him a peculiar gaze, the dark green eyes staring down and away, fixed on something that could not be bound within the picture, as if Cesare were peering into a realm even the painter could not imagine.

Opposite Cesare, on the other end of the wall, Pinturicchio had placed Juan in the guise of a Turkish sultan, the sort of costume this most beloved son had indeed favored in life, a great linen turban around his head, his cape and loose trousers a tapestry of Oriental patterns. Juan was darker than his siblings—Cesare and Lucrezia are quite fair-complected—and in this portrait his gaze is predatory, a falcon's angry yet wary stare. In life, if Juan ever looked thus, it was a pose.

◆

My meditation on those fleet years that "carry us to death's sharp spear," as Petrarch would say, was at last interrupted by your grandfather. Beheim at his side, still in his sweaty shirt, His Holiness wore only sagging hose and scarlet slippers, the better to display his legs, which were still sturdy and well-shaped. He advanced to me with the graceful step of a much younger man, toes out as if his dance master were watching. Only when he was close enough to touch me could I see how much he had aged—the liver spots, the thin skin stretched taut over the great obstinate hump of his nose. But his lips were luxurious as ever, pursed delicately, as if he had just sipped a particularly fine wine and was trying to get the taste of it.

He nodded at Beheim, who removed a knife from the physician's box. I prayed for a quick end. But Beheim simply cut the cord that held my gag. My mouth was so dry that I couldn't spit out the wooden plug. Employing the point of his knife, Beheim gouged it loose.

Your grandfather leaned forward and stared at me with those

obsidian eyes. "Damiata. I always knew where you were." His voice was deep but his words hissed a bit, a whisper of his Spanish ancestry, even though the Borgia family—your family, *carissimo*—has been in Italy for generations. The snake in the grass. Or the serpent in the tree.

His fingers flicked at my hair; this gesture was not a caress but that of a stableboy examining the mane of a sick horse. "Dyeing your hair, hiding in some Jew's tavern . . ." He shook his head wearily. "I could have come for you at any time. Each breath you have taken in the last five years has been at my indulgence."

"You are the prince of indulgences, are you not?" I said. Your grandfather sold forgiveness from the altars of his churches like a whore selling candles on the street corner; the only crimes he would not pardon for a price were those against his person, or in aid of the Turk. "Perhaps you can even afford to absolve yourself. You murdered a blameless, dear old man at my house tonight. And your grandson's dear little pet." I did not want to tempt Fortune by speculating on Camilla's fate.

I thought he would strike me. Instead he turned his back and looked up at Juan, the *alla turca* Duke of Gandia, as if beseeching this most cherished son to restore the flesh to his own moldering bones. After a time your grandfather's heavy shoulders sagged and he turned his attention to the prophetic image of the son who yet lived: the Cesare Borgia who is now, as I write this, captain general of the armies of the Holy Roman Church, famed throughout Christendom as Valentino, Duke of the Romagna, the prodigy who threw off his cardinal's cap for a warrior's helmet, the vanquisher of tyrants and the savior of all Italy. The son who will enable your grandfather, His Holiness Pope Alexander VI, to conquer the Kingdoms of the World without rising from the Heavenly Throne of Saint Peter. Perhaps by the time you read this, that papal empire will have grown far beyond its present boundaries, to spread from the heart of Italy across Europe.

Indeed, if all my present fears come to pass, perhaps Fortune has already made you heir to that empire. But if that is so, then the Borgia have told you nothing about me but lies, save where the truth is worse.

♦

At last your grandfather interrupted his own meditation. "Juan was going to your house the night he was murdered. You alone were privy to that. You alone could have informed someone else."

I had sat at this pope's table often enough, and had observed his methods sufficiently, to know how well he crafted false accusations from undeniable fact. Having anticipated such an interrogation for more than five years, I replied, "If you are claiming that I betrayed Juan by revealing his route to my house that night, God and the Holy Mother know that it was far easier for his murderers to follow him from his mother's house near the Esquiline, where he had dined, as half of Rome knew. And you know as well as any man that the Orsini and the Vitelli had their knives out for him. They are the very *condottieri* who would profit most if the Borgia were erased from the earth."

Now, I should explain that we Italians have for several generations placed the very survival of our various states and principalities in the hands of these *condottieri*, a brotherhood of mercenary generals whose bands of thugs carry out, for a very dear price, the martial tasks the French king would assign to a vast army of men in permanent service, led by nobles who have sworn allegiance to him. Here in Italy, however, it is our fashion to hire the agents of our own destruction. These "soldiers of fortune" strut about like pimps in their suits of engraved armor, waging phony war among themselves only to pillage the livelihoods of helpless peasants, transferring their allegiances to whoever will offer the fattest contract. And the two families presently in command of this blood-sucking cabal are the Orsini and the Vitelli.

"You made Juan the captain general of the Holy Roman Church," I accused my accuser. "An office for which he was entirely unsuited and which he in no way desired. And it was you who directed poor Juan to throw his soldiers into one hopeless assault after another on the Orsini fortresses around Rome, which were defended all the better by troops under the command of the Vitelli. Even a cloistered nun could have seen that Juan's assassins were Orsini or Vitelli. Or both. But you did not pursue them, did you, Holiness?" If I expected an answer, it was not forthcoming. "You were too weak to reckon with your own son's murderers. Instead you made use of them."

My meaning was clear to him, though perhaps it will not be to you. The popes who preceded your grandfather had surrendered much of the Church's earthly domain, which at present occupies the entire middle of Italy and is known as the Papal States, to a host of tyrants large and small. Without the assistance of the Orsini and Vitelli, your grandfather and Duke Valentino could only dream of defeating this confederacy of despots. So they hired their former enemies, subordinating these *condottieri* to Valentino's bold and clever command, and were thus able to reclaim the Papal States with a swiftness that inspired awe throughout Europe; we heard of these victories even in the half-buried alleys of the Trastevere. That is why your grandfather, having no wish to implicate his allies, found it far more convenient to accuse me. I had no soldiers for His Holiness to hire.

"You did not come to me when we found Juan"—your grandfather's back heaved a bit—"when you might have offered us these theories. Instead you ran like a housebreaker."

"I was there when they found Juan. I waited beside the river . . ." For a moment I walked into that memory and could hear the shouts of the fishermen. "As soon as I saw him, I knew you would demand my confession. Just as you expect it tonight." I glanced at the instruments of interrogation in the box beside me. "And I knew even then I had a child in my womb. A child I would have spit in the face of Satan to protect."

His Holiness turned, his words hissing more noticeably than before. "Henceforth the boy will enjoy my protection. Here, in the Vatican."

I wailed and wailed, bereft of all reason, these words having gutted me more effectively than any instrument Beheim might have chosen.

Only when I had exhausted myself did merciful God grant me a certain calm—whereupon I found Satan's eyes so close to my face that I could smell the wine on his breath. "*Bene, bene,*" your grandfather said. "I have opened a door and shown you my grief. A few moments of the pain that is for me unceasing. A shirt of fire I will never be able to tear from my breast."

"I, too, grieve for Juan."

He dismissed my grief with a blink. "You call the boy Giovanni.

Of course I have also known that, from the day of his birth. But I don't believe you are certain that my Juan was your Giovanni's father."

"He is the child of my womb and my soul. The Holy Mother and I know the father who put his seed in me."

"After the boy has been here awhile, I will know the father," your grandfather said, with no uncertainty. He nodded at Beheim, who once again displayed his physician's knife.

On such an occasion, you are only wondering where the first cut will be. When Beheim sliced through the rope that bound my right arm to the chair, I presumed he intended to extend my limb in such a fashion that my song would begin with sharp, clear notes. Instead he cut the rope that held my left arm.

"It is in the box, Lorenzo," your grandfather said. "Give it to her."

I closed my eyes and felt Beheim's hand between my thighs, no doubt in anticipation of pulling up my skirts. Against my will I looked down.

He had placed in my lap a little pouch that could easily fit in the palm of my hand. Fashioned of soiled red wool, with a long red string, it was the sort of charm bag that half the whores and procuresses in Rome carry about, hoping to obtain good fortune or cast a love spell.

"Look inside," His Holiness said.

My hands trembling, I got in a finger and drew out a dirty paper card no longer than my thumb, also with a red yarn attached. This was a *bollettino*, which you do not see much in Rome—country people wear these little prayers around their necks. I could still distinguish the inscription, despite the untutored hand and cheap ink, which was not much darker than the stained paper: *Sant Antoni mi benefator*. Scrawled in some peasant dialect, it was a prayer to Saint Anthony, who guards against demons.

But when I turned over the little card I found another inscription, this in a practiced hand, in correct Italian and black Chinese ink: *Gli angoli dei venti*. The corners of the winds.

I looked at the pope and shook my head.

"Empty it," he said.

The rest of the contents tumbled into my lap. Two fava beans, a little lump of gray chalk, a quattrino *della croce*—a coin melted into the shape of a cross; these were the sort of charms that might compel a man to fall in love with their bearer. There was one last item, however, that froze my hands.

I looked down at the miniature bronze head of a bull, no larger than a small bell, with big eyes, short horns, and a ring that seemed to grow from the top of the tiny skull, so that it could be worn as an amulet. It was an Etruscan antiquity, fashioned by the ancient race that preceded the Romans and lent its name to Tuscany. I turned it over, requiring only a moment's scrutiny to find the tiny Latin inscription engraved on the back: *Alexander filius*. Son of Alexander. On the day Rodrigo Borgia had been crowned Pope Alexander VI, taking the name of a pagan conqueror instead of a saint, he had presented this token of love—and worldly ambition—to his cherished son.

"Juan . . ." The pope swallowed as if the wine on his breath had returned to his throat. "He was wearing it that night."

"He was never without it." In a strange fashion, I hoped this would comfort Juan's father.

"It was found at Imola," he said, referring to an inconsiderable city in the Romagna—the Romagna being the northernmost of the Papal States, occupying a vast plain between the Apennine mountains and the Adriatic Sea. Or I should say that Imola *had* been a city of little consequence, until Duke Valentino located his court there early this year. One heard that all the ambassadors, not only those from our many Italian states and the rest of Europe but the Turks as well, had gone there in supplication. Somehow Juan's amulet had journeyed for five years, hundreds of miles across the length and breadth of Italy, to return to his father's hands. In such fashion Fortune displays her love of cruel ironies.

"How—"

"How indeed."

I looked up. "If you have been watching my every breath these five years, then you know I cannot have transported it to Imola, even if it had ever been in my possession. I last saw that amulet a week before Juan was murdered. The last time . . ." I had to turn away the images that waited for me, floating on a copper-colored river I never again wanted to cross. "I did not see it in that boat, either. Although one of the fishermen might have taken it."

The pope glanced at Beheim. "Those fishermen were examined with great care." Perhaps there was a certain dreadful irony to this "care." But if so, His Holiness's face did not convey it. "My boy's assassins ripped this from his neck." His Holiness snatched the amulet from me as if I were its thief. "They took it as their trophy."

"Surely the woman from whom you obtained this charm bag can tell you who gave it to her." I was surprised at the desperate pitch of my own voice.

"She can tell us nothing. The charm bag belonged to a dead woman. It was found in her hand."

"I presume someone recognized her . . . her body."

His Holiness's nostrils pinched, as if he had smelled the putrefying remains. "She inconvenienced us in that regard. Duke Valentino's soldiers discovered her corpse in a field outside Imola." I noted the formality with which he now referred to his son Cesare. "Absent her head, which has yet to be retrieved."

I crossed myself. "Then the murderers presumed she would be recognized by someone in Duke Valentino's household, if not by your own people. Did she have scars or birthmarks upon her body?" I wondered if I would be expected to know these, still being familiar with the distinguishing marks of a number of ladies in our business.

The pope studied me for several heartbeats. "I am sending you to Imola."

"To examine what is left of her?"

His hand flew at me and struck the top of my skull so hard that the stars winked at me; he clutched my hair as though he wanted to rip my scalp away with it, forcing back my head. "You will go to Imola and wait in lodging provided you by the Holy See." The words seethed through his teeth. "You will wait there until you receive instruction from me."

I looked into a satyr's leering face, so close that our noses briefly touched. I could no longer smell the wine on his breath. Instead this was the foul, earthy stench of a long-buried corpse.

I thought: *Hell smells like this.*

After a moment the pope released me, nodded again at Beheim, then left the room.

✦

In the arch above the door where you entered a moment later, Pinturicchio had painted the Holy Madonna displaying her Child to the adoring saints. Your grandfather's people had already dressed you in a little hunting costume, with a padded jerkin and red morocco boots that reached to your knees. In your arms squirmed a dear Tenerife almost identical to our precious Ermes, licking at your face.

"Mama! Mama! Look!" you cried out like a carillon of tiny bells. An angel's voice. "I have met my *nonno* at last and he has given me Ermes's brother! In the morning we shall go back to our house and get Ermes and mend the cut those evil men gave him! I'm going to stay here with the dogs while you are away and receive instruction in fencing and riding!" You bounded into my lap and the fluffy Tenerife now licked madly at my face, eager for the salt in my tears. "Mama, *nonno* says we are all going to live here when you get back!"

I had hardly composed my sobs when I observed that your *nonno* had returned to stand behind you. His Holiness's fleshy lips trembled as they drew a tauter line. "Now you understand why I have every conviction you will go to Imola and do as I say."

"I understand," I whispered, "that you have made your own grandson hostage to my obedience in this errand."

Your grandfather nodded at Beheim, who gently tugged you from my embrace. At once I felt the pain of birth, when a mother first parts with the child of her womb. Yet I knew that if I clung to you, I would only frighten you.

It is through love, Plato said, that all conversation between God and man is conducted. Thus the vow I whispered to you was for God's ears as well as your own. "I will come back and hold you again, my most precious darling. Soon. As soon as I am able. Until then you will be brave and do what you are told. And whenever you think of me, you will know that I am thinking of you and how I adore you more than the love that turns the stars, and that is when you must smile for me.

Even if it is a hundred times every day. Even if it is only once. Each time you smile, my heart will know it."

You had no sooner left my arms than you offered me the first of those winsome smiles, sly and a bit sad at once, reminding me of your father. You turned and offered the second as you passed beneath the immense gilded arch that framed the Madonna and Child, the little dog in your arms peering back at me as well, his wide eyes lingering longer than yours.

Your grandfather did not witness our farewell. Instead, again he stared up at his own lost son. For the first time that night, I was alone with him. And I cannot say why, but I felt between us a communion so powerful that I sobbed, as though we were the last two mourners standing at Juan's bier.

"The Orsini and the Vitelli are no longer in my employ." The pope's voice was hollow. "Last month the *condottieri* met in a secret conclave at the fortress of La Magione and declared an armed rebellion against Duke Valentino, the Holy See, and our entire enterprise in the Romagna. Vitellozzo Vitelli has already attacked our garrisons in the same fortresses and towns I paid him so liberally to secure for me only months ago. *Impicatti*. The Orsini and Vitelli have betrayed their Heavenly Father no less than their duke, their pontiff, and the pledges they gave us."

"So the *condottieri* are no longer useful to you," I replied. "And now I am."

The pope remained fixed on Juan's image.

"Five years, Your Holiness. That is how long you have husbanded your hatred, every day putting away a bit more, like wine in your cellar. But it will be a sour vintage if you believe I had anything to do with those men. Perhaps this unfortunate woman had a connection with the *condottieri*. Most likely she did." My sigh was weary. "But if I ever knew her, it was not because of some mutual association with the Orsini or the Vitelli."

The pope spun about, his eyes as glaring as black glass in the sun. Yet knowing your grandfather as well as I did, I observed a certain subtlety of his expression, from which I drew the faintest cause for hope.

I had seen this same doubt twitch across his face when he raised the golden chalice full of Christ's blood on Easter morning in San Pietro; as often as he had sold God's forgiveness, His Holiness could not be certain he would ever receive it, at any price. He could taste the stink of Hell on his own tongue.

And in the same fashion, he was not entirely certain of my guilt. If I could connect the *condottieri* to a faceless woman who was murdered while carrying Juan's amulet in her charm bag, I might yet prove to him my innocence.

"Very well, Your Holiness," I whispered. "We have an understanding. I will establish myself in Imola and wait there for your instruction."

✦

There is one final thing you should know about that night: Everything your grandfather told you was a lie, except for the Tenerife being our precious Ermes's brother. I am all but certain that Ermes and the little dog His Holiness gave you came from the same litter, born two months before your father was murdered.

II

Fortune is fickle by her very nature. As a dear friend once observed, that malignant bitch knows that she cannot drop us to our ruin unless she first lifts us up. So it was that I returned to my violated house in Trastevere that very night to prepare for my journey to Imola, only to find Camilla there, quite alive. She had already delivered the body of dear, brave Obadiah to our little community of Jews and paid for his services and burial; she had given Ermes his rest in the herb garden behind our house. I found her with a bucket of water and lye, preparing to clean a great patch of blood from the mattress upon which I had last seen her. Before we could even embrace and keen like Trojan women for our lost little boy, our sad eyes met and she told me, "It is not my blood, Madonna." I did not inquire further. Like your mama, our beloved Camilla came from nothing, and that has made her a most resourceful woman.

◆

Before Camilla and I took our leave of Rome, I was able to sell most of my medallions and cameos, thus obtaining the means to purchase those necessities the Holy See would not provide, as well as redeeming some of my best dresses from the pawnbrokers. Within three days of my forced visit to the Vatican, Camilla and I stood in the little garden behind our run-down house, preparing to mount the mules that waited out front, laden with our traveling chests. In our five years in that little house, the two of us had labored so much to make this garden as lovely as it was useful, planting our cabbages, garlic, lettuces, and all our herbs and flowers; grooming the fig, pear, and lemon trees; building paths and a pergola.

A gentle rain provided almost a lens, through which our foliage glowed beryl and emerald. Yet this shower occasioned a foreboding—if we did not have reason enough to fear our journey—because even as we watched, snowflakes began to flutter down within it.

"This will be the coldest winter," Camilla said mournfully, having warm Neapolitan blood. "All the birds have gone already."

I knew how much she and our Giovanni loved to go out into the garden with Ermes, to watch the antics of the swifts and wrens, and sometimes chase them. I folded her in my arms. "I have a little hope," I said. "The pope has left me that thread, and I will cling to it. I believe if I can discover the truth about Juan's murder, I can bring our precious little boy home. That is my faith, my darling. We will come back here. All of us. The sun will shine again."

"I am remembering it," Camilla said, looking around with wonder, as if seeing our garden for the first time. And then she smiled at me, with the remarkable innocence she has kept throughout the most dreadful times. "If you remember something well enough, you are sure to come back and see it again."

◆

I will not waste words on the details of our transit, except to say that we spent a week on the backs of those mules—and the snow on the mountain passes was so thick that where it had been piled beside the road, it reached above our heads.

Imola lies at the very foot of the Apennines, upon that great carpet of rust-colored soil, known as the *pianura*, that stretches to the Adriatic Sea, one of those cities the Romans strung along the Via Emilia like beads on the reed of an abacus. You could fit all of Imola into Rome's Campo Marzio, but the city itself is not a great pasture like so much of Rome. There is a thick stone wall all around it, with everything packed tightly inside, and there are fewer tottering old brick towers than we have in Rome and just as many modern palazzi. With all the soldiers there and the army of opportunists that has followed them, you could count just as many souls in Imola on the day I arrived as you could count in Rome on the day I left.

We entered the city through the gate that faces the Apennines, thus called the Mountain Gate, passing through a wall thick enough to build a house within. Just inside we found a crowd flailing about like crabs in a sieve: candle-shop streetwalkers painted so heavily their faces looked like Carnival masks; porters with bundles balanced on their heads and peasants with baskets of eggs or sausages atop theirs; merchants in fur-trimmed capes, monks in coarse brown cowls, and cardsharps wearing velvet jackets short enough to display codpieces that might have been stuffed with cabbages. Order was kept by the local militia, rosy-faced mountain boys in jackets and puffy breeches, all striped with Borgia vermilion and yellow.

The pope had secured our lodgings at the Palazzo Machirelli. This was a new building, only a few streets up from the Rocca, the immense stone fortress that anchors the southwest corner of the city. My two small rooms were upstairs, barren save for a big walnut chair and a bed with feather-stuffed covers. Camilla threw open the shutters, allowing us to look out over a lovely courtyard of the most modern *all'antica* design, with slender columns and graceful arches.

We spent the next few days unpacking our chests, determining what to buy, and with great effort securing charcoal, wine, bread, and cheese, as everything is scarce here. With the days too cold to open the shutters more than a crack, we saw little of our neighbors. Even so, Camilla and I made a game of spying on them, just as we had when our windows overlooked the Via dei Banchi, in those years before Juan was murdered. Whenever we heard steps crunching in the frozen sand, we peeked out and gossiped about men we did not know.

"Merchant. Venetian," Camilla said of a graying gentleman wearing a sable cap, with sable lapels on his *cioppa*.

"You are correct about the attire," I said, "but a Venetian of his years would dye his hair, and this man has a little stoop from sitting too much—a scholar's stoop. Ambassador. Ferrara or Mantua."

"Poor fellow," Camilla said sadly of a much younger man, who retrieved a mule from the stables and proceeded to pace it dutifully around the courtyard, wearing only thin hose and a short jacket so threadbare that a louse would have slid off.

"Look at his hair," I said with less sympathy, "tossed helter-skelter atop his head like a spring salad. Messer Salad-head. But he is not a manservant. Do you see the ink on his fingers? An ambassador's clerk. And mule keeper. Florentine. They are a republic now. And republics don't pay to dress their clerks."

Having finished his circuits, the mule keeper began to feed the beast hay out of his hand, as if it were his child. He was engaged in this communion when a boy of perhaps twelve, attired in a peasant's horse-hair cape, with bare legs and shoes that might have been carved from gourds, entered through the stables and went at once to him. The two spoke briefly, whereupon the mule keeper plucked from his threadbare jacket a silver coin, which his visitor snatched eagerly before running out the way he had come.

"Madonna?" Camilla said.

I clutched her hand but said nothing.

◆

On the third day after our arrival in Imola, I still had heard nothing from the pope. That morning, when Camilla went out to secure our necessities, she had found the Imolese similarly uncertain of their own fates. "They tell me that Vitellozzo Vitelli took Fossombrone on All Saints' Day," Camilla reported, this being more than a month past and Fossombrone a fortress of considerable importance, though some distance south of here. "They say Valentino's garrison was slaughtered to a man. But since then, Madonna, it is the living truth that no one has heard a thing, though they all fear that the *condottieri* will soon march on Imola, and put this city under siege."

I could presume that Vitellozzo Vitelli's attack on Fossombrone was one of the traitorous acts His Holiness had reported to me in the Hall of Saints, the *condottieri* having wrested from Valentino's loyal troops a fortress they had no doubt assisted the duke in securing only months previously. And like the Imolese, I could only guess what progress the rebel *condottieri* had achieved since then, an uncertainty that made the pope's silence all the more unsettling. I peered anxiously through the shutters, almost expecting to find the invaders in the courtyard.

Having no other occupation, I continued my vigil at the window, after a while observing the mule keeper begin his circuits, just as he had the previous day. But several times when he was opposite our rooms, he glanced up, as if he knew we were watching him.

"Do you think we are spying on the pope's spy?" I asked Camilla. "Perhaps His Holiness has withheld his 'instruction' because he expects that some accomplice will call on me, thus establishing my guilt." I caught myself gnawing at my lower lip. "Darling, go down there and get his accent and try to make some sense of him. But don't provide him any of our particulars. See what he is willing to give up."

Upon exiting our stairwell, Camilla stopped the mule keeper just after he had passed beneath our window; he was not much taller than she was and nearly as lithe. When she spoke, his dark eyes shined at her and his thin lips drew a smile across his narrow face. I was scarcely surprised that he found her agreeable; for her part, Camilla tilted her head in a fashion she has, as he replied to her with lively gestures.

After a little while Camilla came back up, saying, "You were correct in believing he is Florentine, and a learned man—he speaks well-lettered Tuscan. He had a thousand questions about us, but I did not offer him anything, even when he gave me his name. Messer Niccolò. He thinks you are here to do business. Or so he implies." She shook her head. "Madonna, on my oath I don't think he knows enough about you to be the pope's spy."

Here Camilla's smile, which never remained long, fled her face. "But he told me something you will want to know. He wondered if we are staying in because of the murder ten days after All Saints'. When I asked what he was talking about, he said the peasants are still chattering about it, full of rumors of every sort. Madonna, this woman was . . . cut . . . She was cut into quarters." Camilla's eyes were wide. "And these pieces of her were scattered about the countryside. But her head has never been found."

"Ten days after All Saints'," I said numbly, trying to escape the pictures in my mind. "That would be three weeks ago. Sufficient time for the pope to have been informed, to have dispatched me on this errand, and for us to arrive here. God's Cross. She has to be the same woman who had Juan's amulet in her charm bag."

I closed my eyes, to no avail, because the images were still waiting for me in the darkness. Perhaps there had been reason to take off this woman's head. But what purpose had been served by butchering her like an ox at a Saturday market?

This grim revelation led me to a more urgent question. "Why did His Holiness say nothing about the manner of her . . . perishing, when it seems to be common knowledge here? He did not say she had been dismembered. He merely told me she had been found in a field." I peeked down into the courtyard. The Florentine had resumed his rounds. After a moment he glanced up, prompting me to step back. " 'The corners of the winds.' Perhaps her murderers were boasting that they had scattered her to the winds. Just as they left Juan's amulet in the same charm bag, to boast that they had also murdered him. But I cannot imagine why His Holiness did not remark on this connection."

"Madonna. Do you think His Holiness wanted to see if you already knew that connection?"

I smiled, but only because Camilla was so clever. "Perhaps His Holiness believes these corners of the winds are the key to all of this, more so even than Juan's amulet. And perhaps, as you say, he wondered if I already knew. Or does he believe I will discover their meaning for him? But unless the corners of the winds are in these rooms . . . What is His Holiness waiting on? For the *condottieri* and their armies to appear at the gates of Imola?"

The Florentine's young friend arrived, in the same fashion as the previous day. "You are most likely correct in assuming that your Messer Niccolò is not spying upon us, at least on the pope's behalf," I said, watching as the messenger received his stipend and exited. "Nonetheless, this boy is apprising him of something."

Camilla, who by earliest habit always looked for some way to be useful—an instinct without which she would not have survived her childhood—had begun to polish our little copper bathtub with a handful of sand from the courtyard. She did not look up as she asked, "Do you think they are watching for the *condottieri*?"

I did not think so. But I said nothing. Instead, from deep in my memory I heard my mother's voice: *Cercar Maria per Ravenna.* A saying she had taught me when I was just a girl: To search for Maria in Ravenna. If you don't know, it comes from a story about a man who journeys to Ravenna, frantically pursuing a mysterious woman named Maria, with whom he is desperately in love. This man finds the object of his quest, only to uncover a most unpleasant secret about her that proves to be the death of him. So the saying is a warning—be careful of the truth you seek.

I watched Messer Niccolò lead his animal back into the stables. But far more clearly, I could still see the pope standing before me in the Hall of Saints, doubt twitching across his face. And now I saw a deeper fear.

As Camilla scoured the copper, the wet sand screeched slightly. My whisper was so faint that she could not hear me. "That is what frightens you, isn't it, Your Holiness? That we will arrive at these corners of the winds, only to find Maria in Ravenna."

◆

On our fourth day in Imola, once again we observed Messer Niccolò's ritual and the arrival of his informant. An hour after the latter departed, we had a knock on our door, the first of our entire stay in this city. I looked at Camilla and said with false cheer, "You see, His Holiness has not forgotten me."

Camilla had already gone to the door. "Shall I open up?"

I nodded, my nerves raw.

From our bedroom, I could see our caller on the threshold. This youth was nearly as smooth-faced and ruddy as the mule-keeper's boy, but attired at considerably greater expense, in the vermilion and yellow hose and matching jacket of Duke Valentino's household. At once he presented Camilla a little card, dipped gracefully to his knee, and left us.

Camilla frowned as if the missive had been wrongly addressed. "Madonna, this is not from His Holiness. His Excellency Duke Valentino has summoned you to the Rocca this evening. To '*Cena nel Paradiso.*'"

Supper in Paradise. I did not know what Valentino meant by those words; they seemed little more than another riddle, much like his father's. I could not even guess if Valentino had summoned me on the pope's behalf or for his own reasons. But perhaps he knew that a thousand memories would rise around me regardless, like a field of lavender springing up from bare soil, the perfume almost suffocating. For a moment I felt that I could not breathe.

When I could speak, I said to Camilla, "We'll have to wash my hair."

III

The brief afternoon was nearing its end when I put on the gown I had kept in my traveling chest, folded beneath a layer of dried rose petals. This was a *camora* of exquisite loveliness and great value, the cloth a *cremisi velluto* of the deepest red I have ever seen, brocaded with gold-and-silver threads standing in relief against the sheared velvet. At my throat I wore a very rare Roman cameo—carved in sardonyx, the portrait was a young woman or perhaps the goddess Luna—on a string of Venetian pearls; my hair was braided in back in the *coazzone* fashion, my hairnet woven of gold threads.

Camilla had brought along a mirror I obtained in better times, which I now despise, because the quicksilvered glass reveals even the smallest flaw. I swear by the seven churches I had not looked into this glass of truth since the week Juan was murdered, back when my hair was blond. "God's Cross," I said, "who is she?" After five years of dyeing I still did not think of myself as sable-haired. And of course I no longer looked anything like a girl, though perhaps neither did I the last time I appraised myself in that mirror. But the shape of my face had not changed: still the pale forehead, too broad, and long nose, which I have always regarded as too humped; the delicate mouth, too small and puckered; and the chin too narrow. "You know what my mentor, Gambiera, told me the first time she dressed me up to do business?" I said to Camilla. " 'You look like one of those bird masks ladies wear at Carnival.' "

"I think she also said you were a very gorgeous bird," Camilla told me, still fussing with my hairnet. "A ravishing golden songbird. Or so you told me one night when you had too much Vernaccia."

I stood up and put my hands to Camilla's long, grave, ethereal face as if caressing an angel. "You know you are my most precious sister and most beloved *amica*, forever and always." And then I let her go, because Fortune knows when you cling too long to someone.

♦

The Rocca, I remind you, is at the southwest end of Imola, a squat but massive square of gray stone with a stout round tower at each corner, surrounded by a moat full of water that was, by the time I crossed it that evening, already as dark as the oncoming night. As you approach, the walls seem to rise into the sky and when I looked up, the ravens circling over the ramparts appeared little larger than locusts.

Once inside the walls I announced myself to the guard at the gate, whereupon a soldier in a silver breastplate was attached as my escort. He led me through a procession of vaulted rooms, with pikes, halberds, and cannonballs stacked everywhere. The scent of all the greased metal was so much like dried blood that I almost gagged.

Having passed through these foreboding warehouses, I was grateful to enter a quiet little courtyard occupied principally by fruit trees, this bounded on the far end by a graceful portico of modest size. My escort led me to a door within this arcade, knocked, looked in, and gestured me on.

Though the room I entered would have been too small for a grand public event, it was more than sufficient for a private supper; the lofty ceiling allowed the smoke from all the candles to rise into the vaults, permitting an unclouded view of the lavish tapestries on the walls and a long trestle table covered with cloth of gold so gorgeous that it seemed a mortal sin to serve wine on it.

Several of the gentlemen seated around that table, most of them garbed in high-collared black tunics, were familiar to me. Agapito da Amelia, the duke's personal secretary, talked behind his hand to Michele de Coreglia, whom everyone called Michelotto. The latter had the vague features of a shopkeeper; a moment after you turn away you can scarcely recall him, which was perhaps why Valentino was said to trust him with his most "delicate" errands. Ramiro da Lorca was an intimate of the pope as well as of Valentino; though hardly a young man, his dusky, proud satrap's face did not betray his age. Of the several men present who were not among Valentino's circle, one of those I recognized was the Duke of Ferrara's ambassador, Pandolfo Collenuccio, a noted scholar, weary-eyed and hoary-headed; I could presume that a few of the most important envoys had been summoned to this supper, though to what end I could not guess.

The room was warm enough for a dozen ladies to dress as if it were St. John's Day, each one a radiant blossom next to her grave, monochrome gentleman: lips deeply red, bosoms and bare shoulders blushing like dawn, here and there a rouged nipple peeking out amid ruffles, lace, and glistening damask. I was at a loss to find one who was not what we call a "Venetian blonde," with hair that outshone spun gold, a match for smiles more perfect and brilliant than the pearl necklaces that adorned their elegant necks. There is a name for such women, which had just entered the vernacular when I left the business: *cortigiane oneste*, or "honest courtesans," although less charitable lexicographers will say "honest whores."

At the head of this splendid table, seated alone, was Duke Valentino, master of the Romagna, idol of all Italy, the instrument of ambitions his father—our Holy Father—had only imagined when he made poor Juan their fragile vessel. The duke gave a curt little nod, whereupon a page showed me to my chair.

Contrary to his brother Juan, Valentino displayed a preference for sober attire, the tight collar of his black velvet jacket exposing only a thin band of white shirt. The candles glazed his milky complexion; his auburn hair fell straight to his shoulders, framing the lean, saintly face that God had set upon a wrestler's neck. His mustache and sparse beard were closely groomed, so that the latter more resembled rust upon his jaw—which was as solid as iron plate. However, many of Valentino's most striking features were feminine, the soft pendant of his lower lip and a nose so finely sculpted that a woman would envy it. His hawk-wing eyebrows rested closely over piercing eyes, the pupils and dark green coronas surrounded by uncommonly clear whites.

At the far end of the table an *alta* band played and a sweet-voiced young woman sang the sorrowful "O mia cieca e dura sorte." Yet hardly had I perched upon my cushion, when Valentino lifted his finger and halted the music.

All eyes came to their duke—who had nearly closed his own, his eyelids slightly fluttering. "I am certain you are all familiar with the revelation of Saint John of Patmos, as he watched the new city of Jerusalem descend from Heaven. A city built of jasper and gold." Valentino's voice was thin, almost frail.

It seemed he would not go on, when all at once his eyes shot open, his next words so sharp that everyone sat straight up. "His Holiness and I do not intend to wait for great cities to fall from the heavens. I have been speaking with my architect and engineer general—you all know Maestro Leonardo, from Vinci. Our esteemed maestro has authored his own revelations, visions of cities where plagues cannot be spread, where smoke and fetor cannot foul the atmosphere, where the streets are not clogged with whores, charlatans, and ruffians but instead are spacious and open to the most useful forms of commerce. Cities where mills and geared machines will perform the labor of men and beasts. Cities where all men can enjoy justice and *libertas*, regardless of rank or wealth."

Valentino swept his eyes about the table, as if challenging any of us to deny this vision. "Tonight I propose the first step toward such a city, because like Jacob, we must begin to climb the ladder to Heaven, rather than wait for the last trumpet." He lifted his cup. "We have completed the articles of agreement that will restore peace to the Romagna. Only when this treaty is signed can we begin to build our New Jerusalem here on Earth."

All the blood might have drained from my head. Everything I had heard, whether from the lips of His Holiness or from the streets of Imola, had led me to believe that the Romagna would soon become Armageddon, as Valentino was forced to defend his conquests against the very *condottieri* who had helped him achieve them. But this "treaty" could only mean that these soldiers for hire, having declared war against their patron, were to be welcomed back with kisses and embraces. And if peace between Valentino and the *condottieri* was now imminent, every assumption I had made regarding the pope's errand would have to be discarded. It would hardly remain in His Holiness's interest to discover an association between the murdered woman, Juan's amulet, and his former and now future allies.

I heard the rest of Valentino's address as if I had a pillow over my head: "For that beginning I am grateful to our most honored guests." Valentino tilted his cup slightly toward the opposite end of the table. "My esteemed brothers-in-arms, Signor Paolo Orsini and Signor Oliverotto da Fermo, who comes to us on behalf of the most excellent Vitellozzo Vitelli."

The two men seated at the far end of the table nodded and raised their cups; upon entering the dining room I had given this pair only the most careless examination. Now my mind nearly screamed at me: *Juan's murderers are here. At this table.* And those same bloody hands had just been invited to sign a treaty with the father who still mourned their victim and the brother who alone possessed the skill and courage to avenge him.

Paolo Orsini displayed the excesses of his station, his face bloated and sagging; only the arrogant thrust of his jaw and the great hump of his nose gave any suggestion that his lifelong profession had been that of arms. But his companion, this Signor Oliverotto da Fermo, quite resembled a lord of the battlefield. He was perhaps Valentino's age, his features resembling a bust of a Greek athlete; even beneath his velvet jacket, one could distinguish the shoulders of a discus hurler, though they were draped with languorous curls the color and sheen of polished bronze. His pale, wide-set eyes drifted around the table, pausing slightly at each face.

Over the next several hours, I merely pecked at the various courses, the liveried servers parading platter after platter of melon, gelatins, candied fruits, liver sausage, pork loin, ravioli in broth, and sugared pine nuts; the Trebbiano and Frascati wines poured like the waters at Petriolo. The conversation flowed just as liberally, with many citations of the ancients—among them Plato, Horace, Epictetus, and Marcus Aurelius.

Yet Valentino sat silent throughout, eating little more than I, careful to avoid catching my eye. I found this studied indifference no less disconcerting than his announcement regarding the *condottieri*. If this treaty was all but sealed, Valentino, who had clearly attached his hopes to it, would have even less interest than his father in allowing me to investigate Juan's murder. But perhaps I would yet provide him a useful scapegoat, my forced "confession" twisted to absolve the *condottieri* of any guilt in Juan's murder—and spare the pope and Valentino accusations that they had bartered the peace of Juan's soul for peace with the Devil.

At last Valentino pushed back his chair and slipped out, absent a word to anyone. But the woodwinds and the *trombone* played on; faces grew flushed and hands began to slide beneath damask skirts and linen chemises. The supper did not end until Messer Agapito stood up, a faintly pained expression on his small, weasel face as he brushed the crumbs from his velvet jacket, and addressed us as proxy for the departed duke. "The former despots of Imola, whom our duke has deposed as his gift to the people of this city, referred to this wing of the Rocca as the *Paradiso*." Thus my invitation to supper in Paradise. "But now we must all leave Paradise," Agapito added with a reluctant grin, his teeth like grains of rice. "We have been summoned to the Inferno."

IV

Agapito led us all in a long procession through the door at the end of the dining room, whereupon we entered a closet full of grain sacks and barrels of oil, and then another, darker storage room, reeking of gunpowder. A short flight of stairs led to the darkest room of all. Around me I could hear anxious titters, soon followed by the sound of a heavy door closing behind us.

This place smelled like a painter's studio, redolent with oils and lacquers. More sounds: succulent kisses, the whisper of skirts, whining about the cold. I heard someone say that the tower we had evidently entered was called the Inferno because the previous proprietors had constructed it as a prison—

The sun might have burst forth in a moonless night. In the blinking of an eye I saw every person present—I believed I could distinguish each pearl, every stitch, the stubble on men's faces. Yet this unnatural illumination faded in little more than a heartbeat to the sound of a loud, hollow thump, like a dozen people striking a carpet with brooms at the same moment.

Screams followed. One could scarcely think amid the terrified shrieks, and I wondered if someone had dropped a torch onto a barrel of gunpowder stored in the closets below us.

Out of the darkness, skulls appeared, six or eight of them spaced evenly about the room, hung like sconces on walls draped with black velvet. Each had a candle inside, the light pouring from empty noses and sockets. In this fashion the entire "amusement" was illuminated for us; it seemed Valentino's people had ignited those vapors I had smelled upon entering—the explosion entirely harmless, except to our nerves.

Anxious laughter still floated in the air when a velvet curtain parted and a small, brightly painted car such as they use in triumphs rolled into the room with no apparent means of transport. Atop this chariot without horses stood three entirely naked women, backs facing one another to make a sort of human tripod; beneath their bare feet, gilded plaster gryphon heads spouted wine into silver basins. Absent cups, ladies and gentlemen alike began to scoop with their hands. In little time the wine drenched them, their soaked shirts and chemises leaving little doubt as to where this amusement was proceeding.

I found a corner among a few of the ladies who did not wish to stain their Oriental satins and Rheims linens, and was soon engaged in conversation by one of the blondes. "Most of us are from Venice," she said. "Our merchants are always down here in good times and bad, and they like the same dishes they enjoy at home."

To either side of her, several ladies dropped their deepest curtsies; my Venetian friend hurriedly joined them. Guessing the object of these frantic obsequies, I turned and did the same.

Duke Valentino offered a little bow before presenting me a hand formally gloved in black kid. I could not help but tremble as I accepted it. My companions furiously tittered as he escorted me away.

"Your rooms are sufficient?" We strolled with lingering, short steps, more suited to lovers. But Valentino did not wait for my answer. "If I have neglected to send word before now, it is because this treaty with the *condottieri* has got every government represented here in a lather, believing it will put them at some measure of risk. None more so than the Florentines—I must now convince them that this peace of ours will not provide the Vitelli, with whom they have an unpleasant history, the liberty to attack them. I keep offering the Florentines a separate agreement to ensure their security, and in return they have merely sent me an amusing secretary, to interminably delay the matter. Their merchants and bankers find the expenses of peace too onerous, without regard for the far greater exactions of war."

Valentino stopped and faced me, though his eyes were down. "But if you ask me which is more difficult," he said, nearly sotto voce, "the making of war or the making of a peace, I will tell you that it is the latter." Here he pointed his gaze to Oliverotto da Fermo and Paolo Orsini, the two of them standing with heads nodded together, conferring like Pharisees; I could only presume that whatever observations they were at pains to keep to themselves would soon be shared with Vitellozzo Vitelli.

"It is even more difficult to believe that these gentlemen's current treachery is their only offense worthy of pardon," I said in a quavering voice, knowing I would have only a few words with which to save my little boy. "You know as well as I who put Juan's amulet in that poor woman's charm bag."

Valentino took my arm and drew me deeper into our corner of the room, the velvet drapes almost wrapping us up. "We have sent ships across the ocean and discovered a new world that my father has now divided between Spain and Portugal. Perhaps that will be the patrimony of those nations as we enter this new age." He fixed me with a stare so earnest that I did not even wonder what the division of this new world had to do with his brother's murder. "But we Italians now have the opportunity to end this ceaseless warfare and build the new world here, on our native soil. Damiata, you have never seen such things as Leonardo has drawn. We will begin in Cesena and Cesenatico, then the rest of the Romagna, then all Italy. Ports, canals, new roads, all the gifts that *scienza* offers us. Or we can continue with our wars and factions, refuse to move ahead, and watch impotently as our people become the slaves of foreigners." His nostrils flexed. "Let us assume your accusations are correct. Even if I were to walk across this room and wring a confession from those two, Juan would remain buried beneath the floor of Santa Maria Maggiore. His bones will not save Italy, any more than the names of his murderers will bring us peace."

I closed my eyes, as if he had pried up the church pavement to show me those bones. "So this is what you wished to tell me tonight. There will be no instruction from Rome." My throat clutched. "I am finished here."

"You are no longer Rome's concern. I have made clear to my father that I can better determine your usefulness." My eyes flew open and I saw his, bright as polished jade. "His Holiness has agreed."

I returned his stare. Had the pope already ceded him my fate? Yet before I could so much as stammer a question, Duke Valentino gave me a short bow, his arm across his waist, and walked away.

Only then did it occur to me that I still held a card I had not played, so to speak. I called after him: "Excellency."

Valentino turned abruptly, as if I had threatened him. Yet he lifted his gloved hand in a carefree gesture. "You needn't address me as 'Excellency.' You know who I am."

I knew nothing of Duke Valentino. But at that moment a memory I had kept of his former life, when he was mere Cesare, came without bidding. My house on the Via dei Banchi, a winter afternoon, the shutters slightly parted on a rain-streaked sky, a crow huddled outside on the gray stone sill. On instruction from his father, Juan was encamped before the Orsini castle at Bracciano, trying to assemble his troops and artillery in the rain and the mud, a task he hated with all his soul. Cesare was no less bitter that his father had scandalously made him a cardinal, little more than a conduit for the revenues of the office—and otherwise a doorkeeper, a laughingstock. My sadness was occasioned not only by Juan's absence; once he had begun the campaign against the Orsini, Juan had become distant even when he was present. So I played the "O mia cieca" for my lover's morose brother, mocking both of us with the melancholy verses: "O misery of my life, sad annunciation of my death . . ." Soon enough Cesare and I were passing my *lira da braccio* back and forth, singing each tragic verse with ever more exaggerated sighs, miming our remorse like comic actors, laughing until tears streamed down our cheeks.

But perhaps that Cesare had died the same day as my lovely Juan, to be reborn in little time as Duke Valentino. So I put my question to this unfamiliar man, whom Fortune had lifted up, in the five years since his brother's murder, in yet greater measure than she had cast me down. "Why do you think they cut that poor woman into quarters?"

Valentino exhaled as if he were gently blowing on a candle flame. Yet no words followed.

"The corners of the winds," I said. "It is a peculiar phrase. In what fashion does the wind have corners? No doubt it means something."

"It means a great deal." When he blinked I saw a faint glimmer of someone I had once known. "But as I told you, my father has now left this matter entirely to my judgment."

Here he left me again, absent even a nod. And now I knew Duke Valentino well enough to understand that this time I could not summon him back.

◆

I waited only long enough to avoid exiting directly on the duke's heels before taking my leave. Nor did I wait for an escort to accompany me through the armories, which were now silent as tombs. I paused before the drawbridge, the sleet a hissing shower, to pull the hood of my *cioppa* around my face. The moat before me appeared as bleak as the river Lethe, where the dead wash away all memory of their lives.

"Might I see you somewhere?"

When I turned, Signor Oliverotto da Fermo already stood at my side. He looked down at me, his head cocked slightly, eyes as pale and glittering as frost. His athlete's face was nearly unlined, save for the faint creases that framed his subtle, almost sweet mouth like parentheses. "It would be my pleasure to escort you to your lodging."

"I would inconvenience you to little purpose, Signore. I am not going far from here." I had no intention of informing Vitellozzo Vitelli's errand boy precisely where I was lodged.

"You have a lovely voice. Do you sing? We are going to stay in Imola for a little while yet."

Of course I knew what he was asking. But he had also told me, however inadvertently, that Valentino's treaty with the *condottieri* was not yet signed and sealed. Details remained, perhaps to do with Florence, as Valentino had suggested to me.

"I no longer do business," I said. "Can I presume, however, that yours is not finished?"

"It seems that you and Duke Valentino are familiar," he said, perhaps with a note of irony. "So you know that he does not give way easily. But the Vitelli and I have our interests as well." He cocked his head at a more severe angle, as if now required to examine me more carefully. It occurred to me that if this man knew I had been sent by the pope, as well he might, he would have considerable interest in knowing what

His Holiness had established regarding Juan's murder—and how far the pope would go to bring his son's assassins to account. "We intend to work with renewed industry, and see that all parties are satisfied." Spreading his hands, he ducked his bare head in a brief bow, at the same time stepping away from me. "Permit me to say how gravely I will be disappointed, if our work here is completed before I have had occasion to hear you sing."

I watched as Signor Oliverotto crossed the drawbridge, then proceeded down the street that leads past the cathedral of Imola, not far from the Mountain Gate. Thus I assured myself that he could not wait for me along the route back to the Palazzo Machirelli, as my lodgings were in the opposite direction.

Even so, I still could not cross the moat. No longer Lethe, the dark water before me had become a river of remembrance.

◆

Summer, the night of 14 June, *anno Domini* 1497, more than five years ago as I write this. I was still in my house on the Via dei Banchi in Rome, but six months had passed since I played "O mia cieca" with your uncle. Standing at that same window where the crow had watched us, I looked out across the Tiber River toward the Castel Sant'Angelo and its great tower, which your grandfather built atop that ancient round fortress. It was about the eighth hour of the night, the moon full. The Tiber appeared broken into a series of silver pools, revealed here and there in the gaps between the palazzi and warehouses that fronted the river. There was a distant drone of bullfrogs and occasionally a shout or a barking dog.

Juan had returned from his winter campaign against the Orsini and the Vitelli, the pope having pursued an uneasy, fragile truce—much like the present negotiations. That evening Juan had gone to supper with Cesare at their mother's house on the Esquiline, near the ancient Colosseum; one of his servants had brought word that I should expect him at my house no later than the fifth hour of the night. I always begged Juan to wear his armor, because regardless of the truce, I was certain the Orsini and Vitelli would pursue a vendetta against the pope who had attacked them; they knew that if they slit his beloved son's throat, they would with the same stroke bury that knife in His Holiness's heart. But Juan thought it was enough to come to my house by different routes, at various times. By the seventh hour I had told one of the *bravi* who guarded my house to go around and ask if Juan had been seen on the streets; these were very reliable men, who knew the city at night as intimately as a shepherd knows his pasture by day.

And so I was at my window, looking out on the moon-silvered city, when this *bravo* called up to me that Juan had been seen near the Santa Maria del Popolo, which was far out of his way. Either he had gone to considerable length to deceive whoever was following him, or he had decided to see a new mistress.

Juan did not come to my house that night. Nor did he return to his apartments in the Vatican the following day. The second night, the pope sent his most trusted and implacable agent, Ramiro da Lorca, to search my house. As subtle as a Spanish bull, Ramiro turned over every vase and jewelry casket, scattering the leaves of all my books and tossing aside my gowns. Of course he found nothing. In the morning the entire city was turned upside down, the pope's soldiers all over the streets; there were rumors that the sprawling Orsini palazzo on Monte Giordano was going to be attacked.

But soon His Holiness's people discovered a wood dealer who had seen a body thrown into the river on the night Juan disappeared, whereupon every fisherman in Rome was sent to fish the Tiber's depths. I paced the banks from the afternoon of the sixteenth until well into the next day. During that night I looked over the fetid dark river, its surface obsidian black, and whispered to your father, though I could not be certain if he was in this world or another. "I promise you I will give up everything, even my own soul, to protect this child."

You were the child I already felt in my womb.

At noon the next day shouts came from upstream. The Tiber was no longer dark; a coppery haze colored everything. Fishing drogues had gathered in the middle of the river. I ran like a Fury to the bank opposite, where I commanded one of the fishermen to take me out there.

I can never stop seeing Juan's body laid out in the bottom of a little boat floating on the Tiber. The mud had been washed from him and he was completely dressed in his hose and tunic, his purse and riding gloves still in his belt. His features were so peaceful, so unaltered; I had seen him sleeping like that a hundred times. But as his father had pressed him—not so much with endless hectoring as with relentless encouragement—to undertake one military adventure after another, regardless that none had achieved result, the peace had vanished from poor Juan's face, even when he slept. That was why he had begun to go elsewhere in the night, to find new faces that would not mirror how much his had changed.

"Is he dead? He isn't dead!" I shouted again and again. I tore aside his tunic, thinking that he could begin to breathe when his lungs were no longer constricted. That is when I saw the knife wounds, a half dozen on his torso alone. They no longer bled, but the water had widened each into an obscene little mouth, the flesh white at the lips, pale pink inside. Indeed no metamorphosis described by Ovid was ever as horrifying as this; it was as if beautiful Juan, his face still unblemished, had been transformed into some aquatic creature covered with gaping fish mouths. The slash across his throat was far the longest and deepest of these orifices; within it I could see the white bones of his neck. They had nearly decapitated him.

So, my own life, my own soul, now you know what your mama sees whenever she looks upon dark water.

V

I returned to my rooms, only to lie awake in bed. Yet I must have fallen asleep shortly before dawn, because when I opened my eyes again, the sun that pierced the cracks in the shutters was unbearably bright.

"So much snow," Camilla said as she stirred the coals in the brazier beside the bed. "It came down all night."

Wearing only my chemise, I padded barefoot across the icy tiles and flung open the shutters. The light seemed a thousand times brighter than even Valentino's contrived explosion in the Inferno. With my hand I shielded my eyes and hardly noticed the cold.

Our Lord has assigned Dame Fortune—that goddess known to the ancient Romans as *Fortuna*—dominion over this world, much to the delight of evil schemers, whom that bitch often favors over the good and just. But having threatened her worst, Fortune had granted me a brief reprieve. Because the fine points of Valentino's treaty had yet to be sharpened, I might have sufficient time to draw a straight line between the murdered woman, Juan's amulet, and the *condottieri*—thus establishing my innocence in the eyes of the pope, regardless of Valentino's desire to keep the truth buried. And I had no intention of waiting for the latter's determination of my "usefulness."

"I must learn the truth about this unfortunate woman," I said, looking down at the thick snow in the courtyard; the Florentine and his mule had already traced a deep ellipse upon the glistening surface. "Her associations and why she was murdered." I mused for only a moment before I added, "There are considerable ladies in the business here. Some of them must have kept company with the *condottieri* before they left Valentino's employ. And I needn't tell you where we will find them in greatest number—we should obtain invitation to some ambassadors' suppers."

"Do you want me to talk to Messer Niccolò again," Camilla said, having joined me at the window.

I nodded absently. "It might be sensible to begin there. Surely he is a clerk with the Florentine embassy." I blew out a breath. "I suppose I should make his acquaintance. I'll get dressed."

I put on my thickest hose, calfskin half-boots, and the heavy wool dress I had worn for most of our journey here. But just as I snatched my plainest cape from out of my traveling chest, I heard Camilla say, "Madonna. The boy has come."

I went back to the window, observing the same boy we had seen on three previous occasions. But now his face was as red as a lobster's back and I could hear him sputtering away in the local Romagnolo dialect, a tongue so foreign to most Italian ears that it could be mistaken for a German barking his way through some mongrel mix of French and Latin.

The Florentine appeared to understand well enough. He nodded, gave the boy a coin, and as soon as his little informant had run off, himself raced up the stairs at the far end of the court. Almost before you could say an Ave Maria he flew back down again, a heavy wool cape around his shoulders, and without a pause took his mule's halter and led it back into the stables.

"Madonna, he is going out."

"Bar this and open it only for me," I cautioned, having already gotten to our door. "That boy is a spy of some sort. And now he has discovered something."

Camilla asked almost plaintively, "But what, Madonna?"

I was already on the landing when I turned to answer. I could only shake my head.

♦

As Camilla had suspected, I did not find the Florentine tending his mule in the stables. However, neither did I observe him running down the street that goes past the cathedral, so I quickly proceeded alongside our palazzo to the Via Emilia, where I could see all the way to the center of the city. This ancient road, which cleaves Imola in two, was perhaps not as crowded as a Carnival parade, but amid the wagons, mules, and people of all sorts, there must have been a dozen men who wore gray capes similar to the Florentine's and were also headed away from me. Even so, I did not take long to recognize the familiar salad-head, darting from one side of the street to the other, as he first dodged a cart laden with vegetables, then steered around a conclave of tonsured monks.

I began a similar passage, lifting my skirts above the slush. As I made my way I was surprised to see almost as many soldiers as street-walkers, most with youthful plowboy faces. But I remained fixed on the Florentine, who quickly reached the Piazza Maggiore at the center of the city but did not enter the square, instead disappearing down the Via Appia, which together with the Via Emilia makes a cross in the center of the city. Shortly I arrived at this crossroads and located him again, waiting on a corner three streets up.

He had not budged a step when I arrived at the opposite corner, partly concealing myself behind a farmer's wife, so pregnant that she resembled an egg—and she was selling hens' eggs out of her apron, all of them resting on her belly as if it were a shelf.

Just across the street, the Florentine was engaged in conversation with one of the candle-sellers, who had opened her cape to show him her tits. She bit her thumb at him and stalked off, whereupon the Florentine more carefully examined the palazzi on the opposite side of the street; I determined he was eyeing the largest of these buildings, the third from the corner, with an immense, black oak door that more resembled the hull of a Genoese carrack. Melting snow ran steadily from the eaves of the lofty tile roof, spattering on the pavement like a rain shower.

I waited on the corner, grateful to catch my breath, having been goaded into this pursuit by little more than a desperate intuition. The boy who had set me on this chase was no doubt some farmer's son, and I suspected that whatever intelligence he had conveyed to Messer Niccolò would lead us into the countryside, which was still rife with rumors concerning the dismembered woman, as Messer Niccolò him-self had told Camilla.

Now I wondered if some of these rumors were closer to fact, the reports of witnesses too frightened to reveal themselves—perhaps because they had seen something involving the *condottieri*. And per-haps rumors of this sort had reached the ears of the Florentines, who would have good reason to be interested: as Valentino had told me the previous night, the Florentines regarded his imminent treaty with the *condottieri* as a grave threat to their republic. If Messer Niccolò was a clerk attached to the Florentine embassy, as I had surmised, then he might also be the paymaster of a little spy who kept him apprised of rumors and other reports from the countryside—and who might yet lead him to certain witnesses.

But we had not gone into the countryside. Indeed, as I stood on that corner, an uncomfortable suspicion began to roil my thoughts: that boy had not been employed to gather rumors in the *contado* but rather to watch the same palazzo that held Messer Niccolò's rapt attention. Yet even this vigil seemed fruitless. A half hour went by, I would guess, with no indication that anything of note would occur on this street, much less in front of this particular palazzo. I regret-ted that I had squandered my precious time—this gift Fortune would soon angrily snatch away—on assumptions made in haste.

All at once the pedestrian door set within that great oaken portal clanked open, issuing forth a youth of perhaps eighteen, whose appear-ance almost made me gasp. He was as lovely as an angel in an altar-piece, with abundant blond curls falling over his shoulders. His attire was no less blinding—no cape, only pink hose to display well-shaped legs, and a short carnation-hued jacket that did not cover his pretty ass. The effect was spoiled a bit, however, by black farmer's boots; more strangely, he had strapped to his back a considerable implement of some sort, a large wheel attached at the axle to a long handle. The entire thing might have been a wheelbarrow absent the barrow.

A moment later the pretty boy was followed by a man of good height, dressed in a horsehair cape and the sort of black velvet *berretta* a "doctor" of astrology will affect; hair like dirty wool fell from this crown, framing a long, pale face, the nose almost flat, like a Moor's. Upon his back, he carried two spades and a canvas sack. Directly at his heels a third man emerged, taller still. I recognized him at once, though I had never seen him before.

Now, in the years just after the French army first came into Italy—this being before you were born—I often boasted that hunch-backed little King Charles once drooled on my hand, but God knows His Most Christian Majesty only kissed it wetly, although later he slobbered on my neck. Dukes, popes, cardinals, the brother of the Turk sultan—all have bent their heads to me in intimate conversation, if I can be so vain to say. But never until that day had I laid eyes upon the most famous maestro in Christendom.

Wrapped in a beige chamois cape, Leonardo da Vinci might have been Apollo incognito, a head taller than many men, his features almost as lovely as the young man who had preceded him: his brow strong, his long, straight nose flawlessly proportioned. Parted in the middle, his pewter hair fell like a thick lion's mane, the emblem of a god's ageless wisdom rather than a man's weary age. Yet like his companions, this great maestro carried a stuffed canvas sack upon his back. In his hands he held a small wooden box, carefully, as if it were the reliquary of a saint's finger bone.

Here a little parade began, winding through the slushy, crowded streets, led by Maestro Leonardo da Vinci and his two companions, with the Florentine following at a distance of about twenty steps, I another dozen *braccia* behind him. Our route led us back to the Via Emilia, although we were now proceeding to the far end of the city, entirely opposite the Rocca and my lodgings.

In my former business, I learned by hard practice to quickly take stock of a situation and the men involved. Duke Valentino's engineer general had set out upon some peculiar errand, he and his people dressed for the country and proceeding in that direction. And the Florentine who was following him had no doubt been keeping a watch on Maestro Leonardo's house—and seemed to have anticipated this excursion. Now I could only pray that Fortune had not manufactured some cruel fraud, and the maestro's errand indeed had something to do with a faceless, ill-starred woman, whom I knew no better than the charm bag she had carried, yet to whom my fate, and my precious son's, was now chained.

✦

Shortly we arrived at the Faenza Gate, one of four entrances that pierce Imola's massive brick walls. In the little piazza before the portal, Valentino's soldiers had halted traffic so that the customs collectors could inspect cargoes. But these officers merely nodded at Leonardo and his company, who at once passed beneath the arch.

The Florentine similarly avoided waiting behind the several merchants and farmers; he presented one of the tax officers a paper, no doubt a safe-conduct pass. As the officer paused to read it, the Florentine stared impatiently after Leonardo, craning his neck.

It occurred to me that having no pass, I would have to talk my way through the gate, a delay that risked losing sight of my quarry. I scurried to the Florentine's side, clutched his arm, and gave him a peck upon the cheek, saying, "I have decided to come along anyway, regardless of all the trouble you gave me last night." Here I offered the customs officer my most persuasive smile and a fetching curtsy. But as I had hardly dressed for this role, the officer's eyes narrowed.

"If you must." The Florentine addressed me with a sour tone and a wry smirk. "Don't say you weren't warned."

His safe-conduct pass was returned; the officer motioned his head toward the arch. With neither an attempt to disengage my arm nor a word of protest, the Florentine escorted me into the countryside. There I observed Maestro Leonardo's party already some one hundred *braccia* beyond us, making their way over a little plank bridge that crosses the mill canal, which entirely encircles Imola. My new companion and I were not at luxury to stop and converse, and indeed we would have fallen behind Leonardo's leaping strides if the pretty boy had not been such a laggard, staggering beneath his burden like Christ bearing His Cross whenever Leonardo turned to snap his fingers at him.

My companion was not any taller than he had appeared in the courtyard—not considerably taller than I. But now, walking at his side, I felt a stature as lithe and sinewy as Mercury. Still clutching his arm, I recommended myself. "I am Madonna Damiata. From Rome."

"Messer Niccolò, as I'm certain your girl told you. Niccolò Machiavelli, from Florence, secretary to the Ten of War."

So his position, it seemed, was a bit more elevated than clerk and mule trainer; he was a secretary in the higher ranks of his government—and perhaps even of some use to them. Yet in my former trade, I had once considered it necessary to hold in memory the names of all the important families in Italy, and I could not recall the Machiavelli anywhere upon that list. "So Messer Niccolò Machiavelli, I must presume that you are attached to the Florentine ambassador."

He turned his head and studied me, as I did him. He had a scholar's pale forehead and a refined nose, though with a sharp, impish tip, almost on fire from the cold. His dark eyes glittered. "If I were presently attached to our ambassador, it would necessarily be a very long leash. He remains in Florence." He spoke in a rat-tat-tat cadence, lively and careless. I could see at once why Camilla had been charmed.

"Ah, I see. When I supped with Duke Valentino last night, he told me that Florence had sent him an amusing secretary to delay negotiations on a security agreement. I presume His Excellency was speaking of you."

This erased Messer Niccolò's smirk. He observed me again, now as if weighing my claim to familiarity with Duke Valentino. "It is scarcely a secret," he said, "that His Excellency is as weary of listening to my government's circumlocutions as I am of singing him the same *cantafavola* every time we meet."

"No doubt your lordships in Florence will send you a new song," I said, "if Valentino cannot conclude his treaty with the *condottieri*."

He did not hesitate. "My lordships' most devout hope is that this treaty is never signed—they pray to that end three times every day, at lauds, terce, and vespers."

I noted his mocking tone. "You do not believe these prayers will be heard."

"I fear this treaty is all but signed and sealed."

We came to the mill canal. It raced along, nearly as musical as a brook, although the banks were lined with snow; I was forced to clutch

Messer Niccolò more closely than I would have wished as we crossed the icy planks.

By this time Leonardo's party had reached the wooden bridge over the Santerno River, which in this season resembled a turbid lake more than a hundred *braccia* wide. Yet the bridge was a temporary construction that seemed entirely made of toothpicks, despite its enormous size. The thought of crossing it gave me a shudder.

"I will tell you, Messer Niccolò, why I determined to follow you, in the same fashion you are following Maestro Leonardo." I gave him a moment to say something smart, but he did not. "As I told you, I have come from Rome. On an errand for Pope Alexander. His Holiness has instructed me to examine the murder of this woman who was cut into four pieces and scattered about the countryside."

"Five. If you consider her head, five pieces."

I had expected to startle him, but his quick reply gave me a shudder. "Yes, the head," I said. "Which remains absent, when it might identify the unfortunate woman, as well as inform us of her associations."

Here he did observe a careful silence, though I could not say whether I had assumed too much or if he regretted revealing his interest in the matter.

Moments later we reached the Santerno bridge. Leonardo's party not only had crossed already; they had left the road, marching down a slight slope onto the river's opposite bank, which was covered with snow-clotted reeds. As we began to cross, I could hardly keep my feet; these planks were glazed with compacted snow and so carelessly fitted that I could see the muddy water rushing along beneath them. The entire structure swayed before me like a bough in the wind—and there was no railing of any sort.

No doubt I mouthed the Ave Maria a thousand times before we reached the other side. Here Messer Niccolò halted and looked out over the right bank, where we could see Leonardo's pewter head bobbing through the tall reeds, more than a hundred *braccia* beyond us.

"There are gravel pits and quicksand down there," Messer Niccolò said, evidently believing that this would dissuade me from accompanying him farther.

"Yet here you are, Messer," I replied, "all too eager to follow the duke's military engineer into a frozen swamp." I did not bother with much of a pause before I added: "Why is your government so concerned with Maestro Leonardo's excursion into the countryside?"

He stared out over the reeds, searching for his vanishing quarry. All at once he crossed himself like a comic mime, as if making a satire of the perils ahead. "If you are going to come along, we had better go at once."

✦

We had not gone twenty steps through the reeds when I plunged into a soup of icy water, halfway to my knees. Yet I stiffened my resolve and ventured on, the gravel always shifting beneath my feet and often threatening to suck me down, the water sometimes to my thighs. I could see nothing ahead save the slender back of Messer Niccolò Machiavelli, secretary to the Ten of War. Now and then he peered back at me; I could not say if he was anticipating my rescue, or merely hoped to find me gone.

Just when I feared I had lost sight of Messer Niccolò, I nearly stepped on him, as he crouched in the reeds. He signaled me to keep quiet, though I could hardly help snorting like a horse after the *palio*, I was so breathless. Someone was speaking just ahead, a strident tenor: "Start clearing the snow. It is buried somewhere in this vicinity."

I exchanged looks with Messer Niccolò, who pointed to where the bank sloped up from this dreadful marsh. We scuttled along, soon escaping the icy gravel, and ascended perhaps a hundred *braccia* before Messer Niccolò halted amid a small grove of poplars, stripped to gray skeletons by the early winter.

We were afforded a view of the three men thrashing around in the reeds beneath us, the snow-covered rooftops of Imola half a mile distant. I had hardly stood up and shaded my eyes against the glare, when I received a revelation of such stridor that I might have been Saint John of Patmos, thunderstruck by the unearthly heralds of Judgment.

So that my words would not carry, I urgently whispered to Messer Niccolò, "They believe her head is buried down there." And the cold would have preserved it sufficiently to reveal who she was, so that we might soon discover the unfortunate associations that had led to her death.

I observed the little cloud made by his sigh. "I am not certain."

"Leonardo said it was buried down there. I heard clearly enough."

"Oh, I am certain they expect to find something beneath the snow." Messer Niccolò did not offer what else this might be but instead eyed me keenly. "I know you came from Rome, because the caretaker at the palazzo told me. And I saw Duke Valentino's messenger go to your rooms yesterday, so your tale that you dined with His Excellency last night is certainly credible." Here he frowned, no doubt wondering why the duke had not provided me a pass to join Maestro Leonardo in the countryside. "The rumor going about is that the murdered woman had some connection to the Duke of Gandia's assassination."

In this fashion I heard another herald of Revelation: the Florentines already suspected that the woman's murder had something to do with Juan's assassination, though perhaps they were only following vague rumors. But even so, that entirely accounted for their considerable interest in all this—if by any chance they could connect the *condottieri* to the crime, they might provoke the pope to discard the yet-unsigned treaty and seek vengeance, regardless of Valentino's desire to keep the truth buried.

And I had to give Messer Niccolò his due; he was testing my bona fides with this question, which perhaps he and the Florentines had already answered to their satisfaction—or perhaps not. Regardless, I would have to answer, if I hoped to learn anything about the Florentines' inquiry. So I offered this: "I can tell you that His Holiness believes there is a connection to his son's assassination." If Messer Niccolò knew about Juan's amulet he would understand the particulars, and if not, I had no intention of bearing him gifts, so to speak.

Messer Niccolò betrayed little, saying in a musing fashion, "A connection Duke Valentino would find inconvenient if he hopes to conclude his treaty with the *condottieri*. He still doesn't have Vitellozzo Vitelli's signature."

As I had presumed. "And if the Vitelli were to fall under suspicion in the Duke of Gandia's murder," I said, "I can imagine that instead of praying three times a day, you Florentines would shout hosannas for your deliverance."

I thought I would see his ironic little smile. Instead he merely looked down upon Leonardo and his companions. "I would certainly regard that event as a miracle," Messer Niccolò said. "Because lacking this or some similar caprice of Fortune, within two months we can expect to see Vitellozzo Vitelli's army at the gates of Florence."

He narrowed his eyes. "They have found it."

Leonardo and his two assistants had gathered around something within the reeds, from which they urgently scooped away the snow with their hands. In short time they excavated a little pyramid of smooth river stones, which rose to Maestro Leonardo's high waist. However, for all their urgency in finding this cairn, the three men made no effort to dismantle it.

"Surely the head is buried beneath it," I said.

"The head isn't there," Niccolò said flatly. "I believe this is where they found one quarter of her."

"Do you mean that the murderer marked these locations?"

"Not unless Leonardo is the murderer," Niccolò said. "I believe that the maestro constructed this marker so that he could return to the precise location."

Here was my third revelation: Messer Niccolò had kept watch on Maestro Leonardo's house because he knew that the duke's engineer general had already investigated the murder and was likely to return to the countryside for further inquiry. Thus I asked, "So the maestro discovered the parts of her body?"

"No. Peasants found them, before animals could begin scavenging." He raised an eyebrow a bit, as if he found this peculiar. "Leonardo was sent to collect them—the poor woman would not be the first corpse he has examined in his basement. But most likely she was the first to have been previously butchered."

I had not considered that Maestro Leonardo's interest in the corpse might go no further than the science of anatomy; a number of our modern artists, as well as a few physicians, have undertaken this study, the better to decipher Nature's secrets. I had even known learned gentlemen who attended these dissections, as if they were theatrical events.

Even so, I could hardly imagine that Leonardo would have examined this woman's remains without Valentino's permission—any more than he was presently wandering about the countryside absent his employer's instruction.

"Now where is *he* going?" Messer Niccolò said. The pretty boy, easy to mark in his bright jacket, had started off by himself, forsaking his barrow-less wheel. He trudged through the reeds, in the direction of the hills that framed the city on the west. As we studied his progress, a bright light glinted up at us. Here I observed that Maestro Leonardo had placed upon the pile of stones the little reliquary-like wooden box he had transported from his house; the top appeared to be glass, with sunlight dancing upon it. Leonardo repeatedly looked up and down at this device, his head bobbing. Now and then he gave the box a nudge with his hand.

"That is a mariner's compass, isn't it?" I said, having once known a cardinal who kept a *studiolo* crowded with many astrolabes, compasses, and other such navigational and astronomical instruments. The faces of these compasses are invariably marked with a wind rose, a circle divided into an octave, so that each direction is named after one of the eight principal winds.

I almost gasped. *The corners of the winds.* Did the pylon beneath us mark one of these corners?

But I said nothing of this suspicion, even as Leonardo and his assistants proceeded to a baffling series of measurements. Climbing into the shallow hills, the pretty boy halted more than a quarter mile distant and turned around. He took a step or two from side to side while Leonardo moved his arm like a weather vane, evidently placing his pink-clad marker at some precise compass point. This done, the maestro and his astrologer swung their canvas mule packs upon their backs and started off. The latter placed the barrow-less wheel on the ground and rolled it before him over the snow, heading directly for the pretty boy. Leonardo followed with the compass reliquary in his hands, as if he and his astrologer were a peculiar procession of country priests.

Messer Niccolò and I hastened after them. Despite the snow, the gentle hills allowed a much quicker transit than the marshy riverside; soon Leonardo and his assistant arrived at their landmark. Here they turned at a right angle and marched up the steeper slopes more dis-

tant from Imola, where venerable olive trees with massive, corkscrew-
ing gray trunks stood in rows. Occasionally Leonardo knelt on the
ground to consult his compass, whereupon he redirected the path of
the barrow-less wheel.

"Vitruvius described this sort of wheel," I said during one such
pause. "I recall reading—"

"*De architectura*," Niccolò said impatiently. "The wheel has a cir-
cumference of regular measure, I believe—"

"And the rim is marked," I hastened to add, "so each revolution can
be counted, the distance calculated by multiplication."

"Yes. They want to know precisely how far they are from the previous marker." Yet Niccolò offered this without the conviction of his
previous observations.

I remained silent regarding "the corners of the winds." Information, much like the courses of a supper or even a lover's favors, is best
served in small parcels.

Leonardo and his people finally reached a roughly square-shaped
grove of olive trees, bordered by a parapet of neatly stacked stones.
Quickly hoisting their Vitruvian wheel over the low wall, they continued on.

Messer Niccolò and I crept up to the parapet and hid behind it.
We looked down at the city, having climbed as high as the tops of
Imola's slender towers; the brick shafts glowed nearly pink on the sides
struck by the sun. In the opposite direction, to the south and west, the
mountains were vast, white waves.

"*Dieci*," someone called out, his voice as deep as Pluto in a theatrical. As if joining him in a motet, a high tenor responded: "Six hundred
and twenty *braccia*." Observing each set of ten revolutions in this fashion, the two men continued their duet until they were nearly to the
parapet at the far end of the olive grove. But they did not climb over
this wall, instead dropping their canvas sacks just beneath it. Leonardo
and the astrologer quickly took up their spades.

Hurriedly I made my own calculation, as if I were sitting at a *primero* table, obliged to raise my bid or throw down my cards.

I stood up, drew my skirts between my legs, and scrambled over
that wall.

VI

"*Cacasangue che pazzarone.*" This curse came from behind me. Messer Niccolò had followed me over the wall, though it seemed he had not been prepared to reveal himself so soon.

"Let me speak for us," I said, not pausing in my climb.

We had gotten only a short distance up the hill when they saw us. All three of them started down the slope, Leonardo's astrologer still brandishing his spade. Their long afternoon shadows accompanied them upon the snow like phantom janissaries.

"Maestro Leonardo!" I hoped the strength of my voice would conceal my fear. "I am Madonna Damiata. By His Supreme Apostolic authority, His Holiness, Pope Alexander, has sent me from Rome to inquire into this matter!"

As if I had commanded it, Leonardo halted. He stood no more than a half-dozen *braccia* from me, his wooden farmer's clogs half buried in the snow. His face was nearly as unlined as a youth's.

The maestro's lips moved, though no sound was forthcoming. He did not look at me but instead directed his malachite-tinted eyes at Messer Niccolò, to whom he finally spoke: "I know you. You are that Latinist the Ten of War have sent." His voice, a high tenor, more resembled a boy's whine. "Why are you here?"

"A woman has been murdered. If it can be ascertained that she was a citizen of Florence, my government must be informed." Messer Niccolò offered this in his rat-tat-tat fashion, as though he had prepared his answer—no doubt intended to disguise his government's true interest—well before setting out on this chase. "And I believe that this wheel of yours will soon arrive at the fifth part of her."

"You make a false assumption. We are engaged in an *esperienza*." Now Leonardo's alto tenor had a musical authority, like notes played on a cathedral organ.

Messer Niccolò cocked his head. "*Esperienza?*" I presume he took the word as I had, not as "experience" in the familiar sense but as referring to an observation undertaken for purposes of *scienza*.

"Measurement!" Leonardo's exclamation hung in the air like the peal of a bell. "Measurement and experiment are the pillars of all knowledge. There is nothing that cannot be known if it can be measured, and nothing that can be known if it cannot be measured. But I do not expect you to understand—imagine you read it in some ancient text and assume it on your faith in antiquity, as you men of letters do so many things."

"So we can assume this measuring wheel of yours is a new *invenzione*," Niccolò said, sharing a faint smile with me. "What remains uncertain is by what authority, ancient or modern, you determined to survey this plumb line across the countryside."

Leonardo folded his hands over his groin, as if guarding his manhood. The astrologer descended several additional paces, his spade before him like a Swiss pike. The sun glittered on the brooch pinned to his *berretta*, yet rather than the zodiac badge I had expected, this was a silver alchemist's symbol, the circle and cross that represent Mercury. He growled, "Maestro Leonardo is the duke's architect and engineer general. We are surveying this vicinity under the authority of Duke Valentino."

"And did the duke himself tell you what you can expect to find at the top of this hill?" Niccolò raised his chin as if pointing the way. Indeed for the first time I observed that the snow had been disturbed up there, exposing the sandy soil.

Here Leonardo glanced quickly to his pretty boy, whose sullen mouth—his lips were almost purple—more resembled that of a fallen angel, one of Lucifer's brood. This youth drew a nasty stiletto from his belt, examining the blade before he languidly remarked, "I'll put this between his teeth."

"Maestro!" I called out. "In the privacy of his own Vatican apartments, His Holiness has shown me the *bollettino* retrieved from this unfortunate woman's body." Here I bet it all, declaring most stridently, "If you are able to explain to me 'the corners of the winds,' His Holiness will expect you to provide the particulars. Now show us what you have found up there."

Leonardo stared at me as if pondering how a chittering monkey had acquired the ability of speech; "the corners of the winds" was a phrase no doubt familiar only to the Borgia inner circle, within which Leonardo was clearly included—thus I had established, to his considerable surprise and apparent distress, my own bona fides. For a longer moment, he silently addressed the ether. Evidently failing to receive a satisfactory response, he fixed his mouth in a sour expression, turned about, and began to lead us all toward the high end of the olive grove, his shoulders hunched and his hands, now at his sides, flopping like fish on a rock.

♦

At the top of the grove, the olive trees were far apart and the snow glistened in the sun, all save the partial excavation where we halted. Here the sandy, ocher earth had evidently been churned up by the same animals that had left countless pockmarks in the surrounding snow.

"Wolves," Leonardo said, taking up his spade again.

"Then they have carried it away," I said.

"You make an incorrect assumption." All at once Leonardo struck down on the exposed earth with his spade. The tip hardly penetrated at all, yet the earth did not appear frozen. Instead the dull thud might well have been metal against bone.

"Tommaso!" At this command the astrologer—or more correctly, now that I had observed his badge, the alchemist—joined Leonardo in scraping away the top layer of sandy earth. Shortly they revealed several wooden planks, much like the lid of a coffin. Leonardo prized up one, which was probably a handspan in width. "This is a barrier against animals."

Indeed these boards had not been nailed to a coffin but were merely loose planks weighted at the ends with large stones. When Leonardo and Tommaso had removed the latter, they were able to pull up the first plank entirely, revealing a sort of crypt, lined with smaller rocks.

Something pale glimmered inside. I crossed myself. Leonardo and his assistants pulled aside two more planks. Sunlight flooded in.

What I saw resembled a fragment of an antique statue after it has been unearthed and scrubbed, the white marble almost like chalk. But this was the right half of a woman's torso, truncated at the neck and cleaved from there directly down the middle, the cut precise, as if made by a physician's knife. The lone breast was entirely intact, although the nipple was not visible at all. The arm rested peacefully at her side, bent so that the hand lay just beneath the ribs, the white fingers gracefully curved. This strangely lovely artifact ended where I would have expected to find the navel, had the upper body not been cleaved from the absent lower, just above the pelvis.

As you know, I have seen death before. Yet just as Juan's wounds were all the more terrible to me after I had witnessed the peacefulness of his cherished face, I found this fragment of a woman, presented like an antiquity in a cardinal's *studiolo*, more horrifying than a hanged man with piss dripping from his toes. I thought I would swoon.

"The imbeciles have dusted it with quicklime." Having offered us this observation, Leonardo knelt atop the remaining plank. "They believe this procedure will hasten decomposition. Were they to conduct an actual *esperienza* rather than rely on the wisdom of washerwomen and grave robbers, they would know that quicklime retards putrefaction." Here the maestro reached down, his hand now entirely steady, and drew his finger across the whited torso just beneath the breast, removing the quicklime dust and exposing a finger-width swath of claret-hued skin. He put his finger beneath his nostrils and sniffed audibly.

Without remark Messer Niccolò knelt beside the maestro and similarly ran his finger over the belly of the corpse, leaving another claret streak, whereupon he also put his finger to his nose—and quickly turned his head, as if he had found the odor most disagreeable.

I was occupied with my own observation. "The quicklime is crusted," I said, "where I presume her nipple to be." My stomach turned over as I said this.

Leonardo stared into the stone sepulcher. "It has been sliced off." He shook his head tremulously. "We observed this with regard to the previous remains."

Messer Niccolò's mouth was as tight as a vise. No doubt we shared the same question: Were these the remains of a second woman?

I addressed the maestro, trying to speak against the heartbeat rising into my throat: "Both halves of the previous victim's torso were absent the nipples?"

Leonardo nodded.

"So the quarters of one victim were discovered almost at once," Messer Niccolò said in his musing tone, "because they were left out in the fields." I presumed Niccolò's little informant had told him this. "Yet the quarters of the second victim have been carefully buried in this manner."

"You make an incorrect assumption," the maestro refrained. "We have not located the remaining three quarters. If they are to be found."

So this was the first of four pieces of her. Or five. And now I understood why Messer Niccolò had previously inquired as to the "authority" that had directed Leonardo to this place. "Maestro," I said, "we must know who informed you of this location."

Leonardo silently mouthed something.

"Peasants," offered Tommaso. "Some of them observed a pack of wolves pawing the earth. We did not place these remains here."

Messer Niccolò looked up at me. He wore the expression of a boy who has brought a bullfrog to Mass, under his coat, so that it can croak during the homily. "It was not suggested that you had," he said to Tommaso. "Only that you seemed to know your way here. And took great care to chart and measure your path."

Silence followed, save for the cawing birds. At last Tommaso spoke, but not to the question Niccolò had raised. "What is in her hand?"

Leonardo again reached into the crypt. His long, elegant fingers appeared to crawl about like the legs of a pale tarantula, unwrapping a red string from a chalky hand that was not as stiff as I expected. The maestro was able to gently open her fingers, almost as if she were sleeping, to reveal the little card resting in her palm. After he had delicately removed this *bollettino*, he brought it quite close to his eyes.

Almost as if the words he read had disgusted him, Leonardo quickly presented the prayer card to me.

This *bollettino* was no different than the one the pope had shown me, the cheap, rough paper inscribed in a crude yet legible hand. *"Gevol int la carafa,"* I recited for all present. This audience did not include the pretty boy, who had suddenly vanished, as if snatched away by wolves. I added, "I presume this is the Romagnolo dialect."

" 'Devil in a jar.' " It did not surprise me that the alchemist, Tommaso, knew this phrase. "The Devil appears in the flask of water and conjures images of lost—"

"An imbecilic superstition," Leonardo blurted out. "Of all the foolish beliefs waved as proud banners by the ignorant herd, the existence of spirits is the most asinine, no less offensive to Nature than it is to science. By the very powers imputed to them, these spirits are incorporeal quantities, which Nature defines as a vacuum—"

"Perhaps this is nonsense, but it does not appear to be some peasant's superstition." During Leonardo's anathema of spirits and those who believe in them, Messer Niccolò had reached up and snatched the *bollettino* out of my hand. Now he held the little card so that both the maestro and I could see the reverse side, which we had yet to examine.

There, in black Chinese ink, in the same well-lettered hand I had witnessed in the Hall of Saints, was an inscription in Tuscan Italian. I read it aloud, as I had the previous, finding this new message no less obscure: "The circle within the square."

Messer Niccolò stared into the crypt, puffing out his gaunt cheeks before he blew in weary fashion. Whatever he might have considered saying, he thought better of it.

Leonardo bolted up. "Giacomo! What have you found?"

The pretty boy stood some two dozen *braccia* distant, on the other side of the parapet, in thick brush up to his waist. He might have been a mile away, his lazy Milanese drawl was so faint. "Something has been up here. There are tracks. Not a man's."

"The wolves," Leonardo said impatiently.

"Not a beast, either." Giacomo appeared to enjoy this riddle.

"Then what is it, Giacomo?" Leonardo asked this as if his assistant had no more credence than a child.

Against the stiff north wind, Giacomo's voice now seemed scarcely to reach us; his words wavered. "The Devil has left his footprints up here."

VII

"Stilts." Maestro Leonardo stood erect, having bent over to peer at the tracks, which we had followed a short distance through thick, wiry brush that much resembled the shrubs common to the Campagna around Rome, though it had grown in the shadow of enormous oaks. Leading away at a right angle from a snow-covered path pocked by wolves' paws, these footprints, though paired like a man's, were considerably smaller, a few of them preserving the distinct impress of a cloven hoof no larger than a goat's.

"He was walking on stilts," Leonardo went on to say. "The impressions are entirely uniform in contour, as well as in depth. He carved the ends of his stilts in an imbecilic effort to deceive us."

"To deceive *us?*" Niccolò cocked his head. "Possibly he wants the olive harvesters and acorn hunters to credit this crime to the Devil. To keep them away."

It seemed none of these men intended to make further remark. Thus I offered my proposal. "While we still have the light," I said, "we must follow these tracks, and see where they lead."

Messer Niccolò at once started off. But I believe that the maestro, trailed by his reluctant assistants, followed us only because he did not want to risk that we would learn something he would not.

◆

For perhaps a mile we followed the tracks toward the distant mountains, always on rolling hills, occasionally crossing a vineyard, the bare grapevines sticking up from the snow like the quills of a porcupine. But mostly we traveled in the darker half-light beneath the ancient oaks. Even where the undergrowth was thick, we did not lose the tracks, our quarry having stayed to the narrow paths made by acorn collectors.

Chastened by what we had seen in the olive grove, we walked silently. After a time I took Messer Niccolò's arm and drew him back, so that we fell behind Leonardo and his people. "So you believe it is hardly an accident that peasants found the pieces of these bodies," I whispered to him. "Do you think they were paid to inform the duke's people?"

"It wouldn't be difficult to persuade them," Niccolò said into my ear. "This countryside has suffered terribly, with so many soldiers living off it. A quattrino would be enough."

"But if the *condottieri* have done this . . . I can understand why they might wish to make mischief here, perhaps provoke the pope by murdering a woman connected in some fashion to the assassination of his son." Again I did not think it wise to reveal that the *condottieri* had taunted the pope with his dead son's amulet. Instead I went on: "Presumably that poor woman back there is somehow intended as a similar provocation. But why now, when the *condottieri* have come to Imola to secure peace?" Indeed I feared I had misjudged this matter entirely.

"I am not certain all the *condottieri* want this peace, at least under the present terms. The Orsini, yes. The Vitelli . . ." Messer Niccolò shrugged as if to say "not so much." He looked at the ground for several paces before he added, "Every day that passes, the *condottieri* hire more soldiers. And Valentino divests himself of his mercenaries because he cannot rely on them. I believe the Vitelli want to keep the thistle, let us say, up the pope's ass, hoping that they can delay the signing and continue to improve their position. Their object, I would think, is not to discard the present treaty entirely but to force the duke to make additional concessions."

"What sort of concess—?" I broke off because we had walked nearly onto the heels of Leonardo's party.

Giacomo pointed toward a shadowed oak grove off to our left.

"Have you seen him?" Niccolò said.

Giacomo dropped his arm in a weary fashion. "He's gone now."

I asked, "Was he on stilts?"

Giacomo shook his head. "He wore a monk's cowl."

"Did you see his face?"

Giacomo answered Niccolò with another slight headshake. But then he said, "He had a white beard. Just like a goat." I would have said Giacomo was fond of these *invenzioni*, except that he had been correct about the Devil's footprints, even if they had been a fraud.

"He resembled a goat," Leonardo said in a fashion more disdainful than affirming, before he started off again.

"Carnival stilts. And a Carnival mask," Niccolò said, giving Giacomo a favoring nod. "We'll look out for this false Devil."

"Yes," I said. The cold wind blew against my back. "No doubt he is already watching us."

◆

The Devil's tracks at last led us to a large farmhouse constructed of pale clay bricks. The stables were on the ground floor, with the farmer's lodgings above them. This dwelling was perched on top of a hill overlooking the Santerno River, which made a gurgling sound as it flowed swiftly between steep, rocky banks. The farmhouse and several wooden sheds framed the yard, garden, and pigsty, though neither the herbs nor the mud were in evidence beneath the snow. Nor were any animals present.

The paired "hoofprints" ended where the snow did, at a dirt-floored porch in front of the stables. Niccolò pointed to the names chalked in rough letters on the porch's squat, square brick columns. "Soldiers were billeted here—the farmer probably carried off all his fodder and the stores in his cellar ahead of them, so the soldiers moved on. But the farmer has not come back."

I would have been considerably less frightened to learn that the place was occupied.

Giacomo again unsheathed the impressive knife at his belt and blithely wandered into the porch, leaving Leonardo to mouth impotently after him, before he and Tommaso reluctantly followed. Niccolò arched his eyebrows and shrugged. As I joined him, I allowed the butt of the knife I keep within my sleeve to drop into my hand.

Tommaso remained in the porch, to keep watch, while the rest of us walked directly into the livestock stables; perhaps the gate had been removed to serve as firewood. We found nothing but a dirt floor that might have been picked over by a plague of locusts, though the place still smelled of the animals. Niccolò, Leonardo, and Giacomo began inspecting the bare plank ceiling, which was supported by heavy cross-beams. I presumed they were looking for the trapdoor, which usually opens from the farmer's bedroom on the floor above, so that he can quickly look over his stock if he hears some sort of noise in the middle of the night.

"Maestro!" Tommaso called from his post on the porch. "We've been followed."

I looked out and saw the three men standing just beyond the porch. In Imola I had been struck by the handsome faces and proud bearing of many of the Romagnole peasants. But these three, attired in horsehair capes, their legs bare, were so miserably afflicted that they more resembled beasts: One had skin like an elephant on his cheek and neck, all weeping pus—what they call Job's disease—while another had replaced his nose with a scrap of leather shaped into a semblance of the missing item, though it had been painted much whiter than his ruddy skin. The third man's black teeth were as jagged as a lamprey's. He carried a sickle, while his companions were armed with a baker's *forchetta* and a pitchfork. None of them, however, had a white beard or in any fashion appeared to be a goat.

No sooner had I observed these arrivals, than behind me Giacomo said, "I wager he's up there." I turned to find him pointing at the ceiling.

Coming to Giacomo's side, Messer Niccolò squinted through the shaded porch at the three beasts, who were brightly lit by the snow-reflected sun. "Lift me up now," he said, "before they decide to come in here."

Leonardo himself wrapped his arms around Messer Niccolò's knees and lifted him as if he were a child. The secretary pounded the palms of his hands against the seam on either side of the trapdoor but effected nothing; no doubt the latch could only be opened from the room above.

"They are coming!" Tommaso called from the porch, his growl

pitched urgently higher. Indeed the three men had spread out; crouching slightly, they crept warily toward the alchemist like a wolf pack.

With quite a calm demeanor, Messer Niccolò said, "We had better make our numbers known." As soon as Leonardo had put him back on the ground, the two of them, followed by Giacomo and his stiletto, rushed out to the porch. "You stay out of sight," Niccolò instructed me.

The two factions faced each other at a distance of several paces, theirs having superiority in arms, while we were favored by number and stature. The three interlopers looked among one another, shaking their heads, conversing in the belching diction of the Romagna, so that I could understand nothing. But they did not seem inclined to withdraw.

"Are they waiting to be reinforced?" Niccolò asked.

The sound was behind me, but it was as if a great heap of snow had slid off the roof and struck the ground. Just then something dark flew by the corner of my eye and I imagined the ceiling had begun to fall down around me.

I turned to see the trapdoor hanging from its hinges, swinging back and forth like a banner in a breeze. With a gasp I looked up into the dark, rectangular aperture in the plank ceiling.

I ran out to the porch. Here I witnessed the similarly abrupt flight of the three visitors, no doubt also prompted by the noise of the trapdoor. Indeed the Devil might have been their pursuer, so quickly did they vanish around the far end of the farmhouse.

Messer Niccolò shot back into the stables. In a moment all the gentlemen present had assembled to stare at the hanging trapdoor, a construction of wooden slats and cross braces that creaked only slightly before it became entirely still.

You could not hear even a breath, only the sibilance of the wind outside and the rushing river, which now sounded more like a low, rasping sigh.

Messer Niccolò advanced directly beneath the aperture and looked into the darkness above him. He stood there, evidently listening, perhaps waiting for the face—or mask—of a goat to appear. At last he issued a resigned exhalation. "Lift me up again."

Leonardo's mouth turned down like a sour old man's. But after a moment's pause he hoisted Messer Niccolò, who got a handhold on either side of the opening and hauled himself into the room above.

We could see him stand up and look around. Then he vanished into the darkness; soon we could not even hear his feet padding over the floorboards. Giacomo held up his knife, as if he should be sent to Niccolò's aid. But the maestro quickly placed a restraining hand on his arm.

For my part, I silently recited an Ave Maria on Messer Niccolò's behalf. I might well have recited several Paternosters while we continued to wait, ever more anxiously. Now and then I heard dull thuds, yet I could not say if these were blows, someone moving things about, or merely muffled steps.

A pale face floated above us. I let out a little cry and even Leonardo drew a sharp breath in the heartbeat before we recognized Messer Niccolò.

"Nothing," he reported. "There is not a stick of furniture up here, not a piss pot or a grindstone. Nothing except this." Messer Niccolò sat on the edge of the opening, his legs dangling, and reached down to us, holding in his hand a plain clay butter pot.

For some reason the maestro and his people were reluctant to accept this offering. I took it, wishing I hadn't as soon as I smelled the contents. This little pot was half filled with the sort of unguent that ladies in Rome usually obtain from the old women of Israel, whose concoctions of myrrh, sulfur, and hog lard are intended to preserve the skin. But there were other scents in this particular recipe: the foul bitterness of belladonna when it is first crushed and also mandrake, perhaps with henbane and hellebore.

For a strange moment, every foreboding I have ever had in my life seemed to revisit me.

Messer Niccolò dropped almost silently to the ground. When he had straightened up and dusted the sleeves of his jacket, he said to me, "Allow the maestro to smell it. He will recognize the scent."

The breath caught in my throat. Both Messer Niccolò and Maestro Leonardo had sniffed their fingertips after running them across the flesh of that poor, butchered woman. And now I understood Leonardo's apparent indifference to this discovery; he had already known what he would smell in that pot.

"This unguent was smeared over her body, wasn't it?" I offered this more as a plaint than a question. "And it was found on the remains of the first woman as well."

Leonardo nodded in a palsied fashion, his nostrils fairly twitching. "Yes." His tenor was slightly hoarse. "Both of them."

Messer Niccolò cast his eyes up at the darkness he had just explored. "Then I am certain," he said, "this is where they were both butchered."

VIII

All five of us arrived back in Imola at dusk, having returned briefly to the olive grove to replace the planks over the little crypt, to keep the wolves at bay until Leonardo could send soldiers to retrieve the human fragment. I could not make myself go close to the grave. But even as I stood some distance away, I felt a vague yet increasingly heavy presence, until all at once I shuddered.

I ran to Messer Niccolò. "He is watching us right now."

Niccolò looked at me in a piercing fashion, as if I had claimed to see the Virgin.

I pressed my argument. "He was waiting for us at that farmhouse, wasn't he? He had to have gone out a window just before you went up there. Do you think those men came to help him escape?"

"They were looking for him," Niccolò answered. "For what purpose I am not certain. Neither am I certain he was up there. The latch was broken. Perhaps I jarred the trapdoor loose, only to have it fall when our backs were turned." He elevated his gaze as if peering into the dark copse behind me. A moment later his eyes fell to me, almost reluctantly.

I know when a man is drawn to me, even if he hopes to conceal this attraction. That element was present in Messer Niccolò's stare—as indeed in any number of glances throughout that day. Yet there was something else, to which he gave voice. "You should consider leaving Imola."

I wondered if he hoped to cast himself as my protector; perhaps he imagined I would offer him a grateful farewell before I returned to Rome. "Why do you say so?"

"Because I, too, am certain that the Devil has seen us." Of course, I took this to mean a man disguised as the Devil. "And now he knows who we are."

♦

Niccolò and I parted with Leonardo and his people as we entered the Via Emilia. I continued my fraud, telling the maestro, "I will write His Holiness at once and inform him that there has been another murder." Though Leonardo did not say so, I had little doubt he would quickly inform Duke Valentino that I had brazenly followed his engineer general into the countryside and insinuated myself into his inquiry.

The street was raucous with tradesmen and candle-shop girls, the latter calling out, "Take a bite of this chestnut!" "No French pox here!" This cacophony was the greatest in front of the Inn of the Cap, where so many of the streetwalkers had gathered in order to solicit the travelers and couriers going in and out of the stables. Once we had passed and could talk without shouting, Messer Niccolò looked sideways at me and said, "Leonardo is involved in this."

"In what fashion?"

He shook his head. "Certainly he is no murderer. That is not his nature. But he is trying to conceal a great deal. With little success. You saw him. His paintings may fool us all with their semblance to life. But at the art of deception, he is hardly a maestro."

I said into Niccolò's ear, "As a military engineer, Leonardo had to have worked with the *condottieri* before their defection from Valentino. Perhaps they have duped him."

Niccolò nodded. "There is something in all this that only the maestro and this murderer know. Something that makes the maestro behave as if *he* will be hanged for it."

Messer Niccolò and I turned the corner. Not far down the street, the Rocca was an immense gray monolith against a sky as deeply purple as squid ink, the moat around it already black. We entered our Palazzo Machirelli through the stables gate we had both exited separately, hours before, when I had been innocent of a great many things—and considerably less baffled by this whole matter. The animals in their stalls stamped at our presence, as if the very Devil had followed us.

"I have to look after my mule," Niccolò said. I had become anxious even about going into the courtyard alone, so I trailed Niccolò to the stall.

"You are uncommonly devoted to this beast," I said to him. There was just enough light remaining that I could see the animal blink gratefully, as Messer Niccolò stroked his muzzle.

"I acquired him from a charcoal burner who had driven him mad with work—the poor creature was burdened with grapevine bundles piled so high they could reach a balcony, while his belly sagged into the dirt. I persuaded the *cacapensieri* that his animal was worth more to me alive than to him dead. My intention is to restore his strength and ride him back to Florence."

I now understood the nature of Messer Niccolò's devotion: the mule was a promise he had made to himself, that he would return to his home. But even as I believed I had divined his sentiments, I saw that he was peering into me.

And judging from his expression, he had found something that required his sympathy. "I am no longer so certain," he said almost sadly, "that these murders have anything to do with the treaty between Valentino and the *condottieri*."

I could only assume that Niccolò indeed knew nothing about Juan's amulet; otherwise he would surely believe, as I had, that the object of the first murder was to provoke the pope. Perhaps the second murder, seemingly in the same fashion, had only been a taunting reminder, a memento mori of the cruelest sort. As Messer Niccolò himself had said only hours before, it was in the interest of the Vitelli to keep the thorn in His Holiness's side and prolong the negotiations.

But I did not know Messer Niccolò well enough to risk sharing this confidence. I could only ask him vaguely, "What brings you to this opinion?"

"The care taken to dismember the corpse. The nipple sliced away. The unguent, containing narcotic herbs, smeared upon the skin. This business with the corners of the winds." Here he made a sharp little nod that stung more than an overt accusation, reminding me that I had previously withheld this confidence from him. "Leonardo's measurements, the note regarding squares and circles. It is all of one piece. A great rebus or riddle, composed in human flesh. As if all of this were one man's cruel amusement."

"Yes," I said. "There is no end to the riddles and mysteries that amuse men. The Key of Solomon, the Kabbalah and the *Heptaplus*, the mysteries of Hermes Trismegistus and the Pythagoreans—not to mention that I have known several men to find pleasure in cutting women with knives."

Messer Niccolò offered me the rueful smile of a man who knows the world all too well.

"But," I continued, "I believe that this amusement was conceived with a sole purpose: to provoke the pope. To cite your own theory of this very afternoon, perhaps the Vitelli are behind this because they do not see the treaty with Valentino as sufficiently advantageous to them. And if they delay the negotiations with these clever and cruel games, they can obtain these additional concessions you remarked upon."

Here I took Messer Niccolò's arm and led him into the courtyard; all at once it had come to me what I must do next. When we reached the foot of my stairs, I said to him, "I am going to send my girl to your rooms with some food and wine." While I did not intend to serve as a pimp, I thought Camilla's charming—if chaste—company might fire his eyes and would certainly fill his belly; he did not appear to eat well.

Of course I expected poor Messer Niccolò's disappointment, to learn he could dine with me only by proxy. Thus I was surprised—and perhaps a bit disappointed myself, vain as I am—when he did not evidence any regret. Indeed, he appeared relieved that I would not be present. With nothing more than an ironic little bow, he started toward his rooms.

Regardless of his indifference, I did not want to risk that Messer Niccolò Machiavelli might post himself behind his shutters and observe me in the fashion I had so often spied on him. So I trudged wearily up my stairs, gratefully embraced Camilla, and sent her across the courtyard with some wine, cheese, bread, and boiled capon.

As soon as I was alone I summoned my courage, washed my face, and changed my clothes.

✦

Not having a pass to the Rocca, I was fortunate to locate the same guard who had escorted me the previous evening; from long habit, I make it a point that men should remember me, even if there is only a small chance they will be useful later.

Although I had asked to see the duke's secretary, Messer Agapito, my journey terminated at the same *sala* where I had supped the previous evening. Inside, I found the dining room transformed. The bare wooden table appeared almost tiny and the plastered walls were similarly undraped, the tapestries replaced by a single golden crucifix and an ancient icon.

Agapito, his uniformly black velvet unchanged, commanded an entire side of this smaller table, opposite several gentlemen and a copper-haired woman. He speared a chunk of meat with his knife before looking up from the platter. Just as quickly he looked down, wiry jaw pulsing.

I went around behind him and whispered close to his ear, "I have seen something today that will interest His Excellency. An observation his engineer general failed to remark upon." In this fashion I hoped to anticipate Leonardo's inevitable report—yet also tempt Valentino with the notion that the maestro had overlooked something. Of course this was a perilous game. But Valentino would be sufficiently infuriated regardless, when he discovered I had not waited on his determination of my "usefulness."

Agapito merely chewed like an ox, obliging me to stand there as if I had been summoned to hold his napkin. I looked across the table. Two of the men were ambassadors, judging from their sable collars and pinched faces. Next to them, as if conjured by my invocation of Vitellozzo Vitelli not an hour before, sat his emissary, Oliverotto da Fermo. This signor was kept company by the copper-haired woman, a prime slice of Venetian prima donna, with glorious curls and breasts as round and firm as oranges, pushed up almost to her collarbones by a brocade bodice cut straight across in the Milanese fashion.

Without a word to me, Messer Agapito rose and proceeded to the brightly lit stairwell at the corner of the large room, before he vanished within it.

Signor Oliverotto watched Agapito's departure, then gave me a nod.

I returned his greeting. "*Buonasera*, Signore."

"I was all but certain we would meet again." If Maestro Leonardo's words were notes played on a pipe organ, Signor Oliverotto's were plucked from the deepest range of a lute. "As I told you, I am here for a while."

I could not help but wonder if he had been here long enough to murder one woman, wait for her charm bag to be delivered to the pope in Rome, and, shortly after the arrival of His Holiness's emissary, murder another woman in the same brutal yet meticulous fashion.

His lady nodded at me. "That is such a lovely gown," she said in a sweet, cither-like voice. "One does not see *velluto allucciolati* of that quality these days. You must have had it sewn some years ago." I stifled a laugh; she already sounded like a jealous wife. Had I wished to set myself after her signore, I could have quickly turned her jealousy to envy, a far more sour vintage.

But I did not need to encourage Signor Oliverotto. He turned to his little *cortigiana* and said, "Play something. Without words."

Silently the girl took up her *lira da braccio* from the chair next to her, backing away from the table like a waiting lady leaving a duchess. She began to play the *Gelosia*, holding the slender bow between two fingers and her thumb, drawing the taut horsehairs over the strings of her *lira* with the liquid grace of a dancer—although her notes were not so beguiling.

As she played on, her companion turned his attention to a silver plate crowded with miniature olives. Signor Oliverotto's hands seemed twice as large as most men's, yet delicately he began to arrange the tiny olives into some pattern, although it was not at once clear what he intended to make. He did not look up until he had finished his *disegno*, whereupon the ferocity of his stare so startled me that I could not observe what he had created. "She will learn," he said to me, his tone far more gentle than his eyes. "The *lira*, like warfare, requires long practice, while one is still young. She can benefit from instruction." Here he cocked his head, as he had the previous night on the drawbridge. "But I would have no need to teach you, would I?"

Signor Oliverotto smiled thinly and edged his platter of olives toward me. Having made this offering, he rose and left me with a short salute, touching his fingers to his velvet cap. When he collected his girl, he took her arm so quickly that her delicate bow screeched against the strings.

Only when they had gone did I look down at the platter of olives. Signor Oliverotto had made a perfect spiral.

◆

I waited an hour for Messer Agapito to return, whereupon he instructed me I would have to wait some more, before he disappeared again. As the night wore on, the ambassadors were summoned, separately, each to a lengthy audience. Ramiro da Lorca also came and went, in a fury of clicking boots, his dark complexion nearly brick-colored; he was not required to wait at all and his meeting with the duke was similarly brief. He passed me with hardly a glance, though surely he knew I was the same notorious woman whose house he had so thoroughly searched the day after Juan's murder.

At last Agapito came back down the stairs, for a moment standing silently over me like a priest at Mass, as if offering me the absolution of a prudent exit. "His Excellency is ready for you."

The light in the stairway was provided by a large candelabrum; I found this peculiar, since a little oil lamp would have sufficiently illuminated the steps. Agapito knocked on the lone door in the landing, then opened it quickly himself. A woman slipped out like a wraith. She wore a snow-white chemise, her nipples making dark points beneath the thin fabric—I thought due to the cold, until I saw her eyes.

I knew the expression there, though it is a rare thing in my experience, because most ladies in my former business guard themselves well; if not, they are soon lost. And this lady *was* lost, as if upon a vast sea, entirely without stars or instruments to guide her, searching only for the touch of the man she had just left. There is a terrible bondage in such eyes, and always fear.

Even so, in such a state there is also a profound abandonment to one's senses, and this I saw in her mouth, the subtle yet swollen pendant of her lower lip, the flesh above her thinner upper lip still moist with sweat.

Only when I observed that her hair was as blond as mine had been five years previously did I draw away from her with a start, for a moment imagining I had just encountered the duke's sister, Lucrezia, now the Duchess of Ferrara. I was all the more startled because I so firmly believed that despite all the scurrilous gossip that Valentino was Lucrezia's lover—the same had been said of Juan and the pope himself—there was no truth to these rumors.

But I could not see the rest of the lady's face, which was concealed by a birdlike Carnival mask. She kept her eyes on me, turning her head even as she passed, though not as if I were a rival. Instead she seemed to acknowledge some kinship of our souls.

When I entered the dim room, however, it was as if she had been a phantom. Duke Valentino sat behind a single table in a large study that was otherwise unfurnished, poring over some document by the light of a single reflecting lamp, his jacket laced nearly to his chin. The tabletop was covered with stacks of papers.

Valentino pushed away the bronze lamp and sat back, clasping his gloved hands over his breast. He was attired entirely in black, his long, grave face appearing almost to float. He examined me, a silent attention I found considerably unsettling; at best, I expected a grim warning to remain in my rooms until I was sent back to Rome. And I did not want to consider the worst.

"Let me show you something that Maestro Leonardo has drawn."

I knew at once that Leonardo had been to see him while I waited in "Paradise"; no doubt there were several passages to this room. Even as I considered this, I observed a small door in the wall behind him.

Valentino sprang from his chair like a hunting panther, yet he came around his table with the same languid grace those animals display when they have been fed and leashed. He looked down and began to thumb through one of the stacks. After a moment he extracted several drawings, which he placed near the lamp. "Come here," he said. "Look at this."

It was a study of a man's arm, in reddish chalk, the contours of the muscles elegantly drawn in a perfect mimicry of life, save that the skin was absent. The myriad veins thus exposed resembled naked trees, the thicker limbs separating into smaller branches and twigs, so to speak.

"Maestro Leonardo has made a number of these studies," Valentino said. My stomach soured; I wondered if the maestro intended to make similar drawings from the limbs of the butchered women. "Our modern painters have given us a convincing representation of the human form as they believe God created it. But only this maestro shows us the world hidden beneath our flesh. Only in these drawings can we envision man as Nature perfected him, an intricate *invenzione* of tubes and mechanisms." He circled his finger over the drawing, almost as if he were tracing Signor Oliverotto's spiral. "Maestro Leonardo already has plans for machines that can mimic Nature in various ways—devices that can walk like a man, or even fly like a bird."

I had not even begun to digest this ambition, which seemed a challenge to both God and Nature, when Valentino removed this sketch, revealing beneath it a larger drawing, vividly decorated with paint washes upon paper; to my eyes it was some sort of architectural *fantasia*, a plan for a villa or palazzo of fantastical complexity, the bright brick hue contrasted to a thick blue serpentine painted a thumb's span beneath the fantasy palace, like some immense banner curling in the wind.

All at once I imagined myself a thousand feet in the air, my shoulders gripped by an eagle's talons, looking down on the earth, gazing into a walled city—indeed, the very city of Imola I had viewed from the surrounding hills just that day. However, this was Imola as seen by someone with the wings and eyes of a bird, every fortification, residence, and courtyard, each canal and river—for the blue serpent was the Santerno River—in its exact place, but observed from a great height directly above. Now, in my life I have sat upon a cloth-of-gold cushion in a Vatican apartment and held the maps that guided our mariners to the new lands. But I had never seen anything like this.

"Do you see what the maestro has done?" Valentino's whisper was so faint that I strained to hear him, even in the hush of that room. "Just as he can see within our bodies, so he can also portray the world from a perspective we have never before seen. If we measure this distance on

Leonardo da Vinci's Map of Imola

his map"—he stuck the tip of his finger on the Rocca at the corner of the city, which one could easily distinguish by its circular towers, then pointed to the Piazza Maggiore in the center of the city—"and this distance"—he now moved his finger to the Santerno River, outside the walls—"we will obtain precisely the same proportion that results if we pace the ground itself or measure the actual distance with mechanical devices. Leonardo's *mappa* is an image of the world identical in all its features, reduced to a scale that we can hold in our hands."

Yet even as Valentino extolled this extraordinary *mappa*, I could see all too clearly that the novel perspective and uncanny fidelity were not the only remarkable features. The center of the map was also the center of the city, where two ancient Roman roads, the Via Emilia and Via Appia, cross each other. On the map, this intersection was also the hub of a circle, drawn in ink, that surrounded the entire city and the fields outside its walls. Like all geographers, Leonardo had indicated the points of the compass in the form of a wind rose, employing eight lines that proceeded carefully from the center to the perimeter of this circle, dividing it into an octave of evenly spaced slices. Where each line of the wind rose met the rim of the circle, in the fashion of a wheel's spoke, it was labeled in a small, fine hand: *Septantrione*, this being the north wind; *Greco*, the northeast wind; *Levante*, east wind; *Scirocho*, the southeast wind—and so on around the compass, comprising the eight principal winds.

"This is it, isn't it?" I said. I put my fingertip on the map, precisely where the compass line labeled *Scirocho* met the circle scribed around the city, just outside a bend in the Santerno River. "I believe this is where one quarter of the first victim was found. Today I saw the cairn of stones the maestro left beside the river."

Skipping a line each time, in quick sequence I pointed where three other lines of the wind rose also met the circle, as I read the names written alongside them: "*Libecco, Maestro, Greco.*" Southwest, northwest (this being the strongest, or "master" wind), northeast. "Each point establishes the corner of an imaginary square, which we are able to see through the agency of Maestro Leonardo's remarkable map. Thus the murderer was able to boast that he had left one quarter of a woman's body at each corner of the winds. God's Cross. Whoever has done this had to have seen this *mappa*."

Of course I presumed that Valentino's *condottieri* had been privileged to see this map before they betrayed him.

Valentino did not even nod. "But you have not finished," he said flatly. "Show me the rest."

Leonardo's map was so precise that I was able to trace our route that afternoon, from the pile of stones beside the river into the hills south of the city, running my finger directly along the compass line labeled for the south wind, *Mezzodi*. Yet as I attempted to judge the distance on the map in proportion to the distance we had traveled, I understood the flaw in my reasoning: I was forced to move my finger off the map entirely.

"I presumed that he would make another figure of geometry," I said, "following the points of this map. No doubt this is what Leonardo was measuring this afternoon." I shook my head. "Unless the *mappa* itself is in error, what we found today"—I lifted my hand and crossed myself—"cannot be placed on this map."

"The maestro is continuing his measurements." Here Valentino nodded slightly, as if satisfied that he had just measured the depth of my knowledge—and my ignorance.

"In some fashion this murderer intends to create a circle within a square," I said, presuming that Leonardo had already shared the *bollettino* with his employer. "So this figure is not finished. There will be more." By this I meant parts of a woman's body.

But when Valentino did not offer a response, I said, "Have you instructed Ramiro da Lorca to look for the rest of that woman?" I assumed this would be the case, not only because I had just seen Ramiro come and go with some urgency; among all of Valentino's people, he had the most familiarity with Juan's murder, as I knew only too well.

Valentino shook his head absently. "No. I have sent Ramiro to command the garrison at Rimini. His methods of investigation are old-fashioned. The rack, rope, and hot iron. Leonardo employs the methods of *scienza*."

No doubt I made some expression that betrayed my surprise—and dread. Ramiro had been one of the pope's most trusted retainers before His Holiness had attached him to Valentino's household, and it seemed likely that his loyalties remained with the father rather than

The Corners of the Winds

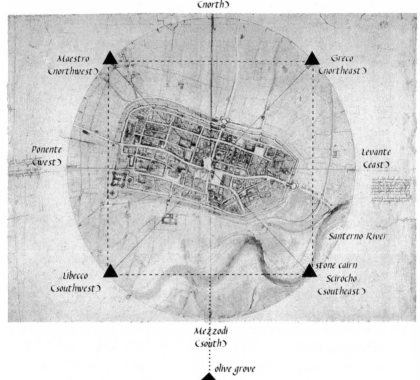

Septantrione
(north)

Maestro
(northwest)

Greco
(northeast)

Ponente
(west)

Levante
(east)

Santerno River

Libecco
(southwest)

stone cairn
Scirocho
(southeast)

Mezzodi
(south)

olive grove

"corners of the winds": remains of first victim

torso of second victim

the son. If Ramiro was to be excluded from this investigation, I could only wonder if Valentino wished to determine entirely what his father would be told. And if this second murder was intended to refrain the provocation of the first, perhaps Valentino saw it in his interest—the interest of his peace—to withhold from his father certain information.

Valentino did not remark on Ramiro's exile, instead returning to my prior speculation. "You presume there will be further discoveries. Provocations." He paused at length, his nostrils dilating several times. "Yes. There will be more."

This conviction was not offered in a fashion that invited further questions but instead seemed to forbid them. I prepared to be dismissed, if not condemned.

Here he glanced at me again, a slight thing. Yet I recalled this expression quite well; it prefaced a silence by which he demanded—or pleaded—that one address some longing hidden within his breast. That was the single key to his seduction: where all but a few men wish only to enter you and fill you up, with their cocks and thoughts and sentiments—in many instances all equally flaccid—he brought a woman inside him entirely. He could not exist until she poured her soul into his.

So after a silence, I gave him something. "That woman who was here. She loves you with every fiber of her being. I hope you will be merciful." Yet perhaps I was merely pleading for myself.

He blinked. "She knows nothing of me. Nothing but flesh. The sentiments that reside on the tips of our fingers."

After a moment Valentino looked down and again took up Leonardo's *mappa*. "We have been given the means to hold in our hands the entire orb of the Earth. We need only to measure it in order to possess it." His next words, almost sotto voce, did not seem intended for me. "But we need not turn this new world of ours over to Fortune, chaos, and war."

The duke motioned his head toward the door. "The maestro will continue to examine this matter," he said with less sentiment than one could find on a fingertip. "When he has completed his observations, we will talk again."

IX

On this night I ran across the drawbridge, imagining that hands grasped at me from the dark moat. When I reached the street my breath made a cloud before me. In the time I had waited on Valentino, the snow had blown down from the mountains again, tiny, wind-driven grains that stung my face.

Thus blinded, I confronted the truth I had not wished to face in Valentino's study. In the same blithe fashion that the duke would discard the poor woman who loved him so nakedly, he would discard me. I would not be strangled or "interrogated"—if he simply wished to have me out of the way, he might have done so tonight. Instead Valentino would leave me at liberty to nose around Imola; I might even learn something that would enable him to exact more favorable concessions from the *condottieri*. Indeed, I presumed this was why he had instructed a courtier as valuable as Leonardo to continue pursuing a truth he only intended to bury. But all too soon Signor Oliverotto would convey the documents to Vitellozzo Vitelli for his signature, at which time the treaty would bind all the parties.

Whereupon I would return to Rome with life intact, but too late to ransom my little boy. The name of his father's murderer would no longer have any value, except to poison the wound in his grandfather's breast. With no other vengeance left to him, His Holiness would seek his solace in my lingering and painful death. And even if the Holy Madonna were to intercede for me in Heaven, I would suffer an eternal torment far greater than any punishment of Hell, knowing I had left my precious son behind to grow up in the Devil's house.

◆

After I had entered our palazzo, I ventured the length of the courtyard, ascending the stairs to the piano nobile on the wing opposite ours. I pounded on Messer Niccolò's door, only to be greeted by a ghost, or so it seemed: the boy in a nightshirt was so pale and slender that it was a miracle he had worked the latch, much less lifted the bar. He couldn't have been seventeen, but he had the vitality of an old man—he fixed me with one rheumy eye, the other nearly crusted shut, and stumbled back inside.

I followed this scarecrow into the bedroom, where he collapsed upon the mattress with a pitiful groan. Just in front of the shuttered window was a small table, lit by a tallow candle and piled with books and papers, with scant room cleared for an inkwell.

Messer Niccolò had fallen asleep at this little desk; he remained sitting in an old chair, still dressed in his shirt and hose, his head at the angle of a hanged man. I spied a bit on his researches. In addition to the stacks of folded letters and diplomatic dispatches, I found a Latin text, the *Decades* of Titus Livy. A missive also appeared to be in progress, this beginning with the salutation *"Magnifici Domini,"* no doubt intended for the secretary's lordships in Florence.

I gave him an indelicate poke in the shoulder. "Messer Niccolò," I said, "I hope you found your supper agreeable."

He sprang to his feet, blinked, and gave me a little hand roll that seemed to mock us both. "Antonio found it particularly agreeable—he was able to rise from the dead and eat. The miracle of Imola." He glanced at the boy on the bed and whispered, "My manservant has made my mattress his sickbed, leaving me the choice of his cot or this chair. When he is not ill, Antonio must endeavor only to restore his health; when he is ill, I must endeavor to restore his health while providing for myself." He added, "I have lost my enthusiasm for Terence," referring to those comedies wherein the servants dictate their masters' lives.

"Is that why you find your amusement in the more serious Latins? Your copy of Livy is marked up well enough."

He ran his hand over the salad atop his head. "Titus Livy tells us that the study of history is the best medicine for present ills."

"Ah. So you are not merely your manservant's physician but Italy's as well."

He lifted an eyebrow a bit.

"Well, Dottore," I went on, "I find myself in agreement with something you told me today. All this has to do with whatever Maestro Leonardo is measuring."

He rubbed his eyes. "It has to do with considerably more than that. But we must begin with whatever Leonardo is measuring, if only because it will lead us to this man's necessity. And his nature."

"His necessity?" This seemed some philosophical invention. "I do not care about this vile murderer's necessity or his nature. I want to learn his name." But I did not think this was the time to reveal how strongly I suspected the name Oliverotto da Fermo.

"Nevertheless, I do not believe we will know his name before we learn his necessity," Niccolò replied. In the candlelight it was hard to say if he wore the expression of a mischievous boy or more resembled the Devil himself.

Here I saw an opportunity to aid both of us. "I have now seen the corners of the winds." Whereupon I proceeded to tell him about Leonardo's *mappa* of Imola, describing how the quarters of the first woman had been placed precisely on four equally spaced points of the wind rose.

When I had finished, Niccolò looked down and placed the tips of his fingers on his Titus Livy. "Yes. A *disegno*, drawn with human flesh. But Leonardo already knew that. So now what is our maestro measuring?"

I shook my head. "The point the maestro measured in that olive grove is not on his map. You said yourself this was all a riddle or a rebus. I think the location of the olive grove is some sort of key to that riddle. Perhaps Leonardo believes his measurements will direct him to the head of the first victim."

"I never took to geometry." Messer Niccolò's fingers remained on his Titus Livy. "The question I would first consider is this: Why the riddle?"

"To taunt the pope," I said impatiently, recalling all too well His Holiness's fury in the Hall of Saints. "To confuse and enrage him with these games, so that the pope himself will remove the burden of delaying the negotiations from the Vitelli—whose fellow *condottieri* are far more eager for peace. I believe it was you who instructed me regarding these 'additional concessions' the Vitelli hope to coerce, when they are allowed time to hire more soldiers and achieve superiority in numbers." I could not fathom why I had to continue reminding Messer Niccolò of his own words.

"I don't know. Perhaps that is in fact this murderer's necessity—to torment the pope. Or perhaps it is merely his nature."

I had all too little time for more of this philosophical nonsense. "Let me make you a proposal, Messer Niccolò. I intend to examine Maestro Leonardo's studio for whatever drawings and notes he has recorded with regard to this murderer's figures of geometry. I invite you to come with me."

"You intend to call on him? Will you send Camilla over with supper before you pound on his door in the middle of the night?" He made no effort to disguise his amusement.

"I intend to call on him," I said, "this very night. But I do not intend to knock."

Once again I had erased his smile. Messer Niccolò drew his fingers over the page beneath him, as if caressing a child's face. When he looked up at me, his black eyes were sparked by the candlelight and I could see the desire he had previously taken pains to hide. Yet I could also see that he did not trust me.

At last he shook his head, evidently perplexed at his own decision, because he said, "If you mean to go at once, I have only to get my cape."

Messer Niccolò having obtained his wrap, I brought him across the courtyard to my rooms, so that I could quickly change my clothes yet again. While he waited outside my bedroom, I told Camilla where I intended to go and she dressed me accordingly, in hose and a boy's short jacket, my hair pulled up under a *berretta*.

When we had returned to Messer Niccolò, I instructed Camilla,

"Bar the door, of course. But I am not even going to say farewell, because I will return so soon."

My darling smiled at me, in a fashion that struck through my heart like a stradiot's spear.

◆

I suppose here I should tell you a few things about your *zia* Camilla, who could shame the Seraphs with her goodness. She came to me in *anno Domini* 1494, the year the French came to Rome. Charles VIII had arrived with his enormous army in the last days of December, driving Pope Alexander out of the Vatican and into the Castel Sant'Angelo. But His Holiness, though weak in arms and soldiers, was far too clever for the drooling, watery-eyed little king. With the aid of my dear old patron, Cardinal Ascanio Sforza, a truce was negotiated that proved more profitable to the pope than to His Most Christian Majesty.

The French soldiers were allowed into Rome like panthers on leashes. Most of them were held in check, but enough got loose to sack scores of houses, making bonfires of the tables and chairs while they drank our finest wines and sampled without recompense delicacies of various sorts—though King Charles himself had issued a decree that no *cortigiane* were to be harmed. Even the houses of the pope's chamberlain and the mother of His Holiness's children—your grandmother—were not spared. And unfortunate servants and Jews often fared little better than the furniture.

I was twenty-six years old in that year, and there was not a man in Rome, from the fuller treading piss in his vats in the Trastevere to the pope on the throne of Saint Peter, who did not know my name; the wages of my notoriety had earned me the best house on the Via dei Banchi. Even now I can still smell those rooms, the orange water and lavender; the flowers I had every day in spring and summer: roses, carnations, jasmine, and hyacinth.

But there was little such *bellezza* on the day I met your *zia* Camilla. I was out in the cold rain, seeing after the *bravi* who always guarded my house—in those difficult days they also informed me as to the whereabouts of the French looters, in the event we should have to flee. I watched the evacuation of the neighborhoods just above the Ponte

Sant'Angelo, where hazy plumes of smoke rose into the leaden sky. These refugees had loaded their mules with whatever they hoped to save: money chests, dresses, silver plate, what have you. I took in several of these distraught souls, who had credulously believed the French pledges, and was about to shut my door when I observed a couple mounted on a mule, trotting right down the Via dei Banchi, but in the direction of all the trouble. He had two good lumps on his nose and white scars on his stubbled cheeks. She was half his age, not more than fourteen, with a child's slender face and charcoal eyes that had already seen everything.

Surmising that both the mule and the girl had been stolen, I waved the thief to a stop. "Messer," I said, "where are you going with my friend's mule?"

He threw back his cape and reached for the sword at his belt—until he saw my *bravi* step out from my doorway. "Who did you say your friend is?" he asked, his eyes slits.

"Donna Vanozza Catanei," I said, this being your aforementioned grandmother, although her ownership of the mule was entirely my invention. I wanted this thief to think he had just met a better thief.

He gave me a scoundrel's toothy smile. "That is so. Madonna Vanozza gave me this mule with orders to sell it to the *oltramontani* before they could steal it." He nodded toward the smoke plumes.

I knew what he intended to sell to the French. "Who is the girl?"

"My sister. When I heard what the monks were doing to her at Santa Cecilia, I took my own flesh out of there, may a better God now protect her."

"Truly? And here I am looking for someone to recite the Litany of Saints." I could see from the girl's bare, purple feet that she had come from the dye vats instead of the convent, but you couldn't say which was worse. "For which do you think the French are likely to pay more, your little sister-sister or the mule?"

He pumped his heels at the mule's ribs but I nodded to my boys to grab the halter. I told the rascal, "I think it will matter less to the *oltramontani* that the mule has already been ridden." Then I looked carefully at the girl. "Do you want to go with him?"

I knew what her eyes said. After a moment she shook her head.

"Messer," I said, holding out my arms to the girl, "I leave you the mule."

So that was how my Camilla came into my house.

She did not trust me for two weeks, although she ate my soup and roasts and took in everything with those agile, all-consuming eyes. Of course she believed that I would use her as I had been used when I was her age—like the girl of Andros. But one day she followed me into my bedroom and stood looking about at all my Greek vases and Roman medallions—with those eyes I didn't know if she intended to snatch something and run off. Instead this tiny voice emerged: "Madonna, can I live here until Easter?"

I took Camilla in my arms for the first time since I had lifted her from that mule. And I gave her at least a dozen kisses before I said, "You can live here forever."

That was when she began to tell me her story. Like me, she was born in the dirt, in her instance the red dust of the Neapolitan Campania. The rest was a tangled tale, much of which even she couldn't unravel, but it is sufficient to say that she was sold like a basket of fat Spanish olives to another family, to serve as a companion to their daughter, only to be put on the street when the little girl died of plague. After that she suffered in as many guises as Ovid's Mestra, until at last she found herself treading cloth in a dye vat near Monte Mario, from which she was soon enough chased by the French soldiers pillaging there. Having no place to go, she had been offered the poisonous charity of the lout from whom I had retrieved her.

I taught my darling Camilla to read, as my mother had taught me, and that was the beginning of our love. In the end she did not profit, because she spent more years with me in the Trastevere than in our palazzo on the Via dei Banchi. But without Camilla I would not have survived the day you came into this world, and when she might have made her own life, she stayed with you, my precious son, as if you were her own. She was my first baby, you were my second. I was your first mother, and she was your second.

I will say no more, except that our angel's love is woven into the weft of your soul as well as mine, and nothing can ever draw it out.

X

When we reached the corner where Messer Niccolò had earlier kept watch on Leonardo's palazzo, I said, "There is an alley alongside," having studied the great house well enough myself. "Let us see what they have in back." The towering façade offered only barred windows and the massive oaken door.

The unpaved alley led us to an ill-kept garden where flowerpots lay tumbled amid a small, overgrown orchard. Behind a low brick wall was cleared ground, mostly planted with squash, lying beneath a pale carpet of snow that extended to the city wall. For a moment I looked about in melancholy wonder, remembering our own little garden in the Trastevere. I saw you and dear little Ermes running about, Camilla chasing behind you both. Now all I wanted in this world was to hear your laugh again.

Messer Niccolò and I examined the back of the house. The smaller windows on the ground floor were covered with iron grates; the arched windows on the piano nobile were merely shuttered, though a good ten *braccia* above us. After thrashing about in the snow-sprinkled shrubs, we located a crude ladder, merely a long pole with scraps of lumber nailed to it every *braccia* or so.

When we had wrestled the ladder against the stone lip of one of the windows, I told Niccolò, "I will go in."

He looked at me as if I were mad.

"Can you say that you have earned a living stealing from men's houses?"

His smile was quick but sad. "As an honest servant of the Florentine republic, I earn no living at all. I am in debt for my expenses here
and still waiting for my appropriation."

I began to climb, the scrap steps creaking, my gloves shredded
by splinters. Upon reaching the shutters I forced them open with my
knife and sat on the broad windowsill, letting my legs hang into the
house. I was able to make out quite a large room; probably it had once
been a bishop's *sala grande*. Indeed it appeared to have been set up for
a banquet, the three large trestle tables already having a great many
objects on them, though I could not say what they were.

It was not a long drop to the floor beneath me, but before I could
leap my breath caught in my throat.

The blank, ghostly face hovered almost directly opposite me. I
thought, *I have found her head.*

But this was something only a bit less ghastly. Evidently a whited
human skull had been placed upon the broad cornice that ran around
the walls, in the fashion that small antiquities are often displayed.
Wondering if this room contained other items Maestro Leonardo had
obtained from corpses, I decided to search it first.

I observed the faint glow of a brazier near the open doorway and
padded over to light the candle stuck in my belt. When I turned around
again I discovered, tumbled and strewn upon those banquet tables, a
new world.

With each step, my flickering light illuminated one marvel and
then the next: A bleached thighbone might sit next to a Herodotus
bound in leather, atop of which rested something like a miniature mill-
works, with sequences of tiny wooden cogs and wheels. Drawings were
scattered about like leaves in November, many portraying the human
body from without, but others were similar to those Valentino had
just shown me, whole lattices of bones, tendons, nerves, and veins, as
though they had been stripped intact from the surrounding flesh, like
the skeleton of a filleted fish. The light glimmered on mirrors, lenses,
calipers, and scales. On myriad scraps of paper measurements had
been noted, quantities added, geometry proofs recorded. Yet what
most teased my eye were those forms repeated from one thing to the
next: a petrified spiral seashell metamorphosed into the cog of some

strange wooden machine, only to be found next in fantastic drawings of spinning whirlwinds and whirlpools.

I wandered for some time, so rapt I almost walked straight past the most important drawing in that room—at least with regard to my quest. Carelessly surrounded by several notebooks and wooden polygons, this diagram had been inscribed in red chalk upon a piece of thin, translucent paper, such as artists employ for tracing copies.

"God's Cross," I said aloud. "This is what you were measuring."

This tracing tissue was somewhat larger than the map Valentino had shown me only an hour or so before. Maestro Leonardo had drawn a circle divided into an octave identical to a wind rose; indeed it appeared that Leonardo had traced this figure from his own map of Imola. He had also made red dots at each of four equally spaced points on the rim of the wheel, so to speak, these no doubt corresponding to the corners of the wind, as Valentino had shown me. And Leonardo had drawn lines between these points, creating a square perfectly fitted within the circle, touching it at only the four corners.

This much I could have expected. But Leonardo had further drawn a larger square around the circle, which touched it at only four points, these tangents being the four corners of the winds; the larger square was in this fashion rotated at an angle to the smaller square, thus giving a sequence of square, circle, square, all fitted perfectly together.

"The circle within the square," I said aloud, though at that moment I did not entirely understand it.

All at once, it appeared that my candle had waxed considerably brighter. I spun about.

Maestro Leonardo da Vinci stood in the doorway, attired in a farmer's shirt and an apron, the latter covered with irregular dark spots, which I thought to be paint. With his right hand he held a candle lamp; the tarantula-leg fingers of his left hand appeared to claw at the apron where it covered his breast. Only when I recalled that Leo-

The Circle within the Square

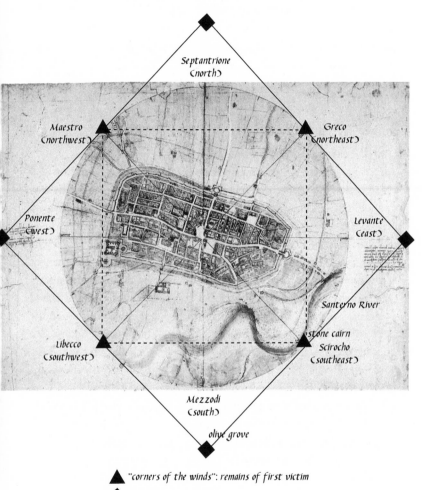

Septantrione
(north)

Maestro
(northwest)

Greco
(northeast)

Ponente
(west)

Levante
(east)

Santerno River

stone cairn
Scirocho
(southeast)

Libecco
(southwest)

Mezzodi
(south)

olive grove

▲ "corners of the winds": remains of first victim

◆ remains of second victim

nardo was said to dissect corpses in his basement did I understand that the apron was a butcher's smock, the dark spots blood, which he was attempting to wipe from his fingers.

"What do you think you see?"

His sharp tenor now had an authority absent in the olive grove; he seemed to draw strength amid the dazzling disorder of his own intellect. He came to me with the padding gait of a great lion.

Yet for some reason, I was not frightened. When he had come to my side, I said, "The duke has shown me your map. And the corners of the winds."

"You make a false assumption." His pitch was higher now, querulous. "These corners of the winds are not my construction."

"No. But the murderer has imposed them on your wind rose." I placed my finger on the tracing tissue, directly upon one of the corners of the larger square. "Let us presume that this point represents the location we visited today, in the olive grove. Where we found one quarter of the second woman's body." In quick sequence, I moved my finger to each remaining corner of this larger square. "The corners of this square are the locations where you have since found the remaining three quarters of her." I reasoned that Leonardo and his assistants had gone back out that night, or perhaps Valentino's people had visited the other three locations during the day. "Once you had measured to that olive grove, you understood how to draw the circle within the square, because the circle was your own wind rose, and you had the first point of the square."

"Again you make an incorrect assumption. We have yet to recover anything from the other three locations. The duke's soldiers are guarding them until we can conduct our *esperienza* in a suitable light."

However hasty my assumption, I had little doubt that the remaining quarters of that poor woman would be found buried in crude crypts. "Maestro, this murderer is using your *mappa*," I said sharply. "He has traced his own *disegno* from it, as your drawing here demonstrates. Who would have had an opportunity to examine your map at such length?"

His lips moved silently and I thought he would merely address the ether. "I am a military engineer," he said at last. "The defense of this city requires an exacting set of measurements."

"Then I presume that the duke's officers and intimates were familiar with your map." As I had observed to Messer Niccolò, the duke's engineer general had no doubt worked with the duke's *condottieri* before their recent defection. And as Leonardo had not contested my previous assumption, I leapt at once to another, hoping to take him by surprise: "Maestro, did you have an association with Signor Oliverotto da Fermo?"

The tarantula legs returned to Leonardo's apron, as if his hand wished to burrow into his breast. "Only inasmuch as he was attached to Vitellozzo Vitelli."

So he knew both of them, evidently being more familiar with Vitellozzo Vitelli—who among all the *condottieri* had the most to gain by sending his emissary to Imola with instructions to secretly and most deviously impede the peace negotiations. But the maestro had confirmed my suspicion of Signor Oliverotto only because he had not expected such a direct inquiry; he would not answer me so readily again. Thus I simply said, *"Mille grazie*, Maestro. Now will you allow me to exit through your door?"

Leonardo silently led me down a creaking wooden staircase to the entrance vestibule. When he paused at the great oak portal, his eyes transited carefully over my features, as if examining the tissues beneath my skin. At last he stooped to unlock the smaller pedestrian door.

"Maestro," I said, "someone has taken considerable care to cut two unfortunate women into pieces and place them in conformity with your *mappa*. Is it incorrect to assume that whoever has done this might take similar care to see that someone else is blamed for his crime?" By this I implied that Vitellozzo Vitelli, once he had succeeded in gaining the upper hand in the negotiations, might find it useful to provide a scapegoat for the very crimes that had postponed the agreement—a fate the duke's engineer general and I might well share.

His eyes still on me, Leonardo pushed open the door. "Whenever good Fortune enters a house, Envy lays siege to the place." He blinked, with that expression one has when remembering. "And Envy's chief weapon is false accusation."

✦

As soon as the door closed behind me, I scurried through the alley to the back of that great house. Messer Niccolò remained faithfully beside the ladder, a dusting of snow on his head and shoulders. Startled to see me come around the corner, he began to push the ladder over before he recognized my face; in my costume I might well have been the maestro's servant or *bravo*. I took his hand and led him at a trot into the street, not slowing until we were back on the Via Appia.

"What happened?" he said. "I saw the light. Did you rouse the entire house?"

I let go his hand and told him everything I had seen in Maestro Leonardo's study. We were halfway down the Via Emilia before I concluded my recitation: "This butcher has made a square within the circle of Leonardo's compass rose and another square outside it, all fitted as tightly as an egg in its shell. The maestro believes that whoever has done this will endeavor to accuse him, out of some envy or rivalry." I recalled how Valentino had extolled Leonardo's plans for the Romagna; perhaps the *condottieri*, men who had mastered only the arts of destruction, both feared and envied an engineer general who threatened to build new cities where all men could share peace and prosperity. "That would explain why this murderer has followed so faithfully the maestro's *mappa*."

I waited a dozen steps, the thick snow flying furiously into our faces, before Niccolò offered his commentary. "Yes. This man has a great deal of interest in Leonardo," he said in his musing fashion. "Envy? Possibly. But I lean toward a different opinion. The murderer is most concerned with his own amusement—an amusement principally derived from confounding all of us. Each time we look at this *disegno* he has created, we find it more difficult to see what he is getting at." He shook the snow from his salad-head. "No. He does not wish to bury the maestro with false indictments. He wishes to engage him in a dreadful game."

I could hardly listen to this. "Now you imagine that"—my pitch rose sharply—"that this butcher and the maestro will sit together and play *triche-tach*?"

Niccolò gave me a cautious glance. "You recall Maestro Leonardo telling us he was informed by peasants as to the location of the remains we found today. Yet from what you just told me, Leonardo has deduced the whereabouts of the other three quarters solely from his measurements regarding the first."

"Having one point of the square," I said impatiently, dodging a hole filled with slush, "he could easily measure the other three, knowing their position on the wind rose."

"Yes. Just so. The remains of the first victim were placed on the corners of the winds. The murderer paid peasants to report their locations but not to disturb them, so that they would be found precisely in that pattern—and Maestro Leonardo would be certain to recognize it. Peasants likewise informed Valentino's people regarding the crypt we opened today. But the murderer did not pay peasants to report scavengers at the locations where he buried the remaining three quarters. Instead he challenged Leonardo to discover his new figure of geometry." Here we turned onto the street that ends at the Rocca, though the fortress itself was no longer visible through the veil of snow. "Do you see? With the first victim he established the rules of his game. With the second, he invited Leonardo to play against him. That is why he buried the quarters of the second victim—so that they would not be disturbed before Leonardo was able to make his measurements, discover this new square with his own circle or wind rose within it, and find his way to them."

I had it at the tip of my tongue to tell him about the Duke of Gandia's amulet, thus establishing beyond question that the object of this otherwise meaningless "game" was to provoke rage in the Vatican—and, it seemed, cast false suspicion on Valentino's engineer general. But instead I merely remarked on Messer Niccolò's dubious method, in the hope I would no longer have to hear his theories: "As Lucretius says, 'We draw large deductions from small indications, and so bring ourselves to deception and delusion.' "

I was not entirely surprised that he laughed, even if he was the joke.

◆

When we reached our building, we entered the stables through the pedestrian door, finding the animals inside huddled together against the cold. As we entered the courtyard, I looked up to our shutters. They were closed, but the light from Camilla's lamp glimmered reassuringly through the cracks.

Almost directly above our shuttered windows, a motion caught my eye. Through the falling snow I saw what appeared to be the ghostly, pale face of a great barn owl, perched upon the spine of the roof. Almost at once this enormous bird vanished into the gray sky.

"Did you see it?" I said, turning to Niccolò.

Niccolò bolted into my stairwell and I could only watch in utter confusion as he leapt up the stairs and disappeared onto the landing.

For some reason I looked at my feet. Two sets of footprints led to my stairwell, the second having just been made by Niccolò himself.

I flew up after him, unable to feel my feet touch the steps. The door was wide open and I could see straight into the bedroom. The candle still burned on the little table beneath the window. All at once Niccolò appeared at the bedroom threshold, his face as white as the owl I had just seen.

I ran toward him. "Tell me she is still here!" I screamed.

Niccolò pushed me back as if I were an intruder, his hand at the back of my head, burying my face in his cape. I could see nothing but the abandoned farmhouse where two women had already been butchered.

"She is still here," he said. In Rome, Camilla and I had once climbed the Esquiline hill to visit the ancient ruins of Nero's Golden Palace and had called to each other from within those vast, echoing chambers; Niccolò's voice was hollow and distant like that. "And you must not go in there."

XII

I would not have survived that darkest of nights, or the next days, without Messer Niccolò. First he kept me from my bedroom, though he nearly had to suffocate me to do so; afterward, as I fell into a black stupor of grief, Niccolò also made those arrangements the living must make for the dead. I slept upon the servant's cot in his rooms because I could not bear to cross my own threshold, relying instead on Niccolò to bring me my clothing and other necessities.

I began to climb from the abyss on the second day, when Niccolò compelled me to bathe. He transported the copper bathtub from my rooms and had the hot water brought up by the watchman, then left me while he attended to his mule. I fitted myself into the little tub that Camilla had polished for me; as grateful as I was for this last token of her unceasing industry on my behalf, I became as angry as Electra that I had only this metal shell to wrap me, and not my angel's loving arms. Even after the water had turned cold I continued to sit in the tub as if it were armor, guarding me from a grief I could not otherwise defeat.

I might have stayed there forever, if Niccolò had not discovered me, still curled up like a fetus in the womb. "*Cacasangue*," he said. I had some vague notion of him bustling about, draping me with towels. "You must dress yourself."

I rose, unconcerned to cover myself, but Niccolò had already withdrawn to the bedroom. I scarcely toweled at all and pulled my shift over wet skin. My feet were still in the tub when Niccolò looked in and came to me at once, snatching up several of the towels that had tumbled to the floor. He turned my back to him and began to dry my hair, much as Camilla had always done.

"You handle a woman well, Messer Niccolò." It was as if someone else were saying this. Yet I knew it was true; most men wish to put their hands on a woman, but few know how to truly handle her, although all the men in your family are among the latter. No doubt this gift is also your patrimony.

"You know women, don't you, Niccolò? And not just wives and sisters." In my brief interludes of reason during our mourners' vigil, I had learned a few things about him. He had a young bride, who had come to him from a wealthy family but with scant dowry; one could see why this spoiled girl and the secretary in threadbare clothes did not enjoy an epic love. Indeed his wife, Marietta, refused to write to him here in Imola, although they already shared a little daughter, who was not a year old.

Yet Niccolò had a comfort with women that did not come from bedding a scarcely pubescent bride. "You know us," I went on in my oracle's voice. "You watch us, circling like a hawk. Waiting for the moment..."

I faced him. I might have torn open the wounds of my soul, bleeding not only grief and anger but also a desire I had not obeyed since the last day of your father's life.

Casting my eyes down—a demure invitation that came to me by habit—I observed that the hem of my shift trailed into the bathwater. I gathered it into a ball and wrung it out, the water dripping from between my legs.

When I looked up at Niccolò, I expected a carnal variation of his blade-thin smile. But only his eyes flickered with temptation. In my former life I had always found these subtle expressions of desire the most welcome affirmation of my vanity—and all the more so in this instance because of Niccolò's previous indifference. His flesh had only to make an equally subtle gesture and I would devour it like a bacchante.

My mouth was not a palm's width from his. I whispered, my own words giving me a little shudder, "This is your moment."

I could feel the slight warmth of his sigh. When he closed his eyes, they trembled beneath the lids.

He opened his eyes again. And in them I saw only compassion.

I shut my own eyes as if praying. "Niccolò, I am a liar, a thief, and a whore." I made this confession in my own infinitely weary voice. "And whomever I love is cursed by Fortune, because out of malice toward me, she snatches them away."

I hoped he would heed this warning. Yet he was still there. "Dry yourself," he said. "Put on your clothes and get under my coverlet." I vaguely wondered why he had not brought the much thicker coverlet from my rooms. "I'll find some *minestra* we can heat over the brazier."

When Niccolò shut the door behind him, I cringed at the dull thump. In the silence that followed, I observed that if I died in the Romagna, the confession I had just recited would be my sole epitaph. Of all that I have made in this life, of all whom I have loved, you alone would live on. But as a prisoner in your grandfather's house, to remember me only with questions. And anger.

It was that thought alone that gave me the courage to step from my cold bath and begin to climb, hand over hand, from the pit of Hell into the healing oblivion of sleep.

✦

By the next day I had begun to recover my reason, as well as my purpose. I obtained a good fifty pounds of wax candles for Camilla's funeral Mass, which we held in a lovely old Benedictine church near the center of the city. We buried her in the shadow of the church's bell tower, where the gravestones were ancient, crowded together like an old woman's teeth. But before we put my precious girl in consecrated ground I took Niccolò aside, into the dingy arcade of the stone-carver's shop that opened right onto the cemetery, where they were chiseling her stone with a verse I had chosen from Petrarch: "There comes from her a brave and lovely soul, that put us on the straight path to Heaven."

I opened my cape and took something from around my neck, pressed it into Niccolò's cold hand and asked him to place it in the coffin. I could not look inside that oak casket, but neither did I want my angel's mortal remains to be absent any token of her family.

"You can look at it," I told Niccolò as he closed his hand around this little necklace. "It is a cameo portrait I had carved of my Giovanni, when he was a baby." During our vigil, I had told Niccolò many things about you. But I had not told him who your father was.

Niccolò studied me for a careful moment. When he started off, I pulled him back. "Dearest Niccolò," I said, looking at him directly, "when His Holiness sent me here, he kept a hostage at the Vatican to ensure my cooperation. My Giovanni. My little boy is the pope's surety for my obedience in this errand. I should have told you. But now I know that the well-being of your little daughter is also at stake in all this." And I knew how desperately he missed this baby girl. "I can no longer ask you to risk your hopes for her, even for the sake of my son."

Niccolò pursed his lips tightly. Steam drifted from his nostrils. I wasn't certain what sentiment he was at pains to contain. But after a moment he turned, to pick a path among the jagged gravestones.

◆

When we were finished I said to Niccolò, "I cannot go back there." Of course I meant the place where Camilla died. I took his arm and we walked up the street to Imola's central square, where people of every sort had gathered: sufficient workmen in rough cloaks to dig a canal, yet their numbers were almost matched by the foreign merchants and wealthy townspeople, their collars, lapels, and caps trimmed with sable or ermine, many of them accompanied by pages and *bravi* in bright-colored hose and short padded jackets. The ladies were out as well, not just the candle-shop girls but *cortigiane* with jewels glittering in their hair. Valentino's ruddy-faced soldiers were everywhere, wearing their steel helmets and leaning on their German pikes.

"They believe something is about to happen," Niccolò said. "They are hearing rumors that Valentino will soon leave Imola."

"Are they true?" If so, I would probably be sent back to Rome, to a yet more bitter fate. "Where would he go?"

"Here is my prophecy," Niccolò said. "When Vitellozzo Vitelli is finally conceded all the terms he requires, Valentino will be obligated to decamp from Imola and take his army south, to join the armies of the *condottieri* and prepare plans for the spring campaign. And when this reconciliation takes place, we Florentines will lose everything—money, life, *libertas*."

"Are you so certain Valentino will allow Vitellozzo Vitelli to devour Florence?"

"If only I were less so. Vitellozzo is the conspirators' dance master—the Orsini and Oliverotto da Fermo only step where he points. Three years ago the Republic of Florence hired Vitellozzo's brother Paolo to retrieve our seaport of Pisa from rebels whose paymaster was the Duke of Milan—the very same *impicatto* who previously invited the French into Italy and made us all servants in the House of Valois. With the walls breached and our infantry waiting to rush into the city, Paolo Vitelli took it in his mind to suspend the attack, a decision that was unaccountable—unless one took account of the bribes he received from the Duke of Milan. The Pisan rebels repaired the walls, and we are still without our seaport. Some men among us had the courage to see that Paolo Vitelli was executed for treason—and since then Vitellozzo Vitelli has kept no god before him except the destruction of Florence."

We had approached one of those open-air kitchens with a big iron grill set over a great pile of glowing charcoal. A cook wearing an oxhide apron attempted to entice us with several eels skewered on a spit.

"I believe that in order to achieve this peace of his," Niccolò went on, shaking his head at the vendor, "Valentino will be forced to put a secret codicil in his treaty, offering Florence to the Vitelli."

I stopped and turned to him. I had previously considered the destruction of the Florentine republic a possible consequence of Valentino's treaty; it had never occurred to me that the sacrifice of Florence might well be a condition for it, absent which Vitellozzo Vitelli would not even sign. This revelation was heralded by a shrill ringing in my ears: Florence herself was the "additional concession" Vitellozzo had all along intended to extort, in the most unspeakably cruel fashion.

"And you understand," Niccolò said, "that Vitellozzo Vitelli and Oliverotto da Fermo will enter Florence under the same terms they offered Capua."

"Capua?" Even in the Trastevere the name of this fortified city, which bars the approach to Naples, had recently become familiar among those who gossip about events. And the very name had become fearsome.

"Valentino led a considerable army against Capua last year," Niccolò replied, "on instruction of his father, the pope having contrived a scheme to deliver Naples for his French and Spanish allies, who contributed their own troops to the campaign. Although Valentino was nominally in command, most of the soldiers at Capua were Gascon and German mercenaries hired by the *condottieri*. When the walls were breached, the city was put to the torch and the many thousands who could only cower in their houses were forced into the streets to be speared, hacked . . . Men . . . women . . . children. Without discrimination. Without mercy." Niccolò shook his head as if refusing to see these things. "We see how the duke now hangs his own soldiers for looting, and he is to be credited for keeping them from the throats of the Romagnoles. But he will not be able to restrain the *condottieri* and their mercenaries, even if he wishes. He could not at Capua. When Valentino completes this treaty with the *condottieri*, they will drag his soul down into Hell."

My ears still ringing, I said, "Perhaps Valentino believes that his pursuit of peace and justice for all will erase the stain on his honor."

"And my most profound fear," Niccolò said, "is that the duke can only secure that peace at the cost of another Capua."

◆

Continuing our melancholy progress, we reached the aged Civic Palace at the far end of the piazza. Just beneath the rusticated stone façade was a small circle of laborers and workmen, wrapped up in mud-colored cowls. They had gathered around a street-corner storyteller perched atop a wine crate, his limbs jerking about like a marionette's while he strummed his lute and recited the oft-sung *cantafavola* of Ginevra degli Amieri—a Florentine lady buried alive by her rich husband, who thought she had died of the plague. The song peddler sang the husband's lament, wonderfully miming his insincere grief, before he even more persuasively played Ginevra on her bier, this as he remained standing with his lute in his arms; he closed his eyes and became so still that the crowd stirred uncomfortably, then gasped and cheered when his eyes suddenly flew open and darted about an imaginary tomb. To similar effect, he enacted Ginevra's escape from that crypt, followed by her determination not to return to her husband's house. Instead, in this second life, she found refuge with a poor man whom she had always and truly loved.

When it was over and we had made our way out of the cap-waving crowd, I whispered to Niccolò, "You know that Plato believed that when we die our souls are born into new bodies, and that we are free to choose our next life, although often we are guided only by our desire to avoid the mistakes and evils of the previous." This comforted me just a bit, to think that Camilla had already chosen to live in a home she would never have to leave.

"Then I was previously a wealthy man," Niccolò said, "with few lords to serve, and those few were uniformly wise and courageous." His slight smile was as sharp as his eyes were opaque.

"Niccolò, what if with your next step you could walk from here, this very moment, into a new life, just like Ginevra degli Amieri? Would you?"

He closed his eyes as if miming the dead Ginevra. I feared he regarded this question as another temptation put before him by a woman who had yet to restore her reason.

But on this occasion, when Niccolò looked at me again, I saw an entirely different answer.

◆

We walked on and shortly came to the Inn of the Cap, where a good dozen couriers in riding boots and short jackets milled about in front of the stables. When we had passed through that crowd, Niccolò looked back the way we had come—as he had done several times since we left the piazza.

"Do you know him?" He pulled me aside and gestured with his head at the tall, robust-looking man in a long *cioppa* with a sable collar, who stood perhaps twenty steps behind us, in the loggia of an apothecary's shop, where the tables glittered with glass flasks and vials. Making no effort to disguise his interest, Signor Oliverotto da Fermo touched his fingers to the little velvet cap that crowned his long, sand-colored curls. His smile deepened the creases beside his mouth, so that they resembled scars.

"He killed her. He killed my angel." This was my oracle voice. But Niccolò already stood in my way, his hands like vises on my arms.

"If he did," Niccolò said between his teeth, "you cannot settle with him here." He grunted as he pushed me back, even as I whimpered angrily at his intervention. "We will gather the proof against him. You can do nothing for Camilla or your son if you confront him now."

We did not speak again until we reached the entrance to our stables. Niccolò studied me, his face flushed, breath streaming from his nostrils. "Why do you think Oliverotto da Fermo killed Camilla?"

If ever Niccolò needed and deserved to know the truth, this was the time. "Niccolò, as you suspected, this has to do with the Duke of Gandia's assassination. An amulet His Holiness gave to his son was in the charm bag carried by the first woman . . ." I fought the images that came to me. "That amulet can only have been removed from Juan's body the night he was murdered."

He nodded slightly but I could almost hear the gears of his brain, so to speak, grinding away like a millstone. "So the pope does in fact believe that the *condottieri* murdered his son."

"I believe His Holiness knows in his soul they did," I said. "But he has desperately wished to evade that truth. Because if he accepts that the *condottieri* murdered Juan, he must confess that he himself cast his most beloved son like a lamb into a den of lions when he sent him to attack the Orsini and the Vitelli."

Niccolò looked at his feet, thus sparing me whatever accusation or suspicion I might have found in his eyes. "Yes. At the time the Duke of Gandia was murdered, the Orsini probably wanted peace with the pope—even if Gandia succeeded in nothing, the cost of defending all their estates and fortresses had certainly become onerous. The Orsini value their prosperity above all else. But the Vitelli in fact did much of the fighting on behalf of the Orsini. They have no properties around Rome to defend, so a war between the Borgia and the Orsini was only to their profit." This was also as I remembered. "And Oliverotto da

Fermo is a creature of the Vitelli—they took him in as an orphan and raised him like a son, and now he is married to Vitellozzo's daughter." I had not known they were actually *famiglia*. "Was he in Rome when the Duke of Gandia was murdered?"

"I don't know."

"He is certainly capable of worse." Niccolò eyed me warily. "I presume you know about the business with his uncle?"

"I know that Oliverotto da Fermo's name is nearly as notorious as Capua. But in the Trastevere it is difficult to obtain reliable particulars."

"Early this year Oliverotto came home, after some time away campaigning with the Vitelli. He hosted a supper to honor his uncle, the reigning Lord of Fermo, in company with most of the other leading men of the city. After they had gone through the courses, Oliverotto invited his uncle and the guests into a smaller room for a private dessert . . ." Niccolò audibly exhaled a cloud. "They were all murdered. And then Oliverotto's thugs rode to these gentlemen's houses . . ." He hung his head as if he shared their guilt. "Suffice it to say that Oliverotto no longer fears any challenge as the sole and legitimate Lord of Fermo."

Despite Niccolò's laundered language, I understood that Oliverotto had ordered the children of the leading noblemen slaughtered as well. But I could not conjure the images he had intended to spare me, regardless; in my mind I could see only a landscape of gray, smoldering ruins, scorched to ashes and cinders by the ambitions of men like Oliverotto, and indeed the pope himself.

"Niccolò, I came to Imola with a simple faith," I said desperately, as if in confessing that faith, I could still cling to it. "I believed that the *condottieri* who murdered the pope's son also butchered that poor woman, that I would discover her association with these evil men, that Camilla and I would return to Rome with the proof of this, that I would use that secret to ransom my precious son and leave the pope to seek vengeance against those who bear the actual guilt, rather than harrying the innocent—"

I stopped because my first sob threatened to choke me. Niccolò held me and I wept and heaved as if retching up my entire soul. When

I was done, all that remained to me was a little boy patiently waiting for me in Rome, who could not yet know that behind his grandfather's charming smile and glib promises was the Devil's grin.

At last, I blinked away my tears. "Niccolò, I must go up there now." I meant my own rooms. "You needn't guard me from the truth any longer. It is time for you to tell me what you found."

XIII

I presume Niccolò had locked the door to protect my possessions, because he produced the key and opened it. A little light came in through the cracks in the shutters. A basketful of charcoal sat on the floor next to our box of wine, the bottles still packed in straw. The coals in the iron brazier had long ago burned to ashes and the room seemed colder than the streets.

I went to the threshold of the bedroom and stood there for a moment. "Open them," I said to Niccolò, who had gone to the shutters but seemed to wait for my permission.

Our walnut traveling chests were still on the floor at the end of the bed, Camilla's with the legend of Patient Griselda, which so suited her, painted on the side, mine decorated with a scene of Saint George spearing the dragon, a tale I have always loved. The secondhand sideboard was to the right of the bed, upon it our blue faience pitcher and basin, our towels, combs, and cosmetic jars arrayed beside them. On the little table beneath the window, the brass candleholder was nearly buried beneath congealed wax; even Camilla's copy of Petrarch's canzone was still open. Only when I saw this little book did I think I would sob.

Evidently Niccolò had been careful to disturb nothing, except that the cotton mattress was now barren of the down coverlet. I gestured at the bed, unable to ask the question.

"The caretaker burned it."

I continued to look at Niccolò, only then realizing that his drawn, pained face was no doubt a mirror of mine. "Tell me now," I said. "It will never be any easier. For either of us. She wasn't cut into quarters, was she?"

His face was almost as pale as it had been that night. "Her head . . ."

"I know, Niccolò." I had known when he insisted I could not see her. "Was it like that woman?" I meant the woman whose half torso we had found in the olive grove, her neck a neatly trimmed collar of flesh, the cut clean and careful. I wanted this same dreadful mercy for my beloved Camilla.

"He cut partly through her neck . . . with a knife. The rest . . . the flesh was torn away."

I shuddered so violently that I thought I would fold up like a marionette. This creature had nearly ripped off her head. "He was a powerful man," I said, thinking of Signor Oliverotto's huge hands. "What . . . else?"

"He did not remove her clothing, much less apply the unguent to her. He . . . removed . . . her arm. Her right arm. Just as he did the head. First the partial cut . . . then . . ."

Perversely, my mind tried to picture it. "Is there more?"

"No. And he left no objects or messages with her."

"But he took her head. And her arm. The same arm that held the other messages." It astonished me that I could observe this.

Niccolò shook his head. His eyes roamed a bit.

I shouted at him, "What is it?"

He swallowed as if the words were stuck in his throat. "I believe you will mislead yourself if you see poor Camilla's murder as of a piece with the first two."

"Madness!" I shrieked. "Can you possibly believe this? They are not related?"

"I believe they are related. But they did not have the same necessity. I do not even believe that the same man did them."

At the very least I owed Niccolò a hearing. Yet it occurred to me that having seen the horror in this room—and now forced to relive it—he was perhaps closer than I to the precipice of reason. "Why do you think this, Niccolò?"

"The meticulous nature of the first two murders. No physician could cut more precisely. The nipples carefully sliced away. The unguent applied to the skin. The riddling messages he left on the *bollettini*, the figures of geometry derived from Leonardo's map—"

"You have already noted these things."

"And they have led me to this man's necessity."

"It is necessary for him to torment and provoke the pope," I said. "Or if you must believe your most recent theory, he merely needs to draw us into his cruel game."

"I see now that he regards this as more than a game. Vanity is his necessity. He has created this *disegno* with human flesh, and he is no less vain of it than any maestro of painting, sculpture, or architecture. We are his audience, who must admire the cleverness and accomplishment of his creation."

"The pope is his audience," I said, returning to my first faith. "He does not care about the rest of us."

"No. From the very first he was as much interested in Leonardo as he was in the pope. And now . . . As you observed, he was watching us the other day. Watching you, I fear." The late-afternoon sun must have come from behind the clouds and reflected off the opposite roof, because a brilliant light haloed Niccolò's head. "Once he knew you, he sent someone to your rooms, to search them, to learn something about you."

"He 'sent someone'?"

"He cannot do this on his own. Like any maestro of a painter's *bottega*, he must employ assistants or an apprentice—in his case there are probably only one or two, because of the nature of his art. The man who impersonates the Devil is almost certainly one of them. I would guess they assist their master in measuring the countryside and placing body parts on the points of a wind rose. Little different than Leonardo and his people." From his look, Niccolò might have tasted rotten meat. "But I believe that his apprentice also abducts these poor women beforehand."

I clapped my hand to my eyes. "He intended to take my Camilla to that farmhouse. But she would not have let him take her across this threshold. The Devil himself could not have forced her. She would have fought . . . Did you find her knife?"

"No. He might have taken it with him. But you must understand this: The apprentice killed your dear friend in anger. Because he could not do what he wished with her. He could not do what I believe his maestro instructed him to do with her. The maestro of the shop would not have permitted him to . . ." Niccolò held up both hands like a priest giving the blessing. "This evil maestro does not kill in anger. He murders with calculation. With a remorseless disregard for his victims. I do not believe he kills with any sort of passion at all."

I was suddenly so weary that I collapsed into the ancient chair beside the little table. Where my beautiful Camilla had sat, in her last moments among us poor and miserable sinners.

"Niccolò, I know who he is. I have looked into his face. His very eyes. And it does not matter to me why he kills if I cannot establish that he has done so." I spoke to him as gently as I could. "All I require now is proof. Perhaps Maestro Leonardo will find something in these figures of geometry, some key that will lead us to the . . . heads." Perhaps my lovely Camilla's as well. "The cold will have preserved them. When we have the first woman's head we will know. We will connect this evil man to his crimes."

Niccolò blinked rapidly. "No. Leonardo's measuring wheel, maps, and figures of geometry will lead you nowhere. The journey we must now take is inside him. Within his head. Whether this maestro of the shop is Oliverotto da Fermo or another man, we must first inhabit his mind."

We live in an age of marvelous *invenzioni*, where even an obscure secretary might stand upon the shoulders of the ancients, aspiring to some sort of *scienza* of men. But having seen Leonardo's anatomical drawings, I regarded the maestro as considerably more likely than Messer Niccolò to journey inside a man's skull.

"*Mille, mille grazie*, my dearest Niccolò," I said to him. "I can never begin to thank you enough for all you have done for me. And for my Camilla. I will always be grateful to you." I got up to embrace him, although it seemed I carried the world upon my shoulders. "Now I must try to be alone with my grief."

Niccolò looked guardedly at me. Perhaps he was as much concerned with the state of my reason as I was with his. He opened his mouth to speak but stopped himself, closed his eyes, and turned and left me.

✦

When I sat again, I was no longer in that room. Like Simonides reconstructing the ruins of his memory palace, I went back to our little garden in the Trastevere, which my beloved Camilla had committed to her memory hardly a fortnight ago. She was already waiting for me, as she had on our first day there, eight months to the day after your father's murder. In that time we had not spent more than three nights in a row under the same roof, staying with various ladies I had known in the business, sometimes hidden away in some *guardaroba* where a servant slept, sometimes in a latrine under the stairs, always making our farewells before our hostess could no longer resist the temptation to draw her thirty pieces of silver from your grandfather's prodigious and ill-gotten treasury. It was Camilla who found us our sanctuary in the Trastevere on the first day of your life, bringing us there in a tanner's cart, hidden beneath stiff, stinking cowhides, the afterbirth tied to my thigh with a string because the midwife, not having time to deliver it, did not want it to draw back in and poison me. On that day the little garden had seemed a Gethsemane to me, so certain was I that your grandfather's people would track us there—a place as wicked as the world we had fled, dark and tangled, the pitiful trees strangled with vines, a nest for rats.

Yet Camilla and I transformed that Gethsemane into our Eden. That is the memory garden to which I returned, to those long spring days hoeing, pruning, planting herbs, flowers, and fruit trees, grading gravel paths, and hammering together our trellis. Watching you grow, as our little boy more resembled his father every day.

I remained in that garden until dusk, when the cold wind rustled across the pages open on the table beside me. I had given Camilla this little Petrarch years ago and she had inked tiny medallion shapes beside those lines she favored. I saw that she had marked this: "And should time work against my sweet desires . . ."

I got up, closed the shutters, and stretched out on the barren mattress, covering myself with my fur-lined *cioppa*. I did not believe I would sleep, yet it seemed I drifted from one dream to the next, fitful images populated with the living, the dead, and the many faces of regret.

I remember only the last of these visions. I was in my lovely bedroom overlooking the Via dei Banchi. A man stood at the shutters. The sun had transformed him into a creature of light, no more material than a golden flame, glowing and shimmering. He turned to me, slowly; though I could not make out his face, I knew he was Juan, because his body was pierced all over with dark gashes, shadow instead of light pouring through these wounds, quickly congealing into black blood.

I tried to awaken but a pale face came over me, his hand on my mouth so that I could not breathe. I thought he whispered to me, "I would like to hear you sing."

Then I heard myself scream, entirely within my own mind: *This is not a dream!*

XIV

The weight pressing upon my mouth and nose seemed little more than a down pillow but I could draw nothing into my lungs. Another voice whispered my name in a diminutive I have not been called for years. I thought it was Juan calling me back to my dream, and death.

"Dami, Dami. Don't scream. It is Cesare. Don't scream." The man all Europe knows as Valentino lifted his hand from my mouth.

"Mother of God," I gasped. I could vaguely see the features of his long, somber, beautiful face, as if Christ Himself had come to sit on my bed.

"I had to come in here like a housebreaker." His whisper was harsh. Perhaps even fearful. "The watchman is sleeping. I couldn't risk his attention."

"Why? You are the duke."

"I can trust no one. Not even my own father. The watchman here is in his employ. I could not even send Michelotto to you. Dami?" He removed a glove and gently placed the back of his hand to my face. "You are so cold, Dami. You have no heat in here." Yet it was his hand that seemed cold.

"I remember her. Your Camilla. She was so lovely. So lively. If I could, I would offer you the comforts of the faith I long ago lost. If I ever had faith." Even as little as I could see of his face, he suddenly appeared sadder. "My father should not have sent you here. He should have left Juan at peace. And left the boy with you. Now this . . ."

He sat up, his trunk as erect as if he were standing. "When the searchers came from the river to tell my father that Juan had been found, he would not even turn his head to me." His voice was distant. "I thought it was merely that he could not bear to see that Fortune had spared me and had instead taken the icon of his heart. I remember the first occasion when he did look at me again. He had shut himself up in his bedroom for five days without food or water. I brought a candle into that tomb and could no longer recognize my father. His eyes were great bruises, everything except the pupils entirely purple and red, as if he had attempted to snatch them out of the sockets." I could hear the sigh escape through his nose. "Yet when he stared at me through these wounds I thought for the first time in my life: *My father sees me.* And I knew at once that he believed I had been an accomplice and instigator, not only of Fortune but of the men who wielded the knives." Valentino's eyes had appeared shut during this remembrance, but now I could observe a faint glimmer. "Sometimes I think there is no one His Holiness does not suspect. To this day."

"Then it is all the more urgent that the *condottieri* be held accountable."

He shook his head, yet I could not be certain if he was signaling disagreement or had instead resigned himself to pursuing justice. "Dami. There is something else you need to know about Leonardo's map. The maestro did not finish it until mid-October. By then my *condottieri* had already announced their defection and rebellion. None of them have been in Imola since early this summer."

"What about Oliverotto da Fermo?"

"He arrived here a week ago. With Paolo Orsini."

I couldn't accept this; the first woman had been butchered at least three weeks ago.

"Dami. Do you understand what I am saying? I have a traitor in my house. Likely more than one. Not all of the conspirators declared themselves in October."

So Niccolò had indeed been correct: the murderer—the maestro of the shop—had received assistance of some sort. And it would be all the more difficult to connect these crimes to the *condottieri* if they had employed proxies—presumably Valentino's own people—to commit them.

Valentino leaned over me and placed his hands beside my head, almost as if he were preparing to mount me. "Juan demanded nothing of himself," he whispered. "Yet he was a magnet to others, demanding—taking—everything from whomever he touched. It is still so. Even in death. At times I believe that it is not the New Jerusalem His Holiness sees descending from Heaven. It is the resurrected Juan."

I whispered back to him, "You, too, demand everything."

He lifted his right hand, remaining braced by the other, and brushed the back of his fingers across my cheek; now his touch was like a hot brand. A touch that returned me to my bedroom overlooking the Via dei Banchi. Late on a summer afternoon, the sun turning everything to pale stone, as if the entire room and all its furnishing had been carved in white sardonyx. Even my sheets and naked flesh had that hard luster.

His fingers trembled. His face was so close to mine that I could smell the rosemary on his breath. "I know some things that you do not. Matters not even my father has been told. And I did not think I should tell you . . ." He sat up again. "About the woman. The woman who had Juan's amulet."

My heart seemed to kick at my ribs. "You know who she was?"

"Not her name. Not the farmhouse—or hut—in which she lived. But you can see why I kept the secret. She was Vitellozzo Vitelli's whore."

"God's Cross." I presumed that they had already found her head, evidently even before I had last spoken with him. "Have you seen her face?"

"No. No one has found the head." He paused, as if he regretted disclosing this. "But I knew that when he was here in Imola, Vitellozzo had a woman in the brothel next to the Franciscan establishment. A country girl. He likes to see the dirt on the soles when he turns their feet up. This woman was in a *gioca* with some other whores."

"You mean they played the *gioce di Diana?*" Witch games. Everyone in the Trastevere and the little towns where I grew up knew about the *stregoneria*—the religion of witches—and the *gioce di Diana*. The *streghe*—witches—call their covens *gioce*, for those games.

"Their games are principally dancing naked about the wheat fields at night and rutting like dogs with plowboys who call themselves wizards," Valentino said. "I don't condemn them, much less believe we should burn them. But I am told that these witches' *gioce* also include divinations."

"*Gevol int la carafa*," I said. According to Leonardo's assistant Tommaso, this was some sort of augury, employing a jar of water. "The Devil in the jar."

Valentino nodded. "That is one of their games. There is also the goat ride. A state of entrancement induced by a narcotic ointment."

My memory flooded with the reek of the pot we had found in that cursed farmhouse.

"The *streghe* believe it enables them to fly to distant places, on the back of the Devil, who takes the form of a goat," Valentino said. "Leonardo found this ointment on all the bodies. On all the parts. They were covered entirely with it."

"So the murderer uses the witches' magic against them. Like a thief who robs the butcher with his own knife."

He nodded. "It assists in the abduction."

"But why? Why not a buffet to the back of the head?" Or a hand over the mouth. "Why all the rest of this? The *mappa*, the games, the riddles . . ." All the things Niccolò had observed. "And my darling Camilla . . . Why?"

"I can't say regarding Camilla . . . I don't know." He shook his head with some animation. Or frustration. "But I think the butchered *streghe* were more than conveniences for this riddle you and Maestro Leonardo have described to me." He paused as if the next words would be a binding oath. "I believe the two *streghe* knew something."

"Something about the *condottieri*."

I heard another sigh. "Something that goes back to Juan's murder. In a way that even Juan's amulet does not."

"Something that Vitellozzo Vitelli's whore overheard? And then told to her *amica* in this *gioca*? Something that required them both to be silenced."

Valentino got up, for a moment staring down into the brazier beside the bed. "You must burn some charcoal." He turned and faced the shutters. "This is no longer about war or peace. It has to do with the honor of our house. My father has waited more than five years for his vengeance. Nothing else lives in his breast . . ." He was entirely still. "I could have dealt with the *condottieri* in my own time. But Juan must have his way. Always. We must open his grave and parade his corpse up the Via Alessandrina." He did not try to disguise his bitterness. "I can no longer contain this. We must discover what these women knew. Until Juan knows the peace of the dead, Italy will not have peace."

"Do you want me to see what I can find at that brothel?"

"I don't know. I must consider the next . . ."

All at once he started to the door, leaving his answer hanging in the air. I called to him when I heard the latch.

"Cesare. Your father suspects that Giovanni may be your son. He said as much to me. He said he would soon enough know his father."

I heard only the door closing.

◆

Shortly after dawn I crossed the courtyard. The spectral *garzone* answered my knock, but on this occasion Niccolò himself was sleeping beneath his cape on the boy's cot, and indeed, with his unkempt hair and youthful face he looked like a poorly kept manservant.

Out of habit I slipped into the bedroom, cracked the shutters a bit, and again examined the books and papers on the table. No dispatches to Niccolò's lordships in Florence remained in plain sight, but his Livy's *Decades* was open as before. Atop the printed pages was a little scrap no doubt torn from some missive, upon which Niccolò had made two lists. The first was composed of names:

Alexander of Pherae
Perseus
Demetrius
Sulla
Caligula
Nero

I believe the first three are mentioned in Plutarch's *Parallel Lives*. Of the others, Sulla was, of course, the cruel Roman dictator, while

Caligula and Nero earned their infamy as depraved emperors. Beneath this evil litany, Niccolò had written:

Amusement
Arrogance
Vanity
Ambition
Remorselessness
Reverence

I shook my head in perplexity. I couldn't imagine the meaning of the second list, but the first suggested Niccolò intended to find this murderer among the principal villains of history—men long dead having somehow returned to butcher witches in the Romagna. I determined that the time had come to awaken him, in more than one sense.

"Niccolò!"

He did not jump up, but his limbs did arrange themselves helter-skelter into a seated posture. He put his hand to the back of his neck as he tried to turn to me.

"Put on your jacket." He had slept in his shirt and hose. "We are going to my rooms. I have a great deal to discuss with you."

◆

After firing my charcoal with a taper I had lit in Niccolò's brazier, I took him onto my mattress and sat him up against the pillows, before covering us both with my *cioppa* and wool cape. I did not imagine that either of us gave much thought to the intimacies I had so recently invited, when deranged with grief.

"You have been so good to me, Niccolò. Better than this sinner deserves. So I must tell you something you deserve to know." I waited until I had his eye. "My boy Giovanni, who waits for me in Rome, is the Duke of Gandia's son."

Niccolò's eyes did not betray surprise. But I felt his body startle, like one of those little spasms before sleep.

"There is more, Niccolò. His Holiness believes that I was complicit in the murder of my son's father. As I told you, His Holiness has made my precious little boy his hostage, and I cannot hope to have him back until I can prove that the *condottieri* murdered Juan. I do not tell you this to seek your sympathy and beg your further assistance. I tell you as a warning, so that you will know what the stakes are for me and what I am prepared to risk. And then to ask you, Niccolò, what you would risk for this republic of yours, which has thrown you into the lion's den without a care for you or your little girl. It is a disgrace that they have not sent an ambassador in all this time, nor paid your expenses."

He heaved a bit with the mirth a man can enjoy only when he knows the worst is true. "My appropriation is always promised with the next messenger—as a city of merchants and bankers, promises are our method of accounting. They hope I will be dead before my appropriation actually passes."

"Niccolò, would to God I had taken the counsel you offered me in that olive grove. But now let me return it to you. Leave Imola. Leave today. If it is a matter of money, I can give you whatever you require. No one with a fair bone in his body would accuse you of abandoning a mission that can only end in a terrible calamity for all Florentines. Go home. Your little daughter needs you, regardless of your wife's affections."

"I have only one wish for my Primerana." Niccolò's voice might have been played on the raw strings of my own grief. "The same dream my poor dear mother and father had for me. That she grow up in a free Florence."

I resisted the temptation to put my arms around him. "Niccolò," I whispered, "the woman who carried Juan's amulet in her charm bag was Vitellozzo Vitelli's whore."

"How did you learn this? Leonardo?" But he did not sound incredulous.

Previously I would have allowed Niccolò's own speculation to obscure the truth. Now I said, "Duke Valentino told me." I did not, however, reveal the circumstances of that meeting. "He believes she worked in that brothel near the Franciscans. Perhaps the second woman worked there as well. Evidently they belonged to the same *gioca* of witches."

"Yes. That would be a reasonable connection."

"There is more, Niccolò. Have you heard of the goat ride?"

He nodded. "My father owned a little farm near Florence. As a boy I'd listen to our tenants talk about how the *streghe* could fly at night to Diana's games. On the backs of goats."

"It is a trance of some sort. Valentino says they grease their bodies with a narcotic unguent. That is what you found when you searched the farmhouse. And what you smelled on those women's bodies. The duke believes this narcotic aided in their abduction."

Niccolò turned to me and I knew the question in his eyes: *Why did Duke Valentino wait until now to tell you this?* But he was a sufficiently skilled diplomat that he remained silent; often the unasked question receives the best answer. And perhaps he had already answered for himself: *Valentino does not trust his father—and is uncertain about the reliability of his father's emissary.*

I went on. "Niccolò, I should beg your pardon, because Duke Valentino also believes as you do, that this murderer has employed an apprentice. Oliverotto da Fermo was not present in Imola when the first murder occurred, so I presume he dispatched his plan rolled up on a sheet of paper like a painter's cartoon, and relied on his assistant to color it in, so to speak."

"So the duke believes as you do," Niccolò said, "that Oliverotto da Fermo is the maestro of the shop?"

"Duke Valentino did not offer his opinion."

Niccolò's chest rose and fell several times before he said, "You and I must be entirely certain as to who did this. If we say it is Oliverotto da Fermo, and if instead the maestro of the shop is Vitellozzo Vitelli, then the *condottieri* will do far worse than simply make fools of us. We are dealing with Italy's most powerful and vicious men—and most practiced liars. If we can be proved wrong in any accusation, any particular, they can turn all of this against us. We will be squashed like bugs. Even the duke will not be able to avoid harm."

I drew my wraps to my chin. "You are correct, Niccolò. Until I have proof, the murderer has no name. But you must likewise put aside this business of inhabiting a murderer's mind—or searching for him in your histories. I saw your notes. What do Alexander of Pherae and Nero have to do with this, other than encouraging us to reflect on the evil nature of men?"

I was almost heartened to see the wry flicker of a smile. "To truly understand the nature of men," he said, "you must learn what is common to all men, in all places, at all times."

"Ah. So you do have your own *scienza*." I said this in a fashion neither credulous nor skeptical. "Should I presume that you are looking for principles that govern the nature of men, just as the mathematician seeks principles common to the cone and the circle?"

"Why would I not? The times change. But the nature of men does not change."

I began to see the slender thread of his logic. "So you believe that if you examine the evil deeds of a Nero or a Caligula, you can understand the nature of this murderer."

"With careful study, one can make useful comparisons. Just as Plutarch did in his *Parallel Lives*."

"I give you that Plutarch shows us how one man's character can determine the fortunes of a state or even an empire. But Niccolò, I wonder if your Titus Livy, or Plutarch or Suetonius, truly tell us what was in the minds of such men, or merely what was in the minds of Titus Livy, Plutarch, or Suetonius?"

He extracted an arm from beneath our covers and drew his hand over his unkempt hair, as if trying to flatten it. "The astute historian can weigh a man's actions against the circumstances that compelled him, and arrive at an assessment of his character."

"Even so, you are merely relying on the ancients to judge these men."

"No." Niccolò sat almost straight. "I look beyond the judgment of historians. I must fish deeper, as they say."

"Ah. So now you must cast a net into the Abyss—and hope to pull something up."

He grinned as if his appropriation had arrived. "Let me haul up an example: Hannibal. If I truly wish to understand Hannibal, I must turn to him as if he is standing beside me, as real to me as you are at this moment. And I say to him, 'After Cannae, your wisest men advised you to be content with your victory and use it to win a peace with Rome on terms favorable to Carthage. But others in your senate believed that there were yet greater victories ahead, that Rome itself could be conquered. Why did you choose the course that led to your nation's ruin?' And if I have studied the matter carefully enough, I can transport myself entirely inside Hannibal's mind." He touched a finger to his forehead. "That is where Hannibal will answer me."

"Yes, you have found something in your net," I said, "though I cannot say if it is fish or fowl." Indeed I understood Niccolò's reasoning, though many would regard his conversation with Hannibal as madness, if not a peculiar form of necromancy. "You believe you can in similar fashion ask this murderer why he has done these terrible things. But I would think it far more difficult to speak to this butcher than to Hannibal, the latter having been described in so many histories, and whose words and deeds are known to every schoolboy. Yet you are the first to insist that we cannot even presume to know this murderer's name. And all he has written for us is 'the corners of the winds' and 'the circle within the square.' "

"That is my difficulty at present." Judging from his untroubled tone, Niccolò was little concerned about this deficiency of his method. "But I have faith that this man will begin to answer me. And soon enough I will recognize his face."

I found his hand and clutched it tightly. Perhaps Messer Niccolò Machiavelli's strange *scienza* of men would someday prove its merit; more likely it was a folly even he would quickly forget. But he was a good and courageous man, and if he wished to escape this vale of tears into his histories and conversations with ancient generals, it was not my place to judge him.

"My dearest Niccolò," I said, "if any of the dead women's *gioca* are still alive, it is possible they are still in that brothel. I intend to go there tonight." I had taken Valentino's ambivalence—or confusion—regarding this matter as permission enough. "But once again, I will require your help."

I had the sharp fear he would refuse me. And I could scarcely fault his prudence.

His "*Sì*" was a sigh. "I will do whatever must be done."

"If Fortune gives us anything at all," I said with renascent hope, "by tomorrow morning, you may well be able to add this murderer's name to your litany of history's monsters."

XV

What Valentino had referred to as the "Franciscan establishment" was a massive old cloister of this order, the brick gray with age, joined to the even older church. When Niccolò and I arrived that evening, the street was crowded with candle-sellers, these ladies having opened shop, so to speak, for all the sturdy artisans and workmen who had just closed their shops. There were also many other peddlers displaying all sorts of goods, from mirrors and matches to soap and biscuits. Their torches traced through a dusk descending quickly into darkness.

Our destination was a brick building of even greater antiquity than the church and cloister. It had probably been a bishop's palace at one time—the Church finds no sin in leasing to brothels while anathematizing the sin from which it obtains this profit. A lone *bravo* stood guard at the massive oak door, his stiletto in his belt. He was a sour-looking young man attired in a shirt sliced open at the sleeves like a courtesan's and a little jerkin that did not come within a palm of his ass, the better to display a codpiece as big as half a melon.

I took Niccolò aside. "I need you to stay at the door," I instructed. I had learned a great deal more about this sort of establishment than I had ever wished to in the Trastevere, where I had sheltered some runaways from such places. "If I find the right woman, it is likely she will run as far from me as possible, given the danger she is in. So you must prevent her escape. The *bravo* will no doubt assist you, as he will want half of whatever he believes she has stolen from the pimp."

The shallow stone steps of that aged building were so worn by countless visitors that they appeared to sag in the middle. Yet as I contemplated my ascent, I swear by the seven churches that those few steps appeared to rise up before me like the Mountain of Purgatory.

✦

My darling, if you hope at all to understand the profound fear that whorehouse occasioned in my breast, you will have to put away any childish sentiments that might still linger in yours, and at last see me face-to-face, as the Apostle of our Lord would say. And this will require that I tell you a bit more about your own mama than perhaps you would like to know. Now, if Fortune has determined to keep you in the house of Borgia, then no doubt your family has already told you what I was. In this the Borgia were always republicans rather than monarchists: all their children were begotten equals, whether they entered the world from the *potta* of a *puttana* or the perfumed snatch of a duchess. So do not apologize to your cousins who were squeezed out of the latter; your house is full of uncles and cousins who, like you, were born of the former.

In the same fashion, neither will I offer an apology. You see, any child born of the seed of the left testicle is offered these opportunities, and these alone: wife, nun, or whore. Where the father can afford a dowry, the first choice is made; she surrenders her virginity, property, and liberty to her husband, and prays to the Holy Virgin that her father has bought her a good man. The father who does not have a dowry, or has squandered it on his firstborn or wishes to save it for the prettiest of the brood, can always choose Christ as his son-in-law, a convenience that has made our convents so populous—and has made those parasites who call themselves monks so relentlessly eager to cuckold their own Father in Heaven.

And then there is the whore. In the beginning, she has no more choice of who picks her fig, and when, than does the dowered wife or the Bride of Christ, and it is as true as the Gospel that it was no different for me. Here is my story:

My mama—your grandmother—and I moved from town to town when I was growing up, simple places such as Carpi and Lucca; she did not bring me to Rome until I was twelve years old. The city struck me dumb with fear, these countless people from all over Christendom and the Levant rushing about on the streets, jabbering away in a Babel of tongues; to make it worse, Mama had to go into an *ospedale* because she was suffering from a dreadful catarrh, which had plagued her for months. So one day she left me in the care of a certain Madonna Taddea, who had rooms on the third floor of an ancient palazzo near the Campo dei Fiori, where she lived among ponderous old furniture and fragments of antique statues. She was the first woman I had ever seen in a wig and her aging face was painted like a saint's effigy.

After several weeks Mama still had not returned, and one afternoon Madonna Taddea was visited by a much younger lady who resembled no living creature I had ever seen. It was as if she had been conjured from the canzone of Petrarch or the fables of Pulci. She required only a little rouge to color a face like cream, with eyes like agates and lips so red that they seemed to bleed.

"I am Madonna Gambiera, the natural daughter of the Prince of Squillace," this vision told me, her words flowing like water from a spring. By this she meant she was the prince's bastard; I was too innocent to know that even this parentage was her *invenzione*. Having recommended herself, Gambiera proceeded to poke at me like a physician and examine my teeth as if I were a horse in the market down the street. When she had finished she announced, "You are my sister. Who is called Sancia." She nodded as if a divine messenger had whispered this name to her. "Now you will come and live in my house."

"But my mama is coming back," I said. "How will she find your house?"

Gambiera's agate eyes appeared almost golden as she looked up at Madonna Taddea. Then she gave me the most charming expression I had ever seen in my life, as if she were an angel sent to assure me that this trifle shouldn't trouble either my mama or me in the least. "I live on the Via Giulia, so close that you can throw a stone from here to there. Nothing at all to concern your mama."

So began my life as Gambiera's little sister, and I would require all the words in two Bibles just to tell you the half of it. Her house on the Via Giulia was not so splendid as the one I would own, within ten years, on the Via dei Banchi; nonetheless I thought I had gone to

Paradise when she took me up the stairs to her salon, where the scent of flowers and perfumes made me swoon. I did not leave that house for months, while Gambiera prepared me for my trade, dressing and painting me like a doll on countless occasions, before at last she took me out with her.

My first "business" supper was at the palazzo of "His Excellency," whom I now know to have been some cardinal's secretary and abacus-rattler, but to little me he might have been the pope. He was not a young man, and though he dyed his hair, his drooping eyes betrayed him. Several other men were there and Gambiera engaged them all with her brook-like chatter, mostly in Italian, though from time to time she issued little phrases in French or Latin.

The supper itself was perhaps the most astonishing wonder of that house—I had never seen desserts that resembled sculptures and statues, and as much pork and capon was taken from that table as scrap as I had likely eaten in all my life. But after I had finished nibbling my spun-sugar unicorn, Gambiera took me into the latrine and said, "His Excellency is going to have you tonight. Now look at me. He has not paid for anything more than this." Here she pretended she was a man holding his works in his hand, thrusting between my thighs. "You just pull up your skirts and hold your legs together no matter how he tries to push them apart, and let him rub his thing between your thighs. He has not paid to touch you here." She gave my hairless little monkey a hard squeeze. "If he does, you scream and I will come. That cock will spit its seed between your legs, so come back here and wash when he is done. He can kiss you, but don't take his tongue or anything else in your mouth. I am saving you for something better."

I will only tell you that I did as instructed and afterward went into the latrine, where I began to wash myself with a towel I had wetted in the basin beside His Excellency's bed. I stood in the dark scrubbing that vile secretion from my legs—I had never imagined that a man's "seed" would be any different than the dry seed a farmer tosses upon a field. And at that moment I knew my mama was never coming back for me.

I did not sob as you might think I would have. Instead I recalled the *Inferno*, the first book I had ever read, when the poet enters the gates of Dis and looks out over a vast graveyard of fiery tombs, spread in all directions as far as he can see. Still just a girl, I saw before me a life no less terrible and inescapable than the city of Dis, to which I believed my own mother had abandoned me. In this fashion I blamed my poor mama for the choice others made.

Just then Gambiera burst into the latrine, her eyes dark and darting. "We'll go now," she said in a harsh whisper. She grabbed my hand before I could even drop my skirts, yet instead of taking me downstairs to the street she dragged me deeper into the house, where shortly we entered the most remarkable room. It was lit by only a single lamp, but I could see antiquities and books everywhere.

Gambiera's head swiveled like an owl's as she appraised all these treasures. "Take something," she whispered malevolently.

A moment later, she lunged at one of the tables, her fingers like talons, and snatched her "gratuity," as she always referred to these thefts. I could only see that she had pinched what looked like an immense coin, though no doubt it was an antique medallion of some sort. "If you don't take something every time," she said, drilling me with those raven eyes, "you will end your life in a whorehouse, with every malformed, half-witted gallows bait in Christendom shoving his donkey dick into your little perfume bottle."

Terrified even to imagine a fate worse than that to which I was already condemned, I grabbed a book, smaller than most of the others, the leather binding almost black from grease—and clutched it like my last hope as Gambiera dragged me out into the street.

When I returned to my bedroom at Gambiera's house, I read the title on the front page: *Regulaes grammaticales*. I did not know that this was a Latin grammar, or that it was the first book any child encounters when he ventures beyond the vernacular. But as I turned the pages, I gazed in wonder at those strange and beguiling Latin words. To me they seemed like the answers to all the mysteries of the universe.

From this humble beginning, I accompanied my thieving "sister" to suppers, garden parties, concerts, theatricals, and balls for almost four more years, halfway through giving up the chastity Gambiera had so carefully husbanded to the highest bidder, a fat old German cardinal who grunted and groaned like a quarry worker throughout—after having paid four hundred ducats for a pleasure that did not seem worth a *carlino* to either of us.

But I also advanced from my *Regulaes grammaticales* to Ovid and Horace, and then to Cicero and Tacitus. And soon I became wise enough to understand that I could pluck knowledge from a learned man's brain as easily as I could steal a manuscript from his *studiolo*. In this fashion I earned a distinction that eventually brought me to the tables of the most distinguished men of letters, as well as the princes of the Church. When Rodrigo Borgia became pope, an office he could not have purchased without the singular aid of my great friend and patron, Cardinal Ascanio Sforza, I was among those who dined with the new pontiff the next day, at twenty-four years old occupying a chair any man in Rome would have given his right hand—and his right testicle—to claim.

I did not stop my climb up this Jacob's ladder of learning and wealth until I met your father. After several years in Spain, Juan had returned to Rome to become captain general of the papal armies, a position coveted by everyone, it seemed, save him; your father was the only man I had ever met who valued love, however reckless and mad, over his own greed and ambition. They all laughed at Juan's vanity, his silly *alla turca* costumes, but they could never see that he was mocking their vanity and self-importance, that he wished only to live every day as if the sun that set on it would never rise again. I adored his virtues and did not understand that he could not survive his faults. And I only pray that you will be heir to the former and possess few of the latter.

So my darling, in such fashion I made the best of the choice that was made for me. Year after year I added to my treasury of knowledge and earned a liberty that few nuns or wives could ever imagine: I owned my own property and was free to converse with whom I chose about topics of interest to me. I found myself at the center of great events and knew well, often to my profit, not only the persons of great men but also their peculiarities.

Yet even the *cortigiana onesta* fortunate enough to have mastered her trade must fear the inevitable loss of her assets—beauty and youth. When Geras clasps us to his wizened breast, there are those few *cortigiane* who have husbanded their income well enough to retire in modest comfort. But there are a great many more who must continue to labor, even as they become husks, the sad remains of their youth rattling around inside them like seeds in a dry gourd. If a courtesan must take up residence in a brothel, she is not likely to go out again, except in her coffin. And every day she will pray that it is her last. It is the living truth upon the Body of Christ, that a *cortigiana onesta* would rather walk into a graveyard and throw herself into her own tomb, than walk through the door of a whorehouse.

XVI

Far more than the whorehouse, however, I feared leaving you in your grandfather's house. So I waited until my heart had let go of my throat, forced myself to take a breath, and climbed the steps.

The *bravo* met me at the front door, his drowsy eyes wandering all over me as he let me into a room of considerable size, lit by greasy tallow candles and a blazing fireplace with a terra-cotta hood as broad as the roof of a small farmhouse. The tables were bare planks littered with jugs, glasses, platters, and bones, with men of all sorts seated on the rude benches: secretaries, farmers, merchants in fur-trimmed caps, cavalry officers in gold-stitched jackets. The girls who paraded about for them were attired in wool dresses a servant wouldn't wear on Sunday. Some showed the grinding years—as well as the pox scars and pustules—that even a jar of ceruse could not conceal. But a few still had the unadorned beauty that country girls so often possess. I prayed for a blessing on all these ladies, knowing full well that what little grace God had already shown them would be withdrawn bit by bit every day they were here.

Despite the crowd, the pimp wasn't difficult to find—no man with any other sort of livelihood would wear Spanish shoes so long and pointed that you could spit a capon on the toes. I raised a hand to obtain his notice.

He came to me with hips forward, his four-color hose so tight that it was pink at the knees, his codpiece no doubt obtained from the other half of the *bravo*'s melon. The French pox had left his face as rough as a peach pit. Faster than a cardinal's chamberlain can reach for a tip, he had his hand on my *culo*.

"I'm not here to work for a poxy shit-rag like you," I said, which made him so mad that he raised his hand as if to give me a knock on the ear, lowering it only because I had already drawn a few ducats from the lining of my cape. "I want some girls. I've got a Florentine wool peddler back at my palazzo who's swallowed every piece of meat we've thrown at him and still won't get up from the table. If you'll move your runny ass, I'll go up and give them a look."

The pimp followed me upstairs, where curtains had made many rooms of several. An unseen trombonist played with sufficient wind that only occasionally did I hear the grunts and cries of fleeting passion; I had to shout a bit to issue further instruction. "I must have a pretty girl and a Tuscan-speaker—he likes to tell them to do this and that and he'll pay ten ducats if he doesn't have to point. And I would like her to be familiar with the tastes of better men, if you understand my meaning." Of course I meant gentlemen such as the *condottieri*.

Grunting, the pimp moved past me, going nearly to the end of the hall before he drew aside a curtain made from a bedsheet that had been much used and never laundered. The lady inside, still in her shift, knelt upon a straw pallet scarcely better than they sell to pilgrims during Jubilee, her head obscuring the works of her guest, who had raised his rough country tunic.

I was about to protest that this girl did not seem much familiar with the better class of men. But at that moment her farmer smiled at me, as if I had been summoned to pull his rope as well.

I recognized his black lamprey teeth, which quickly vanished when he similarly identified me; evidently he had seen me well enough out at that dreadful farmhouse. He pushed away the girl's head and sprang toward me with such alacrity that I had time only to turn my back and cringe. I was waiting for the blow when he flew through the door, still pulling up his hose.

"Stop him!" I shouted.

The pimp turned to the girl, who had risen from the altar, so to speak. "Did he pay?"

I could see she had bleached her long tresses during the summer, because a palm's width of dark hair, like a helmet of sorts, had grown out since then. Her face was a mask of ceruse, her mouth a pink scar far less brilliant than the spots of rouge, as big and round as French tennis balls, on her cheeks. Her dark eyes darted from side to side. She nodded at the pimp.

The pimp cocked his head in a shrugging gesture. With this, the girl flew past both of us. I had not seen a woman in her underclothes move so swiftly since Gambiera, my mentor in theft, ran across the Ponte Sant'Angelo with the Venetian ambassador two steps behind. And you have not seen a woman in mourning clothes run as fast as I did in pursuit.

The front door was absent its guardian and I entertained the hope that the *bravo* had chased after the runaway whore. But it seemed he had instead gone to break up a fight or some such thing, because when I reached the steps I saw Niccolò at the bottom, the girl clawing at his face like a virago and the lamprey making his way up behind him. But as the lamprey had no visible weapon and I had my knife out of my sleeve, I held it over my head and called out to him, "You! When I tell my *bravo* to release your girl and turn his attention to you, we will both hold you down and make certain that you savor the same meat she was trying to swallow! Will that be to your pleasure?"

Men always fear a lady with a knife more than a similarly equipped man, because they do not believe we are subject to reason. Whatever interest the lamprey had in securing his lady's freedom vanished as quickly as he disappeared into the crowd. And no doubt we already had in our net a bird more inclined to sing.

I yanked this screeching songbird's two-color hair so vigorously that she stopped screaming at Niccolò and threw up her talons in hopes of keeping her scalp in place. Having gotten her attention, I showed her the knife that had so effectively routed her companion. "Now, if you shut up and talk to us," I said through clenched teeth, "this night will end for you much more profitably than it began. If not"—I held the knife to her cheek—"there will be less of you than there is now."

The fight went out of her, if only to await a better opportunity to escape.

✦

On our way out of that street, I made several purchases: some rope and a torch from the sundries peddler, a cloak from the secondhand dealer, and a nice roast pheasant from one of the charcoal grills. Having no intention of parading this poor girl through the city, where she might draw unwanted attention to all of us, I determined we should do our business in a nearby alley. This we found behind an enormous palazzo just across the street, a modern building that had recently been the home of one of the local despots whom Valentino had banished. Because there were no staircases or balconies for loiterers, we were quite alone.

Niccolò held our captive while I tied her ankles together and bound her hands behind her. Once she had been secured I thrust the sputtering torch close enough to her face that I could see her clearly. Beneath the mask of ceruse was a girl not even twenty; her narrow eyes glittered with frightening malice. I asked her, "Who was the man with his works down your throat? He thought you were worth rescuing, until he was asked to risk his own cock."

"*Carogna*," she spat back.

"She's calling you a carcass," Niccolò said to me, having been in the Romagna sufficiently long to know such things. Then he stated flatly to the girl, "Your friend is a *meg*." He looked at me and translated: "*Mago*." Meaning a wizard, a man who would most likely come to the *gioca* to provide protection for the *streghe*—and if he was fortunate, to play the Devil to the Devil's whores when their rituals became a bacchanal. "I think the men who came to the farmhouse that day were all *magi*," Niccolò added.

The girl began to murmur "*Sant Antoni mi benefator*," at the same time struggling to get her arms loose. It seemed she wanted to cross herself, or perhaps make the *corne*—the sign of the horns—against the evil eye.

I said to her, "If you speak Tuscan, we can help you. I know why your friend ran. He knew I had seen him before. But you could have been any whore to me. Why did *you* run?"

Her entire jaw quivered. "We all going to die." Her Tuscan was good enough, though with the buzzing local inflection.

"Who is going to die?"

"Me. Them. You."

"How will we die?"

"Goat ride."

"Did your friends take the goat ride?" She knew what I meant, but she blinked defiantly. So I added, "The two girls in your *gioca*, who are now dead. They took the goat ride. You know someone is looking for you, don't you? Do you think I came to that whorehouse to take you on the goat ride?"

Here she spit at her feet and began to chant again and again: "*Sant Antoni mi benefator.*"

It was only then that I observed the red string around her neck. I pulled the *bollettino* from beneath her shift. Her refrain had been written on the little card: *Sant Antoni mi benefator.* The appeal to Saint Anthony. I turned it over, to find another such invocation: *Angelo bianc, per vostr santite.* This was close enough to Tuscan: White Angel, by Your holiness. The White Angel was another name for Lucifer.

But beneath the invocation of Hell's angel another name had been scrawled: *Zeja Caterina.* I looked up at the girl. "*Zeja?*"

"*Zia,*" she said, eager to make a fool of me.

"Ah, an aunt," I said to Niccolò, who was nearly squinting at the girl. "No doubt the sort of auntie who will tie a man's handkerchief into knots to make him fall in love with you—or dig up a mandrake root watered with a hanged man's piss to forever protect you from curses. Every whore in Rome has a *zia* like this. And everybody else calls this *zia* a *strega.*" I returned to the girl. "Are you this Auntie Caterina?"

She curled her lip and snorted with contempt. "You won't find her. Not here. Not there."

"Truly?" But rather than ask her directly why Auntie Caterina was so concerned to make herself scarce, I approached the matter by way of Calabria, so to speak. "How long have you worked in that whore-house?"

"Ten *mes.*"

Ten months; she had been in that whorehouse while the conspiracy of the *condottieri* was still incubating. "Do you know a girl who did business with a soldier? A very important soldier. A *condottiero*."

Her eyes became slits, like Judas in a painting.

"Was his name Vitellozzo Vitelli?"

"*Vitello*," she said, using the Tuscan word for "calf," from which the name was indeed derived. But then she shook her head as if I had described someone half beast, half man, like a Minotaur. "No *Vitello*."

"Oliverotto da Fermo?"

Now she shook her head rapidly yet wearily, as if she were listening to some *pazzarone* recite nonsense names.

I took her chin in my hand. "Have you ever seen an amulet no bigger than the end of your thumb, shaped like a bull's head? A very ancient amulet."

She almost sneered at this, as if I had invented it entirely. Niccolò put his hand on my arm, cautioning me that I was going nowhere.

I might have been entirely frustrated had Valentino not confided to me his belief that the murders involved more than Juan's amulet. "Your friends who took the goat ride and did not return," I said. "They knew something, didn't they? A secret this soldier told them."

"*Secrét*," she said in a hissing fashion; this was the Romagnolo word, rather than the Tuscan *segreto*. She frowned as if I had made some sense, but not entirely.

"What is the secret?" I said gently. "Does it regard a man who was murdered?"

The Judas eyes widened and she drew back her head, as if it were I who had revealed this secret to her.

All at once Niccolò reached out as if he were about to grab the girl by her throat, but he only put his fingers on her *bollettino*. She did not regard this interest as benign, however. The serpent's malice in her eyes came spitting back.

"*Zeja* Caterina knows this secret," Niccolò said, having no doubt deduced for himself that *Zeja* Caterina had good reason to hide. "How do we find *Zeja* Caterina?"

"*Caz*," she barked. Prick.

Niccolò glanced at me. "*Zeja* Caterina is at the center of this."

When I had nodded my agreement, he added, "If we hope to find her, we are going to require sterner measures."

Indeed, I had prepared for such measures, with the hope they would not be needed. I snatched up the secondhand cloak I had laid on the ground and the roast pheasant I had placed on top of it, ostentatiously taking a bite of the latter. "No doubt this tastes better than that sausage you had earlier," I said. "I can wrap you in this cloak and send you off with the rest of the bird. Or I can keep my cloak, eat my pheasant, and send you off in your shift. And to remember you fondly, I'll keep your nose."

I might have plunged my threatening knife into my own belly when I saw how defiant she remained. "We want to speak with *Zeja* Caterina," I said in desperation. "Nothing more. We can help her. The men who are looking for her will take more from her than a nose."

"*Angelo bianc per vostr santite! Angelo bianc per vostr santite! Angelo bianc per vostr santite!*"

Pushing her against the brick wall of the palazzo, I shouted, "Now the saints of Heaven aren't strong enough, are they? Now the *Gevol* is your *benefator*, isn't he?" I stuck the tip of my knife between her nose and eye, drawing blood. "But neither Heaven nor Hell is going to save your face."

Knowing what I had at risk—and had already lost—I had set my own soul to cutting her when Niccolò caught my wrist. "Wait." He drew back my arm, pried the knife from my stiff hand, and took it in his. I hadn't decided whether I should damn him or thank him when he shot the point of my knife straight at the girl's neck. She screamed at the same moment I did.

In a single motion Niccolò cut the string of her *bollettino* and plucked it from her breast.

"*Angelo bianc per vostr santite! Sant Antoni mi benefator!*" The poor girl refrained her invocation of both Heaven and Hell until tears cut tracks in her ceruse.

She was still heaving when Niccolò quietly said, "You will have your *bollettino* back when you take us to *Zeja* Caterina."

At last she shuddered violently and nearly belched up the words: "You come to fawn stone. *Dmanansera.*"

"What is this 'fawn stone'?" Niccolò asked.

"To Bologna, three miles. To the fawn stone. You see it. Big stone. Fawn on it."

"Go on the Via Emilia toward Bologna for three miles," Niccolò said. "And she will meet us at the fawn stone? Tomorrow evening?"

"Sì. Dmanansera. They will come."

Niccolò's thin lips were nearly bloodless. "I hope *Zeja* Caterina won't disappoint us. I intend to leave your *bollettino* with her. Otherwise I will use it to make a *maleficia*." A curse.

She swallowed and nodded.

"We should untie this woman," Niccolò said. "And pay her what she is due."

As soon as the girl had wrapped herself in the cape and snatched up the pheasant, she fled like a shadow into the street beyond us.

I was suddenly so weary, sad, and frightened that I could not keep from saying aloud what my soul already knew. "Niccolò, I don't like the turn this has taken. We are going to die out there."

"Yes. I think it most likely that someone will try to kill us." Niccolò was almost mumbling like Leonardo. "And I would very much like to know who."

XVII

Niccolò took me home and sat on the bed beside me for a time, though we did not exchange a word. I believe he knew, as do I, that if this is to be the last night of our lives, our thoughts belong with those for whom we have lived and will soon die. Yet even as we sat silently side by side, I had the most peculiar and profound sense that in some fashion our souls had met long before this, perhaps in that Elysium where Plato says we determine our next lives. And there our souls had conspired to meet again here in Imola, to share the same fate.

After perhaps a quarter hour, Niccolò offered that he had dispatches to write before we departed the next day, and left me with instruction to bar my door.

❖

My dearest, most darling Giovanni, I began this account even before Camilla and I left Rome, with the hope that some day you would be able to understand the circumstances of our separation. But I also recorded the pope's instructions to me, and the subsequent events, knowing that powerful men would try to twist the truth against me, and I would most likely require a chronicle of my actions so complete and precise that none could doubt my honest intentions—and from which I could cite particulars I might well have forgotten otherwise.

But I did not intend for a little boy to read any of this. I was twelve years old when my dear mama left me in Madonna Taddea's house, and for years it was easier for me to try to forget her than to remember her with confusion and anger, wondering why she did not come back for me. If I cannot return to Rome, you will grow up in the house of Borgia. And it will be far easier for a little boy to forget me than to defend a vague memory against accusations he cannot even understand. Yet I also know, from my own life, that the day will come when you will have questions, and the truth that has been buried will become a deep ache in your breast—and in your case, the lies you have been told may even become a threat to your security in that house. That is why I was comforted to believe that our beloved Camilla would survive, even if I did not, and somehow deliver you this truth, when you were ready to hear it.

But the bitch of fate had other designs. Now it is my intention to wrap up this bundle of pages and dispatch them by courier to the Fugger Bank in Rome, along with a letter of instruction that this parcel be delivered to you on 10 February, *anno Domini* 1518. Your twentieth birthday, when you will be a man, preparing to find his own way in this terrible and beautiful world. And perhaps you will also be ready to remember me.

So you see, my most precious, most adored son, I am writing these words with the entire faith that if you are reading them, by the grace of God you are already a man. And by the malice of Fortune I am bones and dust, already fifteen years dead.

That being so, here my story must come to an end. I can best finish by telling you its beginning.

✦

My tale begins with a little girl, born in some village or farmhouse in the Po River valley, I think, though I have never been certain. Her mama, though she never said so, was probably left with bread in the oven and empty promises by some country scoundrel; if she didn't want to throw her bastard baby in the Po or some ditch, she probably was no longer welcome in her own house or the village where she had grown up. Thus driven from their home, this little girl and her mama, who couldn't have been older than fifteen, wandered from one village or town to the next, Mama selling the only goods she had to sell, which were usually made in that workshop between her legs, moving on when the village bitches chased her out with stones and curses. There was never much to eat, just chestnut polenta or beans with a piece of bacon or sometimes only what the country folk call snake bread—the root of the lords-and-ladies flower, boiled like a thistle. Can you imagine how much that mama must have loved her little daughter, when she might have left her on a doorstep—or worse—and gone off on her own, to become a pretty virgin again? Even our dear Lord doesn't love us that much. Oh, I know He suffered on His Cross, but it was only for a day. What did that mama suffer all those years, every time some fat, farting oaf, with a beard like a porcupine and a mouth like a latrine, got on top of her?

There were a thousand adventures they had, going from tiny towns to places like Modena and Lucca, learning the turns of the streets, so to speak. By then the little girl had her basket of baked apples she carried on her head, selling them all around town while her mama was home selling herself. When the girl returned in the evening she could always smell the men, their perfumes and pomades, and she loved that scent, because often it meant more than bacon in the beans. Sometimes they had pork cutlets or thrushes, and the girl got her first wooden clogs, so that she could imagine she was one of those important ladies who clomp-clomp all over the cobbles in their tall pattens.

Then just after Carnival one year, it got worse. The same man came again and again—the girl never saw him, but she knew his smell, a bitterness like almonds. For months he came every day, until they were back to eating chestnut polenta and boiled thistles. Mama became a wraith, her skin like the scraped parchments used to cover windows. The girl cursed God because she believed her mama was dying.

But one day, when the girl came home with her empty basket, her mama said she had something to show her. Mama brought out this leather binding that seemed as old as a saint's relic; you could see where the mice and insects had nibbled away at it. And then she opened up this ragged thing, to show her daughter the pages within. No doubt they were the cheapest thrice-used parchment, covered with atrocious copying. But to that simple little girl, for the first time in her life looking at the pages of a book, those rough leaves were as wondrous as something you would find today in the printshop of Aldus Manutius. "*Divina Commedia*," the girl's mother said, pointing to the words on the first page. "Dante Alighieri." She looked at her daughter and her gaunt face was like Beatrice's when she first removes her veil, dazzling Dante with her radiance. "This is ours now. Almost as long as I carried you in my womb I have been learning how to read this book. And now I am going to teach you."

So all those months, this mama had not only been selling herself to buy that book; she had also been buying a grammar tutor. The priests would say that she bought that book, and that knowledge, with the sinfulness of her corrupt flesh, but that is not true. She bought that book with love—pure, beatific love, a love beyond all understanding. A love as great as the infinite compassion that turns the eternal spheres. A mama's love.

✦

I am writing this over the speckles made by my tears, which will be dryer than old bones after fifteen years, but perhaps you can see where they have blurred the ink. As you now know, that same dear mama who gave up so much for me never came back for me. I am certain my mother died soon after leaving me with Madonna Taddea in Rome, but I cannot say exactly how she went to God, just as you will probably never know precisely how the journey of my life ended. But I believe in my soul that my beloved mama died in the *ospedale*, carried off in a delirium of fever, with my name on her last shallow breath: Laura, the name of Petrarch's great love. Laura, who became Sancia, the bastard daughter of the Prince of Squillace, and then Damiata, the Aphrodite of the Vatican Curia. The name of a little girl from the dirt of the Po valley, who was loved above all things in Heaven and Earth by her sainted mother of eternally blessed memory. The same little girl who now writes her last testament from a cold room in Imola, in the middle of the frozen Romagna.

So I must go now, my darling Giovanni, my beloved little boy now become a man, who can only know his mama through a haze of memories of a tiny house in the Trastevere and these thin words, her last fitful dream before the final, endless sleep. But I beg you to drink these words into your soul, even if you find them a poor vintage. Then look into the eyes of those you most adore, and try to see the reflection of my love for you, which has no end.

Magnificent Francesco Guicciardini
9 January 1527

ere Damiata's chronicle ends. Much as the Aeneid *follows the*
Iliad, *I now present, in three parts, my continuation of her account. Like
Damiata, at the time of these events I understood the great importance of even
small things I witnessed—hence I wrote down many of the conversations
and incidents related here at a remove of mere hours or days. But not until
several months ago did I endeavor to assemble those observations into a single
narrative. Nevertheless, I did not attempt to fashion a tightly knitted summary
of events; rather, I have provided you what Caesar in his* Civil Wars
*described as the "new wool of history." When you begin to write your own
history of these times, it will be your task to shear my words, comb and spin
them, and weave them into a fabric of your own design.*

*Plato believed that every child born is a soul returning to life. As I
compiled these pages, so entirely was I absorbed into my memories that I believe
I came back a lesser distance, to inhabit my own life as it was twenty-four
years ago, when I was a young man and it seemed that new worlds awaited
our discovery, that our republic might prosper, and that our Italy might yet be
saved. Alas, as Seneca wrote,* Sed fatis trahimur: *But we are drawn on by
the Fates.*

Farewell,

Niccolò Machiavelli

PART TWO

The Nature
of Men

Imola and Cesena: December 9–26, 1502

It is much better to tempt Fortune when there is a small possibility she will favor you, if in not tempting her you face certain ruin.

The aforesaid dictum is cited from my treatise *The Art of War*. I offer it in place of a preface describing everything that ensues in this chapter, because the latter would make me a poor excuse for a dramatist. But as you read along in this account, you will understand why I ran toward certain perils, rather than choosing to barricade myself in my rooms, awaiting certain ruin.

When I left Damiata after our excursion to the brothel, I spent most of the night at my writing table. Once again, I exhorted the lords of the Palazzo della Signoria to send an ambassador with full plenary powers, in order to arrive at an agreement with Valentino, which, in light of the duke's evident suspicion of the *condottieri*, might well encourage him to withdraw the treaty he had offered them—and have the useful effect of saving our republic. But I had little hope that the blind would soon see.

The next day I prepared for the possibility that I would not return from the evening's journey, my foremost concern to ensure that my little Primerana and my wife receive my appropriation, which had yet to be sent from Florence. But I also had to provide for my mule and my piti- ful manservant, who would need someone to look after them. These were no easy matters and I did not finish much before our departure.

Nevertheless, Damiata and I exited the city gate at the time we had appointed, some two hours before dusk, reasoning that this fawn stone was not much more than an hour outside Imola on the Via Emilia. We would arrive while we still had full light, the better to loiter nearby and see if anyone was laying snares in the vicinity—or determine if someone had followed us from Imola. I had rented a mule sturdy enough for two—not wanting to tax my own mule before he was ready—but I walked alongside while Damiata rode, in order to save this beast's strength for later, when our survival might require it.

Outside the city, both the road and the surrounding *pianura* were entirely covered with a January snowfall that had arrived a month early, the snow heavy but dry, like coarse-milled grain. The north wind sweeping across the plain was bitterly cold, and icy specks still blew down from a sky that resembled a sheet of lead. But we had prepared as best we could. Damiata's hood and cape were lined with sable; when she was seated on the mule, I could see that she was wearing thick woolen hose and an extra skirt beneath her black mourning dress. I wore most of my wardrobe, along with a farmer's wooden shoes, these at least keeping my feet dry. Nevertheless, we would have to quickly finish our business with *Zeja* Caterina or the cold would mock—and make us forget—all our other fears.

With the rust-colored soil of the *pianura* freshly whitewashed, or so it seemed, one could see more easily the stamp the ancient Romans had placed so indelibly on this land. Not only was the straight line of the Via Emilia the testament of their surveyors, who possessed skills we have since lost; the entire plain to its east was divided into a vast checkerboard of fields, perfect squares of equal size, all precisely aligned with the Via Emilia like bricks against a mason's plumb line. Over many centuries, the boundaries among these squares came to be marked by various means: irrigation ditches; narrow dirt and gravel roads; lines of mulberry trees or cypresses; rows of shrubs and hedges.

This vast grid was entirely different than the countryside I had known as a small boy. My father had owned a little land and a house at Sant'Andrea, near Percussina, about six miles outside the walls of Florence, from which he obtained nearly all his income and most of our food. There the fields, olive groves, vineyards, and forest draped the low hills in a patchwork that might have been sewn at a secondhand shop. On a glaring August morning, I could run through stalks of blue-flowered flax almost as tall as I was, and if I squinted my eyes I could imagine I was in an ocean; in the next moment I had vanished into the sunless woods where we cut our kindling, listening to the rabbits and pheasants scatter, only to emerge a moment later into a chicken yard or hog sty.

We had little company on the road that cold afternoon, aside from a train of several mules burdened with great baskets of charcoal and a small band of cape-clad peasants, one of them with a pair of dead rabbits over his shoulders. The scant traffic, like the hunters' pitiful yield, evidenced the scarcity of everything in this region, due both to the climate and to the army that had been living off the countryside. Seeing that we were foreigners, the peasants spit in the snow and made the *corne* against the evil eye.

The wind made conversation difficult, but it did not slow us much; I estimated that we had been gone barely an hour when I shouted, "I see our stone!" We had passed about a dozen crossroads, but these four corners were different, in that all were entirely exposed. Jutting from the earth at the corner nearest to us was a great slab of limestone, worn by time and probably half buried in the snow, although what remained was close to my height. I expected we would find that someone had carved a fawn on it, many centuries ago.

Yet when we came close enough to examine the carving, we discovered this was not so. The deeply cut letters were as tall as my hand, the Latin inscription still easy to read: SANCTISSIMIS FAUNIBUS, an ancient devotion to the Holy Fauns.

"Faun stone," I said, wondering if this would be merely the most trivial of my mistaken assumptions. Across the road from this monument, in the far corner of the field, was a well, a gray masonry cylinder against the snow, beside it a wooden crane for the bucket hoist. "We'll go over there and wait," I said. "If we have to conceal ourselves, it will do."

The road we crossed appeared to run beyond the flat horizon, perhaps going all the way to the Adriatic coast. This perfectly straight white path was bordered by endless rows of naked mulberry trees, their spiky limbs branching into delicate webs of twigs, these almost resembling black lace against the snowy fields.

Damiata stopped and stared down the road, studying this design of man and nature as if it were an augury of our fate. "Leonardo has made drawings like this," she said in a nearly entranced voice. "I have never seen the like of them. He has flayed away the flesh to expose the veins, nerves, and sinews that run throughout us like rivers, streams, and creeks. Or like these mulberry branches." She turned to me. "The maestro has found this secret world beneath our skin."

She had her hood up, exposing only her face, and this dark frame made the blue of her eyes deeper than seemed possible. If the most profound blue available to our painters is the *ultramare* that comes from beyond the sea, you would have to sail the sea between here and our friend of blessed memory Amerigo Vespucci's *mundus novus* a thousand times to obtain this hue.

Yet this gaze could metamorphose in a single blink, haunted in one instant, as sparkling as light off a wave in the next. To watch Damiata for more than a moment was not merely to become fascinated, in the sense of our modern Tuscan *affascinare*, but also to be reminded of the ancient Latin *fascinare*: to cast a spell.

So if in her eyes I appeared wary, it was only because I regarded them as the incorrigible thieves of all reason and good sense.

⸭

With tiny steps Damiata approached the well's stone rim, which was frosted with snow. She peeked in but quickly drew back.

I came to her side and looked down, wondering what she had seen, finding nothing but a lightless void. At this time in my life, I had only begun my study of men's natures—my *scienza* of men—and the well provided an allegory of my own efforts to imagine the face of this murderer: peering into the darkness with the conviction that something lay at the bottom, yet utterly unable to see it.

"Let us assume that two witches have already died for some secret regarding the Duke of Gandia's murder," I said, knowing that Damiata already believed this. "But were the *streghe* murdered in an effort to conceal this secret? Or to obtain it?"

"No doubt to conceal it," Damiata offered at once. "The *condottieri* know the truth they hope to keep hidden."

"That is the reasonable conclusion. But then why display the bodies in a manner that only drew attention to the victims?"

Damiata warily cocked her head. "What are you saying, Niccolò?"

"Possibly there is a secret these *streghe* have concealed. But I do not believe it will tell us who murdered Juan of Gandia. Or those women."

She made a little scoffing sound. "Then you believe we have come out here for nothing, except to invite our own deaths."

"We are looking for a man of a peculiar nature," I elaborated. "A very rare nature. And I believe that we cannot know him until we understand another sort of secret. A *segreto* that will not be found out here on the *pianura* but within him. Something that makes him different from other men."

Damiata gave me the merest frown and a tiny pout—which made me almost insane with desire. So I required a moment to see this expression as one of deepest skepticism. "Do you intend to once again cite his vanity? His interest in games and riddles, Niccolò? Because far from being rare, this is the nature of so many men I have known. Particularly those of high station."

Certainly I knew I could not easily convince Damiata of my arguments, when in truth I had not entirely convinced myself. Yet often in those days I committed myself to a rhetorical leap, hoping that before the end of my fall, I would discover something to which I could cling.

"I believe that this man is rare," I said, "because we so rarely find him in our histories."

"I have read Herodotus and Tacitus just as you have, Niccolò." In fact, Damiata's well-lettered challenge to my intellect had beguiled me no less than her beauty. "History is nothing if not a catalog of vain and cruel men."

"Men who almost always kill at the prompting of some human passion or sentiment," I said. "Ambition. Jealousy of other men's power. Upon reaching the heights, they are consumed by the suspicion and fear they will lose everything to men much like themselves."

"Yes. You have previously said you do not observe such sentiments or passions in these murders." Her tone was peevish. "But isn't it more reasonable to believe that this man's greatest fear is that the full revelation of his crimes will compel the pope and even Valentino to seek vengeance, thus depriving him of both his station and his life?"

"I give you that reason does not provide us an easy explanation of this man's actions—"

"Then you believe he is afflicted with a sort of madness. Some excess of choleric humors in the brain."

"No. Consider his forethought, his calculation, his fastidious dismemberment of the corpses. He appears to have entire command of his faculties." As I spoke, my sleeve brushed snow into the well; the glittering little shower vanished before it was consumed by the black water. "Not even the greatest of the ancients truly understood this sort of man."

Damiata pushed a few stray hairs from her forehead; her delicate hand, sheathed in gray kid, was more lovely than a marble Aphrodite's. "But Niccolò, you believe you have made a list of such men, do you not?"

I shrugged. "Plutarch tells us that Alexander, the tyrant of the ancient Thessalian city of Pherae, massacred entire populations for no reason at all, butchered men merely for his own perverse amusement, and worshipped as a deity the spear on which he had impaled his predecessor—yet he regretted nothing and wept only at the sufferings of Hecuba and Andromache on the stage. Nevertheless, Plutarch did not observe that Alexander of Pherae was a rare man, even when compared to other tyrants. Our histories tell us of a few others who also derived a perverse amusement from their murders and cruelties. Demetrius and Perseus. The Roman dictator Sulla. The emperors Caligula and Nero. Plato believed that the cause of all such depraved behavior was a 'disease of the soul.' But this man's disease or deformity of the soul is so rarely seen that no Hippocrates or Galen—or Marcus Aurelius or Augustine—has ever described it."

"Niccolò, if this man is so different from other men, shouldn't we know him at once? Didn't the Romans know well the madness of Nero and Caligula, even though they were powerless to oppose them?"

"That is what confounds me so. Because for a time the people of Rome, even those closest to the tyrants, were deceived. This was true regarding Sulla as well. As though these men were able to mask their nature until their power was sufficiently established to permit their worst excesses."

"What sort of mask?" She gave me a subtle wry smile. "I presume you do not mean this Devil's mask Leonardo's assistant has witnessed."

Despite the importance of this question, I had no answer. Instead I stared into the well as if it were a black mirror. "Perhaps that is his secret," I said. "The Sphinx's riddle."

It was not lost on Damiata that travelers who failed to answer the Sphinx's riddle quickly found their ignorance fatal. "Perhaps you are correct in that respect, Niccolò. Tonight either we answer his riddle or Fortune will bring our journey to its end." She took my arm and drew herself close. "I know I asked you before, Niccolò. You are familiar with women of my sort, aren't you?"

At that point in my life I had enjoyed "conversation," let us say, with the less gifted courtesans at the French court in Lyons, not to mention *interludi* dancers and singers in Florence. But I could hardly say I had known a woman of her sort.

Reading my silence if not my face, Damiata added, "Is that why you don't trust me?"

"I trust that you were honest when you said I could not," I told her lightly, not needing to recite the sins she had confessed to me: liar, thief, and whore.

Her smile revealed teeth as perfect as pearls. "If only I had known you in Rome, before everything . . . We would have been great friends. And I would not have required your trust."

"If you had known me in Rome, I would have been merely one among the court of three dozen scholars camped on your doorstep, not daring to hope for more than a nod." This was a kind way of saying that a single night with her would have cost me a year's expenses.

She cast her eyes down. "No. I believe I would have found you different than the rest. Or perhaps it is myself, not you, whom I flatter. Perhaps in those days, as I climbed to the heights, I was not so wise . . ." When she looked up, she might have put her finger on my heart—and a hand on my *cazzo*. "There is a connection between us, Niccolò." Her teeth worked at her lower lip. "And it frightens me no less than I know it does you. As if long ago our souls conspired to bring us to this place. On this night."

I would not have described this connection in such terms, yet in truth I felt it no less. I looked into the ocean of her eyes, unable to say if Damiata was Dante's Beatrice, who would lead me to the Higher Spheres, or if she was a Circe, who had already bewitched me body and soul.

CHAPTER 2

It is always the case that where little is known, more is suspected.

By the time the boy came to the faun stone, stars had appeared in half the sky—and a quarter-moon had begun to peek through the clouds that remained. "He must be their scout," I said as we crossed the field to meet him, leading the mule along behind us.

He was even younger than the local boy I had employed to spy on Leonardo's house; I did not reckon him more than ten or so years old, fair-haired, but with the same strangely grave and dour face found on so many of the Romagnole children, as if they had never been taught happiness. Those children's faces were but one reason I believed so profoundly in Valentino's vision, a Romagna where all citizens might enjoy the peace and justice they had long been denied. Presently, however, war had made this countryside a yet harsher place.

The boy wore the uniform of the *contado*: the hemp shirt and horsehair blanket, the wooden shoes. We had only said our *buonasera* when his high-pitched question rang in the darkness. "You want *Gevol int la caraffa?*"

"With *Zeja* Caterina," I said.

"*Sì.* She is there."

"Where is she?"

His hand shot out and he pointed to the north, straight down that endless, mulberry-lined road. "*Pianura.*"

Damiata and I both mounted the mule, as I did not want to give these people an easy opportunity to separate us. I had little cause to regret my caution: the boy quickly snatched the halter and started off at a courier's run, a pace I would have had difficulty following in my own clumsy clogs. By the time he had led us down the crossroad a good two miles, the clouds had almost vanished and the waxing moon was joined by the great band of stars across the center of the sky, as though a celestial road mirrored our route.

Quicker than a flea can jump, the boy turned us onto a narrow path we had not seen until we were on it. At times the barren branches nearly made a pergola over our heads. There was a perfume to that night I will never forget, the freshness of the snow wedded to the scent of Damiata: oranges, the merest tincture of roses, and a sharp, lily fragrance that still comes to me at times when I am not even thinking of her.

We entered nothing more than a footpath beside an irrigation ditch. The boy had to coax our mule onto it—or into it, as the case might be, because the mulberry branches were a dense thicket on either side, reaching out like fingers. When the mule had been set in the proper direction, the boy went around behind, presumably to push it by the rump. Instead I heard him say, "You go. *Zeja* Caterina." With this he slapped the mule's flank and by the time I turned to look for him, he had vanished into the grid of silver fields.

We had gone only several hundred paces when Damiata whispered, "Do you hear that, Niccolò? That little chiming. Like coins in a witch's charm bag."

"Someone is shadowing us."

The chimes became a steady ching-ching-ching for a short time, then faded, leaving only the sound of the wind rattling the mulberry branches.

We might have gone another quarter mile when we heard a growl of sorts, somewhat like an old man clearing his throat. The hair on my neck rose.

The mastiff was as big as a boar. It had appeared so suddenly, its dark form distinct against the snowy path, that it might have been conjured by a *strega*. As it padded toward us, I could see well enough the pale teeth and a head little smaller than a sower's basket. And then the man crouched behind it.

The mastiff stopped, trembling in anticipation of its attack, the keeper shortening its leash like a crossbowman drawing his string.

The man's words seemed to drift toward us, each a separate, huffing exhalation. "You. *Gevol int la carafa?*"

We both answered at once. "*Sì, sì.*"

The mastiff keeper allowed his lethal pet a snarling lunge before he put his entire weight against the leash and wrestled back the great oxen-like head. "Then this way you come."

◆

Taking the halter in the manner of our previous guide, the hooded mastiff keeper led us on a journey more wayward than Odysseus's route from Troy to Ithaca: crossing field after field, sometimes going in one direction only to turn and go back the way we came. I took pains to keep my bearings by the stars, but otherwise found no recognizable landmarks.

I don't know how long we had been on this voyage when Damiata turned to me with the suppleness of an acrobat, throwing her arm around my neck and pressing her forehead and nose against mine. Her eyes glittered and her scent swept every thought from my brain.

"Niccolò," she whispered urgently, "if anything happens tonight you must leave me behind and go home. Go back to your baby daughter and learn to love your little wife. She is still just a girl. Love her and she will grow up for you." Her lips were so close to mine that I could literally feel the warmth of her words. "But you should know this as well. I would not have offered myself to you, even in my grief, if I had not also desired it. If we survive this night—"

An owl flew over us, wailing like a spirit. As if he were following its flight, our guide yanked hard on our mule's halter and we crashed over an irrigation ditch, breaking the ice and splashing cold water onto our feet. I clasped my hands beneath Damiata's heart, to keep her from being thrown.

In short time I observed orange sparks at the edge of a large field, then the outline of a watchman's hut. This rude dwelling was larger than most of its sort—a family could have crowded into it—but no less a rag-and-bone-man's shop of stones, reeds, and scavenged planks, the roof a trash pile of shattered tiles. The mastiff keeper gestured for us to dismount beside it.

Damiata said with little humor at all, "So this is Ravenna," recalling the familiar saying. And I could only wonder if the truth we found here would, in fact, be the death of us.

The door was a flimsy screen of woven branches. Our guide gestured us inside, although he and his dog did not follow. A fire of grapevine and dry brush burned down to coals directly on the dirt floor. Behind it, illuminated like the enthroned Virgin in a sacred play, sat a woman whose chair was entirely concealed by her huge skirts and layers of shirts. Her features were strong, mannish, but she had plucked her eyebrows into thin curves, like a banker's wife; a green kerchief covered her head. She appeared to be twenty-five, but perhaps she was only seventeen. On the *pianura*, a woman becomes a *vecchia* at Damiata's age.

With a sudden, feral movement she looked up at us. Damiata made a little gasp and I could feel the fear down to my numb toes. Her pale eyes had a quicksilver sheen, like a wolf's. Peasants call this peculiar coloration *occhi burberi*—fierce eyes.

She spread her hands over her lap as if brushing crumbs from her mountain of skirts, displaying rings on every finger and the cheap bracelets that sheathed her wrists. "I am Caterina. What do you want to find?" Her Tuscan was surprisingly good.

"A murderer," Damiata answered, far more quickly than I could. "A man who has murdered my dearest friend. And two other innocent women."

The witch's fierce eyes narrowed, a cat peering into torchlight. "You want to ask *Angelo bianc?*"

"Yes," Damiata said. She glanced at me, uncertain. But we could no longer turn back.

The makeshift door creaked. Another young woman entered. Taller, darker, and more slender than Damiata, she wore only half as many peasant skirts, rings, and bracelets as *Zeja* Caterina. Her head wobbled a bit and her eyes were unfixed, as if she had used opium. Or as if she had returned from a goat ride.

This *strega* was followed by a man in a wool tunic, at once identified by his unnaturally white, leather nose; as I had suspected, the men we had seen at that abandoned farmhouse were *magi*. More to my surprise, behind him trailed two children, a boy and a girl, neither older than eight or ten, both wearing hemp shirts and sorrowful little expressions; as if they were choirboys in the Corpus Christi procession, each carried a lighted wax candle. They made their way behind the witch's throne, where a little tent had been constructed of two horsehair capes thrown over a frame of boughs. The children scurried inside like mice returning to their nest.

Leather-nose moved the enthroned *zeja* and her chair just enough to reveal another prop: upon a small table rested a clear glass flask sufficient to hold the contents of a wine bottle, although it had been filled only with water.

Zeja Caterina again made that whisking motion with her hands, as if brushing something from her lap. But now a book rested atop her skirts, already open; she was pressing the leaves flat. I was certain I had missed the introduction of this item while I observed the children; the book had probably been concealed in the folds of her ample skirts. Nevertheless, had I been more credulous, I would have regarded its materialization as magical.

As the *zeja* turned the pages I could see that it was not a printed book; the text had been copied in a single column with wide margins, the stiff parchment nearly as soiled as the leather binding. It appeared to be a schoolboy's text, probably a geometry. I believed I glimpsed squares and circles drawn in the margins, although the lines were faint.

"There are many great spells in this book," the sorceress said as she continued to turn the leaves, her companion *strega* and the leather-nose wizard looking on as if she had produced a relic of the True Cross. At last *Zeja* Caterina appeared to obtain a suitable incantation. She peered into the tent and addressed the children inside, her Romagnolo so rapid and high-pitched that I could no more discern her words than I could understand a sparrow addressing her chicks.

This instruction was followed by a silence, except for the crackling coals and the creaking of the flimsy hut, as it shuddered in the wind.

The children began to speak in chirping Romagnolo, their cadence herky-jerky but their words recognizable. "*Angelo bianc, per vostr santite e mia purite.*" Here I divined the importance of these little sparrows: Holy Lucifer could only be summoned by the *purite*—virginity—of a child.

I never saw the *zeja* extend a sly hand over the flask on the table before her, but she must have done so, dropping some sort of agent into it, because the water billowed, taking on a reddish hue dotted with sparkles, some bright as fireflies.

"The clouds have cleared," the *zeja* said. "The king has come." A pen had materialized in her hand and she leaned forward and dipped it into a small clay inkwell; neither had I seen this previously, although the little vessel now sat in plain view on the table. "Who asks him?"

"Damiata." She fearlessly raised her chin.

"Then you writes it," the *zeja* said, turning the book sideways in her lap.

Damiata navigated around the fire, her hems stirring embers from the blazing coals. On the opposite side she took the pen and bent over. Damiata's cape, belled by her own layers of skirts, blocked my view of the book and I could no longer see her face. I studied her back intently, but she offered no revealing shudder, no hint at all as to what she saw from her new vantage. Hence I could not say if the question Damiata asked, in a trembling voice, was a performance or a fear born of some childhood superstition: "Will this put my soul at risk?"

The witch's wolfish eyes devoured Damiata. "Many great lordships has signed it."

You can imagine how desperately I wanted to know the names of these "great lordships." If one of them was Oliverotto da Fermo or Vitellozzo Vitelli—or even Paolo Orsini—his signature might connect him directly to the murder of the pope's son. But I also knew that Damiata might well be dead in an instant if I so much as coughed.

Damiata began to turn the pages herself, the parchment whispering like dry oak leaves. With each movement of her arm, her shoulders rocked very slightly. Hence it was quite noticeable to me when this motion stopped. Her shoulders rose with a quick heave.

Damiata's trembling voice was certainly not a performance. "Did you see these men sign it?"

The witch's nostrils twitched. Behind her the children tittered. Her fierce eyes still fastened to Damiata's face, the *zeja* nodded just a bit. If she said anything, I did not hear it.

Behind me, however, I heard our guide's voice, coming from outside. "*Licorn*." This was certainly *licorno*. Unicorn. I assumed it was a password.

The mastiff keeper flew past me as if blown in by a whirlwind.

Damiata turned just as quickly, her face white. "Get the book!" she shouted at me. "They are all in—"

The mastiff keeper seized her braid and put his knife to her bared throat. Yet before I could leap across the fire a cannonball might have struck the back of my neck, occasioning a brilliant light in my head, followed by a blackness that threatened to swallow me.

I was blind only a moment but sufficiently long that when I could see, I was on the floor and Damiata's attacker was stepping over me on his way through the open doorway.

"Follow him!" Damiata screamed. Leather-nose restrained her now, grasping her arm as well as her braid. "He has the book!"

I stumbled outside. The field of snow before me was illuminated like mother-of-pearl and I could see the fugitive and his dog slipping through a line of low brush at the perimeter.

Behind me, a little chime.

I turned and glimpsed only what appeared to be the flaring nostrils of a horse and a goat's white beard.

This time the cannonball struck my temple, the light was an exploding sun, the blackness entire.

CHAPTER 3

*M*en are motivated much more by the hope of gain than by the fear of loss.

I awakened in Hell, my punishment tailored to all the defects of my life.

I, who could never remain still or in one place—as my family and friends have endlessly complained—was frozen for eternity into the position a child assumes in the womb, legs and arms drawn up as if to guard against the world and all its ills.

I, who always gathered the gang and led the conversation, was both mute and entirely alone in a darkness without end.

Yet I could see, in a fashion, because I, who never stayed with one idea for more than a moment, had been condemned to behold thousands of visions in a single instant: a procession of everyone I have ever known and loved and many other creatures and demons that have never existed; great battles such as Carrhae and Pharsalus teemed beneath me like anthills and I could make no sense of them; the entire senate of ancient Rome went past and I did not have time to ask one of them a single question. I visited places I had been—Lyons, Siena, Pistoia, Forli—and flew like a bird over places no man has ever been, cities like chests full of gleaming jewels, walls made of ivory blocks studded with pearls, flying endlessly through wonders my frozen body could never touch and my humbled brain could not hope to grasp.

There is sleep in Hell, however, or at least there was in this one. When I awakened again, the light was no less brilliant or painful than it had been in the last instant of my life, as if vinegar had been thrown into my eyes. I could move, although I wished I could not. My hands clawed entirely without volition; my knees heaved almost to my nose in excruciating spasms.

And I could speak. My father reappeared and we babbled for hours like washerwomen: the law, the Medici, Savonarola, Biondo's histories, Aristotle's *Ethics*, Cicero's *De officiis*. My sisters made me sing the lauds Mama was always writing: *O castita bel fiore, che ti sostiene amore . . .* Yet this laud went on and on, not dozens of verses but hundreds. I had a furious argument with Albertaccio Corsini, paterfamilias of Marietta's entire clan, about sending my little Primerana to her wet nurse at Terranuova. Marietta was there, weeping, yet when I held out my arms to her, she turned away, this being what in truth occurred when I still lived.

When at last I began to comprehend, however vaguely, the true nature of my situation, I imagined I was Archimedes in his bathtub and had just divined the secret of the cosmos. The light was one of several shafts the glaring sun had shot through the gaping chinks in the walls of a watchman's hut, although this shelter was much smaller than the one I had previously visited. The bare floor was as cold as a grave and I was as naked as a newborn. And the place smelled as though a thousand country healers had filled it to the roof with all their disagreeable ointments and poultices.

I recognized that stink.

I bolted up, my head throbbing as if I had been kicked by a horse. A malodorous gum stuck to me everywhere—legs, nose, chest, back, balls. I wiped the stuff from my eyes and looked about. I had been covered with a horsehair blanket, my clothes and wooden shoes left in a pile at my feet. Whoever had moved me there had not wanted me to die. But he had also left on the floor beside me a small clay pot. It was almost empty, but there was a residue of the substance that had been smeared all over me: an unguent of hellebore, henbane, mandrake, and belladonna.

During the preceding night, I had been taken on the goat ride.

◆

Despite the spasms in my legs and my seizing hands, I was able to put on my clothes and stumble outside. The sun on the field of snow nearly blinded me, but after a time I distinguished the footsteps of the lone man who had carried me there; his feet had been large but unmistakably human. Yet the single set of tracks that proceeded away from the hut were the Devil's. That is, a man walking on stilts carved to resemble cloven hooves—the same man who the night before had also worn a goatlike Devil's mask.

I numbly began to follow those tracks, hopeful that they might lead me to Damiata, certain that they would take me to a road. As I stumbled along, the truth began to trickle into my brain. The unguent that had frozen my limbs for the duration of the night had also been applied to those poor women who had not awakened the next morning. Instead they had been rendered into a paralytic state—a "first death" of sorts—so that they could be precisely dismembered. Yet for a reason I could not fathom, I had only received this first death and not the second.

Almost certainly Damiata had been immobilized in the same manner. And I feared in my cold bones that the Devil would not spare us both.

I soon came to one of the frozen irrigation ditches that often divide the fields. It seemed the man in the Devil's mask had met an accomplice—or someone—because the ice was broken in both directions. I ventured some distance one way, only to find no sign he had walked—either on stilts or on foot—past a row of cypress trees. Returning the other way, I similarly discovered that the broken ice ended at a thicket of naked mulberry trees. It was as though both these creatures had either leapt from tree to tree, or simply flown away.

My senses still confused, I tramped through the fields until the afternoon sun began to turn snow to slush, calling Damiata's name until my throat was raw. I did not even succeed in rousing the natives of this boundless plain. Again and again I saw gray columns of smoke against the gesso-white *pianura*, yet whenever I reached the farmhouses, the fires appeared to have been put out and there was never an answer to my shouts and knocks.

At last I determined that I could best aid Damiata by returning to Imola and organizing a search. When I found the Via Emilia, the sky was already turning a charcoal hue, the scent of snow again in the wind. Yet strangely, my feet were lifted by a stern if not cheerful resolve. This was inspired by Damiata's last words to me: *They are all in*—certainly she had meant that several of the *condottieri* were the "great lordships" who had signed *Zeja* Caterina's "book of spells." If so, that book was the sacred text, let us say, that would connect the *condottieri* to the murdered women—and indict them in the murder of the pope's son.

And as I crunched over the gray clods of frozen slush, it occurred to me that somehow the Devil's apprentice responsible for my present distress had followed Damiata and me to the *Gevol int la carafa*, despite every effort of the *gioca* to elude him. Yet if he had in fact obtained the book he was seeking, he would have had no further use for me—and my goat ride would have ended differently. I could only have been spared because that book was still out on the *pianura*, in the hands of some desperately frightened *strega* or *mago*—and I was still regarded as someone who might yet locate it.

For the same reason, I could assume Damiata had also been spared. In truth, after knocking me senseless, had this Devil's apprentice sensibly pursued the mastiff keeper who fled with our sacred text, Damiata might have had considerable opportunity to escape him entirely.

♦

I arrived in Imola after dark, to find the city transformed since the previous afternoon. Wagons and pack mules flooded the streets, laden with every sort of goods, from folding chairs and weavers' looms to sacks of seed and baskets of chestnuts. The entire population seemed to have joined this procession: frantically bustling merchants and their *bravi*, sullen candle-shop girls, bewildered street vendors, greedy-eyed priests (who find in every tumult the hope of profit), and frightened workers in their horsehair capes.

Such was the instability of my mind that I hardly gave this activity a thought. Instead I went at once to the Palazzo Machirelli and ran up the stairs to Damiata's rooms, insane with the hope that I would find her waiting just as desperately for me. I must have pounded on her door like a *pazzarone*, because the little watchman, Sebastino, smelling like the bottom of a wine barrel, had to come up and tell me she had not returned.

I trudged across the courtyard and climbed the stairs. Against my door I observed what might have been a bundled cloak. And a pale leg sticking out.

With equal measures of horror and hope, I leapt up the final steps.

The penitent at my door lifted his buried head.

"Lucca!" I shouted. "What in the name of God and Mankind are you doing here?" This was my youthful spy, whose commission I had extended in my absence, largely because he needed the little enough that I paid him.

"*Msir* Niccolò, they bring more things."

The fears I believed I had put behind me on the Via Emilia, not to mention all the poisons that had leached into my body, seemed to rush straight to my heart.

I knew precisely the sort of "things" that had been brought to Leonardo's anatomy workshop.

CHAPTER 4

Those who are besieged should not trust anything they see the enemy do continually, but instead should always believe that beneath such repeated actions lies a deception.

I pounded on the pedestrian door set into the immense oaken gate of Leonardo's palazzo, barking "I am expected!" when the viewing grate slid aside. The door was opened for me without challenge—the aforesaid greeting often obtains this result—and I found myself in the well of a large inner courtyard lit only by a peculiar light, this issuing from a doorway at the far end.

"Where is the maestro?" I addressed my question to a poorly shaved but well-dressed servant; I could only envy his green damask tunic. Nevertheless the unfortunate man had but one eye and one hand, probably a punishment for theft and some other transgression; Leonardo's household was evidently a refuge for criminals, defectives, and frauds. Before he could reply I heard a peculiar noise, a distant "Aaahhh."

I tasted something foul, a fetor that clung to the back of my tongue.

"Aahhhh." Now the sigh was louder and higher. A boy. Or a woman.

"Agh! Agh! Agh!" These were the sort of cries I would hear years later, when the Medici lodged me in our Stinche prison.

I ran through the illuminated doorway into a dank hallway that smelled like a church in July, when the bodies buried beneath the floor begin to stew. With each frantic step I perceived the light waxing and no sooner had I turned a corner than it erupted from the tile floor.

I stood there blinking, until I was able to see the wooden steps beneath me.

A cellar. The smell more resembled a funeral in August.

"Agghh! Agghh! Aggghhh!" This was neither a woman nor a beast but some unholy choir assembled of both.

I clattered down the stairs, all too certain I had arrived at the very moment Damiata was being cut into pieces.

◆

My descent ended in a pit no painter of the Last Judgment has ever portrayed. A zodiac of illuminated globes appeared to hang in the air above Satan's own banquet, the main repast the entire bloated corpse of a woman, set upon a trestle table and opened from throat to groin like a gutted sow. I shouted, "What the *cazzo diavolo* are you doing to her!"

"She was discovered this morning at a farm near Cantalupo, absent a single mark of violence upon her." Through the glare of the floating globes, I observed the author of this pedantry: Leonardo da Vinci stood near the back wall of his cellar, attired in a butcher's smock, upon which he wiped his hands.

Reluctantly, I renewed my examination of the corpse. A fleshy woman, entirely naked, her pale arms at her sides and legs spread a bit, she had been laid out on linen so stained and soiled an Englishman would refuse to dine off it. Her dark hair framed a somewhat livid face, yet even in the brilliant light her eye sockets were empty black pits. Evidently the violence had been done to her in this place, by means of the saws and polished blades that lay beside her. But no anatomist's instruments could have metamorphosed my Damiata into this. For the first time since she had vanished, I was relieved to know I would have to look for her elsewhere.

"We have proved the cause of her mortality," Leonardo said. He stood before a lead tub, which was shaped like a coffin and raised on a stone platform, so that the rim reached to the height of his waist. At each end of the metal tank a miniature sun rose atop a lampstand; the light source was a candle somehow enclosed in the center of a large glass globe, despite the latter appearing to be filled with water. Evidently this medium rendered the brilliant light unnaturally steady.

"As you might expect in this capital of all stupidities," Leonardo continued in his theater-organ tenor, "the wheat-field sages attribute her death to some demonic agent. With presumably every means of destruction at his avail, Satan instructed one of his minions to insert a large piece of dried apple at the entrance to this woman's breathing tube. Giacomo. Show him."

I turned to find Leonardo's Adonis, Messer Giacomo, presiding over his own table, upon which had been distributed various organs that appeared to have been removed from the corpse. To my untutored eyes, this arrangement resembled a *zampogna*—a peasant bagpipes—although this instrument had but one pipe, as thick as a barge rope but only half as long as my arm, crowned with a sort of crest. At the other end of the pipe was a pair of glistening purple bladders that put one in mind of fresh ox livers. Messer Giacomo clutched the crest atop the pipe with one hand, while with the other he pressed down on one of these bladders.

"Ah! Ah! Agghh!"

Hence I came to the understanding that the bladders were lungs, the pipe a windpipe; Giacomo had been squeezing his inelegant notes from that poor woman's dead flesh. Of the countless frauds and fables wherein a corpse speaks, no storyteller had ever imagined a truth such as this.

Finished with his playing, Leonardo's maestro of lungs plucked something from his table and displayed it delicately between his thumb and finger. The brown chunk was hardly bigger than a Spanish olive.

"I think it reasonable to propose that the woman herself swallowed it," Leonardo said. "As we have demonstrated, her lungs and larynx, indeed the whole apparatus of her breathing, remain entirely without damage. Had she spit out that single bite or masticated it more thoroughly, she might have lived another forty years."

"Then Fortune was her murderer," I said, regaining my bearings. "Maestro, I am looking for—"

I stopped, having noticed something that made the hair dance atop my head. "What do you have in that vat, Maestro?"

Not waiting for an answer, I made my way to the rear of the cellar, finding my suspicions confirmed even before I reached the long metal tub, which in fact was a coffin of sorts. A lead pipe ran in one end and out the other, conveying the water that both filled this vessel and coursed through it like a gentle brook.

Beneath the surface lay two alabaster objects. One was a single buttock cut just above the pelvis and through the crotch, with the thigh still attached, although I was able to orient myself to these anatomical features only by the remaining patch of pubic hair, which drifted in the current like moss at the bottom of a perfectly clear creek. The second object was the matching lower leg, severed at the knee.

I could not even begin to accept the dreadful defeat that lay before me. "Damiata was abducted out on the *pianura* last night. Did they do this to her?"

"We will see."

"See?"

"If they are the same." I had only a vague idea, if any, what he meant by "they," or why they would not be the same. Leonardo collected a notebook from one of his tables. "You must demonstrate to me, as precisely as you can, her height."

I knew where Damiata's eyes were, relative to mine, when we faced each other. With a trembling hand I showed the maestro. With a great long stick he measured to my mark, then made notations in his notebook. "She was wearing her half-boots?"

I nodded stiffly. With his bare hands Leonardo hauled the remains out of his vat like a fisherman clearing his net, placing them both on the stained sheet that covered his third trestle table. When he placed a measuring stick alongside the glistening shank, I could no longer watch.

From time to time, I heard the scratching of Leonardo's chalk, after which he noisily turned the sheets of his notebook like a court musician looking for a song. Here and there he also said things like "g is to h as the value r is to s . . ." But mostly he mumbled in fits and starts.

The maestro was still engaged in this nerve-scraping *esperienza* when footsteps shook the wooden stairs. Down came the alchemist

Tommaso, although you could see nothing of him save his head—with all that black wool sticking out of his idiotic *berretta*—and his big black boots. He was otherwise obscured by one of those great wicker baskets used in the grape harvest, these being shaped like an urn so that they will stand up, but so wide at the mouth that even Tommaso, with a span like a pelican's wings, could hardly get his arms around it. When he had conveyed his harvest basket to Leonardo's table, he emptied the contents onto the sheet.

The butchered parts tumbled out like the fragments of a shattered marble statue, yet the almost rose-hued edges where these pieces had been cleaved from the whole were perfectly straight and even. Half a torso, absent the arm, which had been severed at the shoulder joint, the glassy, pale blue breast having no nipple, only what appeared to be a blackened, crusted areola where it had been sliced away. The two parts of another leg, the upper portion also having a fine dark fringe of pubic hair alongside the cut that had divided the trunk. The arm and hand, half clenched, that had evidently been sliced from the partial torso.

Nevertheless, it was not the sight of that flesh but rather its reek—the same bitter scent that still clung to me—that made my head light. The room around me began to wobble.

Leonardo had already begun to move the ghastly pieces about on the table, as if trying to reassemble the corpse. Distantly I heard him say, "Did you precisely ascertain the locations?"

"All excepting the arm," Tommaso answered. "Some boys had passed it about."

Here Leonardo paused to study the remains as if he were painting a fresco, musing over his pots of colors. After a moment I thought he muttered, *"Dimmi"*—Tell me—as though imploring the body parts to speak. Whatever his inquiry, the lifeless flesh did not reply, because the maestro knitted his brow, then turned away and rushed up the stairs.

◆

I caught up with Leonardo in his studio. Here, too, several candle globes were lit, allowing me to see this immense disorder that Damiata has previously related. The maestro was already leafing through a bound manuscript—Latin, as I soon observed—that he had snatched up from among several other volumes on the tabletop, all piled together as carelessly as if he intended to make a bonfire of them.

"Vitruvius determined that the members of the human body were in mathematical proportion," Leonardo said, poking a great finger at a page in his book. "A man's height is equal to twenty-four palms and the other members are multiples or fractions thereof—my dear friend Fra Luca Pacioli has an equation to represent this. Dottor Savonarola, the grandfather of the fanatic, made useful tables based on similar principles . . ." Trailing off, Leonardo wrinkled his brow and wrote a few more numbers in his notebook.

I was suddenly as frozen as at any time during the previous two days. He had seen something. "What is it?"

The maestro once again produced his chalk and notebook, making a final notation. He shook his head.

I shouted, "In the name of God who was the woman Tommaso brought in the basket!"

"Not her."

My heart filled my entire chest. Yet I was only able to say, like a slow pupil, "So you are saying that those pieces of the body would not match someone of Damiata's height."

He looked at me as though I had just asked him how to empty piss out of a chamber pot. "Neither is proportionate. One of those unfortunate women was three-sixteenths of a *braccia* taller than Damiata. The other woman was one-eighth of a *braccia* shorter."

I returned only the blankest of stares.

"They are not symmetrical," Leonardo said. "The length of the lower leg is not proportionate with the section of the pelvis and femur." He was referring to the two fragments I had seen in his tank, upon which he had evidently based his entire deduction. "When we measure the parts Tommaso has collected, we will find the same variation."

I closed my eyes. "You mean—"

"They cannot have been obtained from the same body."

I stood there, insane with hope. Damiata might yet live.

But in her place, two other women had been butchered: *Zeja* Caterina, I was all but certain, and the *strega* who had joined her; the latter had appeared to be taller than Damiata. The taste in my mouth was suddenly as vile as the stink on my skin.

Having offered me this cold comfort, Leonardo began to sort through the vast accumulation on his tables, as if I were not present at all. If Damiata had been astonished to find amidst this chaos a clandestine order—those numbers and measurements that the maestro had imposed on all these models and devices—I had the fleeting but inescapable sense of something quite different: Nothing was ever completed. Every drawing had later notations or corrections in the margins. Every wooden model, be it of a fortress or a contraption of gears and wheels, sat among pieces that either had been taken away or were waiting to be added.

Like Damiata, I had no personal acquaintance with Leonardo da Vinci before I came to Imola; once there, I had only observed him, on a few occasions, coming and going to the Rocca. My interest in Valentino's engineer general began only after I heard reports that he had collected the pieces of a woman dismembered in a peculiar fashion—this followed by rumors connecting the crime to the *condottieri* as well as to the pope. Whereupon I employed the boy, Lucca, to watch the maestro's palazzo and inform me as to who—and what—went in and out. But I had never traded words with Leonardo until that afternoon in the olive grove.

Nevertheless, I was familiar enough with Leonardo's particulars to regard his disordered studio as a metaphor of his life. Thirty years before, he had been exiled from Florence on charges of sodomy, from which the Medici who had sponsored him should have protected him. His subsequent labors came to naught when the Duke of Milan betrayed him as well as all Italy, after which the esteemed maestro was run out of Mantua and Venice. It was our republic that had welcomed him back, two years previously, the brothers of Santissima Annunziata having provided him a commission. Yet when Valentino took him on, Leonardo left the friars with nothing but an immense drawing—which crowds came to gawk at nonetheless, as if Botticelli had taken up the brush again.

From among the clutter of his unfinished prodigies, Leonardo shortly produced one of the few items he had presumably completed:

his *mappa* of Imola, which Damiata had described to me in some detail. I assumed the duke had returned it, evidently to assist Leonardo's investigation. And I must confess that when I saw this map for myself, the sense of looking down on the earth like a bird nearly made my jaw drop.

Leonardo at once covered the *mappa* with a sheet of tracing paper that just as quickly engaged my interest: the square, circle, and square he had already drawn upon it in red chalk were the same figures of geometry he had displayed to Damiata. This drawing perfectly matched the *mappa* beneath it, the circle on the tracing paper and the circle of the wind rose being exactly the same diameter, although the tracing tissue itself was larger than the *mappa*.

"Tommaso," Leonardo bid his assistant, who had come upstairs on my heels. With Tommaso at his side, the maestro lifted the sheet of tracing paper, again exposing the map. "Indicate where they were found. As best you know."

"This was the first." Tommaso stuck his finger upon the empty little square at the center of the map. This was the Piazza Maggiore, Imola's main square.

"Yes, the buttock and femur," Leonardo said, certainly meaning the considerable haunch I had seen in his anatomist's vat.

"The lower leg was here." The alchemist pointed to the miniature street in front of what was recognizably, despite its tiny scale, the Dominican church; in the city of Imola as it existed in our world, this building was located several hundred *braccia* north and east of the Piazza Maggiore. "I am told the arm was here"—he pointed just outside the Appian Gate, several hundred *braccia* directly east of the Piazza Maggiore.

Each time Tommaso indicated a location, Leonardo placed the tracing tissue back over his map, marked this spot with a single point and wrote beside it the name of the body part that had been found there. This procedure went on, seven in all: The armless half-torso was found outside the Faenza Gate, just to its east, between the mill canal and the city wall. The second buttock and thigh were found on the other side of the Santerno River, south of the city, at the very edge of the big circle, or wind rose, drawn upon Leonardo's map; the lower leg outside this circle, in the hills southwest of the city.

Here I was prompted to ask, "Were these parts buried or found on the surface?" I presumed the latter.

"They were exposed." Having finished marking the locations indicated by Tommaso, Leonardo had taken up a straightedge and was busily connecting various points. He did not actually inscribe chalk lines between them but one could see that he was drawing geometric figures in his head, composing triangles and various other polygons.

"Yet animals did not take these exposed body parts," I remarked.

"We have sent word among the rustics that we will pay them if they discover such things and do not disturb them or allow animals to scavenge them. As it is, we have yet to collect them all."

I calculated my own ghastly inventory: given the new division of the bodies into eighths, nine fragments were still missing. Not to mention the heads.

Leonardo had begun to converse with himself again, moving his measuring stick about almost as if it were the bow of a *lira da braccio*. Yet again and again he shook his head, as if he could not find the right notes.

At last I said, "Maestro, possibly in this instance there is no figure of geometry, in fact no *disegno* at all."

"Having gone to such pains to create this device"—Leonardo gestured at his tracing paper—"why would he abandon his work?" Evidently the maestro who had left so many of his own works unfinished did not see the irony of his question.

"Perhaps this man intended the *disegno* to be absent," I said, "because he is varying his methods."

Still bowed over his tracing, Leonardo glanced back at me. "He has varied his methods only in the dismemberment and disposition of the bodies. He varies between inhuming the remains and leaving them exposed. And now he has divided the limbs in a fashion to provide a greater number of points for his constructions. But the *disegno* is here. We presently cannot see it."

I noted to myself the similar natures of Leonardo and the murderer, in that both could regard butchered limbs as "points" for some figure of geometry. "Certainly he intends that we expect some new *disegno*," I said. "But perhaps in this instance his intention is to confound us by not meeting that expectation."

"His intention is to create a riddle employing figures of geometry."

"To what end, Maestro?"

"That would be speculation."

"It is his intention to engage us. He does not want us to lose interest or to find his *disegno* predictable. Hence he has varied his methods by not creating a figure of geometry, where one is expected." I put my finger to the tracing. "In truth, we do not need to understand these figures of geometry if we can instead discover the necessity that has led this man to create them. What is the necessity in all this?"

Leonardo shook his head so vehemently that his gray curls swept about. "Why must we have this endless orgy of speculation! Let us return to the terra firma of *esperienza!*"

Here the maestro again searched among his tables. Half the things strewn upon them were of no use to his art or science, but instead belonged in a dry goods *speziale*: napkins and bed linens; terra-cotta pots full of brazier charcoal; a box overflowing with nails. And glass jars containing all manner of things, from glistening mercury to pearls of rice; sorting among these, the maestro finally selected one and returned to my side. He began to pluck from the jar a succession of dried black beans, placing them one by one on his tracing, at the points indicating where body parts had been found.

Yet Leonardo's beans only better illustrated the terrible perfection in the distribution of the first two bodies and the anarchy in the placement of the most recent remains. In his frustration he dumped the entire jar on his tracing paper, crying out, "There is more here! The *disegno* is in relation to that which has preceded it as the sphere within a cylinder is to the planar construction by which Archimedes . . . Where the base is the greatest circle in a sphere . . . the surface together with its base is three halves . . . But I cannot see it. The points are not complete." He extended his great index finger and gently tapped the beans in a random sequence, as if he were a fool who intended to count each one. "Archimedes. I must read my Archimedes." Suddenly he swept the beans aside. "Tommaso! We have to prepare for our journey. We have much to do. Much, much to do . . ."

"Journey?" This word struck me like a great stone dropped from a mason's crane; I was all the more stunned because I should have known at once, after witnessing the activity on the street. I could only croak, "Where is the duke now?"

"He departed for Cesena this morning," Leonardo said absently. "In company with the entire army. Owing to the urgency of this matter, the duke has instructed us to complete our *esperienza*. But we must leave here tomorrow."

Like Job sitting in the ashes, I stared at Leonardo's tracing paper, still dotted with a few remaining beans. The departure of Valentino and his army could only mean that the treaty negotiations had been all but concluded; the duke and his *condottieri* would meet at Cesena or somewhere to the south, to seal their accord and join their armies in a common purpose—which would almost certainly be the conquest of Florence. And I was bound by my government's instructions, reiterated to me in my most recent dispatch from the Palazzo della Signoria: to follow Duke Valentino wherever he went, regardless of his fate, or mine. I, too, had much to do, if I hoped to catch up with the duke and his army.

I had but one remaining stone to hurl at malignant Fortune. "Maestro, when you see His Excellency the duke, you must tell him there is a book, presently possessed by the same *gioca* of witches whose bodies you have examined in your cellar, that will connect the *condottieri* to his brother's murder. Damiata and I both saw it on the *pianura*, a moment before she disappeared and I was struck senseless by the same masked Devil's apprentice your own Giacomo witnessed. I believe that this book and possibly Damiata herself are still out on the *pianura*. The duke could dispatch horsemen from Cesena to conduct a search." In truth only a canvass of this sort, conducted by a great company of swift-moving cavalry, was likely to bear result.

Leonardo looked up at me and nodded. He began to pace among his tables like a gray lion, pressing his hands to his temples, pushing back his mane as if he wanted to shear it off entirely. *"Dimmi!"* Leonardo spit out the *d* as if he were an angry cat, the rest of the word a strange whine. *"Dimmi! Dimmi!"* Tell me! Tell me!

I looked to Tommaso, who quickly shook his head. Having said all I could until I saw the duke myself in Cesena, I went to the door but paused at the threshold.

Glancing back at the disordered studio, I wondered if Leonardo's panoply of unfinished marvels had also become a metaphor of a yet more ambitious undertaking, which would in similar fashion never see completion: Valentino's new Italy, a vision the duke had evidently surrendered to the designs of the *condottieri*.

CHAPTER 5

Whoever wishes to see what is to be, should consider what has been.

Early the next morning I was able to find a courier who needed a horse delivered to Cesena, which lies thirty miles south of Imola on the Via Emilia. This animal was scarcely a blessing; it was poorly schooled, difficult to handle, and finding fodder for it slowed my progress considerably. A journey I would ordinarily have completed in half a day required three.

I shared my misery with the great army of priests, monks, prostitutes, thieves, peasants, peddlers, and opportunists of every stripe that had followed Valentino's army throughout the Romagna campaign. Whether on foot or bowing the backs of pitiful starving mules and oxen, day and night all proceeded almost single file along the Via Emilia, for to go where the snow had not been trampled was to quickly come to a halt.

At Cesena, at last I received a grain of good news: Valentino and his army had stopped there, apparently for a stay of some length. Certainly Cesena was capable of sustaining the army for a little while, as well as being defensible; it is a walled city much like Imola and of similar size, but the principal fortress is a true citadel, perched atop a steeply sloped summit, with the city itself directly at its foot. If Valentino were to regret his accord with his brother's murderers prior to the irrevocable union of their forces, he would find Cesena a suitable redoubt.

Like the surrounding countryside, the city had been taken over by Valentino's soldiers, who were billeted everywhere. But by various devices I was able to find a room in a large palazzo near the central piazza. The narcotic unguent that had been smeared on my flesh had evidently leached into my blood, afflicting me with weakness and fevers; for the next few days, as I attempted to recover from these ills, I struggled to find food and charcoal and attend to my dispatches, this requiring that I begin to reliably ascertain the strength of Valentino's forces. I gravely feared that the duke's troops, a great multitude to the Cesenate who had to lodge them, were nevertheless considerably outnumbered by the combined forces of the *condottieri*. Hence I saw nothing to relieve my suspicion that Valentino was marching south to consummate a peace that more resembled a surrender. My appeals to Agapito for an audience with the duke, in which I might have raised the conjoined fates of both Damiata and Florence, had fallen on resolutely deaf ears, this all the more evidence that Valentino was no longer concerned for either.

As much as I was plagued by the demands of each day, each night found me host to yet more troubling desires. Like Petrarch's Laura, whose distance—and death—only strengthened the poet's attachment, my memories of Damiata bound me more desperately to her as the days passed without word. At night she came to me as a succubus, sometimes as feverish as I, her flesh like a bed warmer, at other times her eyelids rimmed with frost and her arms as cold as a corpse.

Each time, I awakened with an almost unbearable regret, believing I had abandoned Damiata out on the *pianura*. In truth, I mourned for her as if my soul knew she was dead. It was as though I were a Ginevra degli Amieri of a far less fortunate sort, waking to discover that I had escaped death, only to find myself in a darkened tomb that would remain forever sealed.

✦

At the end of my eighth day in Cesena, still laboring over my dispatches, I leapt up at the knock on my door. The soldier who waited outside, a heavy cape over his cavalryman's breastplate, did not have to tell me that the duke had sent him; he had similarly summoned me in

Imola. I assumed I had been called to present what might well be the final performance of our Florentine *cantafavola*, which had so wearied both the singer and his audience.

Our destination was the Governor's Palace, a building no larger, excluding the considerable tower, than any number of private palazzi in Florence. Messer Agapito waited in the cramped vestibule. "His Excellency will see you now."

The duke's secretary led me to a much larger chamber, well-lit by brass candelabra and a fireplace. Tapestries—one depicting a unicorn hunt—and purple velvet curtains draped the walls. Two cushioned chairs had been placed before the fire and Valentino stood beside them, attired in a white shirt tucked into riding breeches; his long, reddish hair, which appeared damp, fell to his collar.

Never had the duke received me with such informality. In Imola, where I had often waited for him until well after the fourth or fifth hour of the night, I had become accustomed to a certain ritual: the bright light outside his study ensured that one was all the more discomforted by the lean, vigorous, yet almost doleful face that waited in the oblique light of his reflecting lamp.

But it was not the duke's features that made the deepest impression. At twenty-six, Valentino had the gravitas, as the Romans put it, of a far more mature man—along with an air of authority and power so resolute that I had seen the most experienced diplomats and *condottieri* leave his presence with trembling hands and blanched faces. Yet afterward one learned that voices were never raised, threats never issued.

"Secretary." This much had not changed; Valentino never addressed me as anything but "secretary," to emphasize that my lords of the Palazzo della Signoria had been unwilling to send an actual ambassador. He gestured that I should sit in front of the fire and he took the chair beside me, his hands draped at ease over the gilded arms.

Without another word, he stared at the fire for sufficient time that I might have recited a half-dozen Paternosters. Finally he spoke in a low, distracted voice. "You know the people here cast drops of oil on their Christmas log. They say they can prophesy from the various colors of the flames that flare up."

More silence followed, and then he asked me this: "How would you defeat Fortune, Secretary?"

In our previous meetings, the duke had conversed with me seriously regarding affairs of state, and I believed that he credited my opinion on such matters—even if he did not take seriously the positions of my government. So I replied to this question, which seemed more suited to supper-table philosophy, just as earnestly. "First one must remove the blinders all men wear when Fortune is preparing her worst—when events are about to sweep them away. To defeat Fortune, men must anticipate such evils before they arise, and take prudent steps to avoid them. When the waters have already risen, it is too late to build dikes and embankments."

He made a flicking motion of his hand. "But men take action only when Fortune—or other men—have already undermined the foundations of their security. And when that edifice begins to topple they can only run for the doors. Why do you suppose that men refuse to anticipate events?"

"It is the nature of men to see things as they are, not as they will be," I answered. "But we have also abandoned the science of anticipation, which the ancients established. Instead, since the fall of imperial Rome, men have surrendered their fates to God, Fortune, and the Church—none of which will save us when the waters rise or the pillars of the house begin to fall."

"The science of anticipation. To see ahead, to peer through the clouds of complacency without relying on the fictions of prophets, seers, and stargazers." Valentino spoke as if he were in a *studiolo*, examining some new antiquity or curiosity. "To anticipate events before Fortune herself can turn her great wheel. How would you create such a science?"

"Here I would also follow in the steps of the ancients. Historians such as Titus Livy and Herodotus. I would look into the past, as they did, and speculate that the same forces that compel nations and empires to rise and fall will always be repeated, in endless cycle, throughout history. Understand the past, and one can anticipate what is to come. Understand the nature of men, and one can anticipate what men will do."

He nodded, but as if he did not entirely accept my prescription. "Then that is the error in this science of anticipation. The nature of men. Surely in this new age, this rebirth of humanity, we are changed men, different even than our own fathers. How can you anticipate a new man?"

He had mined the very foundation of my science; had I been less fixed in my fundamental conviction, or had his question been more oblique, I might have accepted this chastisement. Instead I said, "The times change. Events favor one man's character or nature over another's. Yes, a new age will prefer a new sort of man, and he will rise, while men whose natures are less suited to the times will fall. But the nature of men does not change. From age to age, our desires, fears, and necessities are always the same."

He turned slightly, still not looking at me directly. "But a man can change his nature."

No man in Christendom was better suited to wage this argument; within a few short years Valentino had metamorphosed from an insignificant, scorned cardinal to a warrior-prince whose intelligence and ambition were fairly comparable to those of his namesake, Julius Caesar.

"Just as the nature of men does not change," I said, "the nature of a man does not change. Perhaps when his true nature has remained hidden, to outward appearances he is a new man. But he has merely discovered the gifts that were always within him."

"The gifts Nature has given him." Here the duke nodded emphatically, as if I had resolved this question of a man's immutable nature to our mutual satisfaction. The smoldering coals popped and a flame shot up, as though the elements shared our agreement. Yet Valentino scarcely contemplated this little prophecy at all, because almost at once he said, "You know nothing of her?"

The tone of this remark was so ambiguous that I was not entirely certain that Valentino had posed a question, rather than stating a fact. But I was certain I knew the "her." It seemed Leonardo had conveyed my message.

"I have heard nothing from or of Damiata since she vanished on the *pianura*," I told him. "The day before you marched out of Imola."

In the silence that followed I cautioned myself: now that Valentino seemed to have committed his entire army, as well as his own fate, to reconciliation with the *condottieri*, he might earnestly hope that *Zeja* Caterina's "book of spells"—and its imputation of his allies' guilt—was never seen again.

Valentino turned fully to me. We were face-to-face, with a disquieting intimacy; certainly this had been his intent when he had set this stage.

"This book you mentioned to my engineer general." Valentino placed his pale hands on his thighs. "Did you see what it is?"

I had to swallow the rock in my throat before I could shake my head. "Damiata saw it. The names in it."

"It is Euclid's *Elements*. A schoolboy's geometry. But to our credulous peasants it might well be the magic of Solomon. Those women—the *streghe*—brought it to the Rocca. Not recently. More than a year ago, when all my *condottieri* were in Imola—Vitellozzo, Oliverotto, Paolo. Another Orsini cousin as well." My scalp prickled. "It was an amusement for everyone. These country *streghe* with their fraudulent prophecies. And the *gioce* that followed. Witch games of the most basic sort."

I needed to say nothing in response; he had himself indicted the *condottieri* for his brother's murder.

Yet Valentino next spoke in a musing tone, as if he wished only to distract himself from the grim truth written in the pages of a schoolboy's geometry. "To truly defeat Fortune, Secretary, it is not sufficient merely to anticipate the changes and catastrophes she will inevitably bring. At best you will merely become Fortune's accomplice and more often her servant, waiting on her human proxies to do their worst. No. To defeat Fortune you cannot merely peer into the past and find a mirror of the present. You must look ahead and see what has never been seen. A future even Fortune has not imagined." He returned his gaze to the fire. "Secretary, I have a very great enterprise under way here in the Romagna. What we build here will shortly secure the salvation of all Italy. That is why Fortune has chosen this moment to bring a very great intrigue against me."

I waited for him to elaborate. Then, unwilling to let my desperate hopes simply slip off into his silence, I said, "The *condottieri*—"

His hand came between us so quickly that I expected he would strike me. Yet he merely held it there, fingers spread, perhaps a palm's width from my face. "Yes. You see the *condottieri* as the principal agents in all this, because you know of their past enmity toward my family. But Secretary, I do not need the fingers of this hand to count the gentlemen under my own roof whom I can trust without reserve, who would not betray me for a price."

I did not find this entirely surprising; Damiata had told me that Valentino suspected some treachery among his intimates. While it was hard to believe that the duke's entire household had turned against him, I could easily conclude that at least one traitor remained under his roof: a man familiar with the details of Leonardo's *mappa*, who had conveyed them to the murderer.

"And Secretary, you are overlooking something else." Valentino lowered his hand. "Listen carefully now." His voice was only faintly sibilant, like the breeze that sighs among the beech leaves in summer. "You know nothing of her."

This, I was certain, was not a question.

CHAPTER 6

Don't you know how little good a man finds in the things he long desired, compared to what he expected to find?

"The day I first saw Damiata . . . I was twenty years old." Valentino leaned back, his chair creaking slightly. "It was spring, a cerulean day after a rain, in that marvelous garden at Ascanio Sforza's palazzo, with all those topiaries and an entire grove of trees—pomegranates, lemons, oranges." He spoke as if the intervening years had vanished. "She was standing in this little grove, her shoulders bare, all alabaster, her dress fitted so closely that the gold embroidery seemed like veins of fire on a skin of satin. Until that day I had thought my own sister the only truly beautiful woman . . ." He shook his head with tiny, rapid motions. "Damiata was not a woman who had strolled in there in her gown and pearl slippers. She was Diana glimpsed at her bath. Her hair was golden then, and the breeze gathered it with phantom fingers, each strand a thread spun of light."

He looked into the fire as if this vision were present in the glowing coals. "I was a little cardinal, a fool in a red cap who served only as a basket for the benefices and other income of the office, scarcely allowed to hold the door at even the most meaningless events. Pissing my life away in the Vatican latrines. But in that garden, on that day, I saw a goddess come down from the stars, a divine messenger meant only for me. And on that day I promised myself something." The sibilance in his voice had become a slight tremolo. He closed his eyes. "A new life."

I did not dare say that I, too, understood that promise.

"I want to believe her, Secretary. I want to believe in her, because she is part of who I am." Here he began to lightly tap the fingertips of both hands on his thighs. "But my father has heard nothing from her. You have heard nothing. I have sent soldiers back to Imola to search for her. We have looked everywhere and have found not a hair of her."

I was relieved, in part, to learn that Valentino's people had in fact undertaken the search I had so desperately urged. But why was he only now inquiring of me, when I might have been more useful than anyone in this endeavor?

He went on: "We have found nothing to suggest that she has come to a sad end. Nothing to tell us that she has gone elsewhere. Nothing at all." He continued to tap his fingertips against his thighs. "Yes, I want to believe in her. But she betrayed my brother." Valentino allowed this accusation to hang in the air, as if content to echo his father's suspicions. His elaboration, when it came, was murmured like a prayer. Or a confession. "We both betrayed him."

An abyss had opened at my feet.

"She became my lover only weeks before Juan was murdered. I will not tell you I was seduced."

Now I could only think: *What else did she withhold from me?*

"Of all that Juan had been given, of all that I, in turn, had been refused, I coveted her most of all, even more than I coveted glory and wealth. And believe me, Secretary, beneath that absurd cardinal's hat my father clapped on my head, I craved glory and wealth no less than the gut of a starving man screams for a crust. And she knew my desire." A single fingertip tapped up and down. "We betrayed my brother twice. In her bed. After the first time I vowed that I would not go back to her. But I could not . . ." He shook his head as though marveling at Damiata's singular powers of attraction. "The second time was the last day of my brother's life. In the afternoon, because he was coming to her that night. She expected him to come from the Vatican, across the Sant'Angelo bridge. I told her no, that I was dining with Juan that evening at our mother's vineyard on the Esquiline, next to San Martino ai Monti. I believe she knew then that Juan was lying to her, that when he left our supper he intended to visit the Contessa della Mirandola's house near the Santa Maria del Popolo." The duke's exhalation was audible. "To this day I don't know. But to this day I still question . . ."

He opened his eyes and sat forward. "Everyone knew that the *con-dottieri* had their knives out for Juan. First, because he had enraged the Orsini with his campaign against them, even if he achieved nothing. And second, because the Vitelli, who did most of the fighting for the Orsini, saw it to their profit to continue the hostilities with my father, even when the Orsini began to discuss peace. Yet Juan did nothing to secure his person. When he went out at night he took along a drunken groom or two and rarely wore his armor. His only defense was his wandering nature—no one could say when or where he would go." Valentino now tapped his thighs so rapidly that his fingers might have been playing a *moresca* on a flute. "I have always wondered if Damiata told them where he was that night, and where he would go later. Told this to one of the Vitelli, I believe. Or perhaps Damiata simply told someone who told the Vitelli. She was furious about Juan's dalliance with the contessa. Ordinarily she could conceal her anger. As she concealed so many things. But I was with her that day. I saw . . ." He blinked as if trying to see his former lover through the veil of years. "Damiata had ears and mouths all over the city. She had a thousand ways to accomplish her betrayal."

His fingertips ceased their tattoo. He stared at his hands, as if wondering why they had stopped. "And I, in my own way, was her accomplice. I told her the fatal truth about Juan's plans for that night, fully knowing that I would feed her anger over his new lover. Of course I was mad with desire for her. But I also believed she was another gift, much like the captain general's office, that Juan had so carelessly squandered. So I, too, willfully betrayed my brother." The words drew his lips tight, as if he had swallowed sour wine. " 'The Lord set a mark upon Cain, lest any finding him should kill him . . .' "

"Excellency, I believe she loved your brother." If Damiata had not loved Juan of Gandia, how little truth was there to this "connection" she had cited between us?

"She loved him. Yes, I believe that." Valentino acknowledged this as if love itself were a sad and tawdry crime. "But I must ask if she has

betrayed not only Juan but both my father and me—and you as well."
He turned to me again. "Secretary, is it possible that Damiata escaped
the divination with this book?"

Hope pulsed through my veins at the mere conjecture that Damiata was alive. And fear followed: if Valentino's speculation was correct,
perhaps she had kept the book from him because she could not trust
him.

I tried to steady myself, reasoning that even if I could tell Valentino
little he did not already know about the events on the *pianura*, the manner in which he received my information might reveal more of his own
intentions. Hence I described for him in detail the *Gevol int la carafa*
and the mastiff-keeper's flight with the "book of spells," as well as my
own encounter with the masked Devil's apprentice, withholding only
those particulars of the goat ride that had occurred within my own
mind.

"I do not see how Damiata could have pursued the mastiff keeper
with better result than the masked man who knocked me senseless," I
concluded. "And as I told you, I do not believe this apprentice obtained
the book, because if he had, he certainly would have put an end to my
involvement in the matter."

The duke's eyes, though half shut, were so fixed on the embers
before him that he might have been willing the genesis of some great
conflagration.

"You must think carefully on this, Secretary." After Valentino's
long silence, this instruction was as sharp as a stiletto. "Did you see
this *mago*, this 'mastiff keeper,' in possession of the book itself when he
ran from the hut?"

"I was knocked down. I . . ." I saw what Valentino was asking. I had
simply assumed the truth of Damiata's words: *He has the book!* "No. I
never saw that he had it."

"Consider it, Secretary. Is it possible Damiata intended you to pursue this man, so that she would be at liberty to bargain with those
people? I would guess she kept a considerable sum on her person. And
as you know, she is both clever and persuasive." And a confessed liar
and thief. "You would not be the first man she has deceived."

And she would not have been the first woman to deceive me.

"My father made a grave error in involving Damiata," Valentino said, his tone mirroring my regret. "And all the more so in using the boy as he did. Her desire to retrieve Giovanni is entirely sincere. Never doubt that. His Holiness has only given her a grievance and a cause."

I nodded. If she must, Damiata would enlist Satan himself in that cause.

"You say that if we are to defeat Fortune, Secretary, we must anticipate events. If Damiata had this book in her possession, what would she do with it? Would she go to my father and trust him to release her son? Or would she wager that the *condottieri*, offered the opportunity to destroy the evidence of their association with the murdered women, would secure the boy's release in exchange for the book?"

I presumed Valentino meant that the *condottieri* would "secure the boy's release" with the sort of subtle coercion that had already compelled him to leave Imola—or perhaps they would overtly threaten to attack the pope's fortresses or the Vatican itself. That Valentino had even raised the question evidenced his steadily weakening position.

"Given Damiata's difficulties with your father," I said, "she might have reason to favor the *condottieri*."

"I agree. More so if they have had a previous connection."

This "connection" being a conspiracy to murder his brother. Yet the duke had also left the "if" hanging in the air.

Valentino settled back into his chair with a weariness I had never observed in him, his shoulders slumped and his chin down. "Secretary, do you know this nun from Mantua?" Now it seemed he was, in fact, only talking in his sleep. "This seeress or prophetess they all chatter about? Osana, she is called. She prophesied that the reign of the Borgia would be like 'a fire of straw.'"

A faint moan came from the fireplace, the sound of vapors in the wood escaping.

"At our first breath, we begin to race Fortune." Valentino spoke as if he had already surrendered his hope of defeating her. "She draws a map of each man's life, marking the distance that bounds our mortality, requiring of us that we race against her, ever faster, toward the oblivion that lies beyond. Santa Maria, that distance is short, the contest brief." I thought I saw a glimmer at the corner of his eye. "Perhaps the nun of Mantua simply saw Fortune's map of my life. Because if I do not find this schoolboy's geometry, then all this, all my hopes for a new Italy, will be consumed more quickly than straw in a fire."

CHAPTER 7

Whatever is entirely clear, entirely without suspicion, is never found.

Upon leaving the Governor's Palace, I wandered the streets of Cesena for what seemed an age, trudging from one corner of the little city to the next, hopelessly perplexed. I believed with every fiber of my intellect that Valentino's suspicions of Damiata were sincere and not without foundation; he knew her better than I could imagine. He had held her, breast to naked breast, inciting in my own a jealousy I had once thought alien to my nature; this alone should have warned me that I was not in my right mind. Yet my entire soul still believed in Damiata with a conviction my intellect was powerless to defeat. It was possible that Valentino, plagued by his own guilt, was simply mistaken; certainly someone other than the two of them had also been privy to the Duke of Gandia's route the night he was murdered. Nevertheless, even my soul had to concede that Damiata had known full well what I had at stake in the investigation of Juan's murder, yet she had maintained a silence that was no less than a lie about the manner in which she *had* betrayed the Duke of Gandia, when she had taken his brother as her lover.

On the other hand, Valentino's own intentions were scarcely clear; even his presentiment of doom had been ambiguous. Did he regard any evidence that would obstruct his accord with the *condottieri* as the foremost stumbling block to his new Italy—or did he regard the *condottieri* as the principal threat to his most immediate ambitions, or even his very life? If the latter, then his withdrawal from Imola, and for that matter his entire treaty with the *condottieri*, might well be a madness feigned to deceive the architects of this "very great intrigue" against him, until he could secure the *Elements* and produce the evidence that would damn them all. Yet if the former were true, he desired the book only to destroy it—or deliver it as an offering when he submitted to the *condottieri*.

In this manner my arguments went in circles, like my own repeated circuits of Cesena.

◆

I must have walked until well past the seventh hour of the night before I finally stopped in the doorway of a palazzo not far from my own rooms, suddenly unbearably weary. My feet made a little screech on the icy pavement as I found my footing. Cesena had become as quiet as a graveyard around me.

After a moment I heard a familiar, clamoring noise, although it was not of this place, or the present.

This was the rising din of another city, as Florence awakened to another day: a vast crowing, barking, and braying of both men and animals; a rattling of carts, a carillon of smiths' hammers and stonemasons' chisels. In some netherworld between memory and a goat-ride vision, I was once again only a few months past seven years old, standing in the doorway of our little house on the Via di Piazza.

It was my first day with my new Latin tutor, Ser Battista, whose *studiolo* was at the San Benedetto church, next to the Duomo. I had never crossed the Arno by myself, much less half the city, so at breakfast my chin quivered a little. Mama had certainly observed this, because she fried little flour cakes and filled them with a cherry paste, singing one of her own lauds all the while: "The Lord who brings justice to the oppressed, the Lord who feeds the hungry and frees our bonds . . ."

Having wrapped one of these confections in a napkin, she presented it to me at the door. "My darling Niccolò, my first son," Mama said as I tucked away the treat in the bag with my slate. "Your life will be out there." Mama nodded in the direction of the city. "You will become a learned man, a man of letters. Like your papa. But I have the deepest faith that you will also have an office. You will take your place in the government of our republic."

This prophecy seemed utterly fanciful to me. Papa had never held an office in our government and could never hope to do so; he was not one of the favored "Medici men" who alone were accorded wealth and influence. The republic itself was only the dream of little people like Mama and Papa, who closed their shutters whenever Lorenzo de' Medici rode past at the head of yet another gaudy Carnival parade, his chorus of sycophants and retainers following behind him like an immense, multicolored snake.

Mama caressed my cheek with dry, rough fingers. She had been almost forty years old when I was born, and on this day she seemed an old woman to me, her forehead hatched with lines, her lips thin and almost without color. "Niccolò, long before you were born, I made the most solemn promise to our Lord. I vowed that I would give the first son I carried in my womb to our *bella* Firenze and her *libertà*." Her wide-set, vaguely catlike eyes peered inside me. "Today you will begin to redeem that promise. You will come to love our Firenze, and then you will understand why you must save her. Why you must restore her *libertà* to all her people. Not just the few."

With these words my mother gave me to Florence. As I crossed the Ponte Vecchio, tears clouded my eyes, because I knew I would never again follow my beloved mama around our house like a little pet. And I did not fall in love with *bella* Firenze that first day; I was too frightened.

Nevertheless, not a week had passed before I bounded out the door after breakfast and raced across the bridge, within a few hundred steps finding myself in the roaring heart of all Europe's commerce. To my mind the buildings on either side of the street resembled great sailing ships, the towering façades of the silk shops always draped with enormous, shimmering damask banners, while from nearly every window of the wool factories, each the size of a palazzo, long bolts of newly washed fabric, nearly as fine as the silk, flapped in the wind. Swept along in a great tide of traffic, I crossed the city on the Via dei Calzaiuoli, named for the many hosiery shops that lined it, although most of the shop-front arcades displayed some other trade beneath their long tiled canopies: shoemakers, goldsmiths, illuminators, bookbinders, our first printer's shop.

But amidst all this commerce, which to my eyes resembled a great and fascinating battle, I found an even more astonishing beauty. On the Via dei Calzaiuoli, I could wander around the great gray block of the Orsanmichele church, looking up at the statues of the patron saints of all the guilds, like Donatello's Saint Mark and Saint George, their lifelike appearance nearly miraculous compared to the stiff scarecrows carved in the centuries before our *Rinascimento* of ancient arts and letters. At the end of the street was the immense Duomo, clad in white-and-green marble, crowned with Brunelleschi's prodigious brick dome; every time I passed, I craned my head back so far I thought I would fall over, and floated away with pride, to think that the men who had made these *invenzioni* were Florentines like me.

Yet I found the greatest wonder of my *bella* Firenze in the austere Piazza della Signoria, bounded on the east by the rustic stone palazzo where, many years later, I would serve our republic, just as Mama had prophesied. The Piazza della Signoria was a vast marketplace of discourse, where ideas were exchanged like coins at the bankers' counters that lined the streets feeding into it. Here gathered men of all stations, from smiths in thick leather aprons to lawyers and wool merchants in fur-lined capes. They discussed things I hardly understood, even when I could hear them amid the great din; nevertheless I was enchanted simply to watch them speak, to study the manner in which men gestured with their hands, nodded, grimaced, reflected, turned from one to another.

Perhaps some part of me still stood in a doorway in Cesena, but my mind was entirely absorbed in this vision of the past; I was nothing more or less than a boy seven years old, sweeping my eyes about the Piazza della Signoria, transfixed by the life ahead of me. And even when this living memory faded, it slipped away so slowly that for a time I was lost, neither in one place nor another, empty save for a deep longing to hear my mother's voice and to walk the streets of our Firenze.

When I once again realized where I was, I had my answer. I had not come all the way to Cesena because I trusted anyone—neither Valentino, nor Damiata, nor even the Ten of War.

"I belong only to the republic, our *libertas*, and our *bella* Firenze," I whispered, watching my words in the still, cold air, rising like smoke from a priest's censer. "Whatever is required to save the city I love, I will do."

◆

No sooner had I issued this oath, than I observed a witness to it, although he seemed as much a phantom as the faces I had left behind in Florence, and time. He was perhaps fifty *braccia* distant, standing in a street-front arcade. His cape appeared little more than a shadow against the shop-front shutters, his face so enveloped by the hood that it seemed merely a bone-white Carnival mask—in this instance, the skeletal face of Death, rather than the goat-bearded Devil's mask I had so briefly glimpsed on the *pianura*. Yet at once I had the terrifying conviction that this man had been present that night.

I saw little security in taking another route. If he was in fact the murderer's apprentice—or perhaps even the maestro of the shop—my escape would only postpone this reckoning to an occasion when I might have even less warning.

I started toward him, my breast like a drum. When I had halved the distance between us, I could still distinguish nothing more of his face—or mask—than a pale cipher.

I called out with the desperate bravado of an unrepentant heretic, standing before his stake: "You there! Have you a new mask?"

A peculiar metamorphosis flickered within his hood, as though a bleached skull had begun to clothe itself in pale flesh. I could see the dark sockets, if not yet his eyes.

His cloak fanned out as if he were an eagle about to take flight and I braced for his charge. Instead he turned, striding away so quickly that he had exited the far end of the arcade almost before I could take a breath. Only when he had vanished entirely did it occur to me that this route would take him directly to my lodging—about which he could find any number of places to conceal himself and wait.

My pursuit was so swift that the cold air blurred my vision, my feet nearly slipping from under me as I raced around the corner—

I slid to a stop no more than an arm's length from the point of a stiletto.

"Did you see that?"

I looked up. The face was entirely human, though the mouth seemed frozen into an O. I recognized him in the same moment that I placed his voice. "Giacomo?"

"He ran right past me," Maestro Leonardo's assistant said with indignation. "He would've knocked me over if I hadn't stepped aside."

"Did you see his face?"

He shook his head. "That wasn't a man."

"But not the mask you saw in the woods that day." The same mask I had seen on the *pianura*.

"No. The face in the moon. Or an owl." Giacomo studied his stiletto, which he had yet to slip back in his belt. "Or no face at all."

I nodded at this last description, finding it more apt than the "mask of Death" I had observed. My science, if I could call it that, had so far failed to provide the murderer a face. He had allowed me to see only masks. Or no face at all.

Only after musing on this did I think to ask, "Giacomo, why are you out here?"

"Waiting for you." He offered this as if I were the cause of both his discomfort and his encounter with a faceless demon. "The maestro sent me to fetch you."

Now I could answer at least one question: certainly Valentino had already reported our conversation to Leonardo, who had evidently summoned me at the duke's request. "Will the maestro still want to see me at this hour?"

Giacomo nodded, his Milanese diction as languorous as ever. "The maestro never sleeps."

CHAPTER 8

To many things that reason doesn't persuade you, you are persuaded by necessity.

Giacomo led me to the opposite side of the city, where we halted at what appeared to be the refectory of an abandoned church. Through the cracks in the shutters, I could see that this brick building, which was as plain as a warehouse, was lit up like day inside. We ascended the two steps, whereupon Giacomo barged through the door as if he were an officer of the jail making an arrest.

I girded myself for another visit to Hell.

The considerable space had in fact once been an austere dining hall; if ever the walls had been frescoed, they were now plastered over. The two big trestle tables in the center of the room might have been left behind by the monks, although their refectory had been put to a use the soup-slurpers never could have imagined. Nor could I.

Save for the two tables, the entire floor was occupied with devices the maestro had actually constructed: any number of machines with gears and cogs; small boats; peculiar ladders; an enormous crossbow; a great wheel that reached almost to the ceiling beams, with no less than two dozen buckets attached to it. These and a myriad other things I could not even describe.

Attired in his chamois cape and a red satin vest, Leonardo stared fixedly at a drawing of several toothlike, irregular shapes that appeared composed almost entirely of numbers. Believing that these calculations had something to do with the murderer's *disegno*—or with the stature of his victims—I went at once to his side.

"We are going to build an entire city, the duke and I. Here in Cesena." Only then did I discern that he was examining a rough map, with detailed measurements of this city's dimensions; his *mappa* of Imola had probably begun with similar studies. "A new city even the ancients would envy. With plumbing, sewers, canals, locks, hospitals, courtrooms, public edifices that celebrate reason and liberty. I have drawn them and together the duke and I will construct them. A world without squalor, hunger, or darkness. It will begin here."

I would have thought him mad, had I not believed with equal conviction that Valentino, of all living men, was most capable of building a new world. But certainly the duke had not instructed his engineer general to summon me for this demonstration. "What cannot wait, Maestro?" Again I steeled myself for an anatomy lecture.

"This was brought to us two days ago. From Imola. It was retrieved by the soldiers His Excellency dispatched to search for Madonna Damiata." Perhaps I, of all men, should not have been surprised at the reverence with which he invoked her name, almost as though she were the Holy Madonna.

Leonardo stuck two fingers into a leather purse attached to his belt, first drawing out a length of red yarn; when he extracted the little card attached to this string, I had to close my eyes. "How was it found?"

"Within a hand. From an arm we could not locate before we left Imola."

"You mean an arm belonging to one of the two *streghe*. It could not be Damiata?"

"No. Not her." He presented me the *bollettino*. "Does it signify anything to you?"

The card might have been colored by body fluids or simply by slush and red earth. Despite these stains and the rough scrawl, I could still read the contradictory invocations: *Sant Antoni mi benefator. Angelo bianc, per vostr santite.*

"The ink and hand are identical to the *bollettino* we found in the olive grove," I told Leonardo. "I presume that *Zeja* Caterina wrote this." For a moment the dead witch's pale eyes haunted me. "I am reasonably certain that she alone of that *gioca* could read or write, if only in the vernacular."

I turned over the card, little surprised to find another inscription, this in tiny but elegant Tuscan script. "And this hand and Chinese ink," I said, "are the same as the reverse side of the previous *bollettino*. Maestro, I assume you saw the first of these *bollettini*, before it was sent on to the Vatican." Here I referred to the *bollettino* the pope had shown Damiata; Leonardo had recovered the butchered remains of the woman who had carried it in her charm bag, hence I had good reason to believe he had seen everything found on her person—including Juan of Gandia's amulet. "And I presume 'the corners of the winds,' " I continued, "was written in the same hand as this *bollettino*."

Leonardo looked at the card, which still rested on the tips of my fingers, as if he expected it to burst into flame. "You assume correctly. On both accounts. But you must read this one."

I had to squint a bit to decipher the tight, miniature script: *Il quadrato è il primo cerchio.*

" 'The square is the first circle,' " I said. "Then this is a figure of geometry, in the same manner as the previous two. Likewise presented to us as a riddle or conundrum. But the first circle was your own wind rose, inscribed around your *mappa*. And the square, I would venture, was drawn between the corners of the winds. Is he recalling for us his first figures? Perhaps to direct our attention to something we have not yet seen?" No sooner had I said this, however, than I saw the game this man was playing.

"This inscription describes the new *disegno* he has made." I was not surprised that Leonardo clung to this notion. "Giacomo!" Giacomo appeared to be shuffling off to bed. "Has Tommaso found the Archimedes?"

Giacomo shook his head as if infinitely weary of such requests. I sympathized with him; the chaos of Leonardo's intellect, his disposition simply to toss his thoughts about in a manner little different than his belongings, was already wearying to me—though in this he matched my own practice more than I would have wished.

"We will locate the Archimedes," Leonardo said, although his affirming nod was less than firm. "And then we will have our solution.

I have every conviction this 'first circle' can be found among Archimedes's proofs."

Evidently unwilling to wait on Tommaso, Leonardo began to rifle through various manuscripts, some bound and some loose, already accumulated on the table before him. "Because we have moved, everything has become disordered," he explained—again with no hint of irony.

I took his distraction as an opportunity to examine some of the loose leaves, which recalled to me all the unbound manuscripts in my father's little library. Many of these papers, mostly copied in Latin but a few, quite old, written in Greek, did in fact concern mathematics, the dense script often accompanied by diagrams with lettered points or elaborate drawings of various polygons. I could get nothing from them.

Shortly, however, I found a page written in Latin, and not in Leonardo's hand; on closer scrutiny it turned out to be an account of a man who suffered a disease of the brain the Greeks knew as *kephalgia*, which "alienates the mind, induces loss of voice, and at last withdraws the vital power." As Leonardo continued to sift through his volumes and pages, I found an entire stack of leaves by this same hand, evidently that of a physician, or his copyist, describing illnesses of all sorts as well as necropsies performed on persons who had expired. More than a few of these concerned maladies of the brain: delusions, memory loss, mute entrancement, and a violent madness the Greeks called *phrenesis*. One such case, which involved an executed criminal, interested me sufficiently that I dared to intrude on Leonardo's fruitless exploration. "Maestro, these physician's accounts. Where did you obtain them?"

"Those are Benivieni's cases," he said, as if I were a farmer asking for the source of the dung on my boots. "Antonio Benivieni," Leonardo snapped at my blank expression. "The Florentine physician."

I recovered my own lost memory. Benivieni was a dottore of considerable renown; like Leonardo, he was reputed to have undertaken many dissections of corpses.

"You cannot come to any labor of anatomical science without good knowledge of mathematics," Leonardo said. "As you can see, Benivieni's work is entirely worthless. He has measured nothing."

I was hardly one to raise a defense of physicians. Nevertheless I said, "When you have measured and identified this new figure of geometry, my dear Maestro, what do you expect to discover regarding the nature of the murderer who has created it?"

"We will see."

I believed it was time to take the maestro to school, let us say. "Your Giacomo and I saw this man or his apprentice on the street tonight, Maestro. Evidently there are no less than two different Carnival masks these men wear when they go about their evil labors—one the Devil and the other Death, as nearly as I have been able to observe. And I believe this maestro of death will continue with similar deceptions, displaying to us various other masks, riddles, and figures of geometry, by these means making his works known to us—even as he does not wish us to know him. That is why he is determined to obtain this Euclid's *Elements*, in which I am certain his name has been recorded."

As Leonardo listened, his mouth worked, but he said nothing aloud.

"Maestro, I believe this man ordinarily goes among us without any sort of mask, yet by some means he is able to conceal his true face. And as I have previously told you, it is my most firm conviction that we will not be able to identify him until we have entered his mind and understood his necessity—"

"Necessity?" Leonardo's voice was suddenly as shrill as the high notes of a *piffero*. "Do you understand at all this word of yours, this *necessità* you ceaselessly invoke? You—you are nothing more than a Latinist, your nose stuck in ancient texts!" Leonardo drew his head back as if recoiling from this horror. "Do you think that proofs of the sort I am seeking are established by the ornate words of orators like you? What have you measured? Where is your *esperienza?*"

"You can place your measuring stick next to a man's skull," I answered, "but it will tell you nothing of the desires and necessities that reside within."

Leonardo wagged a great finger at me. "Tell me then, my esteemed man of letters, what instrument you have acquired to measure these desires that exist only in the minds of men—when I, who have dissected the very ventricles of the brain, have yet to discern this mechanism. Do you propose to extend your arms like some barefoot fool measuring his vegetable plot, and tell me that it is you alone who have calculated the length of a man's desire? You are better off measuring his *cazzo* instead!"

"My instrument, if you must have one, is the wisdom of those who have observed history and derived its lessons. Herodotus. Plutarch. Thucydides. Titus Livy! They have provided us with every measure of humankind's desires and ambitions—as Livy says, 'In history you can find human experience in all its infinite variations.' *That* is my *esperienza!*"

"I do not deny that the study of history is a nutriment to the intellect," Leonardo said less vehemently. "But you—you offer no direct observation of the artifacts of the crime itself."

" 'Artifacts,' Maestro? Do you mean the mortal remains of these unfortunate women? I have already taken into account the manner of their dismemberment, how we were expected to discover them, and how their arrangement—or lack of it—has sent you wandering in a dark woods, searching for some *disegno* that can be found only in the ventricles of *your* brain!"

I paused and studied Leonardo carefully. All at once my skin crawled. "There is something else, isn't there, Maestro? Something you have withheld."

His prodigious fingers plucked at his cape as if trying to remove burrs, each hand working independently of the other. "The heart is a muscle . . . of exceptional strength and vitality," he said at last. "So ingeniously has Nature designed the valves . . . to permit a constant flow in but one direction, that our blood courses through our arteries with such turbulence . . . much as a river rushes through a narrow channel." The maestro described this vigorous action in little more than a halting whisper, as though delivering aloud one of his silent addresses. "When we study the course of rivers, we observe that water is capable, over time, of carving passages in solid stone . . . In the body this flow attains such force that it can burst a vein in the head . . . Among older men it will eventually cause a callousing and thickening of the walls of the veins, until the blood no longer circulates in sufficient volume . . . to . . ."

My own blood felt cold in my veins. "Finish your thought, Maestro. I know that these women did not perish due to a thickening of their arteries."

"Blood will pool in the inferior portions of the limbs . . . after circulation has ceased. But that . . . that settling was not observed in the remains that were brought to me." Leonardo's trembling face was gray. "Exsanguination had to have occurred during the dismemberment."

I recalled all too well my own goat ride. The concoction had paralyzed my body but had not rendered me insensible to pain; as my limbs struggled to regain movement, I had imagined awls were piercing my muscles and joints. Those poor women had been butchered while they were immobilized by the narcotic agents; probably they could not even scream. But they had remained entirely sensible of fear, pain—and the dreadful sundering of their flesh.

I looked down at the pages I had previously examined. "Maestro," I murmured, "if you regard Dottor Benivieni's papers as worthless, might I have a few of them?"

Leonardo gestured like an old woman shooing a fly. "Take whatever you wish," he whispered. "As I told you, Benivieni has measured nothing."

◆

As soon as I had barred my door I lit a candle and sat at the little table I had obtained for my writing. Clearing away my own manuscripts, I replaced them with Benivieni's papers. The case that had so interested me in Leonardo's refectory concerned a certain worthless miscreant named Jacopo, a habitual thief who had been hanged for his manifold crimes. Yet upon being removed from the gallows, Jacopo had turned out to be alive, and upon treatment he had recovered. Nevertheless, because of his wicked nature, Jacopo had disregarded the miracle of his resurrection and had returned at once to the same crimes—for which he was once again hanged, this time to the intended effect.

Having conducted a great number of necropsies to ascertain the anatomical causes of various diseases and deaths, Dottor Benivieni was similarly determined to find the cause of Jacopo's incorrigible behavior.

After opening the man up entirely, the physician had fixed his interest on the back of Jacopo's head, where one finds the ventricle of the brain known as the *memoriae sedes*—the "seat of memory," or more nobly, the "throne of memory." Benivieni observed that this region of the brain contained far less matter than was typical. On account of this deficiency, the physician wrote, Jacopo "scarcely remembered his prior crimes and the punishments he received, and so returned many times without shame, like a dog to its vomit, to his crimes, so that at last he put his own head in the noose and ended his life."

I sat there in my creaking chair, tapping a finger on this last sentence. Certainly Benivieni's conclusion was nonsense. It was entirely beyond reason that Jacopo, regardless of his anatomical defect, had forgotten his crimes; instead he had remembered all too well how to commit them. Nevertheless, I was not able to dismiss the physician's observations entirely. It seemed to me that this Jacopo, a very common man, had been stamped from a similar mold to those rare men I had plucked from my recollection of history: Alexander of Pherae, the Roman dictator Sulla, or the emperors Caligula and Nero. All of them, regardless of circumstances, had habitually repeated their crimes without shame, guilt, or regard for punishment (yet history shows us that tyrants, no less than criminals like Jacopo, rarely die a peaceful death). The insignificant Jacopo had lacked the license of power to fully indulge his evil nature, yet he had pursued his trade to the end. Nero had enjoyed absolute power, but I believe that even as a shepherd or a cobbler he would have found an inexplicable delight in cruel acts. Benivieni's description was in fact apt: "like a dog returning to its vomit," these men were driven by some animal instinct to return again and again to the crimes that had already stained their souls.

As I had told the duke, just as the nature of men does not change from age to age, so each man is born with an unchanging nature. Hence I could not help but lean to Dottor Benivieni's opinion: this defect, whether it was Plato's "disease of the soul" or some deficiency of the brain itself, had always been present in the men afflicted with it. Nature had made them thus, and neither man nor Fortune could ever alter them.

A cold wind rattled the shutters. Clutching my jacket around me,

I imagined myself on the threshold of this rare man's mind, much as I had entered the intellect of Hannibal or Caesar, and had queried them there. Although instinct told me to run, instead I stared into his dreadful Labyrinth and silently addressed him.

Your necessity is simply to destroy life, to feast without compassion or conscience upon the suffering of your innocent victims. This has been your nature since your life began to quicken in your mother's womb. Yet in some manner, you have always been able to conceal your monstrous face behind the mask of a man.

The wind whistled through the cracks around my poorly fitted door.

But now I know you, if not yet your face or name. Because I alone know the secret that from your first breath has set you apart from all of us. It is not a secret you keep hidden in a diseased soul. It is a far more dreadful deception.

You were born without a soul.

CHAPTER 9

The best remedy against an enemy's plan is to do voluntarily what he expected you to do by force.

Two days later—the day following the winter solstice—there was still no word of Damiata nor any sign of Valentino's intentions. Instead the city of Cesena witnessed the most notable entertainment it had evidently ever seen.

The *ballo* took place in the Civic Palace, which bounds the city's principal piazza on the north, lying at the foot of the brooding citadel. Its façade composed of two tiers of arched windows, the Civic Palace is attached to a fortress of the same nearly featureless architecture as the one high on the hill—although it is much smaller, a *rochetta* rather than a *rocca*, with only a single great tower. Joined end to end, the Civic Palace and the *rochetta* present an immense massif of stone. On this particular evening the *rochetta* half of this enormous wall was as dark as the bottom of a well, while the Civic Palace was lighted like an armorer's factory.

The Cesenati had admirably transformed the palace's great hall, hanging the walls with every tapestry the town could provide, along with a forest-full of boughs and pine wreaths studded with pomegranates. The adjoining rooms were furnished with sideboards that could only have been gathered from a dozen other palazzi, provisioned with a vast variety of hot spiced wines, meat pastries, spun-sugar confections, and candied fruits.

The festive music was provided by no less than five *tromboni*, about twice as many shawms and flutes, and an equal number of *lire da braccio*, along with a portable theater organ. Most of the diplomats—and *cortigiane*—who had spent the autumn in Imola had remained to welcome the winter in Cesena. Even the famous hermaphrodite known as Il Portuguese had come this far; she might have been a sad, pudgy adolescent boy, a satin bodice pushing up breasts like a fat man's.

As to the other ladies, the matrons of Cesena were content to leave their husbands standing at the sideboards while they received the attentions of worldly men, a company in which I was grudgingly welcomed, this because the ambassadors had come to value my keen ear for useful information. Surrounded as I was by all these eager ladies, I found myself nearly trampled when a fanfare occasioned a great rush of the good wives into the entrance hall, pealing away: "The duke has come! Our duke is here!"

Valentino did not disappoint his audience; he regally bowed and began to lead us all in the *Lioncello*, his partner an exceptionally comely representative of the local nobility, her bosom well displayed and well deserving of display. Yet she was a mere pendant to the duke, upon whom all eyes were fixed. Appearing slender but not slight in black jacket and hose, he danced with equal measures of lightness and strength, never sacrificing one for the other.

I was taken in hand by a local girl not much older than my wife, and so much like her in some ways that she crushed my heart; she was not as fair as Marietta, but she had the same small nose and the same girlish pride that kept it in the air as she performed with the same impulsive grace, with one glance diffident, the next eager. For the first time since I had left Florence I wanted to hold Marietta in my arms, although my only desire was to comfort her and tell her how terribly sorry I was for this marriage neither of us had wanted.

But my stars were little better with this partner; we ran into some difficulty in the *Gelosia* and I found myself spit out of the circle like a melon seed. Retreating to a sideboard in one of the anterooms, I poured myself a Sangiovese and tried to forget another silver cupful of my cares. The band launched into a *moresca*, the cheeks of the *pifferi* like bellows, the dancers spinning.

I nearly choked on my wine. Seemingly from nowhere, Signor Oliverotto da Fermo appeared like the Devil in a passion play, whirling about with his copper-haired Venetian diva, their lavish, curled tresses tossing—his were almost as long as hers. I had not seen or heard of Signor Oliverotto since I had arrived in Cesena, hence I found his appearance here a most unwelcome sign. Most likely he had come to arrange the final reconciliation between Valentino and the *condottieri*.

As I contemplated this evil omen, the swirling chaos of the *moresca* became a suitable accompaniment for the events unraveling around me, the music in time with my own spinning head. Suddenly feeling a soft touch on my hand, I required a moment to focus my eyes on the sort of Carnival mask that had become something of a fashion at Valentino's court, in and out of season; cut from green silk, it was beaded all around the eyes. A parrot's beak obscured the lady's nose.

She did not lead me to the dance but instead pulled me through a doorway at the back of the anteroom, this allowing access to a narrow hallway or closet. Deeper within, I observed pale legs wrapped around pale thighs and heard amorous grunts. Vainly I attempted to recognize my new companion's face, the mask leaving in evidence only her lips and eyes.

"Do you want to know what happened to your friend?" Her thin voice wavered.

I knew this "friend" at once. "Is she alive? Where is she?"

The masked lady grasped my hand more firmly and dragged me past the coupling pair. The hallway ahead of us was cold and smelled of damp stone. At the end of it she opened a little door. I stooped beneath the lintel and found myself outside.

A sheer wall loomed over us like an immense shadow; this was the rampart that connected the Civic Palace to the single tower of the *rochetta*, which at present was employed solely as a prison. My guide pointed to a frighteningly tall ladder that extended from the icy courtyard to the top of this massif.

"Who sent—"

She had already closed the door behind me. When I tried to open it, I was surprised to find it unlocked. Nevertheless I quickly discarded the idea of going after her; some intermediary had probably given her a few ducats, and it was unlikely she could tell me who in fact had dispatched her on this errand. Now my mind spun with possibilities. Had Valentino found Damiata and confined her in the *rochetta*? Or had Oliverotto, as proxy for Vitellozzo Vitelli, insisted on Damiata's imprisonment—or worse—so that she could not return to the pope with her account of what she had found on the *pianura*?

I clambered up the towering ladder with nearly as much skill as a monkey, and perhaps as little sense. Reaching the top of the rampart, I looked down onto the walkway that ran its length, framed by a shoulder-high stone parapet. I was alone up there. I dropped to the icy pavement and ventured to one of the crenellations notched into the parapet on the side overlooking Cesena. The sky was veiled with thin, high clouds. Chimneys throughout the city shot up sparking embers; out across the *pianura*, scattered farmhouses sent columns of smoke high into the cold air. In the darkness at the limit of my vision lay the Adriatic coast; below Cesena the Via Emilia begins to run alongside the sea. And somewhere on the shores of that dark water, the armies of the *condottieri* were waiting.

The tower at the far end of the walkway—where the prisoners were most likely kept—was eight-sided rather than perfectly round, with a large portal opening onto the rampart. I crept inside with due caution—and nearly fell into a rectangular opening in the floor, where narrow steps descended to the rooms below.

I peered into a darkness so thick I could have scooped it into my hands.

The face emerged so abruptly from the murk that I believed a disembodied head had been thrown up at me. I stumbled back and fell, my head striking the pavement.

By the time I recovered, this phantom was standing over me, his muscular legs sheathed in black hose. The head far above was a shadowy cipher.

"Get up." He held out a thick hand and wrenched me to my feet.

I beheld the dusky face of Ramiro da Lorca, the man the pope had entrusted with the initial investigation of his son's murder, five years ago—and whom Valentino had recently sent to Rimini, to get him out of the way. Ramiro reeked of cloying perfume and pomade, his hair plastered to his scalp like a thick black poultice. Yet even with this sleek carapace, his head was too blocky and heavily fleshed for his almost delicate, Oriental features.

"My people are still searching the cells down there," Ramiro said, as though they enjoyed full authority to do so. "You should not have poked your Florentine nose into this. But you have . . ." Vapor streamed from his nostrils. "You are not the first man to be duped by the Duke of Gandia's whore. Do you understand why Duke Valentino might want to confine her?"

I nodded, scarcely able to think.

"I created him." Ramiro's voice was distant, his eyes fixed on the empty, icy rampart behind me. "After the Duke of Gandia was murdered and it was decided to settle Cesare in a secular office, His Holiness asked me to take the boy to France, to see that he received a duchy and was married as promised to Carlotta of Aragon, the price we had arranged for King Louis's divorce." I noted the "we had arranged"—it seemed Ramiro had regarded himself as the pope's partner in such decisions. "You would not have recognized the fop who rode into Chinon on a charger with pearls in its mane. The entire French court howled at his vanity and called him the 'little duke.' "

Ramiro abruptly looked into the dark stairwell at our feet, holding up his hand to caution my silence. I heard nothing. After a moment he returned to his account: "When Carlotta of Aragon joined the chorus of ridicule and refused Cesare's suit, it was I who prevented him from fleeing France and returning like a humble little friar to his tonsure and cap. It was I who negotiated his marriage to Charlotte d'Albret and obtained the Duchy of Valentinois from her father. I created the man we call Valentino." Ramiro's eyes were entirely dark, as if belladonna had been applied to them. "The Romagna is the Lord Jesus's estate, given to the Supreme Pontiff as his state. It is not Duke Valentino's to give away to these dogs."

Here the dawn began to break, let us say. Despite his suspicion of Damiata, Ramiro was most likely my ally—and probably hers as well—in all this. "What do you intend to do?" I asked. "Take Damiata back to Rome?"

"I must know where that book is," Ramiro said. "Did she get away with it?"

Something cold trickled down my back. Ramiro had probably been present when the *streghe* brought "that book" to the Rocca at Imola; perhaps he even participated in the witch games. But I did not think it likely that Valentino, having exiled Ramiro to Rimini, would now confide in him the details of our *Gevol int la carafa*—particulars I had shared only with the duke and his engineer general.

Ramiro had "interrogated" hundreds of men during his long service to the Borgia; with little difficulty he recognized my suspicions. "I did not take all the good men still loyal to His Holiness with me to Rimini. Only a fool and a traitor would have done so." Again the vapor streamed from his nose. "I had Gandia's whore followed. At all times. Even into the *pianura*."

I could not see all his cards, but I made a wager. "I have seen your man's mask. A Devil's mask, on that occasion, as I recall. I presume he spared me because he didn't obtain the book."

I expected that being guilty, Ramiro would deny it. Instead he gave me a lava-glass stare before he said, "A number of people fled that hut—men, women, children. You and two others did not get away." The "two others" were almost certainly the unfortunate *streghe*. Yet it was still maddeningly unclear to me whether Ramiro's man had been responsible for my incapacity—and the fate of the two women— or had simply been a witness. "After considerable pursuit, my subordinate found one of those who fled. The man with the big dog. Both with their throats cut. The dead man had no book on his person. But the tracks of a horse led away from him."

"A horse," I said stupidly. "Then who was the rider?"

Ramiro elevated his square, arrogant jaw. "We will know shortly. Most probably that man with the dog was a decoy employed by the Duke of Gandia's whore." This accorded with Valentino's theory that Damiata would use the book for her own purposes.

Stepping to the open doorway, Ramiro looked over the rampart again. Quickly he came back to me, his dark eyes sparking with some sentiment I could not distinguish: perhaps fear, or anger. Perhaps both. "Ask yourself this," he whispered harshly. "Why would Duke Valentino protect Oliverotto da Fermo?"

"I presume because His Excellency no longer has any choice in the matter. He must accept the terms dictated by the *condottieri*."

Ramiro sniffed. "If you believe that, you are not in any way ready to answer the question. The murderer was at Capua. Do you understand?" I understood that many of the *condottieri* had been present at the siege and sack of Capua, eighteen months previously. "The same man who murdered the Duke of Gandia and these women here in the Romagna also butchered the citizens of Capua." Again he looked out the doorway, the cadence of his speech markedly quicker. "Ask Duke Valentino about the women at Capua. Ask him what happened to those women."

Almost trailing these words behind him, Ramiro strode out onto the icy rampart. Perhaps a third of the way across he stopped and planted his feet, his posture erect. Clouds of his breath rose before him.

He had issued four such clouds when I saw what he was waiting for.

prince who wishes to guard against conspiracies should be more wary of those for whom he has done too many favors than those to whom he has done too many injuries.

The five men at the far end of the rampart became visible all at once, or so it appeared. The two who were unarmed preceded three crossbowmen; I recognized the outlines of this leading pair before I could distinguish their faces. Valentino, attired in his jacket and hose, appeared slight next to Oliverotto da Fermo, who wore a sleeveless sable surcoat over his tunic.

Oliverotto evidenced no expression at all. But when Valentino came closer, I observed that his eyes almost danced about. Nevertheless he did not halt his advance until he was close enough to Ramiro to clasp hands. Or strike him.

He did neither, instead saying in a voice far less troubled than his eyes, "I instructed you to come directly to me when you arrived." Evidently Valentino had summoned Ramiro from Rimini. "I was told your people are nosing around up here. Why?"

"I am looking for the whore His Holiness sent."

"And you thought she was my prisoner?"

"You suspect her of complicity in your brother's murder," Ramiro said. "As we all do."

"Did you find her?"

"My people are still looking down there."

"You won't find her." Valentino turned to Oliverotto. "Do you know where this lady is?"

"If you want to find Gandia's whore, take your Messer Ramiro down into your prison and ask him." Oliverotto spread his legs and hooked his thumbs on his belt, a pose as confrontational as his tone. "You will discover that he knows all of it. He is the traitor in your own house."

Ramiro's neck corded. "How long will you continue to protect this *impiccatto?*"

Oliverotto blithely said, "Do you wish to accuse me?"

"Excellency, come to your senses!" Ramiro's complexion was so colored with fury that he might have been a Moor. "Your enemies found him in their cess-trench and made him a signore." He faced Oliverotto. "Vitellozzo Vitelli shit this turd out of his bleeding asshole when he was fucked by his brother."

What occurred next is perhaps only an image I assembled in my mind after it had taken place. I believe that Oliverotto lunged at Ramiro, who stepped back at the same moment that Valentino sprang forward, placing himself directly between the two of them. But this happened in the blinking of an eye.

From that point on, my memory is more reliable.

♦

Valentino and Oliverotto were as still as stone, as if transformed by Medusa's glance. Oliverotto had been frozen as he reached forward; his great fist, nearly in Valentino's gut, was wrapped within both of his adversary's smaller hands, which seemed a child's in comparison. The only sound was the distant, dull resonance of the *tromboni* still playing below in the Civic Palace.

Valentino slowly raised his head, elevating his gaze from his own belly to Oliverotto's face, which was no longer pale.

"Another thumb's width . . . and you would have sliced me open," Valentino said, his own strain evident in his voice.

"You know I did not intend this knife for you," Oliverotto said. Yet strangely neither man relaxed his posture, as though this contest of strength and wills, however accidental, would have to be resolved.

"It was your mother's brother who took you in after your father died, wasn't it?" Valentino asked this almost as if they were merely conversing at a banquet. "Yes. Giovanni Fogliano was that gentleman's name," he went on, answering his own question. "And this uncle Giovanni did you an exceptional favor, didn't he? He sent you to the Vitelli *famiglia* for proper instruction. Vitellozzo and Camillo—and let us not forget Paolo, of such blessed memory—became your fathers. You learned the art and science of arms long before you were able to shave." Here Valentino's shoulders heaved slightly, as though he were renewing the effort that had spared his life. "I envy you, Signore. I was seventeen years old when my father gave me a cardinal's cap. He might as well have made me a castrated choirboy." The duke offered a small, bitter smile. "Yet I became His Holiness's most devoted servant. And you betrayed your uncle."

"I remind you that the interests of the Borgia were advanced that night." Oliverotto offered this through clenched teeth. "My uncle intended to ally himself against the pope. Excellency, you as well as anyone should know that such actions are sometimes necessary, if capable men are to succeed those far less competent."

Valentino's eyes steadied. "Do you have an accusation of your own tonight?" His voice was higher, mocking. "I can assure you I have heard it before, so you will merely add your own refrain. But those men did not have the courage to face me. You do—the Vitelli *famiglia*, to its credit, made you hard. So accuse me of my brother's murder, Signore. Tell me explicitly what you have just implied, that with such a betrayal I was able to succeed a man who was not competent to hold a sword."

Oliverotto inclined his head just a bit. Almost at once, his Herculean shoulders relaxed and he drew slightly away from the duke, although he did not step back. Valentino still clutched his hand.

Oliverotto's gaze appeared to slip. "I did not intend any sort of accusation, Excellency."

Valentino nodded and released Oliverotto's hand. The latter nimbly turned the blade of his dagger toward his own gut and offered the engraved ivory handle to his adversary. "You admired it the other day," he said. "It is yours. With my apologies."

"No. Keep it." Valentino's inflection was inscrutable.

The duke turned to Ramiro. "Go down there with your men and finish your search," he told him. "Satisfy your suspicions. Then we will talk."

Ramiro appeared no more convinced than I that Valentino had satisfied *his* suspicions. Before he lowered his head and did as instructed, he gave me an almost plaintive glance, as though I had been the sole witness to his last testament. When Ramiro had vanished into the stairwell, Valentino signaled one of his crossbowmen, who followed him down.

"Signor Oliverotto." Valentino issued this address with cold formality. "I have given you the answer Vitellozzo requested. Now it is time for you to return to our friends and conclude this matter." Of course he meant something regarding his treaty with the *condottieri*. And it was all too likely that "this matter" was the secret codicils promising them Florence.

Offering a respectful bow, Oliverotto began to retreat like a courtier, without turning his back.

"One last thing, Signore." Valentino took two quick steps, erasing the distance Oliverotto had placed between them. "I have always wondered. Did you watch your uncle's face at the moment he knew you had betrayed him?"

Oliverotto tilted his head in his searching fashion, as if in asking this question, Valentino had revealed his own weakness.

"You needn't answer me now. You will only have created some image in your own mind, like a painter who believes he can see the suffering face of Christ. You must think about it at greater length. But your uncle's face will come to you when you do not expect it. Soon, I think." Valentino leaned toward him, almost as if trying to get his scent. "The next time I see you, I will ask you for your answer."

Oliverotto inclined his head a bit more acutely, his pale eyes like snow in moonlight. Then abruptly he spun about and walked off, his back to the duke.

Valentino motioned with his head. After waiting a moment, the two remaining crossbowmen proceeded across the rampart, in the same direction as Oliverotto.

✦

You can imagine the thoughts that teemed in my brain, to find myself alone on that dark rampart with Valentino. He walked to the parapet and looked out silently for a time before he said, "Secretary," gesturing that I should come to his side.

"Do you see the design of this?" He extended his hand and swept it along the horizon. "The Romans divided all the land on this side of the Via Emilia." Across the snow-carpeted countryside, the dark grid of trees, hedges, ditches, and roads that marked the ancient Roman field boundaries was visible even at night. " 'Centuriation,' they called it. Just as the units of their armies were called 'centuries.' They gave these plots to their citizen soldiers, after they had completed their service." He nodded approvingly. "Through their own efforts and will, the Romans put the world in good order." He turned to me so quickly that I flinched. "Ramiro summoned you here."

"Yes," I answered, taking his statement as a question. "He said he believes Damiata is confined in the tower."

"Do you?"

"I understand that you suspect her."

"You have my word on my personal honor that I do not know where she is."

I put more credence in Valentino's sense of personal honor than any oath he might have sworn to God. "Excellency, did you believe Oliverotto when he said he is similarly uninformed as to Damiata's . . . whereabouts?"

He did not answer at once. "My fear is that Signor Oliverotto knows where she is. If so, Vitellozzo Vitelli may already have the book."

As before, Valentino's suspicions were ambiguous, at least regarding Damiata. Did he believe she had been killed by Oliverotto da Fermo that night, as she tried to escape with the *Elements*? Or had she simply brought the book to the *condottieri*, in the desperate hope she could bargain for her son?

Nevertheless, I was inclined to believe Ramiro's account, which suggested another means by which Vitellozzo might already have obtained the *Elements*. And although it had not been Ramiro's intention to absolve Damiata, this possibility did not presume her guilt. "Excellency, Ramiro had us followed into the *pianura*. He claims that a horseman reached the mastiff keeper before his spy did, cutting his throat and perhaps retrieving the book from his person." I paused before assigning guilt—and then did so with a question. "Was Signor Oliverotto still in Imola at that time?"

Valentino almost never evidenced his displeasure, yet here he appeared to grimace—much as he had when remarking on his tenure as a prince of the Church. "What else did Ramiro tell you?"

I assumed he was preparing for an interrogation. And I would have to be careful not to withhold what Ramiro might give up all too quickly.

"He recalled that he accompanied you to France, Excellency. He credits himself for your success there. He asks why you would protect Oliverotto." I ran through this litany quickly, the better to avoid undue emphasis on any particular item. "And he insisted that I ask you about the women at Capua."

Valentino closed his eyes and nodded gently for some time. "Capua . . . At Capua I saw and heard things I cannot . . ." His throat pumped. "I would prefer to witness a thousand soldiers hanging from the scaffolds for looting than to see some of the things our German mercenaries did to children torn from their mothers' arms. And then to their grieving, keening mothers. Beasts. Grunting, stinking animals. Not even that. Demons of the pit. If I close my eyes, just the sound of it, the unearthly din . . ." He shook his head such that I thought he would press his hands to his ears. "I would sooner be struck deaf than to hear that again . . . Secretary, one in ten of the soldiers at Capua were under my direct command. But that does nothing to absolve me. I should have protected the honor of those women. No less than I would protect the honor of my own sister."

He stared out over the Romans' vast *disegno* for some while, as if only in their well-ordered world could he find redemption for the sins of Capua.

"Secretary." Sharply voiced, this address abruptly ended his musing. His question was no less direct. "Who do you believe killed my brother?"

I watched my breath drift out over the icy piazza below us. "The same man who killed those women at Imola." After weighing my words, I added, "And he was also present at Capua," echoing what Ramiro had told me only moments before. "I believe he sharpened his trade there."

"You continue to believe he is a *condottiero*," Valentino said almost absently, like a tutor with his mind now on loftier matters. "But which one? As you know, they are not of one accord or purpose. In anything. That is their chief weakness."

I was heartened at his interest in the weaknesses of the *condottieri*. "This man is different than the rest of them. Different than any other man. But I . . . I cannot determine yet . . ." I trailed off, thinking that perhaps the murderer had stood before both of us not moments before. And even then, I could not say with certainty that I had seen his face. In truth, I could suspect Ramiro as much as Oliverotto or any of the *condottieri*. Ramiro had until recently been the enforcer of all justice throughout the Romagna; he possessed superior knowledge of the countryside and had almost certainly seen Leonardo's *mappa*. And the Romagnoles had come to regard his cruelty as proverbial, widely retailing accounts of arbitrary hangings and the torture of even young boys. That was what so nettled me. None of these men lacked the bona fides of an unspeakably cruel murderer.

Valentino issued a scarcely audible grunt, as though I had offered him only nonsense—this perhaps being so. Nevertheless I clung to my conviction that we would never identify this man by trying to guess his allegiances, which were written in water. Only his true nature was indelible.

"You cannot see it from this vantage, but the Rubicon River is over there." Valentino pointed toward the dark eastern horizon. "*Alea iacta est.*" The die is cast. "So said Caesar when he crossed the Rubicon. Secretary, the die will soon be cast. Within days. But we must not allow Fortune to throw the dice for us. We cannot leave our fate in the hands of Fortune's soldiers. Otherwise, we will all dig our own graves and lie down in them."

The inscrutable Valentino could not have more nakedly revealed his hope that he might yet defeat Fortune—and her soldiers, the *con-*

dottieri. And I believed I still had time, however fleeting, to abet this cause.

Certainly this was precisely what the duke had hoped I would obtain from our conversation, because here he ended it. He walked off toward the dark tower, where I presumed he would learn more from Ramiro da Lorca, somewhere deep within it. But after a few steps Valentino turned abruptly, his soles screeching on ice, as though he had forgotten the most urgent matter of all.

"Secretary, as I said, all of us were at Capua. Vitellozzo and Camillo Vitelli. Oliverotto da Fermo and Ramiro da Lorca. Paolo Orsini and his cousins. And myself." Even in the dim light, I could distinguish the green tint of his eyes. "Not one of us is innocent."

CHAPTER 11

Men are born, live, and die, always with the same unchanging nature.

The Malatestiana of Cesena is, to this day, one of the most modern and beautiful libraries in all Europe, the entrance resembling a small Greek temple. Yet I am less beguiled by the elephant carved above the door along with the motto of its builder, Malatesta Novello: "The Indian elephant does not fear mosquitoes." To my mind this inscription reflects the arrogance of the *condottieri*, who became elephants by feasting on the lives of those poor mosquitoes whom they so disdained.

But on the sun-filled day—so rare in that winter—following the eventful *ballo*, this mosquito was only too eager to get into the elephant's library. With its three aisles and great processions of columns and arches—along with dozens of long reading benches, which have shelves like lecterns, upon which the books are kept—the Malatestiana resembles a cathedral for the worship of knowledge.

Inquiring of a monk as to the location of Suetonius Tranquillus's *Lives of the Twelve Caesars*, I was directed to one of the benches. The object of my search, bound in tooled, amber-hued leather, had been secured to the shelf with an iron chain. It was a copied book, but the Latin script, in two columns on each page, was in a hand so precise it might have been produced by a printing press.

Grateful for the light pouring in from the big arched windows, I began to thumb through the Suetonius as if entering a tavern full of old friends, already being quite familiar with these biographies of ancient Roman emperors. But on this occasion, I was intent on finding the key to the singular nature of a man who yet lived among us, concealing his terrible secret.

After reading Dottor Benivieni's necropsy of an incorrigible and remorseless criminal three nights before, I had arrived at the theory that the man I sought had been born with his rare nature. That being so, it followed that he would have exhibited some signs of this nature even as a child. Suetonius, who had been a living witness to a number of his twelve Caesars and had studied the papers of those emperors who had preceded his time, had been quite diligent in recounting whatever evidence he had uncovered regarding their early years. Hence I believed I could test my hypothesis in Suetonius's pages.

I passed the hours immersed in a narrative that spanned dynasties, the Julio-Claudians succumbing to their ambitions, lusts, and fears, as power warped them into monsters. Only the first two of the Flavians, Vespasian and Titus, seemed to escape this inevitable corruption; the latter, who as a young man had displayed coarse appetites, reformed himself when he became emperor, surprising everyone—except perhaps those who had known him most intimately and had perceived his innate goodness.

But certain characteristics set Caligula and Nero apart. Both earned eternal infamy for their cruelty and crimes, and both displayed indications of this nature when they were young, well before power could steal their souls. The emperor Tiberius, who raised Caligula to adulthood, had once confessed, "I am nurturing a viper for the Roman people, and educating a Phaethon for the entire world"—Phaethon being the god Helios's son, who stole his father's chariot of the Sun and fell to earth, scorching Africa to desert.

Like the monster whose butchery I had observed, Caligula did not want his cruelties done with quickly and found nourishment in his victims' pain; he commanded his executioners to administer death with many slight wounds rather than a single stroke. Caligula's familiar condemnation—"Make him feel that he is dying!"—became proverbial among the population of Rome. Suetonius attributed Caligula's defects to a *mentis valitudini*, a "mental illness" manifested as epilepsy, but I do not believe there is any connection. Epilepsy is a transient mental disorder that visits occasionally; Caligula's "disease of the soul," to again cite Plato, is a defect of birth, manifest at all times throughout life. I believed that the case of Caligula was no different than the man I sought: in both instances the soul (or perhaps I should say those qualities of mercy, sympathy, and remorse that comprise the better elements of our natures) was not diseased or damaged; instead the soul was absent entirely.

The same was true for Nero, who as early as ten years old displayed traits such that his tutor, the philosopher Seneca, had nightmares that his young charge was Caligula reborn. Yet in their youth both Caligula and Nero were careful to disguise their true natures, the former displaying such contrived meekness that it was said of him, "No one was ever a better slave or worse master." Nero became so accustomed to his furtive life of vice that even after he built himself a palace the gods would envy, he continued to plague Rome at night, putting on a wig or other disguise in order to roam the streets like a common cutthroat, robbing and raping the innocent subjects upon whom his whims also preyed by day, ultimately with far greater violence.

I was musing upon such particulars when a shadowy presence swooped down on me, its arrival as sudden and startling as if a great bird of prey had descended to my side. But this creature's pale face was framed by the sable fur that trimmed her hood.

Before I could even open my mouth, she pressed hers to my lips.

CHAPTER 12

How happy the man is, as anyone can see, who is born stupid and believes everything.

Who could describe that kiss? It was one kiss that counted for as many as the grains of sand between Libya and Cyrene, as Catullus once said; a kiss that made me "all sulfur and tinder, my heart aflame," as Petrarch had it; a kiss that melted the flesh and incinerated the soul. It was every kiss I would ever have with every woman I would ever love, the kiss that takes a dying man's last breath, the kiss that brings stone to life.

"God's Cross." Damiata pressed her forehead to mine and caressed my face with gloved hands. "My darling Niccolò."

The whiteness of her skin seemed almost blinding and I believed her scent of rose water and lilies would suffocate me. My mind was a Greek chorus, every sentiment shouting at once, in a different pitch: astonishment, joy, relief. And anger, suspicion, even jealousy.

"Where . . . ?" I could not even finish the question.

"I got away from them and hid in the countryside. In the homes of farmers and huts of tenants. They protected me, Niccolò. Such good people. People of the dirt, like me." She began to cover my face with her searing kisses. "The Virgin also kept you alive, as I prayed a thousand times."

I struggled to find a speck of reason in my buzzing head. I knew I had more questions. Too many questions. "How did you escape?"

"That wizard with the leather nose put his knife to my throat and dragged me out of there. He just kicked apart the back of the hut, it was so flimsy." If she had been taken out the back, she could not have seen me lying insensible at the entrance to the hut. "The children went out with us. We ran for two, three miles before I could escape from him. By then I did not even know which direction I should go. Eventually I found a farmhouse, where they took me in. Niccolò, how did you get away?"

"On the back of a goat. As soon as I went outside I was struck on the head—by a man in a Devil's mask, with this little goat beard, just as Giacomo described it. I awakened in another hut somewhere on the *pianura*, smeared all over with Hecate's foul unguent. The two *streghe* also took the goat ride that night. But they ended it in Leonardo's cellar."

Damiata crossed herself twice. "I should never have taken you out there. I can only beg for your pardon, a thousand times."

She took my hands and held them, blinking at her tears until I could no longer look at her, because even if I had believed her sentiment was entirely feigned, her remorseful face would have turned me into a jellyfish. If only to keep from sobbing, I forced myself to say, "The book. What did you see in the book?"

She wiped her eyes and looked around. Only the monk was interested in us. "It is nothing but a school text. Euclid's *Elements*, translated in the Latin."

Finding her in agreement with Valentino's description, I said, "So these 'all of them' that you said are in it. They were names of the *condottieri*?"

"They signed their names in the margin, just as I was invited to do. Vitellozzo Vitelli. Paolo and Roberto Orsini. Oliverotto da Fermo."

This recitation was like snow rubbed in my face, restoring me to a more reasoned state. "The litany of Italy's foremost scoundrels," I said.

"*Zeja* Caterina performed the *Gevol int la carafa* for all of them." This was also as Valentino had told me. "But Niccolò, she wrote other things in the margins, or where there was space at the end of chapters. Accounts of divinations, the things and people the *Gevol* conjured—or so it seemed to me. Her writing is a *salsa* of Tuscan and Romagnolo. And I did not have much leisure to browse."

"Then *Zeja* Caterina probably wrote the name of the *strega* who had the Duke of Gandia's amulet," I said. "Is it possible there is even a description of the amulet in the book?" In that event, even the blind would soon see that the *condottieri* had been involved in the Duke of Gandia's murder.

"I don't know. Niccolò, do you have any idea what happened to the man who ran out with the book? The man with the dog."

I could not help but wonder if this question was merely a deception—both Valentino and Ramiro suspected, not without reason, that Damiata had used the man with the dog as a decoy, while she snatched up the book. "Ramiro da Lorca had a spy follow us," I said cautiously. "One of his officers, I would guess. Did you see him?"

She shook her head. "I didn't see anyone."

"Ramiro himself told me that this spy of his found the man and his dog, both dead. The book wasn't on his corpse."

Damiata crossed herself again. "Then who . . . ?"

I regarded this as a question I might well pose to her. Nevertheless, I decided to address my doubts less directly. "Where have you been since you escaped the *pianura*?"

"When I finally thought it safe to make my way back to Imola, you were all gone. You, Valentino, the army, Maestro Leonardo. I had to send for money from my banker in Rome. And then make my way here."

I heard another echo of Valentino's suspicions. Perhaps Damiata had waited in Imola to begin negotiations with the *condottieri*, so that she could barter the book for her son. Perhaps that was why she had now come here.

Letting go her hands, I forced myself to look into eyes that resembled the blue part of a flame. "Do you know that Valentino suspects you of complicity with the *condottieri*? In both his brother's murder and this business with the book?"

The blue flames flickered. "I don't believe you . . . He cannot have let his father infect him . . . No."

"Were you his lover?"

She closed her eyes. As Valentino had when he confessed it.

"Yes." Her sigh was as audible as any of her words. "Niccolò, I didn't tell you . . ." It seemed the reason for this omission escaped her. A tear came to the corner of her eye and her mouth trembled.

I scarcely knew how to address this silence, much less my own feelings. Yet from somewhere in the seat of my own memories, I found a parable of sorts, certainly prompted by our present surroundings. "I remember when I was a boy, how my father's library humbled and awed me. In truth, it was only a tiny study on the second floor of our little house. A window, a lectern, and three chairs—it probably held no more than a dozen or twenty books at a time, because Papa sold or traded them so often. But I would go in there even before I could read Latin, to touch the pages and smell the ink and new leather bindings, to try to make sense of the words."

Damiata drew herself closer, the succubus of my fevered dreams.

"Papa had books that no one else in Florence had. Books of ancient Roman law. He would say to me, 'Niccolò, the truth is not in a man's breast or even in his goodwill and good intentions. The truth is in these pages. And men can make even these books lie. But our printing presses will make these laws available to everyone, the better for all of us to see if the words are employed for good or evil. Only with good laws, and the fair application thereof, can we reclaim our *libertas* from the Medici and the oligarchs.' "

Papa had been gone for two years as I spoke; for a moment my sorrow flowed from a deep spring and my words halted.

"So my father cherished the hope," I said, coming to the point of this reminiscence, "that lead type and presses would convey the truth everywhere—and men would recognize it. And certainly today we have at least thirty times as many volumes available to us as we did when my father was a boy and copyists were the only means of production. Yet if the truths and wisdom men have accumulated are multiplied countless times by our printing presses, so are the lies and deceptions. A truth can no longer be credited by its mere publication—or by how often one hears it."

Damiata understood my meaning: I could no longer trust her. She turned to me, her eyes wet. But her subtle lips hinted at a smile. "Then in our modern world," she said, "the best lie would be true ninety-nine times. Only on the hundredth telling would it prove false."

Now I had to smile, despite everything. "And the best truth would be ninety-nine parts a lie and only one part true."

She waited for me to elaborate, but finally I forced her to ask. "Why, Niccolò?"

"Because it would require all our faith to believe in that single sliver of truth."

Damiata squeezed my hands. "Niccolò, have you had enough of your ancients? I think we should go for a walk."

◆

Before we stepped onto the street, Damiata drew her fur hood against her face; as long as she did not raise her eyes, even I would not have known her from any of the courtesans who often enough passed by. Our steps led us to the central piazza, where the *rochetta* that had witnessed so much the previous night had already turned gray in the swift-falling dusk. Beneath the stone massif milled a great conclave of townspeople, traders, monks, and streetwalkers, their aggregate mood striking me as more anxious than usual. I saw two clerks I knew from the Ferrarese embassy, both of them pale-faced functionaries who might have been me in a mirror—except that they would consider my wardrobe fit only for the rag shop. "Tell me the army is not going south again," I said when we had exchanged greetings.

"Ramiro da Lorca is a guest at his own inn." My respondent nodded toward the *rochetta* tower. "The duke is now jailing his own household."

Damiata tightened her grip on my arm.

I asked, "Is Oliverotto da Fermo also a guest at that inn?"

One of the men shrugged. "I would think not. Signor Oliverotto and His Excellency appeared more than companionable last night."

As we moved on, I said, "You didn't know about Ramiro?"

She shook her head. This news boded even more poorly for her than for me, because it meant that Valentino had put further distance between himself and his father. For my part, I had considered Ramiro under arrest when Valentino dispatched him into the tower; perhaps what he had been forced to reveal later that night had resulted in a formal charge of treason. But we were hearing only rumors.

"I was there when Valentino decided to confine Ramiro," I confessed as vaguely as I could. "Oliverotto was also present. A complicated tale. I'm still not certain what I saw. Or what it means."

Damiata didn't press me for particulars. Instead she said, "I should have been honest with you. About Valentino. He told you, then, that I betrayed Juan on the last day of his life."

"He says that was the second occasion you and he . . . were lovers." I was surprised at my difficulty in simply saying this. "He insists that he told you Juan's itinerary for the evening, which he fears you revealed to his brother's assassins. Presumably the Vitelli."

She bit her lip. "But Niccolò, on that last afternoon it was I who told Cesare . . ." I could feel her shrug. "I won't argue with Valentino over who told whom Juan's expected route that evening. But I am sorry he doubts me for the same reasons I could doubt him."

We entered a busy street that flowed into the piazza from the south; Damiata stopped and faced me amid the jostling passersby. "I swear to you by the Holy Virgin's veil and the Cross of God that Valentino is mistaken about me. Just as his own father is mistaken about him." Her eyes narrowed a bit. "Perhaps you don't know, Niccolò, but the pope suspects that Valentino himself was involved in Juan's murder."

Even at dusk, Damiata's coloring, her eyes and carmine lips, did not seem real; it was as if a single ray of empyrean light had shot down like an arrow from the highest Heaven to illuminate only her face. Yet her expressions remained as unfathomable to me as the mystery behind Valentino's jade-hard eyes. In short, I did not believe I could ever read the truth of that lovely face, unless she wished me to. And even then, how could I be certain she was not merely showing me a single truth, in order to disguise a host of lies?

"Then I think you should go to the duke," I said, "and allay his suspicions. While the guilty are gathering strength, we cannot afford to have the innocent divided by mutual distrust." I had to wonder if I could ever fully accept Damiata's innocence, unless Valentino also endorsed it.

Damiata pressed herself to me, her breast pillowing my arm, as again we crunched across the icy, crusted pavement. "No. Valentino can harbor his suspicions a bit longer. As yet I have no proof to offer the pope and ransom my little boy. And I have no assurance that Valentino would not use my information to acquire the book and then bury it, if only to secure his treaty."

"I think he would use the evidence provided by that book against the *condottieri*," I said. "He has intimated as much to me."

"And you believe him?"

Because Papa had been a lawyer, I had known even as a boy how words could be sharpened or shaded—an education that had been much advanced by my service in the chancellery and my diplomatic missions. Nevertheless, I required Damiata's prompting to see that Valentino had sworn nothing to me, nor had he even stated his aims in firm and undeniable terms. He was a man of honor, I was certain, but his intentions toward the *condottieri* had been merely—and carefully—"intimated," to cite my own usage.

Damiata listened to my silence. "For the time being, Niccolò, I think I am better off dead to the pope and his duke." She tugged her hood closer around her face, pulling me to her as well, as if she could hide behind my arm. "To fully establish my innocence I need the book. Just as you need it to preserve your republic."

"But where is it now?" As easily as Damiata had resumed her seduction of my will and reason, I still had to suspect she knew the answer.

"I would believe Ramiro's account," she said. "Someone found that man and his dog before Ramiro's spy did. And you saw for yourself that Oliverotto da Fermo was following me on the street."

"You believe he also followed us into the *pianura*." I was hardly inclined to sound a skeptical note, having suggested this theory to Valentino the previous night. "But if Oliverotto had already obtained the book, then why was I spared? I had no use except to lead him to it."

"Perhaps he knew he would require you as a witness."

This took me entirely by surprise. "To what?"

"Perhaps to testify to the book's authenticity. To say you observed these witches employ it for a divination."

I was still attempting to peer into a dark glass. "Let us presume that Oliverotto obtained the *Elements* that night," I said. "His name is in it, along with that of Vitellozzo Vitelli, his mentor and patron. Certainly he would have burned it before the sun rose."

"There is another name in it."

"You mean another *condott*—" I stopped both my words and my steps. "Are you saying..."

The reluctance in her eyes spoke more convincingly than any furious accusation. "Valentino himself attended one of these *Gevol int la carafa*," she said in little more than a whisper. "His name also appears in the witch's book."

"Yes, he already knew about the *Elements* and the *gioca* when I told him." And now I could see why Valentino had been compelled, as Ramiro had told me, to "protect" Oliverotto da Fermo. "Valentino believes that his own familiarity with that *gioca* could be used to inflame his father's suspicions of him. Valentino, Vitellozzo, Oliverotto ... they are all damned by the same connection to Juan's amulet. Any one of them could have butchered the first *strega* and stuck the amulet in her charm bag, certain that it would eventually be delivered to the pope. But only one of them conceived this dreadful game..." I trailed off, for a moment struck dumb by my worst fear, before I could give voice to it. "And now it is all the more likely that this game will end with Florence in ashes. If the *condottieri* have the *Elements*, they will not even require superiority of arms to coerce Valentino's cooperation. God's *cazzo*..."

Damiata offered nothing in response, as if only her silence could comfort me. Instead she took my arm again and led me along the street for a short while, before stopping beside a palazzo in the Venetian style, the stonework light and lacelike.

"I have a little room here," she said. A faint, sad smile flickered at the sharp corners of her mouth. "And a little bit to share for supper."

I stood there in the icy street, thinking of something Boccaccio wrote: *It is better to do and repent, than to forbear and repent.*

◆

We entered through the pedestrian door to find a *ballo* under way in the central court. Hardly as decorous as the dance I had attended the previous evening, this more resembled a *calcio* game played by a dozen teams at once. Woodwinds shrilled and a *trombone* blared over the shouts of men and squeals of women. You could not distinguish the whores from the good wives of the town, except that the latter had the better jewels and more lascivious disguises. Although Epiphany was still nearly two weeks away, half these people were masked, not a few of them with that great long nose intended to resemble Priapus's half-erect *cazzo*. Others wore the same white skull—the face of Death—I believed Giacomo and I had seen on the street.

The palazzo had been divided into apartments. We ascended the stairs to the third, uppermost floor, wandering through rooms stripped of everything save the most ponderous old cupboards. When it seemed we would run out of house we stopped at a final door. Damiata produced a key and unlocked it, saying to me, "Wait." I watched from the doorway as she lit several candles, placing them in ceramic lamps.

She beckoned from a small bedroom—or a large closet—that in comparison with my own lodging appeared to be a little Paradise: a large bed with an Oriental carpet hanging behind it and a cassone at the foot, painted with a scene from *Orlando Innamorato*—the lovers in the forest, drinking their potions of love and hate from Merlin's Well and the Stream of Eros. The lamps had been set on a small table, along with a knife, some Parma cheese, a salami, and a bottle of wine.

Gesturing that I should sit on the bed, Damiata stirred the brazier. She removed her *cioppa* and laid it beside me, revealing her gown of gray-green satin, her bared neck and shoulders nearly as white as the thin band of chemise that framed the top of her bodice. She poured us each a cup of good Sangiovese, cut some pieces of salami, then sat beside me. "I cautioned you that it was a little bit," she said.

"It would not be the first time you have cautioned me." I was not thinking of her confession after she had offered herself to me, half mad; instead I recalled our night on the *pianura*, when to my mind she had warned me of her desire, should we survive. But now I was less certain of what she had meant—and less so that she even remembered.

Damiata nibbled on the salami like a careless little mouse. But then she said, "I know what I said." Finishing her bite, she cradled her cup in her lap. "Niccolò. Do you truly believe that I would use the life of your little girl to redeem my own son?"

She did not look at me as she asked this—and I looked away from her. Nevertheless I saw her more clearly than ever.

"No. I do not believe you would," I said. "You would not want your son to live with the shade of another child."

She sighed as if my answer had eased a great pain. "When I warned you . . ." The wine in her cup rippled from the slight tremor of her hands. "I warned you because I wanted you to love me. Not with some brief act but entirely . . . But that is the most cruel love, isn't it? Condemned like poor Psyche to endlessly suffer Aphrodite's unbearable burdens."

"How did Petrarch describe love?" I said. " 'A death having the appearance of life.' "

" 'A Hell of which fools make their Heaven.' " I could feel her looking at me. "I think we already love one another, Niccolò. As friends who have seen and suffered the most dreadful things together. And who are so much alike. We both love reading the ancients, we are both little people who have spent our time among great men—and know as few do that they are merely ordinary men. You have your science of men's natures, and I suppose I had my own, at one time, though I did not find it in Titus Livy or Tacitus. But as I told you, there is something more. Something that draws us . . . Perhaps if you believe Plato . . ." Now I could feel her shrug. "Niccolò, we should go down there and dance."

No longer concerned that I had been bewitched, I could scarcely contain the sense of longing and regret I had previously felt only in Damiata's absence. When I left this room, ending this moment of intimacy, perhaps I would escape Aphrodite's torments. But I feared I would leave my very soul behind.

Damiata got to her feet, taking my hand so that I could do nothing but stand alongside her, although I might have been putting my own head in a noose. Yet I knew that in condemning me in this manner, she believed she was granting me clemency.

She slipped her arms around my back, as though we would dance in her room, and placed her burning cheek against mine.

"Niccolò . . . Will we even be alive a week from now? Will we ever hold our children again?"

I could only say, "I have hope."

"You know what Petrarch says about hope."

I had to laugh a bit. We were similar in this respect as well; we could smile at one another even as we stood on the gallows. " 'Truly all hope is false.' "

Her laughter echoed mine, but with a sound like little bells. She nuzzled me with her cheek and nose, before her lips wandered over my face and found my mouth. This kiss deepened in a way even the first had not, our teeth lightly touching, the merest hint of tongue.

"Did I melt your limbs?" she whispered, mocking her own charms.

In truth she had made my legs weak.

She breathed these words against my ear: "I feel it, my darling. Deep down there. In waters deeper than you or I can fish. Something more than Fortune's design or Aphrodite's desire. A secret our souls share."

"Perhaps it is just as Plato says," I whispered, completing the thought she had begun moments before. "I began this life with a choice. Yet only at the end of it did I discover I had chosen you."

Her next kiss was nothing like the two that had preceded it. It was the kiss of Lethe, extinguishing whatever memory of my previous life I still possessed.

CHAPTER 13

M en are driven principally by one of two things: either love or fear.

There are images of that night I will see in the moment before my eyes go dim for the last time. Her lace chemise, as beautiful as any gown, falling from her shoulders and hips as softly as snow. An alabaster form that would have made Michelangelo Buonarotti weep because he had not made her. The fine, wheat-colored hair between her legs; nipples as dark as wine, standing like the tips of fingers. But her skill was not to make love as a hetaera or harem slave, practiced in every technique. It was to make love like a girl who had never been touched but was equally untouched by guilt, or fear. *Amante, carissimo, anima mia*: these words, whispered and gasped next to my ear, caressed me no less than the fingers that explored me entirely. There were moments so wholly feral that it seemed we would begin to consume each other's flesh like bacchantes—and moments when it seemed there was not even flesh between us, as if I were embracing the *Scirocho*.

◆

I opened my eyes the next morning to find Damiata still sleeping beside me. I studied every detail of her face, the down at her temple, the few tiny freckles and moles that flawed the perfection of her skin, the delicate scrolling of her moist upper lip. My new life had already begun.

We spent the first day entirely in Damiata's little room; now that

Ramiro had been arrested she feared that Valentino, who was already looking for her, might find her connection to the pope similarly inconvenient. Yet we also embraced the hope that events were not what they seemed, or that Ramiro would be exonerated and released.

It was probably noon before we ate the rest of the cheese and salami, sitting up in bed, Damiata as innocent of her nakedness as Eve in Eden. "All those years in the Trastevere," she said, "I didn't go out during the day, except into our garden. I had to go out at night to make my living."

I shrugged but felt wounded, as though she had made light of our intimacy.

She wrapped her arms around me and kissed my neck. "I traded antiquities. Roman medallions, coins, cameos, small statues. Things I could conceal. And Latin and Greek manuscripts. I want you to know this, darling Niccolò, even if you can't believe me. Since that afternoon . . ." I knew she meant the day Juan of Gandia had disappeared. "Since then, I have been chaste as Athena."

I did believe her, but not without a sad irony: I would have forgiven Damiata a thousand lovers—and well I may have—when I could not truly forgive my Marietta her one.

Despite such brief regrets, the cares of my old life seemed as distant as the world outside. In one divine creature Damiata combined the perfect partner of my intellect and my flesh; when the latter was satiated and still tingling, she engaged the former, our conversation as inexhaustible as our passion. We spent hours comparing Catullus to Tibullus, Sallust's Caesar to Caesar's Caesar, Pico della Mirandola to Plato. One moment we were recalling the words of Ovid's *Metamorphoses* or Virgil's *Eclogues*, the next laughing about the pleasures a certain cardinal found in his collection of Murano glass cucumbers.

And then once again our flesh would speak in ways only our furtive souls could begin to understand.

❖

The second day of my new life was Christmas. "I had intended to go to Mass," I told Damiata that morning, believing I could hear the faint strains of the *O magnum mysterium* from the cathedral down the street. "It would have been my first since I left Florence, may my own mother of blessed memory forgive me—I pray only that the God who holds her to His bosom does not permit her to witness my apostasy. But now my faith in the Holy Roman Church can sleep well for yet another year, having been spared even a brief awakening."

Damiata crossed herself. "No doubt it hurts the Holy Mother to see what the Church has become," she said so gravely that I might have laughed. But her greatest gift was this innocence she still preserved, despite her familiarity with so many evils of the world—not to mention a Church she knew all too intimately.

Eventually I did go out that Christmas, well after dusk, to see if I could learn anything at the Governor's Palace. Making my way into a vestibule teeming with ambassadors, I was approached by my friend Pandolfo Collenuccio, who represented the Ferrarese interests; his care-seamed face was nearly consumed by his thick sable cap and collar. "Even Agapito has not stuck his head out tonight," he said, frowning. "This court remains a marvel of security. So what do you think it means?"

"When Valentino reveals the fate of Ramiro," I said, "he will show us the die he has cast. If we are told Ramiro is guilty of nothing, then I believe the duke will stay in Cesena and defend himself against the *condottieri*." Still uncertain of Oliverotto da Fermo's fate, I did not venture that if Ramiro were absolved, perhaps the duke would produce Oliverotto as his hostage. "If Ramiro is less fortunate, I believe it will signal that the duke has little confidence in his own luck—and less in his own forces. In that event, Valentino will move his troops down to Rimini and possibly farther south, where he and his people will be absorbed into the armies of the *condottieri*—and compelled to pursue the purposes of Vitellozzo Vitelli rather than the designs of the Holy See."

"Here is wisdom." Collenuccio offered me a rueful smile. "We have some Vernaccia back at our palazzo. Come toast the Nativity of our Lord—or the End of Days, as you wish."

"I had better write the Ten of War instead," I demurred, although in fact I did not intend to write my government until I had a convincing sign of Ramiro's fate. More truthfully, I added, "If Ramiro still lives among us, so does hope."

◆

In the universe Damiata and I alone inhabited, the postponement of Ramiro's fate was proof that we had somehow arrested not only Fortune's spinning wheel but also the motion of the Heavenly Spheres, banishing time itself from our little sanctuary. After a late supper, as we held each other in the darkness, Damiata whispered, " 'We go to sleep and endless night,' " citing Catullus's reflection on death. "Niccolò, this will be our endless night," she murmured, her lips on mine, breathing her words into me. "But we will not sleep."

That night I shared with her a body reborn, emptied of all the dross with which life had burdened us. I imagined myself Dante in the arms of Beatrice, flying like an upward-flung lightning bolt toward a vast, uncharted zenith, transformed by the ineffable brilliance of "the love that governs Heaven." Yet nothing in that Heaven blazed more gloriously than the shrouded glimmer of Damiata's eyes.

Near the end of a mostly silent night, Damiata whispered to me, "Niccolò, when we have to leave this room, can you trust me?"

Until she had asked it, I could not have imagined I would still find that question so difficult to answer.

"I should tell you about my wedding day," I said as prologue. "My engagement to Marietta was the last thing poor Papa tried to do for me, not three weeks before he died—I would have dishonored his memory if I had broken it off. The next August the entire *famiglia* Corsini brought Marietta across the Ponte Vecchio more like Caesar than a bride, seated on a gilt chair that resembled a throne, wearing a white dress with gold brocade sleeves and so many pearls in her veil that she might have been caught in sleet—with half the Wool Guild and what seemed the entire populations of Fiesole and Terranuova following after her."

Here my recitation became more difficult. "On the day we were engaged, Marietta had been a child who more resembled the plaster dolls on her bed. In little less than a year she had miraculously grown into a woman. Of course she seemed no more eager to be my bride than had the plaster doll, but I credited that to nerves and the heat. Only as the wedding banquet wound on through that evening did I observe that Marietta had already given away her affections."

"Her *amore* was there? I hope he was not a relative."

I had to laugh. "In fact he was presented as a relative. He was a pretty boy her own age, with a man's nose and chin and a cherub's complexion. I thought I was a spectator at a comedy, with all their carrying on—the sighs, the glances, even some furtive, fleeting kisses. But I wasn't the only one to observe the performance—their devotion was so obvious that even the relentless Corsini busybodies were compelled to say, 'Oh, look at the sweet cousins, how they love each other.' Yet I soon learned that this boy was merely a cousin of Marietta's brother-in-law. So there you have a story Boccaccio could have written—I had believed that the greatest challenge of my wedding night would be to persuade Marietta from her juvenile indifference for all men. I never imagined that she had already acquired the taste."

"But she slept with you."

"It was the only way to get rid of all the Corsini loitering outside the half-open bedroom door, banging the kettles and pots, waiting for the display of the bloody sheet. I am almost certain Marietta bit her lip to ensure their satisfaction."

"Not every girl bleeds the first time." Damiata stifled a little giggle before she added, "Of course I bled the first dozen times."

"I assure you I didn't accuse Marietta of deceiving me. Jealousy cannot be considered among my failings as a husband . . ." I trailed off into tongue-tied silence. Having gotten this far, I could go no further.

Damiata's shadowed face was above me. "God's Cross." I could see the glint of her eyes. "Now I understand."

"Primerana was born eight months and three weeks after our wedding night." The truth, at last uncorked, was as bitter as a river of gall. "God forgive me. I can't believe that darling little girl is my own daughter."

Damiata stroked my face. "You can't know. Between eight months and ten months, you can't be certain. More likely she is yours. I know how much you already love her. Can you say you don't see anything of yourself in her?"

"I have scarcely seen her, between her wet nurse in Terranuova and this embassy. And now Marietta has already taken Primerana with her, back to her brother-in-law's house—the same brother-in-law whose cousin is her boy lover. If I don't return to Florence, the Corsini *famiglia* will clutch them all to their bosom as if the Machiavelli had never existed. Even if I am truly Primerana's father, she will not have one fleeting memory of me. She will never even hear my name."

I knew that this prophecy had carelessly wounded Damiata, because I could feel the little tremor that preceded her silence. Finally she said, "My greatest fear is that my precious Giovanni *will* remember my name. And on his lips, it will be a curse." Her breath on my face seemed colder. "If nothing else, the Borgia will see he is taught that."

◆

So this night did not bring sleep, but neither was it endless. Still holding Damiata to me, I watched the dawn trace gray lines through the shutters of our small window. Shortly after, sound also seeped into our little sanctuary, but this was not the great mill wheels of fate grinding into motion or even the rising of the little city. It was a gentle buzz, as if several people were conversing just beneath our window or outside our door.

I got up and dressed; I had on my cape before Damiata opened one eye in fetching fashion and smiled at me. I told her, "The army may be preparing for something." I was deliberately vague, not wanting to suggest what I most deeply feared, that Valentino's dwindling troops were preparing to leave Cesena and proceed south, to join the superior forces of the *condottieri*. "I'll go out and see."

I descended to the icy street, finding the sky as gray as an oyster shell. A few lonely snowflakes still drifted down. Past the next corner several be-caped workmen crunched hurriedly along, but otherwise the street was empty. The sound that had drawn me outside, however, was more evident, a murmur that seemed to come from the vicinity of the piazza. A crowd, issuing a quiet and reverent soughing.

Crossing several streets, I reached the piazza, which opened up before me in a single blink, teeming as if the entire city had been summoned there. I did not need to inquire as to the reason for this gathering. The tower of the *rochetta* stood like a Titan in the pit of Hell above a lake of dark wool hoods and fur caps. And the condemned man would soon appear, I was certain, in its highest window.

Among the sea of caps I observed Leonardo da Vinci's conspicuous gray mane, close enough to the foot of the tower that he risked being kicked in the head when the condemned man reached the end of his rope. As I made my way toward him, I was struck that the collective tenor of the crowd altered, the farther I ventured into this lake of men. The hushed speculation in guttural Romagnolo I heard at the periphery gradually gave way to whispered, anxious prayers, and then to the sort of awed silence usually inspired by the shroud of Christ. I had entered this region of mute reverence, although I was still eight or ten *braccia* from Leonardo, when I saw Ramiro da Lorca.

His closed eyes were so swollen and discolored that it appeared plumbs had been stuck into the sockets. The rest of his blocky face was covered with bruises, each the artifact of a question that had not been answered—or an answer that had demanded another question. I had advanced two more paces when I observed that the sole support of Ramiro's battered head was a pike fixed into the meat of his truncated neck.

Stunned by this grim vision, not to mention the death of my hopes, I was unable to appreciate the entire spectacle until I had almost reached Leonardo. A simple linen mat had been placed over the new snow, just beneath the sheer massif of the tower. On this canvas lay Ramiro's body, still attired in an expensive brocade robe, beside it a butcher's block and a bloody cleaver with a blade as long as my forearm.

With his gray hair and drawn face, Leonardo was of a piece with a world that appeared entirely ashen. I did not think he had even noted my arrival, until he turned and said at once, "You must come with me. I have succeeded in explaining everything."

CHAPTER 14

Nothing is worthier of a warrior than to foresee the designs of his enemy.

So quickly did Leonardo's lunging steps lead me across the little city, that I found myself in his warehouse, lit like springtime by his globe lamps, as if I had been flown there on the back of a goat. We stood before one of his banquet tables, now littered with an accumulation of geometric models such as learned men keep in their *studioli*: cones, cylinders, and more elaborate, many-sided forms made of paper or thin shaved wood.

Directly beneath us was a machine, this consisting of a wooden box about a palm in height and a *braccia* long and wide, with a rod and a small crank protruding from one side. Atop this box was a flat, round, platter-like piece of wood almost as wide as the box itself, with a shiny surface like a potter's glaze. The round wooden plate did not appear to lie directly upon the top of the box but seemed to be suspended just above it by an axle in its center, like the wheel of a cart that has been tipped on its side.

I was scarcely surprised that Leonardo did not at once explain the purpose of the contraption. Instead he extended one of his great crane-wing arms and gathered up a volume I had not observed, as it was also concealed beneath drawings. The binding was expensive morocco leather, dyed a rich Tyrian purple.

"Archimedes authored a treatise known as *On Spirals*," Leonardo said as he opened the volume and began to turn the yellowed old parchment leaves. The text was Greek, copied in a fine hand. But Leonardo soon paused where another hand, equally fastidious, had written in the margin, in Latin, with a different nib and slightly darker ink.

"Read it," the maestro instructed me, as if I were an apprentice in this shop.

I did so, aloud, offering my own translation into Tuscan:

> *If a straight line, one end being fixed, is made to revolve at a uniform rate on a plane until it returns to its starting position, and if, at the same time as this straight line revolves, a point moves at uniform rate along this straight line, starting from the fixed end, that point will describe a spiral in a plane.*

My bewildered expression prompted Leonardo to add, "I will demonstrate." Here he returned to his box with the platter on top, at which point I observed that this perfectly round wooden plate was in fact covered with a thin layer of wax. Leonardo employed his right hand to very slowly but smoothly turn the crank, so that the wooden wheel spun with no variation in its speed. With his left hand the maestro produced a silver stylus such as draftsmen use, placing it at the center of the wheel; as it turned, he slowly drew the stylus in a perfectly straight motion toward the outer edge. The effect of this motion, combined with the revolving wheel, was to inscribe a remarkably uniform spiral in the wax.

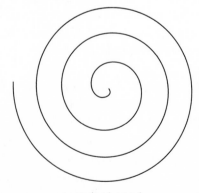

Archimedes Spiral

"I have created an Archimedes spiral," Leonardo said, returning to his bound treatise. "This construction provided Archimedes with important proofs. Proofs that cannot be understood without his definitions." He began to read, offering his own translation. " 'Let the length which the point that moves along the straight line describes in one revolution be the *first distance*.' " The maestro plucked up one of his notebooks and a piece of chalk. He began drawing from a central point in the page, making a line that wound around like the spiral he had made on the wax platter—except that he stopped when he had gone only one revolution around that center point. Without the aid of a measuring stick or straightedge, he drew a perfectly straight line from that center point to where the spiral had completed its first revolution.

Turning to another page of the treatise, Leonardo once again drew in his notebook. He did not require a compass calipers to make an almost perfect circle, using the line he had previously drawn as the radius of this circle. "And here Archimedes tells us, 'Let the circle drawn with the origin of the spiral as its center and the first distance as its radius be called the *first circle*.' "

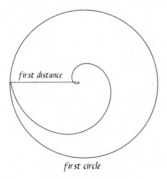

first circle

"The square is the first circle," I said, reciting the inscription on the *bollettino* he had shown me a few days before. The hair rose at my neck. "What in the name of God and Mankind . . ."

Leonardo had already produced his *mappa* of Imola; with none of his customary dithering, he placed atop it the tracing he had previously shown me in Imola, demonstrating the figure of a circle within a square. But now he placed above this another tracing tissue of the

The Square is the First Circle

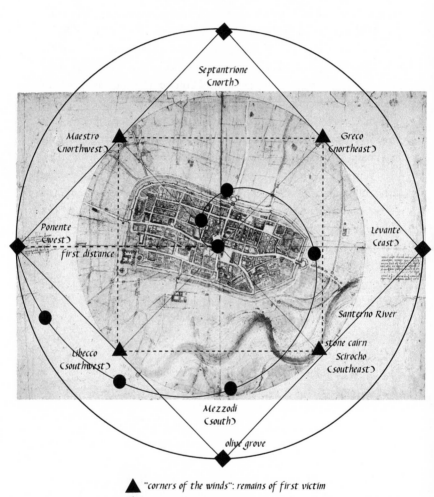

Septantrione
(north)

Maestro
(northwest)

Greco
(northeast)

Ponente
(west)

first distance

Levante
(east)

Santerno River

Libecco
(southwest)

stone cairn
Scirocho
(southeast)

Mezzodi
(south)

olive grove

▲ "corners of the winds": remains of first victim

◆ remains of second victim

● remains of third and fourth victims

same size, smoothing it into place, so that I could see well enough the geometric figures drawn upon it.

Leonardo had proved himself a better prophet than I. Because this was no mere *disegno*.

This was the Devil's map of evil.

◆

The topmost of the two tracings Leonardo had placed upon his *mappa* was similar to one I had seen in his studio more than two weeks previously—which on that occasion he had, in his frustration, covered with beans. The beans were now absent, so that I could again see the points where the cruelly butchered pieces of the two bodies had been found. Although the arrangement of these points had appeared entirely haphazard on my prior viewing, now they were connected by a line that looked as if it had been traced around a nautilus shell—or, to be more precise, represented the first revolution of an Archimedes spiral. Around this, the maestro had drawn the "first circle" with that "first distance" as its radius.

But that spiral was not even the most astonishing feature of this new construction. Leonardo had also indicated the four compass points where the first dreadful set of quarters had been found, and he had drawn the circle on which these points lay—the same circle that circumscribed the city of Imola on his original map. In addition, he had shown the four points that marked the location of the second set of butchered quarters, and he had drawn the square into which that inner circle had been so tightly fitted. This square, in turn, was just as tightly inscribed within the "first circle" defined by the first revolution of the spiral. Circle, square, then circle, all perfectly fitted, one within the other.

"You were correct, Maestro," I conceded. "It is all of a piece. He did not indiscriminately discard the remains of his last victims, as I so incorrectly assumed. He has completed his *disegno* with the most terrible and marvelous of all his geometric figures."

Leonardo took no satisfaction in this victory. His face sagged, a hand greater than his making a portrait of his weary soul. "I wish only to seek the True Light," he whispered. "This *disegno* is intended to impugn me and destroy everything the duke and I intend to build."

I gestured at the morocco-bound volume, certain that the murderer had examined the very pages from which we had just read. "Maestro, where did you obtain your Archimedes?"

"It was a gift. From the duke."

"Did Ramiro da Lorca know about this gift?" I asked this with the considerable hope—and lesser expectation—that the butcher had already received justice on his own block.

"Ramiro considered me his rival." Certainly the duke had favored Leonardo in the investigation of this matter. "We did not engage in discourse."

"Is it possible that Ramiro somehow became privy to this Archimedes and devised this *disegno*? To impugn you and disgrace the duke?"

Leonardo's jaw quivered slightly. His hands went over his groin.

Observing the maestro's typically ill-concealed effort to conceal some truth, I was prompted to ask the question that had burned on my tongue since I had seen Ramiro's head. "Did the duke or any of his people tell you the charges for which Ramiro was executed?"

"Grain speculation. And crimes against the people of the Romagna."

Clearly Valentino did not intend to tip his hand regarding the larger question of his brother's murder. But if the *condottieri* were waiting for signs and wonders, they would find Ramiro's head a most satisfactory indication of the duke's submission.

I then asked a question that bristled the hair atop my head. "Is it possible that one of Valentino's former *condottieri* knew about your Archimedes?"

Leonardo now had the look of a man about to be thrown from a great height. This was the truth he had been hiding in his crotch.

"Maestro?"

"Vitellozzo Vitelli saw it. Before he became a traitor to the duke. He shares my interest in Archimedes. He is an artillerist." In fact Vitellozzo Vitelli was Christendom's foremost artillerist, a maestro of the modern art of war. "As was Archimedes himself, who designed mangonels and prodigious siege crossbows to defend Syracuse. Vitellozzo's concern was equations and propositions regarding parabolas, by which the flight of a projectile can be described."

Nature had given Vitellozzo Vitelli both a savage temperament and great gifts. As an innovator of military tactics, he was rivaled only by Valentino; he had devised how to mass *scoppiettieri* to create an impenetrable wall of gunfire, a singular *invenzione* that transformed this small artillery piece—which can be carried by one man, fires a ball no larger than a grape, and had been previously regarded as a curiosity—into an instrument capable of defeating a charge of armored lancers.

Determined to keep my well-founded suspicions of Vitellozzo inside my vest, I next asked Leonardo a question that fully credited his gifts—and my own demonstrated deficiencies. "Regardless of who this monster is, Maestro, let us for the sake of argument assume he is still among us. What do you think he will show us next? Will he begin an entirely new *disegno?*"

Leonardo began to make shapes in the air with his hands, the fingers of one darting around those of the other like martens fighting. "In the manner that gears of finer tooth . . . acceleration . . . vortices of water and wind . . . compelled by the mass and impetus of their medium . . . toward the center." He blinked at me. "This figure allows him infinite variations."

I did not understand the mathematics of these "infinite variations" any more than Leonardo understood this man's unceasing need to nourish himself with suffering and death. Afraid to leave Damiata alone any longer, I made a final study of the *mappa* of evil. As my eyes traced its elegant geometry, my outraged soul told me that every point represented the flesh of an innocent. Yet whoever had made this obscene rebus had clearly contrived it to mirror not only Leonardo's gifts of intellect but more pointedly his particular enthusiasm for whirlwinds, whirlpools, and various other vortices, which appeared in so many of his drawings. Leonardo had even fashioned gears, cogs, and screws that repeated the outline of this spiral.

Hence another question traced cold along my spine. Had this obscene geographer also drawn something there for me, a *disegno* that mocked my own struggle to enter his mind? Was this spiral also the Labyrinth into which I had so futilely peered, trying to see the half man, half beast at its bone-strewn center?

All the more anxious to return to Damiata, I offered Leonardo this parting thought: "I believe you will once again be proved correct, Maestro. He will soon enough give us another variation."

♦

I ran to Damiata's lodging as quickly as the icy streets permitted. She had locked the door to her room, which told me that my departure had already made her cautious; when she opened up, I found her dressed in a simple black *camora*. She took my hands without a word.

I began with Ramiro, adding something that I had not had occasion to reflect upon until then. "It is likely that I received Ramiro's last testament, just before Valentino arrested him," I told her. "Ramiro implied that Valentino was protecting Oliverotto. And not because Oliverotto and Vitellozzo Vitelli have coerced him with the strength of their troops. Ramiro said the murderer was at Capua. He insisted I 'ask the duke about the women at Capua.' Those were his words. I take this to mean that Valentino and Oliverotto are both concealing something that occurred at Capua. Something to do with the women of the town, I am reasonably certain. You must have heard the rumors."

Damiata shook her head. "They did not trickle into the Trastevere."

"Shortly after the sack of Capua, unsigned letters circulated throughout all the capitals of Italy. Claiming various things. Women hostages who were guaranteed safe conduct but were raped and murdered after they left the city. One report, which was widely published, insisted that forty virgins had been delivered to the Vatican, for the pope's amusement. At the time I regarded it all as a concerted slander, the sort of invention at which the Venetians are so well practiced—they have long considered the Romagna as their own vassal state and have scarcely been pleased at Valentino's ascendance. But perhaps in this instance the facts are close enough to the calumny. Or perhaps even worse. Perhaps Valentino permitted something in the heat of the battle, which he now deeply regrets. Something more infamous than the crimes for which Oliverotto da Fermo is presently renowned."

Damiata let go my hand and crossed herself.

"Who told you," I asked, "that Oliverotto didn't arrive in Imola until after the first woman had been butchered?"

Damiata whispered, "Valentino."

"Then I believe that's it. Valentino is protecting Oliverotto. And not because he needs his agreement to this treaty."

Damiata's bosom rose. "You once told me the *condottieri* would drag Valentino's soul into Hell. Perhaps they have already done so. At Capua."

I nodded. "But however he disgraced himself at Capua, the duke cannot redeem those crimes by abandoning Italy to the *condottieri*."

Damiata bit her lip, lost in her own speculation.

I had to tell her the rest of it, all that I had seen and heard at Leonardo's warehouse. When I described the *mappa* of evil, she had to sit on the bed, her face almost white. With a trembling finger, she traced the spiral in the air.

"The maestro of the shop is playing the Devil's own game," I said. "He knows we are pursuing him. So he is sporting with us."

Damiata sat silently for a long while, as if summoning the resolve to look up at me. When at last she did, her eyes were filled with tears. "You can't say he isn't mad, Niccolò." She seemed angry at me. "You can no longer say it."

My science having suffered sufficiently that day, I had no appetite for disputing her. "Even if he is mad, he has quite cleverly contrived his *mappa* to lead us nowhere. Or perhaps lead us away from the truth. We must not forget that the *Elements* remain the key to all this. Without proof the *condottieri* had a connection to Juan's amulet, we can establish nothing in the eyes of the world."

Damiata drew in a deep breath, bringing back some of her color. "If the *condottieri* have the book, they will keep it. As a surety against Valentino."

"I believe one of them has it. And he will keep it. As a surety against all the rest. The question is, which one? I am inclined to say Vitellozzo Vitelli. With the connivance of his lick-spittle, Oliverotto. But how would we get it? Either one of us would be strangled on Vitellozzo's threshold."

Damiata looked quickly down. She shook her head with frustration and could only utter, "I don't . . ." before she choked on a sob.

I sat beside her and held her cold hands for a time. But knowing the urgency of these events, I soon had to get up. "I must go back to my room and write my government what I have seen. I believe Ramiro's corpse is our sign that Valentino's departure from Cesena is imminent. And we have no choice but to go with him. Because only at the end of this road can we even hope to find the *Elements*." I did not need to add that where this road ended, the *condottieri* would be waiting, regardless.

Damiata stared at the floor. "Yes, we must prepare to leave." She smiled wistfully. "Another little home." Her eyes shot up at me, their blue unfathomable. "Niccolò, whatever happens in the next days or weeks, you must remember this. You must remember it if we become separated. In particular you must remember it if you are blessed to hold your little Primerana again, as I beseech the Virgin you will be. My dearest, most darling Niccolò. The greatest love is nothing but faith. A faith that can bear all burdens, all doubts, and never be exhausted."

Here she stood up, took me in her arms, and whispered next to my ear. "To truly love another person requires more faith than even God asks of us."

PART THREE

BEYOND THE SHORES OF FATE

Cesena–Sinigaglia: December 26–31, 1502

CHAPTER 15

Whoever actually sees the Devil sees him with fewer horns and a face more fair.

Having begun our day so early, with the unpropitious augury of Ramiro's corpse, Fortune determined that it should extend much longer. On leaving Damiata's room, I stopped by the Governor's Palace, finding the loggia as busy with ambassadors and embassy secretaries as was usual much later in the day. I quickly learned that none of Valentino's intimates were available to remark on Ramiro's fate; they had all journeyed down the Via Emilia a good fifteen miles south of Cesena, evidently to assemble the scattered army for the march toward Rimini. Nevertheless I spent considerable time outside the empty palazzo, comparing my accounting of Valentino's troops with those of the other embassies.

When I returned to my rooms at midmorning, I found a courier waiting with several packets from Florence. My friend Biaggio related that my wife was "cursing God" over our marriage and incessantly demanding that I send money, as if I were an alchemist who could create gold out of dross; I threw aside the letter with a weary groan. The second dispatch was from my government, containing sufficient ducats to see me through three more weeks, if I lived like a mendicant friar. This meager stipend was accompanied by further instruction to remain firmly attached to Valentino until I was relieved. Although my lordships in Florence were little concerned for my comfort or security, they attached considerable value to my observations.

In addition to these missives, I had on my table various matters concerning Florentine business interests in the Romagna, which required my attention if I was to follow Valentino's heedless march beyond the Rubicon. Hence I did not send the courier off with my dispatch to Florence, apprising my lordships of the day's events, until just before dusk, whereupon I went at once back to Damiata's room.

I leapt up the stairs, believing that another night in Damiata's arms might somehow transport me beyond Fortune's reach, not to mention the day's disastrous turn. The door was locked, as I had expected. But after I had knocked several times and failed to rouse her, I assumed that her preparations for our uncertain journey had been no less difficult than mine, and that she had gone into the city on various errands.

Hence for several hours I walked the streets of Cesena, yet still I did not encounter Damiata; I also returned several times to her room to see if she had come back. By the third visit my anxiety was at a high pitch. Foremost among my fears, I had to wonder if Valentino himself had discovered Damiata's presence in Cesena, despite her efforts to remain out of sight. He might well have located her hiding place and sent someone to arrest her, given that he now appeared as determined to protect the *condottieri* from the consequences of her inquiry as he was to deliver himself into their arms.

Nevertheless, I could find no one at Damiata's palazzo who had seen her go out, much less anyone come in and drag her out. I contemplated breaking the lock to her door, but that would only put her belongings at risk during the coming chaos, while probably revealing nothing I had not previously observed in her room. Instead, I continued visiting her palazzo every hour throughout a night as miserable as the preceding had been miraculous, my fears taking entire dominion over both reason and sentiment.

I had returned from one of these futile journeys perhaps an hour before dawn, when I paused before my own door. Hearing the faintest little chinging, like coins in a purse, I quickly looked behind me.

The tiny courtyard was empty. Yet all at once a stronger intuition coursed through me in a great spasm, turning me back to my door.

For just a heartbeat, I was surprised that I did not see someone—or some thing—standing on the threshold before me. The little chinging sound seemed to come from the sky. I looked up to the very crown of the roof, two floors above me.

The face of the moon, or perhaps a barn owl. Or no face at all. It appeared to hover above the eave for so fleeting an instant that I could not say what it was, other than a pale apparition. When it vanished, the chinging sound metamorphosed into a light clattering, as if a large rodent were scurrying across the roof tiles.

I raced out of the courtyard and into the street, attempting to observe this creature's escape. Yet I neither saw nor heard anything clambering over the roof. I peered into the alley that separated my building from the next, recalling the night I had found poor Camilla's corpse. I had caught only the most ephemeral glimpse of the "barn owl" that Damiata had noted atop our building, at almost the same moment that I had observed the footsteps leading up her stairs, which I had followed with far more urgency—and what I discovered in Damiata's bedroom had washed away any memory of the phantom on the roof. Yet now I could only presume that this owl-man had also been present that night, an unspeakably brutal apprentice who continued to stalk us behind the mask of Death.

This led me to a more terrifying deduction: the Devil's apprentice had watched me enter Damiata's rooms and had probably observed me leave. Again I saw Camilla's corpse, the fresh blood everywhere, as though we are nothing more than fonts of gore, the bones of her neck and shoulder jutting like pig joints.

I started to run as if I had been struck by lightning, thinking only that I would die myself before I allowed Damiata to suffer poor Camilla's fate.

Yet just as quickly, I stopped. Damiata was not waiting in her room as Camilla had been that night; she had been gone for hours. I would have found her door open, as I had that night, if the murderer's apprentice had savaged her in the same manner. Instead he was here, still watching me. More likely Damiata had been able to flee from him and was still hiding. And he hoped to find her here.

Determined to bait a trap for this creature, I withdrew from the alley and returned to my rooms.

◆

In my haste to search for Damiata, I had left my door unlocked; now I barred it behind me, thinking that I might confound this creature by not returning to Damiata's lodging, as he had certainly come to expect. Instead, I would remain inside until he was provoked to call on me.

I lit a candle and set about examining my room for something to use as a weapon. The search was not at once promising, because I had packed up everything in anticipation of a hasty departure. I might have swept the cold tile floor, it was so clean, save for the brazier and a useless rusted poker. I had even cleared most of the papers and manuscripts from my little table—

I dropped my candle at once. The wick flickered at my feet, still providing a small amount of light. That scant illumination allowed me a fleeting, inchoate fragment of a prayer, that what I saw on my table-top would prove to be only the delusion of a weary and desperate mind.

The next thing I knew I was running down the street, my reason clinging to a single, slender thread.

CHAPTER 16

It has always been no less dangerous to discover new methods and principles than it has been to search for unknown seas and lands.

Maestro Leonardo's globe lamps glimmered through the cracks of the warehouse shutters, these slivers of light as brilliant as molten bronze in an armorer's crucible. The door gave me no resistance and I burst directly into the abandoned refectory, to find Leonardo and his assistants staring at me as if I were a madman. They were engaged in bundling up many of the items that littered the floor; had I my wits about me, I might have observed that Valentino's departure had taken his own engineer general by surprise.

But I did not have my wits about me. I ran directly to the maestro and shouted into his face, "You must come at once! Bring your *cazzo diavolo* measuring things!"

◆

"You know what I am asking," I grimly told Leonardo. Giacomo had placed a reflecting candle lantern on my tabletop, so that we could see quite well enough.

Leonardo crouched, bringing his face within a palm's length of the severed hand. "It is a woman's," he said, his voice lacking its usual melody.

I could not recognize the hand as Damiata's, any more than I could assure myself it was not. Slightly bloated, the fingers swollen most of all, the entire appendage was blotched a ghastly claret and purple. It had been severed cleanly at the wrist.

I had to turn away before Leonardo could begin his measurements. I did not even hear his chalk dreadfully scratching away in one of his notebooks, divining fate with letters and numbers, before he said, "Did you observe this?"

The red string fell from Leonardo's hand like a trail of blood. Yet the little card attached to it was not stained at all. Leonardo presented it to me as if he were a priest offering the wafer at Mass.

There was no prayer to the Devil on this *bollettino*; the facing side of the card was entirely blank. My fingers trembled as I turned it over. The script on the other side was in the familiar, polished Tuscan hand and black Chinese ink. But the words were like something heard in a dream.

Il sale più profondo a Cesenatico.

"The deepest salt at Cesenatico," I mumbled, Cesenatico being Cesena's seaport, a town about ten miles east, on the Adriatic coast. "It doesn't even mean anything."

"There are salt basins at Cesenatico," Leonardo said. Illuminated from below by the reflecting candle, his face appeared distorted, almost monstrous.

Yet it was his silence that alarmed me. "What is it, Maestro!" I knew I sounded as mad as he looked. "Do you already know? Is it Damiata's hand!"

Leonardo shook his head as if entirely bewildered. "I cannot determine that with only . . . this," he said in a croaking voice. "The hand varies too much from the *simmetria* of the limbs. I can only say that it was separated from the living body within the previous day. Or two. There are fluids—"

All at once Leonardo's spidery fingers pounced on the *bollettino*, plucking it from my slack hand.

He examined the cryptic message, his head shaking in his palsied fashion. Finally the maestro found words. "Perhaps the hand was left for you," he whispered, clutching the *bollettino* to his breast. "This is for me."

✦

It was a measure of the skill with which this unspeakably vile murderer had entered Leonardo's mind that within moments of reading the butcher's cryptic missive, Valentino's engineer general had put aside his urgent pursuit of the duke's army; with renewed authority in his voice, he instructed his assistants to prepare for a journey to Cesenatico. He then turned to me and said, "I will require several hours to prepare the apparatus necessary to examine the salt basins." Recalling the great wheel of buckets I had seen in the maestro's warehouse, I wondered if this "apparatus" would be employed for some sort of excavation or dredging. "You must be prepared to leave here later this day. Wear as much clothing as you have—I can tell you with good assurance there is going to be a storm."

Before he departed, Leonardo carefully placed the severed hand in a canvas sack. As I closed the door behind him, I could think only: *Not two days ago I kissed that warm and tender hand, the hand that burned my flesh and healed my soul, the hand that led me to a new life. Now it is nothing but a butchered piece of meat.*

And in Cesenatico would I be condemned to find the rest of her, piece by pale, bloodless piece?

✦

The maestro finally returned for me at midday, alone. He explained that he had already sent his assistants ahead and was now determined to proceed to Cesenatico on foot, as he was certain he could cover the distance more quickly than a mule.

I had no difficulty matching the maestro's lunging strides; such was my urgency to determine Damiata's fate, that I could have run the entire way, despite not sleeping at all since I had awakened early the previous morning. After passing through the unguarded city gate, we proceeded east on a road the Romans had certainly not built, as it lacked the perfect line only their surveyors have ever achieved—a symmetry that was otherwise evident in fields bounded by precise borders.

A mile or so past the city walls, we observed that we were not alone. Traveling in companies of five or six to as many as twenty or thirty, they were not local country folk, although in their rough capes they scarcely appeared different, until one observed that many had only scraps of cloth tied about their feet and some were as barefoot as Saint Francis. These desperate mendicants were my fellow pilgrims, who had also followed Valentino's army from Imola. And while the whores and priests who had journeyed south would always find means to keep from starving, these peasants could only hope to glean from a Cesenate countryside that was quickly being stripped as bare as the Imolese fields they had so recently fled.

"They are looking for farmhouses," Leonardo said, shaking his head with something like pity. "It is the custom of these ignorant farmers to open their dwellings to the dead between Christmas and Epiphany. The imbeciles provision their tables as if the incorporeal spirits they believe are among them fully possess digestive organs."

"Tonight the living will either eat for the dead, or soon join them," I said, observing a group that had already left the road. Like shapeless dark beasts wandering in a little herd, these poor wretches trudged across the snow-shrouded fields, guided by some compass in their empty bellies.

We quickly left behind these plodding foragers. After several more miles, I decided to risk Leonardo's scorn and offer him my observations regarding the evil maestro who had so cruelly dispatched us on this journey.

"I believe that this man has a peculiar defect of his nature," I began, "although I do not know precisely how to describe it. The Church would say he is Satan's creation. But if the Devil truly possessed the art to make this singular being, then why not make a hundred thousand like him and leave all the world beneath a deluge of blood? No. I am more inclined to say that providential Nature, to some purpose we cannot fathom, has throughout history created rare men with this particular defect. They are born without those faculties of intellect and sentiment we would describe as the soul."

Much to my surprise, Leonardo nodded approvingly. "There are no monsters except those that Nature creates. There are men of divine beauty and men of grotesque deformity, and all the variety that lies between them. Why should there not be a similar variation among the faculties of the sensus communis, wherein the soul is found?"

"Then we lean to the same opinion on this," I said, scarcely believing our agreement.

Although we were already walking at considerable speed, Leonardo began to pace more quickly. "We agree upon this particular point. But you must understand that human desires, and the events occasioned by these desires, are random in any instance and are further disordered by the whims of Fortune." His tone suggested he much regretted this state of affairs. "You cannot study the intellects and actions of men, or make assumptions regarding them, as you can the harmonies and proportions that extend throughout Nature and all her elements."

In this manner Leonardo seemed to disregard my studies entirely—although I was flattered that he regarded them as worthy of reasoned disputation. So I replied, "But as many things as Man disorders, through his willfulness or neglect, so does Nature herself. I might look at Nature and say: What does she offer if not a chronicle of chaos—tempests, floods, hail, earthquakes, drought, and plague? How does this differ from the disorder created by men?"

"You are too ignorant to see that natural events are always guided by the same laws, that air is the same whether it moves in a breeze or the most terrible vortices, that no force in nature is ever lost but only transferred from one form to another. Across her entire domain, Nature achieves perfect unity. Do you know that sound, light, and water all obey the same principles?"

"In what manner?"

"Sound, light, and water are all propagated by means of waves."

"Waves?" Yet even as I queried Leonardo like a fool, I began to see in these waves a most useful model.

"I am not at liberty to scatter straw upon water and demonstrate the principle," Leonardo snapped, "nor to show you that the same numeric proportions that govern bodies and buildings also extend to the harmonics of sound—"

"Then why cannot wars, revolutions, and the birth and death of states and empires be governed by similar laws and principles? Because these principles have not yet been observed? I have not witnessed these waves that convey sound and light, but you tell me that they are the very fundament of Nature herself. I believe the events recorded in our histories move in similar fashion. Can we not look at an endless chain of examples, from the Assyrians to the Persians to Greece and Rome, and see that every empire is built upon its virtues and decays with its vices? What is this endless rising and falling of states but a cycle as necessary and unrelenting as the rise and fall of these waves that convey all things?"

Leonardo lifted both hands in the air like a priest elevating the Host. "So you would make an organism of the state, yet tell us that you have explained it in its entirety by merely examining its birth and death. By God! Is anything that Nature has created so easy to understand? Look at what we must know before we can hope to explain the mechanisms of the wondrous machine that is the human body—not merely the configuration of each part but also its function, which sensation each nerve conveys and how each muscle moves and where it is attached to bone, and which of these conspire to create a yawn or pout or move the eyes in unison. How does food move through the digestive organs and how do the eyes restore an upright image in the fashion a camera obscura cannot? You can only determine such truths through ceaseless and interminable study! Measurement! You—can your Livy and Herodotus provide you such *esperienza*? Can you possibly hope to examine all of human history and draw connections among events in such detail that you navigate an unknown sea no man has ever crossed?"

I did not have an answer for the maestro that day. Instead my answer has been the labor of my life, principally my *Discourses on the First Decade of Titus Livy* but also my little *Prince*. Despite what so many say, I did not embark upon this voyage to show men how evil can triumph, but to demonstrate that evil surely will triumph if good men do not strive to learn well its lessons. And now that my usefulness, if not my life itself, has ended, I can say before God and man that I have met the challenge the great maestro of revered memory issued on the road to Cesenatico. For in my life's work, I crossed the unknown sea and charted a route for all men to follow, should they wish to live in peace and security.

◆

As the afternoon turned toward dusk, we had a perfect illustration of the capricious malice of Nature. First the sky became a heavy gray, as if it might collapse upon us. Then this lowering ceiling became a lighter, ashen hue, whereupon snow began to fall in great sheets. A wind came howling from the sea, as if the hand of God was determined to prevent us going farther.

Nevertheless the curtains of snow parted now and then, until at last I could see the town itself. Hardly a great seaport like Pisa, Cesenatico was composed of a few churches, warehouses, shops, and palazzi, aligned on either side of a canal that entered the sea there. The harbor consisted only of the somewhat broader mouth of the canal and some piers constructed along a spit that jutted into the sea.

"It is the duke's intention that we build a great port here," Leonardo said, turning his back to the wind so that his shouted words could be more easily heard. "I have plans to dredge and deepen the canal, greatly expand the harbor, and improve the fortifications so that these new works can be defended! And then we will transform Cesenatico, as we will create anew the entire Romagna!" His words were not directed at me; these cathedral-organ notes were flying straight up to God.

I no longer believed that Valentino would continue to build anything at all. Instead, he would merely leave behind the empire of hope he had constructed in each of our minds. Leonardo's empire boasted cities more perfect than Plato or Augustine could have imagined. My empire of hope was an Italy defended by citizen soldiers rather than mercenary thugs, free of tyranny and foreign armies, with justice for all regardless of rank or wealth. But I feared I had come to Cesenatico only to wander among its ruins.

"There is the salt." Leonardo pointed past the left bank of the canal, just behind a row of warehouses. The salt basins had almost certainly been constructed by the Romans, having been arranged in a grid just like the fields, their borders defined by thick earthen berms roughly half my height. The checkerboard thus created was as broad and as long as the town itself; only a taller berm and a narrow beach separated it from the sea. The square pools of water ranged in color from almost black, where they had been newly filled with seawater, to whiter than the snow, where the water had evaporated entirely and the salt was ready to be harvested. A large mound of this dry salt, which had yet to be sacked, rose before one of the warehouses, its outline vague in the blowing snow.

Leonardo turned and studied the sea. "We must proceed with all haste."

Here I observed the cause of his concern. Great swells were rising with the wind and the gusts continued to drive these waves to the shore; they would soon rise above the berm at the seaward end of the salt basins and begin to inundate them.

We entered the town on the left bank and remained on the road that ran in front of the warehouses, with the salt basins directly to our left. We must have gone almost to the sea—the percussion of the waves was audible above the shrieking wind—when I saw a figure standing on a berm, veiled in snow, long hair and cape flying. I would have imagined this was Lot's wife, had I not at first believed, just as fancifully, that I had found Damiata.

"Giacomo!" Leonardo shouted as he ran to his assistant; in the moment before I arrived, they had some brief conversation. Climbing up onto the berm, I found it constructed of a dense, clinging clay. I looked out upon a basin that was as dark as Chinese ink. The wind had made small waves on the surface, but they were nothing next to those that rolled at us from the sea, pounding the beach in great explosions of spray.

"*Cacasangue cazzo d'iddio!*" I shouted, all but jumping out of my skin.

The demon that shot up from the black water at our feet had eyes as big as saucers, the head of a giant locust, and this great, elephant-like snout. If ever in my life I had believed that Satan's minions dwell beneath our feet, this was the moment. The giant creature, having risen to its full height, began to pull off its own insect head, requiring only several vigorous tugs.

"Tommaso!" Leonardo shouted. "Did you find it?"

Leonardo's assistant Tommaso stood before us, the glass-eyed leather helmet that had entirely enclosed his head now beneath one arm. "I have it here!" With his free hand Tommaso hefted a large canvas sack.

As Leonardo relieved Tommaso of his burden, Giacomo grabbed the helmet's elephant snout, which was in fact divided into two tubes, and pulled on it like a fisherman drawing in his net. This brought to dry land a bobbing, bell-like wooden float to which the hoses were attached. I had little time to observe this aquatic device, however, because Leonardo stalked off, leaving his assistants to transport the apparatus.

Leonardo led us to one of the warehouses that stood beside the salt basins. It was an old building with a red tile roof, with several big doors on each side. In less harsh times, one would expect it to be filled with salt in hemp sacks, but only a few wooden kegs were scattered about. Evidently Leonardo's assistants had placed some planks across two of these kegs to make a small table. Tommaso stood there stripped to his trousers and shirt, drenched, his skin almost white and his lips nearly purple.

"What is this machine?" I inquired as Giacomo carelessly deposited the helmet, float, and tubes on the floor. I assumed it was some sort of *invenzione* that conveyed air so that a man could remain underwater like a fish.

"You must say nothing of this diving apparatus," Leonardo admonished. "If this device became known, we would place the capacity for great evil in the hands of menial intellects. A single fool could sink an entire fleet." As the maestro spoke, he began disgorging the contents of Tommaso's canvas sack onto the tossed-together table.

A great deal of clay still adhered to these bones, which appeared to be arms, legs, and ribs—and a large portion of a skull. *That cannot be all that is left of her,* I told myself, too numb to imagine otherwise.

Sleeves up to his elbows, Leonardo examined the bones one after another, scraping away the mud and studying each from several vantages. Finally he shook his head like a physician who has put his ear to a chest and hears the death rattle. "These bones are of great antiquity. This was all?"

"I was down there a quarter hour," Tommaso said. His teeth were chattering like a Spanish dancer's hand cymbals.

"Then we must go down again." Leonardo looked at me. "There is a sink in that basin, where mud has been excavated, as it is valued for its salutary effects. We discovered it when we were surveying the harbor."

So this sink was the deepest salt—or salt basin—in Cesenatico. Yet I wondered if Leonardo truly understood what he was saying. "Then whoever sent you here not only knew that you had surveyed this area—a fact, I presume, that was known by many at court, in addition to those in this town. But this man also knew the peculiarities you discovered."

Leonardo stared at me mournfully. "They all knew. My survey was performed this August. At that time buckets of the salubrious mud were delivered to the duke and his people. As well as to Vitellozzo Vitelli, Paolo Orsini, and Oliverotto da Fermo." He allowed himself a sigh more like a dying man's last breath. "Any one of them might have . . ."

We had come ten miles to Cesenatico and were still a thousand miles from the truth.

As we stood there in silence, an immense roar issued from outside, the wind and waves having created some terrifying new instrument. Water flooded into the warehouse, soaking our feet in an icy bath.

Leonardo's eyes seemed fixed on a far greater catastrophe. When the water had subsided he strode to the open door. Following him, I observed that the very sea had come to us. It was ebbing away, so that the top of the berm that separated the salt basins from the sea was again exposed, but the smaller berms that divided the basins were under water.

"You cannot send Tommaso back out there!" I shouted.

Leonardo turned and studied Giacomo, as if weighing his fitness for the task. Finally he said, "We are finished here. By tomorrow there will be nothing left. All of it swept into the sea." He blinked away the stinging spray; one could imagine he was weeping. "It is ever thus for those who seek the True Light."

We retreated into the warehouse, although it occurred to me that we could as readily drown in there as out in the salt basins, if the waves rose high enough. Leonardo retrieved his diving apparatus, cradling it in his arms like a shepherd holding a dead ewe.

"Have you considered," I asked him, "that you are thinking too much of your own survey and not sufficiently of the actual words written upon that *bollettino*? 'The deepest salt in Cesenatico.' "

Leonardo was not listening.

I continued my thought, having the attention of Tommaso and Giacomo, who watched me expectantly. "Perhaps we should look not for the greatest depth within the salt basins, but for the greatest depth of the salt itself."

Leonardo turned fully to me. His gray hair like a plaster upon his gray skin, he appeared as aged as Methuselah. "The greatest depth of salt? *Dimmi*." This was a whisper instead of his usual strident demand. "*Dimmi, Papà. Dimmi.*"

CHAPTER 17

Prudence consists in knowing how to distinguish between various disadvantages, and turning the least bad of them to the good.

As I led Leonardo and his assistants to the great mound of salt I had seen upon entering the town, the wind from the sea had only grown more fierce, the great hand now pushing at my back; the snow was falling so thickly that it seemed we would soon choke on it.

"You cannot hope to excavate it!" Leonardo shouted when we reached the pale mound, which appeared to be almost twice my height. "This will require considerable men and machines!"

"Neither can one or two men have excavated it deeply themselves!"

Leonardo nodded, the snow swarming around his face. "We must divide the perimeter by four and each move around it in the same direction." He called to his assistants, "Dig with your hands, at the very base, in the deepest salt!"

The salt was heavy, tightly packed, and coarse; quickly my hands stung with cold and small cuts. I entirely disregarded these new discomforts, so intent on answering the question of Damiata's fate that I paid no attention to a steadily rising roar. The water struck me while I was still kneeling, a wave of such force that it carried me two dozen *braccia*.

Leonardo hauled me up by the collar and kept me on my feet while I spit out brine. We then struggled back to the mound, the water halfway to our knees and the swirling currents grabbing at our feet. I could see that the base of the mound had been narrowed by two *braccia* or so on each side; whatever had been buried there was likely to have been carried away.

"I have her hair! I have her by the hair!" Giacomo's shouts quickly vanished in the wind, but I clung to the desperate hope they raised:

This woman might be alive. She still has her head.

Possessed as if by a demon, I fought the current to reach Giacomo, who was on the side nearest the salt basins, where the flow was most swift. He stood with his arm elevated, as though holding up a lantern.

The disembodied head was suspended from a long tangle of hair. A woman, her face tanned like cowhide, the desiccated skin drawn tight over her skull. Her lips had shrunk away from teeth bared like a salted ling. That was a blessing to me, if not to her, because I could see that her imperfect teeth were not Damiata's lovely pearls.

My relief was more a numbness than any sentiment at all. And it did not last long.

"Here is another!" Leonardo exclaimed. I had only a glimpse of a bobbing head and a face obscured by the black hair plastered to it, when he shouted again, "Another! Tommaso! Come! Niccolò!"

Tommaso arrived before me and plunged his arms into the water. Within moments a head appeared beside him like a fisherman's float. Frantically I turned it to face me, finding only a countenance so withered I could not imagine a universe in which the lips and eyes I had kissed only two days previously had come so quickly to this.

I flailed beneath the turbid water, clawing yet more madly at the salt, when something like seaweed stroked my arms; wrapping these tendrils around my hand, I pulled fiercely. The head popped up like an apple in a barrel. I imagined she was staring at me, yet her shriveled eyelids were entirely shut. Her bared teeth were hardly flawed at all, but as I struggled to find some likeness, I wondered if I would even recognize Damiata when I found her—and how would I retrieve my reason if I did?

We continued this exploration for what seemed a dreadful epoch, though it can only have been minutes. "We have five now!" Leonardo called out, holding them all by the hair like some barbarian chieftain displaying his war trophies.

I stood up, contemplating a terrible calculus. The five heads represented the four slaughtered *streghe* and poor Camilla. If the hand on my table augured a sixth victim, as almost certainly it did, her head might still be in this mound.

"Boxes! There are boxes in here!"

I made my way to Tommaso, who was trying to capture several bobbing wooden boxes the size of infants' coffins—and I could hardly assure myself they were not. I helped him snare one but the others were swept to sea. Suddenly the water rose around me and to avoid being carried away, I had to grasp an outcropping of hard, compacted salt, breaking off a large chunk that allowed the water to pour in and prize away considerably bigger pieces.

Like a swarm of wasps flying out from their nest, dozens of large brown melons infested the retreating wave, some streaming past, others striking my arms and chest. As I pushed them away, I felt the matted hair and skin like a dried fig even before I saw the grinning teeth and sunken sockets.

"He has killed far more than five!" I shouted into the wind. And evidently he had been doing so for some time, as these heads were considerably more desiccated than those of his recent victims.

My mind reeled. I knew that this butcher had always been subject to his evil nature. But I had never imagined we would discover this: the grisly archive of a rare man's cruel history.

Leonardo's ravaged eyes followed the ghastly flotsam into the sea. "We must go to the higher ground now!" he called out, at once starting off, towing his own gruesome collection.

I looked up and saw a wave rising two *braccia* above the surface of the water that had already inundated us. And it was coming with the speed of a charger in the lists.

The next I knew, I was off my feet, spinning, my eyes and nostrils burning. The wave carried me at least a hundred paces faster than I could have run, until I tumbled like an empty clamshell over the ground beneath me. I plunged my hands into the wet clay and clung to the earth, knowing that if I was dragged back toward the sea I might never be seen again.

At last, the water loosened its hold. I got to my feet and ran into the blinding snow, the wind at my back the only assurance that I was proceeding away from the sea. I did not know I had reached safe ground until I found myself trudging through thick drifts untouched by the last tongues of the devouring waves.

I stopped and looked around but could see little more than the hand in front of me. "Maestro!" I called out, astonished at how the blowing snow trapped my voice, as if I had shouted into a pillow.

It seemed I had entirely lost my companions. I could not return to Cesenatico, which might well be under water. My salvation, as I saw it, was that I might chance upon one of the huts or farmhouses I had seen while approaching the town. I would have to put my faith in treacherous Fortune, and hope to find shelter before my limbs became numb and I surrendered to the snow.

◆

As I moved on into the blizzard, I began to see a bit more, although I was little more comforted. The storm was not simply a bitterly cold pall; it was a roiling ocean of snow. At times I even imagined dark leviathans swimming past me, although these were certainly just thicker swarms of snowflakes, hurried along by the winds.

For an instant, one of these apparitions seemed to take a more recognizable form. I shouted, "Maestro!"

This phantom ran toward me, unmistakably a man.

"Tommaso!" I called out, first thinking that he had put the diving helmet back on, which would not have been a terribly foolish thing to do in those conditions. But then I remembered we had left Tommaso's peculiar costume in the warehouse.

A face emerged from the ashen shroud. A white goat's beard. A stallion's long nose and white mane. And in the middle of its forehead, a single long, black horn.

Licorn. Unicorn. The word I had heard little more than a heartbeat before our *Gevol int la carafa* had ended. But it had not been a password. The mask I had only glimpsed that night—and which Giacomo had seen only from a distance days before—had not been the goat face of the Devil but rather this half goat, half horse, one-horned demon. The unicorn, a symbol of both purity and untamed passion, had been perverted into a mask of unspeakable savagery. "Licorn" had been the name a terrified *gioca* had attached to the Devil's apprentice.

The Licorn was armed with the principal instrument of his monstrous trade, more sword than knife, curved like the scimitar of a Turk. It was not the ornate dagger that Oliverotto da Fermo had previously displayed, but the stature of the man who wielded it—not to mention the prodigious fist that clutched it—was so similar to Signor Oliverotto's that only a fool would have been fooled by his mask.

"Signor Oliverotto!" I shouted through the tempest. "I have witnessed your collection of heads! Is this what you summoned us to observe?"

When he was close enough to gut me with a single lunge, he stopped. Another man seemed to take shape behind him, as though the blowing snow had compacted to create him.

My breath burst out of me and my brain offered the distant observation that the scimitar had punched through my ribs with such force that all the wind had been expelled from my lungs. Just as strangely, despite the shrieking tempest, I clearly heard my cloak rip as the blade slashed it.

I was on my back, staring up at the unicorn mask, the snow flying down at me like the ashes of my own funeral pyre.

CHAPTER 18

Those nearest to the Church have the least religion.

My attacker settled to his knee beside me, his blade now elevated, poised to scythe through my neck. Miniature portraits flashed before me, as if illuminated by lightning: Mama and Papa and dear little Primerana; my sisters; even Marietta, a vision for which I was strangely grateful, as if at last I could apologize to her. Yet in that shadow, I lingered longest with Damiata. When I reached the far shore, she whispered, she would tell me the truth of my own soul.

The Licorn's body and blade came down at me in one motion and I closed my eyes, unwilling to witness my own death.

I felt only an immense weight on my chest.

"Are you alive, Messer Niccolò?" These words might have fallen from Heaven.

Giacomo stood over me.

My assailant moaned and his body shuddered atop mine. Giacomo bent down and appeared to reach into the creature's massive back. I could see the knife he withdrew, though not the blood on it. But then the Licorn coughed and I could hear his drowning lungs. He began to gargle an Ave Maria.

With Giacomo's help I was able to push the nearly dead weight off me. I got unsteadily to my feet—and found myself entirely intact. Perhaps my attacker had struck me with a shoulder or arm; his blade had merely torn my coat. Whatever the case, Leonardo's listless assistant had saved my life.

"This man is still alive!" I shouted. I intended to rip off his mask and employ his own scimitar, if necessary, to discover what he had done with Damiata.

"The maestro is up there!" Giacomo waved vaguely into the blizzard.

I determined I would deliver this butcher to Leonardo, who might better understand how to clear the blood from his throat, so that we could take his full confession. Grasping his clothes, Giacomo and I began to drag the Licorn up a slope that seemed only to steepen with each step. I began to feel as hopeless as Sisyphus, condemned to eternally haul this burden uphill, my limbs now entirely frozen. If our dreadful ballast had not occasionally groaned, I would have regarded the entire effort as futile.

Suddenly Giacomo fled into the snow. But even before I could call out, I saw him silently pounding on the vaporous door of what appeared to be merely the ghost of a house. Almost at once, he vanished inside.

Arriving at the same threshold, I found another miracle. Before me was a farmer's dining room, lit by a smoking fire, the table in front of the hearth spread with a Christmas offering: sausages, roasted thrushes, bread, beans, and polenta. The farmer and his family were nowhere to be seen—perhaps they did not want to be further importuned by the starving Imolese refugees—but the dead had most certainly come to feed. Leonardo knelt on the floor next to the table, the five heads scattered around him like a melon harvest, sticking his fingers into the gaping mouth of one of those terrible leather faces, as if he believed he would find something hidden there, perhaps a message from her murderer. Tommaso was also busy, prying the lid from the wooden box he had salvaged.

"I have the agent of their deaths," I said as I dragged the Licorn across the threshold, the snow blowing in with me. "He would have taken another head if Giacomo had not saved me. I am indebted to him for my life." (A debt which Messer Giacomo made certain I paid, although that is altogether another story—that strange business with Leonardo's portrait of Giocondo's mistress.)

Leonardo knelt beside our captive and listened to another gargling Ave Maria. He put his fingers to the beast's thick neck, endeavoring to find his heartbeat, only to discover a little string; pulling on this, the maestro produced a small, red leather pouch.

Quickly I stuck my fingers inside this charm bag and extracted the sole contents: three tarnished, battered, squarish little bells. They rang—or chimed—faintly as I examined them. "Witch bells," I said. "My father's tenant farmers wore them, believing that a *strega* would pause to count each chime and become distracted from her evil designs." Recalling this sound from my night on the *pianura*, I shuddered so deeply that my teeth chattered. These bells had announced to us, and to this creature's pitiful victims, that we were in the unwelcome company of the Devil's apprentice. Or perhaps the Devil himself.

"We must remove his disguise before he suffocates," Leonardo said, now examining the helmet mask, which appeared even more life-like in the light: it had been assembled from the white hide of a stallion, the beard of a goat, and even the horn of an actual antelope. "It is sufficiently well-constructed that it might fool Nature," the maestro added admiringly.

I asked Giacomo, "Could this be the mask you saw in the woods that day?"

Giacomo reluctantly nodded. "He looks enough like the Devil, doesn't he?"

Leonardo glanced up at us before he deftly drew the mask over the dying man's head.

All four of us gasped.

◆

"No face at all." Giacomo repeated his words of a few nights previously, when both he and I had encountered *this* man, as well.

And Giacomo's description was no less apt than it had been that night. Nature herself seemed to have sent the Licorn to us with only the rudiments of a face, most of it a great pink-and-white scar, with two round beads for eyes, two slits for the nose, and another for the mouth. This tormented flesh was less livid than it might have been, however, because it was dusted all over with the glittering residue of some chalky white powder.

"I believe this substance is powdered moonstone," I said; there were great veins of this luminous chalk in the vicinity of Imola. "It would appear that the two masks were in fact only one. This man sometimes wore the mask of the *licorno* and at other times just the ruin of his face, concealed beneath this powder, like a whore hiding the pox with a layer of ceruse."

I knelt beside him, anxious to extinguish the spark of pity I felt for his deformity. "What happened to you?"

His eyes swiveled to me, black as peppercorns, absent lids or brows. He answered in good enough Italian, though with a Romagnole inflection, blood frothing on his slit of a mouth. "I was . . . turned . . . over the fire." Strangely, he seemed fiercely vain of this ordeal and its terrible result. "To save . . . my soul."

"When a child is born feetfirst," Tommaso said, "the midwives here tie him to a spit and turn him over the fire three times. Otherwise he will fall into the *stregoneria*."

"The credulous idiots succeeded only in burning him like chaff," Leonardo said, his mouth sagging with scorn.

Again I had to look at the unicorn's gruesome harvest, if only to be certain of the count. "Did you bring another woman's head to Cesenatico? Within the last two days?" Here I relied on Leonardo's judgment that the hand had been severed within that time span.

His head rolled from side to side. "Three weeks . . . ago. Two *streghe* . . . from Imola."

Hope lifted me a little; evidently *Zeja* Caterina and her colleague had been these last two. But then I had to ask, "The hand you left in my room. How did you obtain it?"

"Imola . . . the *strega* . . . we kept it . . . in snow."

Leonardo's lips quivered. Evidently he had neglected to observe that the hand might have been packed in snow for some time; perhaps he had also failed to consider that he had not collected all the parts from the last two *streghe*.

But a great wave of relief washed over me. Although Damiata's fate remained a cipher, I could reasonably believe that this monster had not butchered her.

Nevertheless, there remained a hard truth I had yet to hear. I grasped the beast's jaw so urgently that it seemed my fingers would puncture his scars, which were not thickened or callused after so many years, but felt as smooth and fragile as frogskin. "You said 'we' kept that hand in snow. You mean you and your master. Who is he?"

The creature cast his unblinking gaze at Leonardo. I don't know how that bloody slit could have suggested a smile, but it did. Yet he did not even attempt to speak.

I asked, "Do you want a priest?" Of course we were not prepared to find one, but I hoped I would be able to offer this illusory salvation in exchange for a full confession.

A little blood spouted from his lips. "I am . . . a priest."

We have become accustomed to the misbehavior and depravities of country priests—not to mention the Vatican Curia—but this man's vocation startled even me.

"This explains why he was entirely free to roam the countryside on his terrible errands," I told Leonardo. "He enjoyed both the sanction of God and the license of the Devil. The master of the shop chose his apprentice well." The peasants knew that even if they reported this priest's crimes to the authorities, he was subject only to canon law. Though the Church was quick to punish clerics for heresy, priests who stole, raped, and even murdered were too often allowed to go about their business—and retaliate with impunity against any who accused them.

Leonardo shook his head in disgust. "That is the consequence when the Church will acknowledge no evil among its own."

"Maestro." Tommaso had finally prized the carefully nailed top from the little wooden casket. Although the room was already filled with the varied smells of the food and salted flesh, a scent of civet and stale roses suddenly came to my nose.

Tommaso removed the aromatic contents of the box: a jar the size of a wine bottle but of the clearest Venetian glass, the mouth plugged with wax. It was filled entirely with an amber liquid and a great number of what appeared to be tiny shelled clams, each about the size of a thumbnail, mostly of a gray or reddish-gray hue.

Leonardo at once seized the peculiar vessel from his assistant, holding it to the nearest lantern and staring as if he had, in all truth, found the Devil in this jar.

"What is it, Maestro?"

"Paps. Human." Leonardo turned to me. "Women's paps. At least threescore."

I had to put my hands on my knees. In every instance I had observed, both in the olive grove and in Leonardo's basement, the nipple had been sliced from the otherwise intact breast. And knowing what I did of the murderer, this had almost certainly been done before death. "At least threescore," Leonardo had uttered. No less than thirty women had suffered this outrage.

I leaned forward and whispered into the monster's ear. "The boxes. Did you put things in them?"

He coughed blood and shook his head. "I only . . . buried . . . boxes."

This I believed. I looked up at Leonardo and said, "Maestro, regarding those wizened heads. From your observation, as little opportunity as you had, is it possible that all of them were killed at nearly the same time?"

Seeing that I had evidently renewed my faith in *his* science, Leonardo appeared almost grateful. "It is not, on the face of it, false to assume that all those heads were severed from their bodies in proximate time." Still chastened by his error, he offered this somewhat warily. "They all demonstrated a similar buoyancy. But we cannot be certain."

"And how long ago would you presume that time to have been?"

"I would have to speculate." Leonardo looked at me as if the very word "speculate" had soured on his tongue. "The medium of preservation is salt . . . postmortem . . . I would say many months."

"As long as a year or two?"

"We would not err within that duration."

"Were they mostly, if not entirely, women's heads?" This had certainly been my observation, judging from the hair, the size of the skulls, and my perception of the distorted features. But they might also have been adolescent boys.

Leonardo only nodded, a grudging assent.

I had heard enough. "Maestro," I said quickly, "the nipples in that cursed jar match the heads that erupted from the salt mound in such quantity. I further believe that the crimes consecrated by these obscene relics occurred before this creature here became an apprentice in the Devil's workshop. Lastly, it is my conviction that these women were murdered at Capua some eighteen months ago." Hence this much of Ramiro da Lorca's last testament was true—as I had previously assumed. The murderer had been at Capua, perfecting his brutal craft.

I returned to the creature, requiring the answer to but one more question. "Who gave you the boxes to bury in that salt?"

He only rolled his head a little.

I approached the matter less directly. "How many did you help him kill?"

"Five," he nearly sighed, as if they had been his lovers. I was certain he meant only the five most recent victims. "Whores!" He spit the word vehemently, spraying blood. "The Devil's . . . whores. Streghe . . . all . . . of them."

I could not help but recall the insane violence he had visited on poor Camilla. Perhaps the master of the shop had encouraged this madman to believe that the Devil's mistresses deserved to suffer the torments of Hell—while they yet lived.

"So this was God's labor." I choked on the words, but I needed to enter his diseased mind.

Again the demonic smile.

"But I have seen your work when your master is not present. A poor imitation."

Blood spewed from the gill-like stump of his nose. Before he died I wanted to exact a last measure of vengeance for our lovely Camilla, if nothing else.

"The woman you killed at the Palazzo Machirelli was not a witch, no matter what your master told you," I said. "The Lord of Heaven knows that." I could hear the bloody froth hissing on his lips. "But without your master present you could not stop yourself. You slaughtered an innocent. And for that good woman's murder, you are about to enter Hell, to suffer far worse than she did, each hour of every day, for all eternity."

His eyes rolled wildly. Though it was little enough retribution, I was certain he would leave this life fearing the Devil.

"But why should the man who showed you the way to Hell live long and well, while you alone are thrown into the pit? Who was your master?"

His throat gurgled.

"I will help you. Was it Oliverotto da Fermo? Or Vitellozzo Vitelli? Or did the both of them put you to this? These great signori who will only mock your death and raise a cup to your everlasting torment."

The wind shrieked against the door. Dante tells us that a man can speak only the truth in Satan's kingdom; it seemed this fiend had heard his last living inquisitor in one ear, and the cries of the damned in the other. "*Speja*."

I thought he had said *Zeja*. "A witch?"

"*Spia*," he said in Italian, the word sputtering out with his lifeblood. "A spy?"

I put my ear to his mouth. His last words were a hiss little different than his last breath, which at once followed. I could not be certain I had understood.

Leonardo observed me with a feverish expression and I thought he would surely scream "*Dimmi! Dimmi!*" Instead, in a dry, catching voice, as if he had witnessed the death of his own kin, he asked, "What was the name?"

"He did not give me a name," I said. "His last words were, 'He watches.' "

"He watches," Leonardo repeated like a slow-witted child.

At that moment I saw Oliverotto da Fermo's face as he stood on the rampart at Cesena, his head cocked slightly, his pale eyes seeming to reach into Valentino's soul. Watching, I believed, for some sign of weakness.

◆

I determined to haul the body of the Licorn back outside, intending to leave him alone on the icy *pianura*, much as he had discarded the remains of his victims. I did not ask for help but merely instructed Giacomo to remain on the threshold and shout "We are here!" from time to time until I returned.

Motivated by a rage I had not felt while watching the beast die, in little time I succeeded in dragging his corpse several dozen *braccia*. I could still hear Giacomo, although only faintly, when I realized I had been a fool not to search this monstrous apprentice's clothing—which might well reveal something more of his master. I knelt and carefully examined all of it, even his leggings and shoes, yet found only a few ducats in the lining of his wrap. Despite my desperate finances, I did not want this money and left the coins for Charon.

When I stood up again, the cold wind hit me like a brick. As before, a portion of the gray, shifting shroud of snow seemed to assume a solid shape. I wondered for a moment if Giacomo had come for me from the farmhouse.

But this most certainly was not a man. Had I just vanquished one mythical beast, only to find myself in imminent and mortal danger from another?

"There was only one of you," I whispered, though of course the thing could not hear me.

CHAPTER 19

Fortune reigns over a palace open on every side, and no one is denied entrance; but leaving is far less certain.

I could see only the hazy outline of a mounted rider, seemingly possessing the forelegs of a horse—hence my belief that whoever had so skillfully crafted the *licorno* mask had also created an equally convincing centaur. Only when the great warhorse fought the bit, swinging its head from side to side, did the illusion vanish.

I did not even sense the men at my back.

At once they had a hood over my head and powerful hands bound my wrists behind me. I was hoisted into a saddle and in a heartbeat we started off. Having no stirrups, reins, or even free hands to clutch the mane, all my efforts were concentrated simply to remain on the horse.

It is impossible to imagine something such as this: clinging to a galloping horse with only my legs, bound and hooded, entirely blind in a world where little enough could be seen as it was, my heart at the base of my skull, asking myself, *Why did they not kill me?*

◆

I have since passed worse nights, several of them in the Stinche prison, where my hands were similarly bound behind my back, the rope attached to them thrown over a beam from which I was hoisted; as my joints popped and cracked I was instructed that I would remain in that excruciating posture until I condemned innocent men—or, failing to do so, until I was taken out to have my head chopped off. (I left that prison having preserved both my silence and my honor, although my shoulders still ache every winter.)

But this night was hard enough for a young man still frightened of death. The sole source of my courage was the scant hope I had obtained from the creature already crawling in the foul mud of Hell. *Damiata is alive.*

For more than an hour, at least, I gauged by the wind that we were going inland, most likely returning to Cesena. This gave me some opportunity to ponder my circumstances—or at least attempt to net a few of the observations that flew around in my brain like harried swifts and swallows. I could only think that in the same manner that both the Licorn and at least one horseman—if Ramiro was to be believed—had followed Damiata and me into the *pianura*, on this occasion the same parties had stalked Leonardo and me. Beyond that, I could not say if the Licorn and these horsemen had worked in concert. Even less clear was where, and to what end, I was now being transported.

Suddenly we turned, so that the tempest now came from the back quarter. Judging from the unvarying direction of the road, we were on the Via Emilia heading away from Cesena, flying south like Boreas.

We continued on this route for what must have been several hours, although in my misery it seemed like days. Then, just after we had changed horses in the manner of couriers, I began to hear the percussion of the sea through the wind. I reasoned that we had likely come as far as Rimini, where the Via Emilia runs along the coast. And indeed the scent of salt again mingled with the blowing snow.

After another interminable passage, at last the sky began to lighten—or I should say, the world inside my hood brightened somewhat. Able to roughly estimate the time, I presumed that at our pace we had gone past the town of Pesaro, which marked the southernmost limits of Valentino's dominion. The territory south of Pesaro was occupied by the *condottieri* and their troops.

Hence I hardly required a *mappa*, or even eyes, to assume with reasonable certainty that at the end of this road I would find one man of a rare and terrifying nature, who had confounded us all with his cruel games and monstrous deception.

♦

Perhaps an hour after I first perceived the breaking dawn, again we turned from the coast. Although we began to go up and down hills, our direction did not vary much, which led me to believe that we were now on the Via Flaminia, heading away from the town of Fano, the coastal terminus of yet another ancient Roman road.

Finally I heard shouts up ahead. We turned and rode up a very steep paved street, which I took to mean that we had entered a town. When we stopped, I was dragged from the horse and could not stand securely, so that I fell down, occasioning much laughter, which I did not mind so much as the kicks in the ribs. I was pulled to my feet, taking slaps as I was forced up a long stairway, this followed by a procession through what might have been several galleries or hallways; the place reeked of gunpowder. I began to tremble, although I was warmer than I had been in a day.

The room where we stopped smelled of wine and damp, like a vintner's basement. But stronger still were the perfumes, of such rare quality that I knew at once I was in the company of some of Italy's great signori. My scent also made an impression, because someone said, "He smells like a fish."

I was forced into a chair and my hood pulled off. Light and shadow flickered around me in amber and brown waves, as if I were submerged in a muddy river. This unsteady illumination was provided by the flames in a brick fireplace large enough to shelter a watchman's hut; I could feel the heat on my face. Above my head ran immense, ancient oak beams. I was seated at a modest round table some distance from the hearth, in company with three men and a woman, their *primero* cards and silver cups strewn across the felt cloth.

The foremost man among them was Vitellozzo Vitelli, sitting like an enthroned cardinal in a great chair ornamented with silk tassels and brass studs. Nevertheless he wore only a satin vest over his linen shirt, revealing a chest like a keg and arms as thick as tree stumps. I had not seen him in three years, since he had been employed by our government to assist his brother, Paolo, in the campaign against the Pisa rebels. At that time he was regarded as a man of proverbial strength, this having been manifest in a neck wider than his head and the jawbone of a horse, if not an ass. In his present incarnation, however, Vitellozzo's powerful face was bloated and the ridge of bone at his brow gave him the appearance of an ape, his close-cropped hair crowning all this lumpy flesh like a boy's cap. His eyelids were so fat and drowsy that he appeared to gaze at me from a near-slumber.

Seated on the right hand of Vitellozzo, as attentive as his *garzone*, was Signor Paolo Orsini. As Damiata has observed, neither did this squat satyr with blubbering lips and sagging eyes wear the last few years well. The third man was separated from Signor Paolo by a woman who was certainly a *cortigiana onesta* and almost as certainly Venetian; as blond and gorgeous as one of Botticelli's Graces, I could only wish I knew her. But the man to her right was immediately familiar to me.

Oliverotto da Fermo was attired as if he had just put his troops through drills, a velvet riding cape draped over his freshly lacquered mail shirt. His eyes roamed in their casual yet watchful manner, as if searching for some small thing that would betray each one of us.

Only then did I observe that my arrival had interrupted a *primero* hand. Vitellozzo lifted the corner of a card and peeked beneath it. "*Fottimi*. Face card," he said, grunting like a Romagnole. "I can hope for a *coro* or throw in now." He sighed theatrically. "Do you know what the Florentines have done?" He addressed this question to the table, his voice now as resounding as an actor's. "Such is their native cowardice that instead of dispatching Duke Valentino an ambassador, they have sent this little secretary. Better this flea die for their sins rather than some splendid merchant with a villa in Mugello—one of those asshole-burgling cowards who lost Pisa and were so desperate to cast blame elsewhere that they murdered my brother rather than confess to their own incompetence. Every *cacasangue*-eating coward in Florence, none of them with the spine to lift anything more than a table knife in defense of their so-called republic, came out to cheer in triumph when my brother was martyred. Were you there that night, Messer Macchia?"

He had abbreviated my name in the way my friends once did with affection—and as my enemies often do these days. *Macchia*. A blemish or a stain that goes deeper than the skin. Vitellozzo Vitelli had erred if he hoped to make a coward of me, because I would rather take the Heavenly Father's name in vain than let pass an insult to my dear father's name.

"We lost Pisa because your brother betrayed us," I answered. "We lost Pisa because your brother waited two days for the breach in the wall to be sealed before he withdrew his troops entirely, protesting that he could not attack an intact defense. We lost Pisa because of your brother's cowardice or outright treachery, whichever you prefer." For a heartbeat, again I saw Paolo Vitelli's head, all white and shadow, lit by the single torch in a dark piazza, black blood dripping from the neck. "And I shouted my own praise to a just God when the executioner raised your brother's head."

I was prepared to die for those words, in some boyish *fantasia* believing that my republic would celebrate my courage. But Vitellozzo did not even rise from his cardinal's throne. "Perhaps we will let you live, Messer Macchia, to see the entry of the Vitelli into Florence—and into your women." He blinked so drowsily that it seemed he intended to sleep. "Or perhaps not." He lifted another corner. "*Fottimi.* Another face card."

◆

After Vitellozzo had lamented his late brother—and his cards— Oliverotto won the stakes with merely a *numero quaranta*. But before the deal could pass to the left, Vitellozzo produced a parcel from his lap. He placed it in the middle of the table, as if establishing the stakes for the new hand. At once, I recognized this slight volume, bound in greasy, soiled cowhide. And I was hardly surprised to see it there.

"It is not much, is it? But I wonder if any of you can afford to play for it." Vitellozzo nodded at Paolo Orsini. "You, Paolo, perhaps. We Vitelli having secured your family's wealth against those who would snatch it away." Certainly he meant the pope.

The preening Orsini warlord could not keep Vitellozzo's gaze, as though the guardian of his family's wealth frightened him more than the prospect of its loss.

"And you, 'Liverotto, would have to kill some more of your uncles. Or sell your hair to a wigmaker." Vitellozzo's sausage fingers mimed a caress of luxuriant imaginary tresses. He lifted a heavy eyebrow and smiled tightly at the man he had schooled since he was a boy—the expression of a harsh father accustomed to mocking his son.

" 'Liverotto" acknowledged this expression with one even less genial, although it was little more than a slight adjustment of his head.

Vitellozzo began to turn the leaves of the geometry text, his eyes now awake, rapidly roaming the pages. "You might ask, 'Why is this eminent artillerist, this maestro of warcraft, so interested in some schoolboy's Euclid?' " He pushed the book, still open, across the table to me. "Perhaps you can tell me, Messer Macchia."

I turned the *Elements* so that I could examine the pages, requiring considerable will not to tremble. The scraped-over parchment had been reused at least once and the Latin text was hurried and careless, the ink fading. The annotation in the broad margin was worse, a childish, scarcely readable scrawl, the ink a cheap oak-gall brown: *Gevol int la carafa.* The Devil in a jar. This was followed by an accounting of the *streghe* present: *Zeja* Virginia. *Zeja* Maddalena. *Zeja* Francesca. And finally *Zeja* Caterina, the white-eyed seeress who had conducted the divination Damiata and I had witnessed—and who was almost certainly the untutored author of this marginalia.

Beneath the list of doomed *streghe* was another brief litany, the script much more elegant than the witch's scrawl, although here each name had been written in a distinct hand: Vitellozzo Vitelli. Paolo Orsini. Oliverotto da Fermo.

The catalog of participants was followed by a familiar invocation: *Angelo bianc, per vostr santite e mia purite.* And beneath this diabolical prayer, *Zeja* Caterina had recorded, in a mongrel of Romagnolo and Italian, a question only the Devil could answer: *Gevol int la carafa,* tell us who here dies before the new year.

I fingered the top of the page, intent on turning to the answer. All at once Vitellozzo shot his great, swollen paw across the table and struck down my frostbitten hand.

"Don't be impatient, Messer Macchia. We will share it with you in a moment. My 'Liverotto tells me that you are familiar with this form of divination. You and the whore the pope sent."

I could only presume that Oliverotto had, as I suspected, followed us to the hut that night—and was in fact the horseman who had pursued the fleeing mastiff keeper and relieved him of this book. "Then certainly Signor Oliverotto also told you that our *Gevol int la carafa* was interrupted."

"Tell us about it anyway. Otherwise we will presume you are a worthless, chittering monkey, whom we have gone to great effort to bring to our table, only to watch you toss your *cacca* on everything. And you should hear how a little monkey howls when you pull its arms off."

I took this as an entirely credible threat. "The *zeja* represents this *Elements* as a 'book of spells' and enlists some young children, virgins, to implore Lucifer to appear in her jar of water," I told him with a dry tongue. "At which point I imagine the demon presents the *zeja* the answers to our questions. But as I said, my divination was interrupted."

Vitellozzo's shoulders heaved with wincing mirth, as if to actually laugh would cause him unbearable suffering. "Turn the page now, Messer Macchia."

The broad margin of the next page had been filled with simple geometric figures drawn with a straightedge and sepia ink, evidently by a student. But at the bottom *Zeja* Caterina had written, in Romagnolo, a curt answer to the question of who among them would perish before the coming New Year: *Tot mort*. All die.

"The white-eyed bitch was only half a fraud," Vitellozzo said. "She and the rest of her *strega* whores have fulfilled their part of the prophecy. Now turn the page."

This margin had been almost entirely covered with annotations. At the top was the familiar list of participants, a litany of the dead *streghe* and the three *condottieri* present at this table. But these names were followed by the words *traget di capra*. *Capra*, goat, was clear enough. *Traget* briefly confounded me. Was it the Tuscan *tragitto*, journey?

Goat ride.

What followed was more confusing. Scrawled over this margin and that of the following page, even written over the Latin text in places, was a hodgepodge of names and nonsensical words and phrases, most in the rough hand of the *zeja* but some in pure yet undisciplined Tuscan Italian. Misspelled names of those present—*Ursin, Vitel,*

Ferm—and those evidently not—*il papa, Duca Valentin*. Places real and imagined: *Roma, Paradisio, Inferno*. Things sublime and profane: *tesoro di mi cuor, milli diamanti, potta, fotta*. My eyes could do little more than race over this marginalia before Vitellozzo's hand shot out again and snatched away the *Elements* entirely. Just as he did so, I thought I saw *Ganda*—which I took as a misspelled reference to the late Duke of Gandia.

"You know what we were doing, Messer Macchia-Monkey. Tell me."

"The *streghe* employ an ointment into which they grind hellebore, henbane, and belladonna, before smearing it entirely over their naked bodies—this recipe induces a state known as the 'goat ride,' wherein the witches and wizards imagine themselves transported to distant places. As I am certain you gentlemen demonstrated to your own satisfaction, ordinarily this goat ride is a suitable prelude to the *gioce di Diana*. Witch games, which more resemble a bacchanal. An orgy."

"That is true, monkey. My 'Liverotto had his *strega* whore babbling before he had even finished greasing her snatch. After that . . . you cannot believe what he got up there. But go on. You know there is more."

"This concoction also induces a paralytic state," I said. "The limbs are frozen, so much so that they might be hacked from the body, yet one is unable to scream." I forced myself to look into Vitellozzo's slitted eyes, wondering if he had witnessed this. "Even as one remains entirely sensible of pain."

Vitellozzo lifted his bloated hand and rolled it limply, in a "go on" gesture.

"As the limbs regain movement," I said, "the narcotics encourage one to converse. Quite liberally, with persons who need not be present."

Here Vitellozzo feigned a little clap. "I adore clever pets. Don't you, Paolo? I found this part of the journey by goat to be most interesting. But our darling 'Liverotto was not at all pleased to see his dearest uncle Giovanni again."

Cold fingers traced up my back. I had the sense that Vitellozzo himself had simply observed, while his associates took the goat ride. The faceless apprentice's last words—"He watches"—took on a new inflection.

Sparks might have flashed inside Vitellozzo's animal slits. He had recognized my fear. "But you know you have not reached the end, don't you, *Macchia*-Monkey. Finish your recitation."

"I can only judge from what you have permitted me to see. But I presume that when their limbs were unfrozen, the *zeja* and these gentlemen were able to record their musings. It is possible they even confessed to certain sins. Or conversed about an object removed from a corpse." Of course, I meant the amulet I presumed someone at that table had plucked from the Duke of Gandia's bleeding throat, five years later slipping it into the charm bag of a *strega* he had so carefully cut into pieces.

Again Vitellozzo's great bulk shuddered, the pained smile fleeing quickly from his bloated face. "So you think you see what I have here, don't you, Messer Macchia?"

I nodded warily, wondering if I had already stepped into his snare.

"Then you are not such a clever little Florentine monkey." Vitellozzo snapped his bloated fingers at Oliverotto, miraculously making a sharp pop, as if he were summoning a serving boy.

As though long accustomed to such servitude, Oliverotto at once got up and went out the black oak door. Quickly he reappeared in company with two soldiers, both in mail shirts like his. Only when Oliverotto declined his own seat and started toward me did I observe the noose he had obtained.

Vitellozzo waited until Oliverotto stood directly behind me. After glancing up at his ward, he began to turn through dozens of pages of the geometry text; I could see that most of the margins were marked up in a witch's scrawl. Evidently finding something of interest to both of us, Vitellozzo stopped and pushed the book back to me.

In this margin was the record of a *Gevol int la carafa* almost identical to the preceding, with the same list of four *streghe* as before. But only one petitioner had signed, offering not his name but his title, in Latin: *Dux Romandiole Valentieque*. Hence I could be entirely certain that Damiata had not lied about Valentino's presence in the book. Beneath the latter's formal signature, *Zeja* Caterina had recorded a new question: *Gevol int la carafa*, tell us who kill Duca Ganda.

"We discovered this *Zeja* Caterina and her *gioca* of whores and witches when we were in Imola almost two years ago," Vitellozzo said. "At that time, our Duke Valentino was only beginning his conquest of the Romagna. He was most intrigued when I told him about our entertainment, but I don't think he amused himself in similar fashion until the end of this summer, after these gentlemen and I had already determined to leave his employ. Well, you can see the question on his mind."

Reaching his hand out as carefully as on the previous occasion he had been impulsive, Vitellozzo again took the *Elements* back. "This will make it more interesting for you, if you can't peek. How do you think this 'Devil in a jar' answered the duke's question?"

I presumed the answer was on the next page. "I would imagine that the *zeja* gave Valentino the answer he expected to hear."

"And what do you think the duke expected to hear?"

It seemed Vitellozzo had simply cast out this net to see if he could discover whom I suspected, given my considerable inquiry into the matter. "The Duke of Gandia had acquired a number of enemies at the time he was murdered. Names familiar throughout Italy. The *zeja* might have told Valentino any one of them. Or even all of them."

" 'Names familiar throughout Italy.' You diplomats have cunts where your mouths should be."

I was jerked to my feet, just as the hood went back over my head. In my renewed blindness, I waited for Oliverotto's noose around my neck. Instead the rope went around my hands, binding them behind my back. As I was rushed to the door, stumbling over my own feet, Vitellozzo called after me.

"Messer Macchia! You should know a thing before we hang you." He waited until his thugs had briefly halted my journey to the nearest window. "Your friend, the great whore of the Vatican, has already come to see me."

CHAPTER 20

When evil comes, you must take it down like medicine, for he is crazy who keeps it on his tongue, and savors its taste.

Still bound and hooded, I was dragged down some stairs, heard a lock clank, and was thrown onto a stone floor. The door rattled behind me. I quickly discovered that this cell could be measured by my head at one end and my feet at the other. It stank like a rotting carcass.

These discomforts were nothing next to the horrors in my mind. I did not believe that Damiata had "come to see" Vitellozzo Vitelli any more than I had; if she had journeyed here of her own volition, she would not have left her room in Cesena without a word to me. Hence I shared that cell with images far worse than any punishment of Hell, condemned to helplessly envision the things that had already been done to the woman I loved.

♦

I know now that I spent only one night in confinement. But when the door clanked open, I had no notion how long I had been there. Still hooded and bound, I was wrestled to my feet and shoved along until I found myself again seated on a horse.

We went up and down hills for some time before I was pulled from the saddle, on this occasion staying on my feet. My hood was whipped off and the light from all the snow burst upon me like a vast explosion of gunpowder. I stood in a small field surrounded by a dozen irregular plots similarly strewn across the hills, all of them pushed together as if they had collided by chance; this was more like our Tuscan countryside than the flat orderliness of the Romagnole *pianura*. In the distance were higher, barren slopes, sheathed in ice and shrouded in clouds.

Amid this melancholy landscape sat Vitellozzo Vitelli, upon the same tasseled cardinal's throne he had occupied at the *primero* table. Strangely, in this considerably brighter light his features appeared less bloated and malformed.

Attending him was Oliverotto da Fermo, attired in the same chain mail and cape as the previous day. The two *condottieri*—Signor Paolo had for some reason not joined them—were accompanied by six or seven soldiers in padded jerkins, most armed with crossbows, although two of them were *scoppiettieri*, the butts of their guns planted in the snow. In the field beyond these men, a dozen grooms tended an equal number of warhorses and mules. I knew there were soldiers at my back as well.

Here I must confess that I have exercised a bit of the fabulist's art in describing this scene, because only after I had been there for a time did I begin to make the preceding observations. In truth, almost as soon as the hood was snatched from my head, I nearly fell to my knees in gratitude and relief.

♦

Damiata stood beside Vitellozzo's throne, the snow a white curtain behind her, her unflawed features framed by her sable hood.

I did not expect her eyes to seek mine; in truth I was grateful that she did not risk even a glance. Yet I could not keep myself from staring at her face, lovely as a bust of Aphrodite—and less animated than cold marble with life or feeling. She did not, however, appear to have suffered the horrors I had imagined.

"We must finish our business quickly," Vitellozzo said, wrenching my attention from Damiata. "Duke Valentino is going to join our forces for the final assault on the fortress at Sinigaglia." One of the most important fortified cities on the Adriatic coast, Sinigaglia had yet to submit to the pope. "When we have Sinigaglia, the Romagna will be entirely secure and our combined armies can move north." Vitellozzo raised his hand to his forehead as if he had sighted this signal victory on the horizon just behind me. "Before the first of January, the duke and I will prepare our plan for the conquest of Florence."

As many times as I had conjured this grim prophecy in my own mind, to hear the words "conquest of Florence" from the man most capable—and most desirous—of effecting it was a kick in the testicles; only by some great exercise of will was I able to keep from doubling over.

No sooner had Vitellozzo announced the fate of my republic, than Oliverotto da Fermo pointed at the men behind me. A moment later I heard the crackle of a burning fuse, followed by the sharp thunder of a *scoppietto*, twice in rapid sequence.

But I did not feel my flesh rip and my bones shatter. Hardly believing that the marksmen could have missed me at this range, I dared to turn.

The two *scoppiettieri* were surrounded by a cloud of smoke. Beyond them, at a distance of about a hundred *braccia*, a man wearing only a peasant's sand-colored work tunic had been tied to a tall stake. The round wooden gag stuffed into his mouth gave him a dreadful, gaping, fish-out-of-water aspect, as he writhed and tossed his head, trying desperately to escape his bonds.

I quickly turned from this ugly game.

"The problem with the *scoppietto* is the man, not the mathematics," Vitellozzo said, pouncing on my terror-filled eyes. "With a fixed artillery piece, assuming the foundry is reliable and the powder likewise consistent, I have only to calculate the mathematics. The wind, also, but that is predictable in most conditions. But the *scoppiettiero* moves to his own momentary tics and whims. He allows his arm to drop slightly with one shot, then stray to the right with the other. The force the weapon exerts on him as the ball is expelled will also cause considerable variation. But that is the usefulness of this weapon, is it not, my sweet 'Liverotto?" He glanced at his pupil, more reprovingly than with expectation of an answer. "Will the gunman's whim provide the correct mathematics? Only Fortune knows." He nodded past me. "The target cannot know. Each errant shot only heightens his terror."

Vitellozzo went on to other business. "This whore the pope sent to find his son's murderer." He inclined his head slightly toward Damiata. "You are familiar with her."

"I know the lady."

"The whore," Vitellozzo corrected me. "At least she has convinced us she is a whore, even if she has not convinced you." Oliverotto smiled slightly, as if at last his mentor had amused him. "She claims the pope trusts her. Should I?"

I presumed that Damiata had used her connection with the pope in a desperate attempt to save herself and her son. "She has the pope's trust," I said, believing the truth could only help her. "Her son is his hostage."

Vitellozzo received this intelligence with no expression whatever. Perhaps he already knew it.

Behind me the fuses spit and the *scoppietti* again issued their dreadful percussion. The two shots were far enough apart that I could hear the brief, moaning flight of each ball. And the impact of the second, like an ox stepping on a melon.

Vitellozzo squinted past me. "Now, that is a turn of Fortune. But let us go on to another matter."

Here Vitellozzo reached into his riding cloak and extracted the *Elements* we had examined at his *primero* table. "We must finish yesterday's tale, mustn't we?" He leafed quickly through the pages. "I believe we left off with Duke Valentino expecting the Devil to appear in a jar of water and tell him the name of his brother's murderer."

Vitellozzo nodded to Oliverotto, the latter drawing from his belt the same ivory-handled dagger with which he had hoped to gut Ramiro da Lorca. Oliverotto lunged at me theatrically, as if he were an actor miming that very attack. Seemingly satisfied with my instinctive cringe, he slipped his arm around my back and sliced the rope binding my hands, so quickly that he nicked my wrist.

"Careful where you are bleeding," Vitellozzo said, offering the *Elements* to me.

I wiped the blood on my jacket and accepted the book. Vitellozzo had opened it to the preceding day's question: *Gevol int la carafa*, tell us who kill Duca Ganda.

Vitellozzo whispered, "Turn the page and you will find the answer."

My hands trembled, even though the seeress's answer could scarcely be considered credible. The parchment crackled, almost as if my fingers had set it on fire.

Zeja Caterina had misspelled the names, but they were clear enough: *Sgnor Vitel. Sgnor Ferm.* And the last: *Madona Damata.*

I met Vitellozzo's eyes and told him the truth as I saw it. "The duke got the answer he expected. As you said, *Zeja* Caterina was a shrewd fraud." It occurred to me that the seeress had perhaps heard Damiata's name, and her alleged crimes, babbled by one of the *condottieri* during their goat ride—or had "divined" it from others at Valentino's court. Yet I observed to myself: *Even a fraud can tell the truth once.* Or perhaps in this case, two truths and one lie.

Vitellozzo winced as his shoulders heaved. "Turn the page."

The only words in the margin of the next page had also been written in the witch's scrawl: *Traget di capra. Zeja Caterina. Duca Valentin.*

"Just the two of them," Vitellozzo said. "On a goat ride together. I imagine that while they were greasing themselves our gallant Valentino showed his *strega* some things even the Devil—or even our dear 'Liverotto—hadn't. But I see you've noticed the odd thing there."

The page that should have followed was missing. I could clearly see the line running along the stub of the parchment where it had been scored by a knife—recently, it seemed, because the cut edge was not soiled like the rest of the book.

"Someone has cut out a page of this book, isn't that so, Messer Monkey-Macchia? I imagine, as I am sure you do, that it was removed because Valentino said something of great import while he was taking his journey on the back of a goat—or on the backside of a *strega*." Vitellozzo offered me his dolorous smile. "So my clever little Florentine pet, what do you think the duke discussed with his *strega* whore—or perhaps chattered to some party not present—while in this narcotic transport?"

I looked at Oliverotto. His eyes, nearly the same hue as the bluish-gray light, appeared to hover before me. Only then did it occur to me that perhaps Valentino was protecting Oliverotto because the two of them had formed some conspiracy against Vitellozzo Vitelli—much as Oliverotto had already betrayed his uncle.

But I answered Vitellozzo with a more likely possibility. "I believe the duke confessed to crimes at Capua."

"We were all at Capua," Vitellozzo said flatly. Valentino had used these same words.

"Then you understand the remorse he might feel." I could not escape imparting a certain irony to my words.

Vitellozzo merely heaved a bit, with what sentiment I could not say, but it seemed he regarded me as a fool. "I have a final question for you," he said, the word "final" freezing me at once. "Who do *you* think murdered the Duke of Gandia?"

I might never have another chance to reveal the truth. "He is the same man who cut a Romagnole *strega* into four pieces and scattered her to the corners of the winds, then proceeded to construct an Archimedes spiral with the flesh of her entire *gioca*, an endeavor in which he was assisted by a faceless priest." I searched in vain for something within eyes open no wider than the edge of a coin. "At Cesenatico, he created a salt tomb for the heads of the *streghe* and a reliquary for the skulls and other mementos of the women he raped and butchered at Capua." I still waited for some sign. "Signore, the man who murdered the Duke of Gandia is a rare and most exceptional individual. Only when he takes life, can he live. He must kill in the same fashion that the rest of us breathe."

Vitellozzo blinked at me like a lizard on a fence, his nostrils steaming the air. After a moment he lifted his swollen hand, then let it fall heavily into his lap.

Several of Vitellozzo's liveried attendants swarmed his chair, quickly turning it about and transporting it like a litter toward the waiting horses. The rest of Vitellozzo's company followed with similar haste.

Before she joined this parade, Damiata at last met my eyes. The poets write of a single glance that haunts a lifetime, casting a spell of desire and regret that can never be broken. But this liquid blue glance, so nakedly pained and remorseful, answered every question of a lifetime. I believed in my reborn soul that Damiata still loved me, even as she had to abandon me.

Then she, too, turned away.

◆

Vitellozzo's party quickly vanished over the nearest hill; by the time Damiata slipped from sight, sitting sidesaddle on a white mare, draped in her red cape, she might have been a duchess in a miniature painting. And then I could hear only the wind sifting the snow.

I took stock of my situation. I had taken no sustenance for almost two days; nevertheless, I was adequately clothed. It seemed that once again I had been deliberately spared; perhaps my recitation of a murderer's history had convinced Vitellozzo Vitelli that I was a keen-eyed and useful witness, if nothing more—much as I was regarded as nothing more than a reliable observer by my own government.

But I was wrong. As I continued to stare out toward the hill that now obstructed my view of Vitellozzo's party, a rider on a white warhorse silently emerged atop it. For a heartbeat, he perched at the summit. And then he galloped toward me, snow rising up from the rapid hoofbeats in large puffs, like the smoke from dozens of *scoppietti*, all firing in sequence.

I wondered if Oliverotto da Fermo intended simply to trample me. Instead he powerfully reined the stallion to an abrupt, rearing stop, its forelegs flailing, then leapt from the saddle and quickly covered the several steps between us, his mail shirt chinging.

He did not, however, lunge at me with his knife—either comically or tragically. Instead Signor Oliverotto planted his feet and combed his blond curls with his fingers, almost as if I were a manservant holding his looking glass. When he did focus his pale blue eyes on me, he tilted his head only slightly, as though he did not require some particularly altered perspective in order to find my weakness. "You spoke with Ramiro da Lorca that night, didn't you? Regarding me."

Certainly he meant those moments before Ramiro's arrest. I nodded.

"What did he tell you?"

As before, I believed that only the truth might save me. "He said that Valentino was protecting you. And he asked me to consider why."

"Do you know?"

"I suspect because you were both at Capua, Signore. And you observed something there that His Excellency would not want the rest of Italy to witness."

He tilted his head more severely. "I learned something even before I could shave." Oliverotto seemed to be citing the phrase Valentino had used on the rampart, even as common as it was, so that I would recall that conversation. "Papa Vitellozzo showed me."

He raised up his immense hands and held them open before me, all his digits spread wide, as if he believed the stigmata had appeared on his palms. Instead he quickly flipped his hands down and made a collar of sorts around my neck, though without touching me. Every muscle in my body clenched, preparing for death.

"If you strangle a woman while you are fucking her, it heightens her ecstasy. She comes at the threshold of death and returns to you, deeply grateful. Almost always she will want it again. But if you do not stop in time . . ." Oliverotto shrugged his massive shoulders. "I can tell you, by Jesus, there is a strange thing about that, as well. She doesn't know fear until the last flicker of her life is about to go out. And that is a marvelous thing to see. At that moment, I don't believe any man could keep from spewing his seed."

Oliverotto lowered his hands and looked down at his sheathed dagger. "Now this," he mused. "If you quickly gut a man with this, at once you can see his astonishment. But then he lingers. He must say farewell to the faces in his mind." He shook his head, as if this stubborn persistence of life had presented him some difficult philosophical conundrum. "I think it is better to observe a man as he watches his wife or child die. Or his lover. Everything leaves him then, except the fear and grief an infant knows when it first enters the world. When that man's anger is spent, he only wants to crawl back into the womb. You will see for yourself. When we come to Florence. Or perhaps even if you are able to get to Sinigaglia quickly enough."

The scar-like creases that framed Oliverotto's mouth twitched more visibly than his lips, as he enjoyed the futility he saw in my eyes. My distress, however, was a trifle he did not intend to savor. He turned and started back to his horse.

"Is that why you spared me?" I called out, voice and limbs quaking. "So that I can witness another Capua?"

Oliverotto tugged at his saddle. His horse issued a long snort. After a moment he looked back at me.

I summoned all my will and took a step toward him. "I have a question to ask of you, if I might, Signore." I knew I was risking even this reprieve. "It is the question the duke asked you that last time you saw him. At Cesena." The question regarding the expression on his uncle's face when he knew Oliverotto had betrayed him. "Have you had opportunity to consider your answer?"

He gave me a smile a woman would have regarded as charming. "My dear uncle Giovan just looked at me," he said blithely, as if this were supper-table patter. "No fear, no anger. *Niente.* He was not even surprised. He had known that day would come, almost since the day I came into his house. Since I was six years old."

My hair danced, given my previous deduction that this rare man would manifest his nature at a very young age. Carefully I asked, "Why do you suppose he knew this, even when you were a boy?"

"Because I was six years old when my uncle sold me into slavery." Unlike the previous, this smile, though nearly as subtle, was intended for an enemy. "That was when my uncle sent me off to the Vitelli brothers. Three of them. Paolo, Camillo, and Vitellozzo. They began my instruction in this empty old house in Città di Castello. The first morning they brought me a little dog as my companion. That evening they made me kill it. With my hands. The next day the Vitelli brought me another dog. That evening..." He shrugged slightly. "And the third day the same. On the fourth day I strangled the little dog as soon as they put it in my arms. That was when I was deemed ready to begin my lessons as a soldier."

This answer startled me as much as anything Signor Oliverotto had said. Leaving me to reflect on it, he swung himself back up on his horse, his cape flying and chain mail ringing. The stallion snorted out a cloud and Oliverotto leaned across the beast's neck, his face emerging from the steam like some sharp-featured demon spawned in Hell.

"It should also interest you to know that I saw the expression on the Duke of Gandia's face when he recognized his killer." He reined his horse to near-perfect stillness. "I was there that night. But I was not the murderer."

Here Oliverotto wheeled the stallion so violently that its rump knocked me into the snow. When I was able to look up again, I saw him at some improbable distance amid the seemingly vaporous landscape, as though his horse had flown him into the sky.

CHAPTER 21

He who deceives always finds those who let themselves be deceived.

I considered following Oliverotto's tracks, and those of Vitellozzo's party, all the way to Sinigaglia. But thinking better of it, I turned in the opposite direction. At once I was presented a vision far less elegant than the splendid party that had abandoned me: the victim of the recent *scoppietto* demonstration remained tied to the stake. The fourth ball had carved away half his jaw.

I freed his bloody corpse and laid him in the snow, prayed briefly for God's mercy on his soul, then took off at a quick pace. Soon enough I encountered some farmers and determined that Pesaro was the nearest city on the Via Emilia—and also where I thought I might find Valentino's army, if the duke was bound for Sinigaglia and his appointment with the *condottieri*.

For much of the journey to Pesaro, I traveled across the snowy fields or along the mule paths and irrigation ditches, having observed too many companies of mercenaries on the roads; the allegiances and discipline of these soldiers were always suspect, regardless of who employed them. As I kept moving throughout most of a bitter night, I saw their campfires winking like the zodiac all across the countryside. I assumed the *condottieri* had cleverly divided their forces into many smaller units, so that their true numbers would not be apparent until they reached Sinigaglia. And I wondered if Valentino was walking into a more deadly snare than I had supposed.

◆

I reached Pesaro at daybreak on 30 December, although I had to inquire at a tailor's *bottega* to be sure of the date; I was also told that Valentino and his army had stayed in and around Pesaro the previous night and had left early that morning, bound for Fano. Here Fortune favored me once again, because I went to the *stufa*, both for news and to bathe and wash my clothes, and there I ran into a courier who was known to be reliable. For several of my few remaining ducats, he agreed to ride to Cesena, retrieve my writing things and papers, along with a few items of clothing, and return as quickly as possible.

I found a cot in a tiny room next to the *stufa* and was so weary that I slept at once, although feverishly. I dreamed I was back in our house on the Via di Piazza, where we had a workroom on the first floor, this opening onto the street on one side, the courtyard we shared with several other families on the other. At the end of the summer the flax was delivered from the fields, already braked and combed, so that it resembled great hanks of grayish-brown hair, as if some giantess had been shorn—or so it seemed to five-year-old Niccolò. Mama always brought in several women to spin these flax fibers into thread, although often she spun as well, as did my two sisters, who were years older than I. On this day a half-dozen distaffs stood in the workroom, reminding me of the scarecrows I saw in the country, because each was just a stick on a tripod, with a bundle of the hair-fine flax stuck at the top, about the size and shape of a woman's head. With the peculiar self-awareness one sometimes has in dreams, I knew that these flax bundles were intended to represent the heads I would see many years later at Cesenatico, so that it seemed little Niccolò was receiving some dreadful prophetic vision.

Yet I also observed that someone was standing on the threshold that led out onto the street. The flax workroom was flooded with light, but it seemed as dark as a moonless night outside, so that our visitor was nothing but a shadow, as faceless as the creature whose death I had so recently attended. And I knew at once that this visitor was the master of another sort of workshop, where living flesh was rendered into a perverse *disegno*.

His voice slithered like a serpent across the floor. Every hair on my body stood up and I felt myself drawn into the air, entirely off my feet. *You are almost here, Niccolò. In the center of my Labyrinth. But you will not see my face until I turn away.*

I awakened covered with sweat as if I were at the bath, my forehead nevertheless like ice, the words this maestro of Death's workshop had whispered into my dream still echoing in my head. As much as my intellect told me this could only have been the voice of either Vitellozzo Vitelli or Oliverotto da Fermo, some baffling intuition stood between me and the certainty that either was a monster in the guise of a man. Vitellozzo remained a cipher, even face-to-face. And as closely as Oliverotto's dreadful words matched the murderer's deeds, a nagging voice of my own told me that Oliverotto was not a rare man; his casual brutality and naked ambition had become all too common among the *condottieri*. He had been bred to violence and murder, not born to it. And I believed that some vestige of his tormented soul regretted the evil tutelage that had begun when he was forced to strangle a little dog.

In truth, I could only see that whatever the differences between Vitellozzo and Oliverotto—those of a stern, cruel father and his rebellious son—they were both conspiring to cast suspicion on Valentino himself. Of course, they were too clever to baldly accuse the duke of his brother's murder; instead I had been led to the missing page of Euclid's *Elements*, which Vitellozzo might well have removed himself, in order to fraudulently represent it as some sort of confession Valentino had made during his goat ride. And with equal subtlety, Oliverotto had implied that he had witnessed the Duke of Gandia's murder yet had not wielded the knife, which certainly left Valentino suspect, given that the duke already appeared to be protecting some secret he and Oliverotto shared.

Hence it occurred to me that this was the witness for which I had been summoned: to cast doubt on Valentino, so that the guilty could continue to elude justice. And in this they had to some extent succeeded, because those doubts had a hard kernel of credence that would not go away, like a seed in one's shoe.

✦

It had been dark for several hours when a knock came at my door, whereupon my courier entered like the deus ex machina in a Greek drama. All of the clothing and papers he brought in a single leather sack were items I had left behind in Cesena, save one large packet, wrapped in fish paper, that had just been delivered from Florence.

Almost since I had arrived in Imola three months previously, I had been begging my correspondents in Florence to send me a copy of Plutarch's *Parallel Lives*. No work of the ancients—much less us moderns—so carefully illuminates the character and natures of various eminent men, and I had been desperate for some insight into the unfathomable Valentino. But I had long abandoned all hope that it would ever arrive.

So to unwrap that packet and find the *Parallel Lives*, after all the misfortune I had experienced, was little less than a miracle to me. My edition had been printed in the shop of Bartolomeo de Zanis in Venice; the work was not bound, although it had been thumbed through a good bit, with some writing in the margins. I took a moment to savor the woodcut printed on the first page, which portrayed Theseus killing the centaur at the wedding of Pirithou and Hippodamia; I regarded this as an ironic emblem for several of the matters that so consumed my thoughts.

Then I went next door and bought a number of candles from the proprietor of the bathhouse. I intended to study the *Parallel Lives* throughout the night, if necessary, knowing I might well be in Sinigaglia before the next day ended, and in sore need of whatever wisdom I might acquire beforehand.

◆

Although Plutarch's method of comparison differs greatly from Suetonius's biographies, he, too, enabled me to distinguish the many tyrants whose cruelties were expedient from those few who took delight in the death and suffering they inflicted. In fact Plutarch draws this contrast directly in his parallel studies of Marcus Antonius, an example of the former, and Demetrius, whom Plutarch found remarkable in that even his sensual pleasures were pursued with such violence and viciousness.

Thus both Suetonius and Plutarch supported my theory that these rare men had a peculiar and unchanging nature, an affliction with which they were born. Yet having established this first principle, I became all the more perplexed as to how these monsters had survived to achieve high office, when any sensible man who observed them as children would have assiduously kept them from the avenues of power, even if that prudence required strangling a Caligula while he was still playing with wooden swords. Evil men might well wish to see such a star rise, much as Vitellozzo Vitelli had schooled Oliverotto da Fermo, however reluctant the latter had been to receive this instruction. But why had good and just men not taken stern—and, if necessary, severe—measures against a child such as Caligula?

I had burned through half a dozen candles before I came to my revelation: all these cursed men had, while still quite young, become maestri of the art of deception. The Roman dictator Sulla, like Caligula, "was submissive to those who might be of service to him, yet severe to those who sought services from him, so that it was hard to say if he was more insolent or servile in his nature." The execrable Philip of Macedon so fooled his mentor, predecessor, and protector, Aratus, an admirable man and "implacable enemy of tyrants," that Aratus did not fully understand the evil he had harbored until he was spitting up blood, Philip having slowly poisoned him. And these rare men did not simply lie when necessary, or even lie often; they seemed to deceive always, as if deception were the very blood in their veins.

This explained to me—and I suppose, forgave me—my inability to see the face of this man, because whoever must deceive us in order to live will by necessity far exceed the skill of ordinary men, who are as much tempted by the desire to be honest as they are plagued by guilt and shame when they have broken faith.

But I remained at a loss to describe how these men acquired their skills of deception while still boys. Some painters are born with this gift, modern maestri who put it to admirable use, deceiving our eyes so that we believe nature has been rivaled if not re-created. And there are many others—diplomats, leaders of political factions, and in particular merchants and bankers—who less admirably promise one thing and do another, often fooling the same man by night that they duped during the day. Nevertheless even the painter or statesman must serve his apprenticeship; a child cannot execute a portrait like Leonardo's *La Gioconda*. How then, contrary to all other vocations, does this man perfect the art of deception at such a precocious age?

In the flickering light of my candle, I put the question directly to him: *How did you learn? What was your course of study, your school, this quadrivium of deception?*

I heard only a spitting wick.

I know why you don't want to tell me, I continued. *This is your deepest secret, isn't it? The most jealously guarded. That is why I must wait until you turn your back. Only then will your mask become nothing but a lucid glass.*

And then we will behold the face of evil.

CHAPTER 22

This more than all else casts down the highest throne: the powerful with their power are never sated.

I was able to lease a horse in Pesaro and left there early on 31 December, arriving at Fano in midmorning—only to find that Valentino's army had departed for Sinigaglia at daybreak. I continued riding south along an extension of the Via Emilia that hews the coast, so that it is never more than a bowshot from the sea; in certain locations the hills appear to rise directly above the waves.

The day, which had begun with a glimpse of sunshine, had become gray, with showers of both rain and snow. I passed many of Valentino's camp followers straggling south, yet encountered no traffic in the opposite direction. I could only conclude that Sinigaglia had already been sealed off, with no one permitted to leave.

I was still miles away from Sinigaglia when I first saw smoke plumes rising from the city, as dark against the ashen sky as the ravens pecking in the snow around me. It appeared that the bombardment of the city had begun.

And here the brilliance of the scheme the *condottieri* had concocted began to glimmer on the horizon. As I had previously suspected, their intention was to lure Valentino and his much diminished army into Sinigaglia, then surround the city with the troops they had hidden in the countryside.

But this breach of good faith would quickly draw the disapprobation of all Europe; the pope would have little difficulty summoning his French allies to assist him in rescuing his son.

Unless, of course, it could be demonstrated that Valentino was guilty of crimes that justified the treachery: the *condottieri* would quickly demonstrate that the duke was a fratricide, driven by jealousy and ambition to murder the pope's most beloved son. And the proof of his guilt was to be found not only in the *mappa* drawn by Valentino's engineer general but also in a page sliced from a schoolboy's geometry, although the latter would almost certainly have more value as mere rumor, while remaining secreted in the hands of the *condottieri* who had cut it out.

Damiata would be sent to Rome to reinforce the suspicions the pope himself had long held; certainly she had been promised her son's freedom—that would be easy enough for the *condottieri* to arrange, once Valentino's defeat had rendered the pope impotent—in exchange for condemning Valentino, who had already accused her. And I was probably one of several players who might have a brief moment in this drama, called upon to witness those facts that pointed to Valentino's guilt. The French in particular would value the testimony of a Florentine envoy.

Within weeks the man who had conceived this entire scheme, concealing not only this carefully laid snare but also a secret so dreadful that none of us could see his true face and still live, would become the master of all Italy.

❖

I reached Sinigaglia at the end of the day. The city sits on the edge of the sea, with the Misa River wrapped like a snake around both the west and north sides. This loop creates a natural moat, hence Sinigaglia is an island of sorts, most of it surrounded by a wall of pale, sand-colored stone, with a *rocca* of modern design overlooking the Adriatic Sea on the eastern side.

As soon as I had crossed the river I could hear the shouting from inside the city. Even before I reached the gate I had to pass a half-dozen looted corpses. Most likely soldiers, they lay beside the road with stiff arms flung out, their naked bodies covered with only a thin rime of snow, some with gutted bellies and blank, staring eyes. I recalled too well Signor Oliverotto's words, informing me of the horrors I might see, if I could "get to Sinigaglia quickly enough."

The gate itself had not been closed. Instead a wall of horseflesh, as it were, had been constructed by some twenty cavalrymen, mounted and in full armor; they were Italian mercenaries who might have been in the employ of either Valentino or the *condottieri*. From within the city I heard a distant scream against the lower, antiphonal shouts, yet the guards at the gate seemed to be waiting only for a joust to begin—or for someone as heedless of his peril as I.

When I rode up, several of the horsemen turned on me, one drawing his sword with a great sweep of his arm. "Venetian?" he called out.

If I was to die for my answer, I intended to do so as a citizen of my republic. I shouted back, "Florentine!"

A captain came forward and spoke to the swordsman; I recognized him as one of Valentino's officers, who had once arranged an escort for some of our merchants on my behalf. He motioned me on. When we had exchanged greetings, I asked, "What is the situation?"

"We have secured the city for His Excellency." Beads of frozen rain speckled the captain's helmet like pearls on a lady's hairnet. "Vitellozzo's infantry and artillery are out there." Here he pushed out with his hand to indicate the countryside, now almost entirely veiled in darkness.

This situation did not, to my eyes, appear secure; instead it differed little from the circumstances I had envisioned on the road to Sinigaglia. Valentino had been lured inside the walls, while the *condottieri* marshaled most of their vastly superior forces outside. The duke was in fact trapped.

I rode through the gate and entered a small piazza covered with icy clods. A narrow street exiting the little square was illuminated by the glow of a fire. As I peered down it, a half-dozen Swiss infantry—these also being mercenaries who might be employed by either or both armies—ran through a crossroads, their long pikes bristling like quills, one of them spitted with a swollen, livid head.

Keeping to the alleys, I ventured toward the center of the city; the entire area within the walls was not more than a dozen streets in length and width. Soon I reached a modest piazza surrounded by sev-

eral large palazzi of fairly recent construction. In the middle of the frozen square sat a single canopied carriage attended by at least a dozen
men on horse and foot. Among the former were several of Valentino's
intimates, most wearing breastplates.

"Messer Agapito!" I called out as I rode toward them.

Valentino's secretary wheeled his horse. "Secretary! His Excellency has been looking for you!"

Without further explanation, Agapito and his companions rode
off, leaving me with the several footmen and their carriage. The occu-
pant of this vehicle stuck his head through the curtained window.
"Messer Niccolò! What do you make of this?"

I recognized the long greyhound face of Messer Gabriello da Ber-
gamo, a grain trader of my acquaintance and a citizen of Venice. "I see
the city unsettled," I said directly, "and Vitellozzo Vitelli's army waiting outside."

Messer Gabriello pointed to the largest palazzo on the piazza, a
great edifice of multicolored stone. "They tell me that Vitellozzo is in
there. Along with Oliverotto da Fermo and Paolo Orsini."

"Do the duke's people say they are holding them as hostages?"

"They say nothing. I myself saw them all go in just after midday. A
handsome parade. But we have seen only Valentino's people leave. And
we hear only the most confounding rumors. On one hand we are told
that Vitellozzo has surrounded the city and is preparing a bombardment, on the other that the *condottieri* will be displayed in the piazza
tomorrow morning, much as Ramiro da Lorca was presented to the
people of Cesena."

In truth, neither did I know what to make of this. The three *condottieri* might possibly be prisoners. Or given the evident superiority
of their forces, they might still be negotiating with Valentino over the
terms of his surrender.

Messer Gabriello nodded toward one of the fires, several streets
distant. The flames, as vivid as Ezekiel's vision, were haloed with
an orange glow that hovered over the rooftops; sparks and embers
swarmed like countless fireflies in the column of smoke. "We hear
rumors that the duke's own Swiss mercenaries are putting the city to
sack!"

"Perhaps to deny the victor his spoils," I said. "Regardless of whose soldiers they are—or to whom they may transfer their allegiance before this night is over—Sinigaglia is in danger of becoming another Capua."

"My concern," Messer Gabriello said, "is to negotiate with someone to protect Venetian homes and property—our traders have quite a sizable quarter in this town. If you need a room, come with me."

I saw no reason not to accept. Until I made sense of these events, I was merely a blind man stumbling around in Fortune's palace.

◆

We needed cross only four streets to reach the Venetian quarter, where I was afforded a small room in a palazzo thought sufficiently secure that Messer Gabriello himself was lodged there. The building hosted a conclave of Venetian merchants; after seeing to my horse and baggage, I joined them by the kitchen fire. These Venetian gentlemen seemed almost cast from a mold, dark stubble against pale, gaunt cheeks; even the younger men appeared careworn.

I had finished a most welcome supper of hot cockerel stew, served from a big copper cauldron, when Messer Gabriello sought me out. "The duke's people have gone back into the palazzo. What do you think happens now?"

I shook my head, a thousand possibilities rattling around inside it. "At this moment I can believe one thing only," I told him. "That tomorrow morning Italy will have a new master."

As I said this, I recalled something I had read in my Plutarch just the night before. When the ancient Roman dictator Sulla had begun his rise to power, it was said that a great trumpet blast was heard from the Heavens, "so loud, and shrill and mournful, that it frightened and astonished the entire world." The Etruscan augurs, who believed that there are eight ages of the world, each allotted to a different type of man, prophesied that this trumpet signaled the dawn of a new age, in which an entirely changed world would be ruled by a "new sort of man."

Now I had to wonder if all our *invenzioni*—artillery, printing presses, *scienze*, our rebirth of letters, art, and architecture, our new world across the sea—had in fact inaugurated another new age, exceeding anything the ancients had imagined. And perhaps the ruler of this new age would be my rare man.

"Yes, Italy will have a new master," I mused. "But God help us if he is also a new man."

Before Messer Gabriello could begin to question this cryptic pronouncement, we were interrupted by several Italian soldiers who had marched right into the kitchen, their breastplates and helmets reflecting the fire, clearing a path for an officer I had never seen before. He stopped in the center of our gathering, propped the butt of his palm on the butt of his sheathed sword, and called out, "The Florentine secretary! Is he here?"

✦

With no explanation whatever, I was returned to the central piazza and the great palazzo that stood over it—the same building Valentino and his *condottieri* had entered during the day, according to Messer Gabriello. I ascended an impressive stone staircase to the piano nobile and was escorted so hastily through a vast polychromed salon that I had little time to observe the dozen or so officers gathered around a map table, all of them still wearing armor, save the tall figure in a chamois cape.

I had not seen Leonardo since I had been snatched near Cesenatico, four days previously. While I could not yet regard him as a *compare*, in our last hours together we had shared grave dangers and great revelations—and his assistant had saved my life. So I was considerably relieved to see him. But until I knew more about the situation, I could not risk offering him more than a brief nod.

Leonardo peered over the heads of the soldiers, his eyes tracking me for a moment. Perhaps his brow furrowed a bit, but I could not find on his transparent face any meaningful sign of his duke's fortunes.

I followed my escort into an empty anteroom and was shown at once into what was certainly the principal bedroom of the house, the large fireplace having a terra-cotta hood painted with an unfamiliar coat of arms. The bed was against the wall, with a small table set up in the middle of the room, covered with scores of documents. The fire flickered brightly, but one of Leonardo's globe lamps provided a more steady illumination.

Valentino sat straight up on a Roman-style camp stool, facing a writing lectern upon which he had propped several parchment sheets half covered with his own elegant script. Unlike the officers outside, he was unarmored, wearing only his black tunic and hose.

He put down his pen and got up, going more promptly than a servant to a small intarsia table that accommodated a carafe and several silver cups; after pouring the wine himself, he approached me with this communion. His face was entirely metamorphosed from the pale cipher I had known for months, his wind-burned complexion that of a farmer—or a *condottiero* during a campaign. There was a natural grace to his rare smile, yet I could not help but find—and fear—a certain ferocity.

"Rejoice with me, Secretary," he said, handing me my cup and nodding to our toast. "I have achieved what God and mere Fortune could not. You must write your lordships at once and tell them that today I have ended tyranny—as I have planned since this summer, even before the conspirators met to form their league against me. I have employed these vile men as was necessary, but always one against the other, with the object that the petty tyrannies of the *condottieri* should end with my victory over the worst of them. Today this is done."

I could not think how to respond.

Valentino gestured me to a cushioned chair. He squatted on his camp stool and leaned toward me, elbows on knees. "Vitellozzo Vitelli is my prisoner, in this house. I could stamp my foot now and he would hear it. The same for Oliverotto da Fermo and Paolo Orsini. Those of Oliverotto's men who opposed us here in the city have been disarmed. Vitellozzo's troops outside the city now receive their instructions from me. Tonight we will conclude our business here and tomorrow we will march on Corinaldo."

Here Valentino offered a wry, tight smile—and once again turned the world upside down. I knew how skillfully he could create an empire of hope with mere words, yet his implacable eyes told me that this was no fable he had invented. Recalling our conversation about the science of anticipation, I was persuaded to put aside all my previous assumptions. I could only believe that somehow he had done just as he claimed: he had anticipated the designs of the *condottieri* even as they attempted to lure him into their snare.

In equal measures stunned and rapt, I listened as Valentino went on in this triumphant vein for some time, describing how he had deceived the *condottieri*, first with treaty negotiations in which he had given the appearance of weakness, then by dispersing his troops in small units throughout the countryside; almost all the campfires I had seen on my way to Pesaro had evidently marked the locations of his soldiers. Without a hint of apology, the duke told me that he had not felt obligated to respect a treaty he had made while under threat by men who had no intention of keeping their own pledges—a maxim I continue to regard as entirely just, however much it has outraged those who believe *The Prince* is the Devil's handbook. Any man who under all conditions insists on making it his business to be good, will surely be destroyed among so many who are not good.

"Secretary, their plan was to lead me here, see to my assassination even before I entered this house, take command of the pitiful remnants of my army, and march against your republic. They are all confessing the particulars down there." He straightened a bit and tapped his toes on the floor. "But I had already envisioned their plan even before they had conceived it. I allowed their own natures to lead them to destruction. Had you been there this morning, when I met them outside the city, you would have seen their false faces, the kisses and embraces these conspirators offered me, as if I were some fool. These masters of deception did not believe that anyone could deceive them, simply because they were blinded by their own evil ambitions. Men are never content with what they have, Secretary." Tilting back his head, Valentino emptied his cup and set it on the floor beside his stool. "Yet a man must never aspire to more than he can seize with his own hand." His pale hand, now empty, appeared to close around an invisible object. "Whoever depends on another man's armies depends on that man's goodwill and good Fortune. But I resolved long ago to rely only upon my own will. Now I have rid myself of the *condottieri*. By my efforts alone, Italy has been saved."

Having offered this instruction in statecraft, which is also cited in *The Prince*, the duke turned with equally artful phrases to another subject. "Surely you recall, Secretary, that months ago I invited your government to come forward and declare its friendship for my person and our enterprise here. And if they would not, to understand that I would have difficulty in distinguishing the Republic of Florence from my declared enemies. Your government, it seems, decided to wait and determine if those enemies would absolve them of that decision, even though the men who conspired against me were the greatest threat to your own state. Now your lordships can plainly see how the success I have had against our mutual adversaries has benefited their interests. I have no doubt that your lordships, when you so inform them of my gesture, will acknowledge their obligation by offering their immediate assistance in my campaigns against Città di Castello and Perugia. By such means they will declare themselves friends."

He rose abruptly, went to the fireplace, and stood before it with his back to me, as if our expected display of gratitude was not to be a matter of further discussion.

I could not breathe. Of course I knew the duke to be a demanding negotiator, and no man who had risked everything to obtain such a victory would be content to offer the spoils gratis to those who had merely sat on their thumbs. But he wanted my government to finance immediate attacks far into central Italy—conquests that would, if one were to plot them on a map, almost draw a noose around Florence herself.

Valentino's mortal enemies had been vanquished, but where was this peace he had so desperately required, so that he and Leonardo could build a new world?

"I will write my government," I said, struggling for words. For once I was grateful that I had no power to negotiate; I could even appreciate the wisdom of the Ten of War in sending a mere intermediary.

Valentino turned to face me once again, a leisurely motion, as if he intended to soften his demands. Yet my heart remained stuck in my throat.

"You know that Vitellozzo intended to accuse me of my brother's murder." His tone was more subdued. "That was to be their pretext to break the treaty." As I had thought. "They intended to use the book. I obtained it from Vitellozzo. Along with the page he cut out of it. I will show you."

Valentino walked quickly to the table littered with documents. From among these he plucked a page folded over twice, judging from its size; most of one side was occupied by an enormous medallion of red wax, impressed with a seal I could not make out because Valentino so quickly put it down again. "Vitellozzo intended for Damiata to deliver this page to the pope."

I had to ask: "Where is Damiata now?"

He shook his head. I did not know whether to be relieved. "But I believe she will come to me. To beg for mercy."

"Will you . . . ?"

"I can't know yet. We are still determining the truth."

"I presume you expect at least one of your prisoners to confess, in the matter of your brother's murder."

Valentino glanced at me, his eyes narrowed and mouth pinched. "I know who murdered my brother, Secretary."

I could not read this. Did he mean that Oliverotto and Vitellozzo had already confessed? But his look forbade me to inquire further, even as a panic rose inside me: Had they also confessed to Damiata's complicity?

Again Valentino gestured at the sealed packet. "Do you know what is written here, Secretary?"

My tongue was thick. "I haven't seen it, Excellency."

He lifted his eyes but did not see me. I knew at once where he was. "Some were whores. Some were not. The women we took captive at Capua." Valentino's nostrils flared wide, as though a hand were over his mouth and he was gasping for air. "I had one of them. One of the innocent. Entirely so, a girl of perhaps fifteen. A virgin. But she was willing—as a servant girl is willing when the master taps her shoulder at night." As Marietta had been willing on our wedding night, her uncles banging kettles outside the half-open door. "Hoping to save herself from worse. And so I wallowed in the same cess-trench as those

Germans and Gascons. I disgraced myself entirely." His complexion had paled. "I shamed myself forever."

Like my question regarding Damiata's fate, I did not want to ask. "What happened to this girl?"

He nodded weakly, still not seeing me. "I gave her to Oliverotto."

I was cursed to envision Oliverotto's huge hands encircling the poor girl's neck, her face a ghastly purple. It was obscene even to think that she had found a moment's pleasure in the strangler's hands, as Oliverotto had boasted; little more than a child, she could have known nothing but fear since she had been wrenched from her home. And I prayed that in the heartbeat in which she had known she would die, she had seen the Mother of God's outstretched arms.

"You must go now, Secretary," Valentino whispered. When he blinked, only once, his eyes glittered. "Go and write your government. We will talk later."

CHAPTER 23

Everyone sees what you appear to be, few truly know what you are; and those few dare not oppose the opinion of the many.

I was not returned to my room in the Venetian quarter. Instead, Valentino's soldiers escorted me to a palazzo nearer the center of the town, where many of the ambassadors were lodged. Installed in a small, windowless room, at once I composed my dispatch to the Ten of War. I wrote with the presumption that the duke's people would read this report, having provided me pen, ink, paper, and a waiting courier. Valentino understood, as had no prince before him, that victory itself is less important than the speed and thoroughness with which news of a triumph is communicated throughout the world.

When I had finished my writing, the small bed beckoned. But on a night when I might have celebrated the deliverance of my family, Florence, and all Italy, I found myself too troubled for sleep. Instead I began to pace the scant floor of that little room like a caged beast, tormented by the thought that perhaps my "rare man" was not so rare at all. We Italians had made warfare our most estimable and lucrative profession, and in so doing had created a state of perpetual chaos, because whoever profits from war would be a fool to value peace. In our Italy, the immortal Cincinnatus, who stepped from behind his plow to lead the Romans to victory and then returned to his little farm, would be thought a risible lunatic. Where war goes on without end, all men are inevitably corrupted by its brutality—and the worst horrors are visited upon the most innocent. Capua was becoming the rule rather than a dreadful anomaly.

And now I feared that Duke Valentino had wallowed in the sty with these evil men so long that he could only with the greatest difficulty rise and build his new Italy. Far more distressing, I also saw the likelihood that throughout our discussions, the duke had secretly coveted *bella* Firenze, perhaps as much as any of the *condottieri*.

At last I got beneath the comforter, only to toss about, cursing myself for failing to anticipate the duke's deception. I had become obsessed with the face of a murderer, when in truth he might well be as faceless as his apprentice—because he could be any man who grasped for power in today's Italy.

Yet for all this, only a single question at last kept me from crossing the threshold of sleep: *Where is Damiata?*

◆

The brief slumber into which I nodded, hours later, was feverish and filled with visions. The last came just before I awakened. I held my father's hand, which seemed marvelously real to me, and walked with him to the Piazza della Signoria. We crossed the Ponte Vecchio and had passed beneath the towering faces of the wool factories, the banner-like bolts of cloth hanging from rails high above, when all at once the sky appeared again, framing the great tower of the Palazzo della Signoria, its crenellated battlements like some Titan's teeth. Spread out over the piazza before me, as teeming as a battlefield, was this immense choir comprising every sort of man I could imagine and some I never had, all of them roaring away. I could not understand their words but I could clearly see that each conversation, whether among two men or twenty, was a stage for the most remarkable display of gestures, nods, smirks, glares, and shrugs. I was terrified; nothing in my life, in large part spent tied to my mother's apron strings, had prepared me to grasp this baffling vocabulary of words, gestures, and expressions.

Suddenly I was returned to my house on the Via di Piazza, to the little room that was still my own, before I began to share it with my brother, Totto. It was dark, the house around me and the street outside entirely silent. I slipped from beneath my coverlet and stood beside my bed. Moonlight pierced the shutters. In that faint silver light I began to make grand rhetorical flourishes, thrusting out my arm, holding up both palms, nodding wisely—these and dozens of others that I repeated again and again, silently in the dark.

What are you doing?

My skin crawled. There was another boy in the room with me. I could scarcely see him in the darkness, but from his size, I judged he was several years younger than I; nevertheless, he was too old to be Totto.

I watch the men in the piazza, I answered him. *I watch them so carefully and mimic them so closely, that they will take my gestures for their own. They will never know I am nothing but an ignorant little boy.*

I had done exactly this as a child, often getting up in the night, just as in my dream, to practice this mimicry. Soon, I also began to listen to the words that shot back and forth among those men, but as I did, I watched more keenly than ever their hands, eyes, nods—even where a man's feet pointed and when he lifted one shoe or another. The faces and gestures of men eventually became books I could read, no less important to me than the words of Dante and Cicero.

The little boy who had joined me in my dream began to whimper. *I hate their faces.*

In an instant, I was inside this boy's head, seeing through his eyes. I was hardly surprised at this, because it had been my waking practice to similarly enter the minds of history's great men; this was no different than surveying the wreckage of a great Roman army through Hannibal's eyes, so that I might ask him where he would go after Cannae. But now I found myself in the mind of a small, frightened child, looking out on the Piazza della Signoria as I had when I was his age. And what he saw was infinitely more terrifying than anything I had ever beheld.

They had no faces. Among the hundreds of men in the piazza, not one resembled anything more than a lifeless plaster mask, with dots for eyes and slits for a mouth and nose.

I bolted awake.

Sitting up in bed, I knew I had returned to the room Valentino's people had provided. Yet as I blinked into the darkness, I was equally certain that the author of this dreadful vision had come with me. He was standing beside the door. And he was no longer a little boy.

"I understand you now," I addressed the icy presence. "You were born entirely indifferent to those feelings that animate our souls and bring our faces to life. In your eyes, our faces are nothing but death masks. And now I know what you had to do, in order to live in our strange realm of souls and sentiments. Because I, too, was once a little boy who desperately wanted to appear to be a man." My teeth were chattering. "And I can only imagine the infinitely greater labor required of a small, bewildered monster, who knew with every animal instinct that he must appear to be human, or he could not survive."

I heard a rustle of clothing, then a grating sound. Near the end of my bed, flames flickered in the brazier.

"Who are you?" In truth, I had no notion of what stood over that brazier: Man, woman, shade, creature of a dream that had not ended?

"The Duchess of Ferrara." The voice was so warped by anger that still I could not say for certain that this "duchess" was man or woman. But I could see a dress and a gauzy white veil. A gown that glimmered with gold embroidery. And then my reeling mind registered that the Duchess of Ferrara was Duke Valentino's sister, Lucrezia—who could not have been within a hundred miles of this place.

She began to strip off these raiments with such sudden vehemence that I grasped about my bedclothes for something I could use as a weapon. The veil, gown, and then a blond wig were cast down on my bed as if they carried the plague, yet almost at once the "duchess" snatched back the gown and held it before her like a phantom partner in a *ballo*. I saw the knife just as she began to thrust it again and again into the empty bodice, ripping the velvet with a sound that recalled all too much a butcher removing a fresh hide.

I leapt up.

"Don't, Niccolò. Don't come near." Damiata's voice remained scarcely recognizable; only the unveiling of her face, her dark hair pulled back, convinced me. She threw the flayed dress upon the bed and turned to me, the knife still in her hand, staring as if she had seen me for the first time.

"I was still deliriously in love with Juan when Cesare began to seduce me." Damiata spoke as if she were dreaming. "Or I began to seduce him. I don't even know. That is how skillful he is. You see him now, the conqueror of the Romagna, feared throughout all Europe, the hope of all Italy. To me he was a lovely bird in a cage. So sad, so forgotten. His melancholy little songs." She heaved with a sob. "In all this, I believed one thing. That on the day we betrayed Juan, we were truly lovers. Cesare loved me." Again her shoulders heaved. "Tonight I surrendered even that slender faith." She glared at the dress on the bed as though she would resume her assault. "Tonight he forced me to mime the only bride he has ever really desired. The same bride he embraced on that afternoon, when in my foolishness I imagined he held me. Tonight he dressed me in his sister's wedding gown."

"Tonight?" I said stupidly.

"I went to him, Niccolò. Tonight."

To beg his forgiveness, I presumed. Yet the price of her absolution, as unbearable as it had been to her—and to me—did not seem sufficient. What else?

"I saw his prisoners. In the room next to his. He showed them to me through a hole drilled in the wall, like a camera obscura. Oliverotto and Vitellozzo. Tied together, seated back to back. The same garrote around both necks. At the end they pleaded for mercy like women. I heard them die. And then I had my wedding night." She blinked furiously. "Your monster is dead, Niccolò. And your city is saved."

"Damiata." I spoke sharply, rousing her from this sleep. "He isn't dead." I halted there, wishing I could not see the face that still floated before me, a materialization of my dream. "Tonight I saw the face of evil."

She shook her head in angry disagreement. "When it was over, he had me look through that little hole again. Their faces were purple. A puddle of piss beneath each chair."

I took a step to her and she raised her knife, warning me to stay back. Clad only in her chemise, she shivered. But then she said, more calmly, "When I was still a girl, I was taught how to steal things from gentlemen's rooms." She smiled as if fondly remembering someone who was dead. "Niccolò, my *cioppa* is also on the bed. I put something in the lining. Will you get it out?"

When I had found the opening in the fur lining, I brought the little packet into the light of the brazier. "I saw this only hours ago," I said, looking up at Damiata. "In Valentino's room. The same page that was sliced out of Euclid's *Elements*." It seemed so heavy it might have been gilded. But now I could see that the large medallion of red wax, which almost entirely covered one side of the twice-folded page, had been impressed with Duke Valentino's seal.

"When I left you in Cesena I went to the *condottieri*, on my own. I knew they had taken the book, that night on the *pianura*. The book I believed would prove my innocence and save my little boy. Niccolò, I left without a word to you because I didn't want you to come after me. I had no doubt that Vitellozzo would kill you at once." Damiata looked at me warily.

I did not believe these words so much as the truth I had seen in her eyes, when she left me in the snowfield.

"Niccolò, Vitellozzo Vitelli wanted me to take something to the pope. Something he expected to obtain here in Sinigaglia."

I nodded. "This page."

"I think so."

"Valentino insists it is a fraud," I said.

She bit her lip. "My only hope is that this page can free my little boy. Niccolò, I believe what you told Vitellozzo. That in it Valentino confesses to things that happened at Capua. Things the Holy See would never want known. Oliverotto himself said as much. I heard him."

The room seemed yet colder. "Tonight?"

"I heard their final words. Through that tiny hole in the wall. While Valentino watched. His eye to that little hole." Damiata shook her head numbly. "They sounded so distant. As though they were already in the pit of Hell. Oliverotto begged that his wife and children be spared. Despite everything I pitied him. 'I know you are watching!' he cried out. 'By the Lord's robe I have kept your secret to the death!' "

I had already prepared myself to hear something like this. Nevertheless, the floor might have fallen away beneath me. "This secret Oliverotto kept. He didn't mean Capua." When Damiata only looked at me blankly, I added: "Oliverotto told me he saw Juan die. But he was not the murderer."

Damiata crossed herself and sank down onto the edge of the bed. "Vitellozzo, then."

An hour before, I could not have believed it myself. In truth, I had to silence my own doubts before I said, "No. Not Vitellozzo."

Damiata got to her feet, retrieved her *cioppa* from the bed, and wrapped herself in it before she looked up at me. Her cheeks glistened with tears. "My dearest Niccolò, you see things the rest of us cannot. Like all great gifts, it is also your curse. But while we were still at Imola, Oliverotto showed me something you have not seen. Weeks later, when I realized what it was, I did not tell you—as I said, I believed they would kill you if you went to them. He showed me a spiral made with little olives." She went on to describe in detail how Oliverotto had carefully arranged the miniature olives on a silver plate, weeks before Leonardo deciphered the Archimedes spiral. "Niccolò, he was taunting me, as he had taunted the pope. As he toyed with Leonardo. He killed them all. Juan. The women at Capua. And the *streghe* at Imola."

My faith in my science wavered like a dying candle. I recalled Damiata sitting on our bed in Cesena and tracing a spiral in the air, when I had told her about the *mappa* of evil. I believed her account entirely, and why she had not told me this until now. But perhaps Fortune had merely employed coincidence to conceal the truth. I could only take on increasingly fragile faith what I had just seen.

"If Valentino has confessed to his crimes at Capua, it will be enough," Damiata said, comforting me. "You must believe that, Niccolò." Her bosom rose. "I have already arranged to leave here and go back to Rome. To trade this page for my little boy. There is a barge sailing to Venice tonight." She cupped my hands, but without touching the packet cradled within them. "Darling Niccolò, I trust you with my life and my Giovanni's life. I must ask you to care for this until I complete my arrangements. In an hour, come to the wharf. I have bribed the guards at the north gate. But if I am arrested, then you must . . . Use this to save your own people, Niccolò. If you can, my son . . . But you must leave the seal intact. Otherwise the pope will say this is a fraud."

Damiata rushed to the door with little more than a whisper of fur. At the threshold, she turned.

"Niccolò, you must imagine something for me . . . You are an old man, in his last days, which you spend in a lovely villa somewhere in the hills around Florence." She blinked slowly, her lashes freighted by clinging tears. "You are in the garden, beneath the pergola, with your Primerana's children playing all around you, and you are reading the *Symposium*, the part where Plato says that love is our desire to be whole, that each soul has a missing half, and although we might spend an entire life searching for that other half, when we encounter it, we know it at once. Yet the soul can never describe the object of its desire until it sees it—until then, that missing half is only a 'dark and doubtful presentiment.' So as you are reading these words, with the bees and cicadas buzzing and your grandchildren giggling, your mind goes back to the loves of your life, and you know that of them all, there was only one who made you whole."

She sniffled, then smiled as if she had truly witnessed this vision. "Promise me, Niccolò. Promise me that when you are an old man, for one moment, you will bring Damiata back into your heart and imagine that my soul completed your own."

My own tears were already growing cold on my face. "I promise you."

CHAPTER 24

Whoever is lucky in love should not play cards.

An hour after Damiata left my room, I went out. The city was now entirely silent, the bodies collected from the streets, the snow falling without a sound. When I reached the north gate, I found it guarded by a dozen Italian mercenary cavalry. Damiata had bribed them well; they did not even issue a perfunctory challenge as I exited.

The road ran beside the wall for about two hundred *braccia* before a ramp descended to the wharf. This platform, which rested on wooden piers sunk into the bed of the Misa River, extended from the city wall like a shelf. Tied up alongside it was a sailing barge of the sort you see on the Adriatic coast, with a single mast and a stout hull, the dark oak planking almost indistinguishable from the river and the open sea just beyond. Nothing moved on the deck, but light glimmered faintly through the cracks in the small shutters of the single cabin.

I waited beside the barge for half an hour, listening to the hull thump gently against the wooden wharf, hearing nothing else save the whispering sea at my back. To my left rose Sinigaglia's *rocca*, the pale round towers not even a bowshot distant. My mind whirled with every imaginable possibility, the multitude of lives I might live before the sun came up again. Few ended well.

Yet when at last I saw Damiata gliding atop the snow with grace-ful dancer's steps, I could believe that she was the only bride my furtive soul would ever desire. And unlike our previous meeting—or my own wedding—this bride walked directly to me and took me in her arms.

"Laodamia had three hours when her husband came up from Hades," Damiata murmured. "We will scarcely have three heartbeats." She looked back toward the ramp. "Everything is ready. I must go." She began to shiver.

"Madonna! Soldiers! Coming!"

A man raced down the icy ramp, cape flying, legs churning with comical fury as he tried to maintain his forward progress. He stopped a short distance from us, hot breath streaming from his mouth and nose, until Damiata gave him a "get on" gesture with her hand, which sent him back up the ramp.

"Niccolò. I must have it now."

At that moment, the little packet inside my vest seemed as heavy as all my doubts. Perhaps it was only a fraud. Or perhaps that single page torn from a schoolboy's geometry text would set in motion fates even Fortune had not imagined.

I doubted I could even move my hand. Yet I did.

♦

As Damiata slipped the packet into her *cioppa*, the first soldiers appeared at the top of the ramp. Through the thickening snowfall, I could also see horsemen on the narrow road next to the wall, at least a dozen, along with as many foot soldiers, all of them armored.

Damiata clutched my cloak and drew me to the swollen waist of the ship. A sailor emerged from the darkened stern and leaned over the railing to help her aboard. But she did not reach for his arms at once. Instead she took me in hers.

"My darling Niccolò, I believe as the ancients did that great love journeys beyond the shores of fate." Her voice already seemed the whisper of a shade. "You must trust me, companion of my soul. I will see you again."

With this promise, she touched her fingers to my lips. Perhaps it was only my imagination, or a beautiful if not reliable memory, but her eyes were transparent at that last moment, as if I could see her soul through blue flames, and the most wonderful smile trembled on her lips.

Then she turned and reached for other arms, to begin her journey.

She had not even gotten over the railing when the first crossbow bolt went by my head, as swift as a falling star, buzzing like a cicada.

Three or four more bolts came as rapidly as a heartbeat, some thwacking wood, at least one making a sickening, split-melon sound as it struck flesh. With a feral grunt the sailor helping Damiata fell back and as he did she slid over the railing like a dolphin pulled into a fisherman's boat, disappearing behind the hull.

I spun about in a crouch and looked toward the ramp, expecting to find the crossbowmen firing from atop it. Instead I observed nearly a parade of horses venturing down that treacherous slope, many of the frightened beasts slipping, none of the riders armed with bows, much less prepared to fire.

The fuses flashed first, lighting like candles atop the pale city wall almost directly above me. One, two, three, all in an instant. Men had begun shouting, so I could not hear the fuses hiss, only the dry thunderclaps that followed as the long beaks of the *scoppietti* spit flames. The balls droned and thwacked, the last slapping the canvas sail. Then another flash, the burst of light already dimmed by the cloud of smoke that hung over the rampart. The ball raised just a puff of snow as it smacked the wharf beside me, making almost the same sound as a ball that strikes flesh.

I thought I might save myself by leaping onto the boat, but the river's strong current had already pushed the barge entirely beyond me. I did not even take a breath before I decided to swim to it. As I tensed to leap into the frigid water, my mind was occupied by only one terrible question: When I climbed aboard that ship, would I find my love already growing cold, the life I so cherished bleeding out of her?

I was struck in the middle of the back, the blow so hard that I thought it would drive me into the water. Yet almost before I could wonder if I had been shot, my feet flew out from beneath me and I was pulled backward with such violence that I went sprawling into the snow. Crystal flakes flew up around me.

Then the entire world became still. I stared up into the unremarkable, *bottega*-keeper face of Michelotto—the last face Vitellozzo Vitelli and Oliverotto da Fermo had seen, only hours before. Valentino's executioner had evidently effected my "rescue." Holding a sparking torch in one hand, he offered me the other.

"Stop your firing!"

I looked toward the ramp. As if God had waved His hand, the veil of snow suddenly parted for the author of this command. Valentino rode his great black warhorse, although he was attired just as I had left him hours before, without even a cape, having merely exchanged his slippers for riding boots.

The stallion advanced with short, prancing steps, as imperiously calm as its rider. The duke rode to the middle of the wharf, glanced up at the city wall as if to confirm his marksmen's obedience, before he gently reined to a stop. For a moment, both rider and horse were entirely still, a living equestrian statue.

A strange thing happened then. The wind had been almost calm most of the night, rising only slightly as it drifted in from the east. But suddenly there was a great inrush of air from the sea, not the sort of gust that accompanies a storm but a vast, whispering suction that seemed gently to pull us after it, once it had passed.

I have always believed that was Fortune sighing.

nd the Devil, taking him up to a high mountain, showed unto him all the kingdoms of the world.

Valentino wheeled his horse about and started back toward the ramp. Michelotto invited—or directed—me to follow with merely a single gesture of his formidable hand. We then proceeded at a pace so rapid that my racing mind was compelled to concentrate simply on keeping my feet. Moments after reentering the city, we began to cross a long drawbridge, this spanning the moat that ran partly around the *rocca*.

I already knew I would be taken to a high place.

Still at a run, we entered the courtyard of the fortress, which teemed like a Saturday market with armored soldiers of every sort, clamoring in a Babel of tongues. Upon reaching the far corner, we ascended the stone steps that spiraled within a great circular tower, finally emerging on the broad platform at the top. This perch was about twenty *braccia* across, protected by a stone parapet high enough to conceal the artillerymen, of whom there were more than a dozen, all employed at moving two ponderous iron cannons.

The artillerymen were under the supervision of Valentino's engineer general; Leonardo stood at one of the large crenellations that notched the parapet in several places. Michelotto delivered me directly to this post, then left us, disappearing back down the spiral stairs.

Leonardo only glanced at me before he returned his attention to the night sea, his brow pinched. The escaping barge was far beneath us, its black hull all but invisible; the canvas sail appeared to float on the inky water. The briefly halted snowfall had already resumed.

"Damiata is in that boat," I said, breathless, my words catching. "I believe she has proof..." I realized I had no time to expound a theory still plagued with so many doubts. "Proof of... crimes. The duke—"

The voices seemed to come from behind us, yet also from beneath us. I turned to see torchlight erupt from the sunken stairwell. Valentino's head rose above the pavement, for an instant appearing to have been presented on the tip of a pike, much as he had displayed Ramiro. But he continued to emerge into view, his torso entirely intact yet nearly motionless, as if some great hand were lifting him from the depths of the earth.

♦

Followed by Michelotto, Valentino strode directly to us, his eyes sweeping quickly over me before fixing on Leonardo. "Maestro, you must calculate drop, weight, and range for the bombardiers." He intended to fire on the escaping barge.

Leonardo's gray-green eyes flickered with movements so fine that he might have been counting the thickly falling snowflakes. I had seen this same stare when he worked with his measuring sticks.

With no word or other indication, the maestro simply turned and walked away.

Valentino's utterly placid face almost at once darkened with rage. "I did not give you leave to go! Do not walk away from me as if I do not exist!"

Michelotto unspindled the Spanish garrote he wore around his wrist and wrapped the ends of the slender cord around his broad fists.

Leonardo halted at the lip of the stairwell. Valentino put a restraining hand on Michelotto's arm.

"Do you know where you will go from here, Maestro?" Valentino no longer raised his voice, but there was an uncharacteristic hoarseness to it. "You will return to the paint shop. You will leave behind only portraits of whores and decorated walls where monks slurp their soup. You will build nothing and be remembered for nothing."

Leonardo appeared to sway slightly before he turned. "I remember the whirlwind that traversed Italy entirely when I was four years old. This great dark cloud that spun with furious and unrelenting violence, tossing up whole dwellings, trees, and herds of livestock before it." The maestro spoke with the wondering, high-pitched tone of a little boy. "A remarkable stillness preceded it, as though the world had issued its last breath and the soul had gone out of it." He blinked rapidly. "When the whirlwind had passed, it left behind an unimaginably obscene fetor, as though the bowels of the very earth had been ripped out . . ." Leonardo bowed his head. "In such fashion Nature destroys so that she can give birth."

"Sì," Valentino said, the word nearly a hiss. "We must destroy the old world before we can build the new."

Remarkably, when Leonardo looked up, his eyes were on me, almost as if demanding instruction from his father.

I shook my head only slightly.

Nodding at me with equal economy, little more than a tic, the great maestro from little Vinci turned and descended the hidden stairwell. Yet even when he had disappeared entirely from sight, I could hear the precise cadence of his steps on the stone, tapping out the harmonics of a universe only he had the vision to see.

◆

"The maestro will come back to us," Valentino said placidly, now seeming to regard his engineer general's defection as little more than a passing whim. "I understand him. A man of such vision must sometimes turn away from more practical considerations." He looked at me with an expression convincingly like pity. "Just as I understand that you have been enchanted by the same witch who seduced me, so that she could betray my brother." He glanced at Michelotto. "Secretary, do you know that Vitellozzo Vitelli and Oliverotto da Fermo are already dead?"

I nodded.

"But I have spared Paolo Orsini. Do you know why?"

I shook my head, struggling to make some connection.

"Because Signor Paolo did not conspire with the other two to murder my brother." Valentino nodded, his nostrils slightly flared. "At that time the Orsini sought peace with us. Seeking profit, the Vitelli wanted to prolong the hostilities. As they intended with this present scheme. Both Vitellozzo and Oliverotto put their knives into my brother. They made their confession before they died. But when they did so, they gave up another confederate." A knife went into *my* breast. "On the night my brother was murdered, Damiata sent one of her *bravi* to Vitellozzo, with details of the route Juan would take after he left my mother's vineyard." Valentino paused and exhaled audibly through his nose. "I assure you I did not want to hear her name, Secretary. To hear Vitellozzo say it—that great misshapen, pestilent pig—was to rip out that part of me that was hers alone. A piece of my flesh."

On this night of revelations, for the first time it occurred to me that Valentino could well be Giovanni's father; perhaps Damiata's precious son was this "flesh" to which he referred.

Valentino looked out to sea. "Damiata knows that evidence of her crime will soon reach my father. She believes she can still save herself with this scheme authored by Vitellozzo. Do you want to know what I wrote on this page she intends to take to His Holiness?"

I nodded, feeling almost as if I were seven again and had not properly prepared my lesson for Ser Battista.

"You see, Secretary, His Holiness declared his preference for my brother long before he made him captain general of the Church, years before my father even became pope. Duke of Gandia was by right my title. It went to Juan . . ." He blew out a scoffing breath. "I could give you a litany, Secretary. But it means nothing now." He swept his arm toward the sea. "During the goat ride, I wrote on that page myself, as if I were addressing my father. I confessed to him that on the night we found Juan's body, I offered a prayer of thanksgiving to the God who had abandoned me until then. The indifferent God who in some fit of mercy or justice—or simply cowardice—had surrendered Juan to the designs of Fortune and the Vitelli. So that, Secretary, is this 'confession' Damiata wishes to take to my father: I wanted my brother to die. Had I grown up with any faith in the power of the Lord, I would have prayed for it every night since I was a boy. But even God knows I had nothing to do with Juan's murder."

Burning with a hiss that seemed equal to a hundred *scoppietti* preparing to fire, the fuse of a bombard illuminated the gunners almost like day. Presumably they had found the range by their own devices. The initial explosion of the powder, however, was almost muted. But a great long flame erupted from the bombard's blunt iron snout and the echo that followed it out over the water rattled my bones, such that the sound of the ball splashing harmlessly into the sea—to my great relief—seemed little more than a stone tossed into a pond.

"Secretary, do you know what my father will do when he reads this so-called confession? My words, though merely babbled in a state of delirium, will rip open wounds that have never healed. His Holiness is an old man. I now regret that I even allowed Juan's amulet to be dispatched to Rome after we found it on that woman . . . It nearly killed him. Just as we feared for his life in the days after Juan . . ."

Valentino shook his head bitterly, blinking away snowflakes as if fighting tears. I scarcely thought he was envisioning the loss of a beloved patriarch. But I little doubted the duke's sincere concern for the merchant of forgiveness, whose sale of indulgences and Church offices had so liberally funded his conquests.

"Get up on the parapet," Valentino said abruptly, as though only from that vantage could I truly comprehend the catastrophe that would follow, if the barge escaped. "I want to show you something."

The pale stone parapet beside me rose to my chest, the flat top less than two *braccia* wide.

"Get up there."

Placing my hands on stone so cold that it seared my flesh, I hauled myself up and knelt atop the parapet. Far beneath me, a silver-foamed fringe of the black Adriatic lapped against the rocks. All at once the blood drained from my head and I could not rise from my hands and knees. Every fiber of my will was suddenly devoted to clinging to this perch.

"Stand up, Secretary."

I lifted my hands from the icy stone and rose unsteadily from my crouch. The sea, although nearly calm, appeared to roil with black swells; the wind, although merely a breeze, seemed almost a tempest.

It was as if Valentino were Lucifer falling from the sky, so swiftly did he land on the parapet in front of me, having leapt with an almost unnatural strength directly from the platform below. But this must have been a more challenging feat than he had expected, because his body gyred as he straightened up. Being only an arm's length from me, he held out his hands.

I thought for an instant that I should let him fall. But I reached out and we clasped each other as if we were playing the "little owl," where you wrestle with only the hands touching. Here, instead of trying to throw one another down, we steadied ourselves.

"You see what we can do together." It was as if Valentino had intended all along to make this demonstration. "I need to work with Florence. Your lordships must be persuaded that our concerns and objects are mutual. And you are the man best suited to lead them into the light. Your merchants and bankers sent you here only to make a perilous art of their craven, ceaseless vacillation. You know that, Niccolò." This was the first time he had ever used my name. "And I know what it is to have one's abilities unacknowledged. You are capable of far more than providing the Florentines a mere mouthpiece. I have come to value your keen observation of events, your deep understanding of men, your gifts of anticipation. Help me convince your countrymen. Let us build this new world together."

At that moment I saw two nations: the Italy we have at present, the prostrate victim of the most foolish men, if not also the worst men; and an Italy that might yet hope to live in peace and prosperity, free of foreign domination, under some sort of *pax Caesareus* imposed by Valentino. And for another moment, one that was less madness than a triumph of reason over sentiment, I glimpsed the new world that I would help him build.

He saw this in my eyes more clearly than I could see it in my own heart. "Look to the sea, Niccolò. Look beyond it."

The black horizon appeared infinite, a dark mirror to the vast prospect of Heaven I had seen in Damiata's arms. Yet after a moment, I had the sense that a great windstorm rushed across this distant realm, so far away I could hear only the merest sibilance, whispers in a dream. Telling me something I had dimly perceived in my conversations with Hannibal and Caesar, a truth that lay out there like some undiscovered world. *A new age.* I began to fly across that night sea, racing beyond the borders of love and hate and all the lesser sentiments that we believe animate our souls, the tempest now singing of a new life I had never imagined, not even in Damiata's arms. A life of such power and majesty that my feet no longer required a tenuous purchase on that parapet, because I was no longer a man bound to the earth. I was an immortal flying to my place in the stars.

I have never felt anything like it since.

"You know now, Niccolò, don't you? This is what life means when you throw aside your human frailties and challenge Fortune, every day and in every thing. You of all men know that if we wait on other men and on events over which we have no control, we Italians will not be free again in our lifetimes." His hands were as hard as iron ingots. "Come with me, Niccolò, and help me defeat Fortune."

"No man sees farther than you, Excellency." My voice trembled. I was so far from the shore, free of all the tethers that might hold me back—family, home, our republic. Even Damiata had slipped from my arms.

He leaned closer and shifted his gaze slightly, as if locating some cranny in my soul where I had hidden my own secret. "But you, too, think you see something, don't you, Niccolò. Something no other man has ever been able to see. You believe you can see me." I would not call the exquisitely subtle expression on his lips a smile. "Tell me. What do you see?"

Valentino did not part his lips at all, yet it appeared that a little steam issued from them. And with hardly more effort, he pushed my hands so that my feet lifted from the stone and I knew I was going into the abyss. Then just as quickly he held me fast, to demonstrate how easily he could win this game. "I want you to tell me what you think you know." Again he pushed, moving both my hands and my feet. "If you have an accusation, make it."

These were almost the same words that had humbled Oliverotto da Fermo. But on that occasion Valentino had left Oliverotto the choice to retreat—to postpone his death, as it were. Here, still holding me fast, he was not offering me even that Devil's bargain. I could plunge silently into the cold black sea, or I could declare my own wavering faith in my untested, unproved, and perhaps worthless science of men.

I began my tale at the beginning. "I believe . . . you started watching us when you were very young . . ."

I had to halt. Looking down, I imagined my body falling upon the rocks. Strangely, only then was my frozen dread overtaken by a profound calm.

"From your earliest years," I said, my voice now steady, "you carefully observed the language of our gestures, our laughter and tears, even our smallest expressions, always perfecting your craft, until you could fashion these masks of yours as skillfully as Leonardo paints his portraits—more real, more true to Nature, than life itself. A simulacrum of life so convincing that only you could know there was nothing behind it."

Another fuse hissed and I could see the flare and feel the heat at my back as flame shot out over the sea.

"But as your intellect matured, you were no longer content simply to mimic us. You began to look inside us, just as keenly observing the desires, fears, and expectations that we believe we keep locked within our breasts. And from the secrets of our own souls you fashioned a mask so malleable that it is no longer a mask, is it, Excellency? It is a mirror in which each of us beholds his loftiest hopes. And deepest fears. When we peer into your illusion of a soul, we see only ourselves. That is the brilliance of your deception. When we look at you, we want nothing more than to deceive ourselves. Only when you turn away from us can we begin to glimpse your true face."

Flames again lit the sky and I could feel the percussion that followed in the stone beneath my feet. Yet Valentino did not even blink. His eyes as much as his hands demanded that I finish.

"Now I understand why you must kill us," I continued, soaring on the wings of my science—and waiting to fall into the sea like Icarus. "Our terror, our pain, the desperate hopes we cling to at the end, the moment when we surrender our souls—these things you see on our faces as we look into the face of Death, are all that bring you life. You, who were born dead in all but the flesh, can only live at the moment we die. Your riddles, your figures of geometry, your shrine of skulls—these amusements only remind you that once you lived and will briefly live again, when you can kill again. You will always have some new *disegno*, a new rebus of human flesh. New massacres. Yet your mound of skulls will never rise high enough to fill the emptiness within you." Something might have flickered in his eyes. "I wonder, Excellency, when you began. Did servants disappear even when you were a boy?" I took in a breath that burned my lungs. "Or did it begin when you murdered your brother?"

Our hands still clasped, Valentino inexorably brought his greater strength against mine, even as I exerted every fiber of my body and will to save myself. With each frantic heartbeat I came less than a fingernail's width closer to my death—a progress far more terrifying than if he had thrown me down in one motion. Yet my adversary never blinked throughout. He did not want to miss the moment when my soul surrendered.

The distant windstorm roared in my ears. But in truth, all I had heard was a single contemptuous exhalation, sighing from Duke Valentino's lips.

"Go, then," he said. "If you wish, inform your lordships of the crimes you believe God has witnessed. Go and publish your lies and nonsense, send your letters and accusations throughout all Italy. This slander will gain you and your republic no profit, nor will you stain my honor any more than have the lies my enemies, to their eternal shame, have already told. The entire world can see that I have obtained justice for my brother, as well as for those unfortunate country girls and the women of Capua, who are no less worthy of it. Their murderers died tonight."

Valentino released my hands. "Go now, my little secretary," he whispered. "Go and tell the world what you think you know."

Before I came down from that high place, I looked a last time out to sea. The blackness that had moments before seemed infinite, promising everything, now appeared to be nothing more than a single dark room, the sanctum sanctorum of a small, forgotten god who was not even present behind the veil of snow. Nothing moved save the fleeing barge, its sail little more substantial than a snowflake blowing past my face, a speck upon the dark water.

PART FOUR

A MOST
BEAUTIFUL DECEPTION

Florence and Rome: January 23– December 19, 1503

CHAPTER 26

*M̃ en have by nature the power to desire everything and from
Fortune the power to achieve little.*

Within days of Valentino's victory over the *condottieri*, word of this signal triumph had spread throughout the courts and capitals of Europe.
All Christendom could not but admire the courage and cunning Duke
Valentino had exhibited at Sinigaglia; the duke's brilliant ruse was
soon widely lauded as *il bellissimo inganno*—"the most beautiful deception." And no longer could any sovereign or state feel safe from him.

As for the "little secretary," to cite Valentino's parting address
to me, I returned to Florence on 23 January, *anno Domini* 1503, to an
empty house on the Via di Piazza, the modest home where I grew up,
bequeathed me by my father. The day after my arrival, Albertaccio
Corsini, Marietta's guardian, dragged her to my doorstep—if not by
the hair, then certainly by the arm. I did not play Agamemnon and
interrogate my wife as to what she had done in Piero del Nero's house,
with the "cousin" with whom she was in love. Marietta's sorrowing eyes
only mirrored my own longing, as every day a life with Damiata rose
anew in my imaginings, infinite in its variety and splendor. Having my
own "most bitter new tears born from old desires," as Petrarch wrote, I
was content to let my wife pine in peace.

But Marietta did not return alone. She brought our little girl back
to my father's house, and there my doubts regarding Primerana's paternity melted like September frost. It was enough for me simply to go

into her nursery, scoop up the *fanciulla*, and hold her to my breast, to watch her little hands clutch and her tiny mouth pucker, babbling and casting her doe eyes about in wonder and amusement. I fell so deeply in love with her that I could hear the wind rush past my ears as I soared, deliriously, to the very zenith of the Heavens.

♦

So Marietta and I resumed our lives, bound only in our love for our daughter and our sorrow for our lost loves. After that night at Sinigaglia, hardly another passed that I did not wake in the dark, wondering if Damiata had been killed by a bolt or a ball just moments after I last held her. The entire credence of my science rested on my belief that the sealed page she had carried onto that barge held Valentino's confession to his brother's murder. And were that true, and if Damiata could reach Rome with the damning document, she would deliver the one blow the empire of Saint Peter and Caesar could never withstand.

Instead, in the months after Sinigaglia, the pope's son was given an entirely free hand to resume his conquests. As I had feared, Valentino quickly abandoned even his lip service to peace, assaulting fortresses and cities throughout central Italy with relentless fury. And Pope Alexander continued to provide his captain general the unceasing torrent of ducats required to conquer both Fortune and the Kingdoms of the World.

By midsummer of 1503, Duke Valentino had determined to discard his alliance with the French king, who alone stood between the new Caesar and the great prizes he had long sought: Bologna, Venice, and, of course, our Florence. At Sinigaglia, I believed, Valentino had not only begun the conquest of Italy; he had already set his acquisitive eye upon the rest of Europe.

As I watched, with dreadful rapture, the rise of Valentino's new empire, I found my sole consolation in ever more desperate conjecture: Even if Damiata's barge had reached Venice, she would not have risked going to Rome by the shortest route; in fact, aware that the vessel's destination was common knowledge—Valentino had known it even as the ship fled from his guns—she might well have disembarked elsewhere along the coast and hidden herself for weeks, if not months.

And once Damiata had carefully made her way to Rome—assuming she had—she could not simply have walked into the Vatican and demanded her son.

But such reasoning could not contain my fears. Despite her promise that I would see her again, Damiata had left me with only one certainty: month after month, as Valentino conquered territory after territory, I heard nothing from her or of her.

Neither did I hear anything more from the murderer who had briefly whispered his secrets to me. In Florence, we received rumors of atrocities that had followed Valentino's campaign in central Italy, among them reports that young women had been abducted, raped, and murdered. But such rumors always accompany conquering armies; in this case most men credited the abuses to Spanish mercenaries. Having heard no accounts of dismembered and beheaded corpses, even I could hardly speculate that one rare man was responsible for these crimes. Try as I would, I could no longer enter the Labyrinth of his mind; eventually I could not help but suspect that his singular nature was perhaps more a creature of my own imagination. Perhaps the murderer had in fact died at Sinigaglia, as Valentino had insisted and Damiata had believed.

Yet as much as I feared that my science had already been proved fraudulent, I feared all the more I would soon see Valentino again. And before that bitter day ended, I would be forced to witness my *bella* Firenze perish in flames, the horrors of Capua in her streets.

◆

Fortune, however, had her own inscrutable designs. In August 1503, at the very summit of his son's success, Pope Alexander VI fell ill with the tertian fever common to that hot season. For a time the pope's recovery was expected, but after a sudden reversal, he died on the eighteenth. Rodrigo Borgia's demise, like his election as pope, was widely credited, even by learned men, to a contract with the Devil, which had allotted him eleven years—and eight additional days, as it turned out—on the throne of Saint Peter, this in exchange for his immortal soul, which he yielded up with his last breath, all witnesses present attributing to him the words, "I come, it is right. Wait a moment."

Thus Valentino lost his essential partner a year before he might have completed the conquests necessary to preserve his power long after his father's death. Worse yet, at the time his father died, Valentino had been on his own deathbed of the same feverish malady; only his proverbial strength and endurance had saved him. These blows notwithstanding, Valentino recovered sufficient health, and secured enough of his father's vast treasury, to ensure that the new pope, Pius III, was elected to serve at his pleasure.

Then almost at once, Fortune struck again: Valentino's consecrated pope died within days of his coronation. When this news reached Florence on 19 October, the Ten of War at once dispatched me to Rome, to observe the election of yet another pope and assess his intentions—particularly with regard to Duke Valentino, a matter of no little interest to us.

Within days of my arrival in Rome, Cardinal Giuliano della Rovere was elected pope, taking the name Julius II. As a cardinal, Giuliano della Rovere had suffered the particular animus of Pope Alexander VI, who had eventually exiled him from Rome. Nevertheless, della Rovere had promised to put aside these former indignities in return for the votes Valentino controlled in the College of Cardinals; these were committed only after the aspiring pontiff solemnly pledged to renew the duke's appointment as captain general of the armies of the Holy Roman Church, the office that had afforded Valentino his vast power and his many conquests.

But as Europe watched and waited, the promised reappointment was repeatedly delayed, on into December. The Papal States quickly enough fell into disorder; citing the need to protect their commercial interests from the growing lawlessness, the Venetians marched troops into the heart of the Romagna. Yet even as this year of three popes neared its end, Julius II, torn between his fear of Duke Valentino and his fear of Venice, still hesitated to restore the former's sacred office. Instead, rumors began to gather like carrion birds: many of the Vatican embassies believed that Valentino was soon to be arrested and exiled from the very Italy he had hoped to remake in his image, much as his own father had denied Cardinal della Rovere an arena for his ambitions.

◆

Hence I remained in Rome, faithfully dispatching the scant news and rampant rumors to my lords of the Palazzo della Signoria. In an effort to peck up more reliable intelligence, on the afternoon of 8 December 1503, I found myself in attendance at the vast Vatican palace, the occasion an ambassadors' reception in the Hall of Saints. This was the same extravagantly gilded-and-frescoed room from which Pope Alexander had dispatched Damiata on the errand to which she devoted her narrative—and which remains the subject of mine.

Beneath that sky-blue vault, which the painter Pinturicchio had adorned with pagan gods, the sacred had already surrendered to the profane, as was so often the case in the Vatican. The dozen or so cardinals present, their red damask robes matched by red noses, cheeks, and lips tinted with Orvieto wine, were doubled in number by the *cortigiane oneste* in the gold-stitched damasks and gold-set jewels of their vocation, their velvet-soft shoulders the color of cream, their breasts as lucent as pearls. Brooches, hairnets, rings, and choker necklaces sparkled as if from a rain shower of gemstones and diamonds.

The ambassadors favored sable lapels and velvet caps, but my reputation for wise counsel had only increased and my intellect continued to admit me wherever my wardrobe did not. I conversed with the embassy from Urbino, the very gentlemen who had fled their city a year and a half previously, when Valentino had attacked them from all sides like lightning from a clear summer sky, forcing the Duke of Urbino to crawl to safety through the irrigation ditches, with only the shirt on his back. But now these Urbinese had come to Rome to seek restitution of their properties, and in this, Fortune had turned to their favor.

One of them, an elegant, mature gentleman, was recounting an event they all regarded as the sign of a great upheaval in the Heavens, this having evidently taken place several days previously: "Valentino had requested this audience for no less than a month, and when at last our Duke Guidobaldo granted it"—the same Duke Guidobaldo who had fled in his shirt—"Valentino threw himself on his knees before him, laying blame upon his youth, his evil counselors, his bad companions, the abominable disposition of the pope and all others who had urged him to that undertaking, even cursing his own father's memory before he pledged prompt restoration of our duke's library, antiquities, and all the stolen items."

"We had better proceed with all haste in recovering these things," confided a colleague, "because Valentino is not long for Rome." This was followed by sotto voce speculation on Valentino's present whereabouts. He was either upstairs, directly over our heads, under close confinement in the Cardinal of Rouen's apartments, or already in a cell in the Castel Sant'Angelo; he was destined either for the latter or a prison in Naples or exile in Spain. His mysterious whereabouts and rumors of his demise seemed no less a marvel than had his sudden ascendance over all Italy, following his brother's murder.

"Whatever the case, we have seen the last of him," concluded the gentleman, secure in his belief—as no wise man ever should be—that Fortune had fairly meted justice.

Seeking my own counsel, I departed this circle of men and found a place beneath the most lavish and lifelike of Pinturicchio's splendid frescoes, the *Disputation of Saint Catherine of Alexandria*. Painted within the massive, gilded arch opposite the window, this enormous pageant spanned the entire breadth of the room. So real it seemed he would speak, the resurrected Juan of Gandia rode his white charger, as vain as a peacock in his *alla turca* turban. His sister Lucrezia was less to be believed as Pinturicchio's learned Saint Catherine, if only because her golden curls and puckered lips rivaled any of the courtesans present in that room. Like others before me, I observed her resemblance to Damiata—although perhaps none had ever made this comparison with such a sharp thorn in his breast.

Nevertheless, it was young Cesare who played the most prominent role, even if he had, at the time this fresco was painted, been far surpassed by his younger brother, Juan. I could see why Pinturicchio had chosen Cesare as his model for Emperor Maximinus, although I was equally certain the painter had not truly understood why he found such powerful ambition and pensive hesitation in the same youthful face. But my science—as much as I could still credit my own studies—offered me another unproved theory: like Nero and Caligula, young Cesare had often hidden behind a mask of meekness, waiting for the moment when his true nature could reign unfettered. And even now I feared that the Duke of Urbino and his gentlemen were pursuing a dangerous folly, if they believed that Valentino's protestations of remorse were anything more than a mirror of their own cowardice and submission.

◆

An alto tenor strolled among us, singing the "Mal un muta per effecto," accompanying himself on a *lira da braccio* shaped like a woman's torso—rounded at the hips, narrowed at the waist, and wide again at the shoulders, with an indentation at the bottom. He played this lady as if he were her lover, his bow floating at the very tips of his fingers, caressing each note.

My senses flooded with memories and for a moment I was achingly convinced I held Damiata again. Yet during my nearly six weeks in Rome, I had found only her apparition—although it appeared whenever I saw a woman of even slight resemblance to her. Certain that I could make no inquiry so discreet it would not endanger her, instead I often walked the muddy alleys of the Trastevere like a lost pilgrim, believing with each step that she would appear in some shadowed doorway, the arms that reached to embrace me no longer a phantom's.

"She whom I keep in my thoughts, where I want her to live forever . . ." the singer trilled, this verse an arrow aimed at my heart by *Fortuna*, rather than *Amor*. Yet it did not seem that I was the only one so struck, because throughout the room the chattering began to fall away, as though those words had silenced two dozen conversations.

Then even the singer let his bow fall to his side.

Evidently Duke Valentino had been comfortably lodged in the Cardinal of Rouen's apartments just above us, rather than in a cell in the Castel Sant'Angelo. By the time I saw him, he was staring up at the *Disputation of Saint Catherine*, fixed upon himself in the guise of Emperor Maximinus. Only when Valentino pointed to this image did I observe that he held the hand of a little boy, perhaps six years old, dressed like a diminutive prince of the Church, in a burgundy velvet tunic and scarlet hose.

I had expected Giovanni to be the image of Damiata, but I could not find her so easily in this boy's face. He had a hint of her mouth, with lips more plump than Valentino's and sand-hued bangs that shadowed his eyes. Perhaps there was also a suggestion of Damiata's long, slender nose, but on a child's face I could hardly be certain. I doubted the boy no more or less than I doubted her.

But of course I had to know. If Damiata's son was still living in the Vatican, either she had failed in her quest to rescue him, or she had perished even before she could attempt it.

Before I could reach the new arrivals, Valentino turned away from the enormous fresco to face his entire audience, as it were, his posture at once stately and casually indifferent. He looked about. And then he lifted his hands, urging the stunned company to resume the conversations his entrance had halted. As if commanded by their priest to recite the Te Deum, they dutifully did so—none more quickly and anxiously than the gentlemen from Urbino.

Holding the boy's hand, Valentino stepped to greet me—I should say, to present his young companion to me. "Giovanni, I recommend to you the Florentine secretary. Messer Niccolò Machiavelli. Give him your hand."

The boy's name was a finger poked into my heart. He held out his hand gracefully but kept his eyes lowered.

"Messer Niccolò." Valentino did not offer his own hand. I cannot say that he appeared a changed man. His face was as pale as it had been during our days in the Romagna, his attire just as black: cap, gloves, tunic, hose, slippers. Only the keenest observer would have found his hair thinner and the cinnabar tint less evident, the skin stretched a bit more tautly upon his arrogant jaw. Nothing suggested that he had recovered from an illness that would have buried any other man.

"All this time you have been in Rome," Valentino said, "I have meant to send someone to inquire of you regarding Leonardo." He offered this so earnestly, that one might have presumed Leonardo's fate was the only matter of our mutual concern. "I am told you have employed him to do something about Pisa."

Leonardo da Vinci had come to Florence a month after my return, in February of that year. And despite no little continuation of our quarrels, we had become true *compare*—as well as partners in a most ingenious scheme to return our seaport, Pisa, to Florentine dominion. Evidently Valentino's spies were still everywhere, although it was unlikely he knew all the particulars of our plan. Perhaps he hoped to sow distrust among us.

"I can only say with certainty that the maestro did not return to your employment," I answered, reminding Valentino that at Sinigaglia, he had falsely prophesied that Leonardo would quickly reconsider his departure.

Valentino nodded respectfully at this barb, as if I had merely repeated his own wisdom. But perhaps his eyes narrowed. "You have not heard from her, have you?"

I had thrown a dart at him; he had replied by sticking a dagger in my throat. And I felt as though I were choking on the truth.

My silence provided Valentino the answer he expected. "She lied to you," he said. "As she lied to me."

"I have not heard from her." I imagined I had achieved some victory in simply confessing this. "That does not convince me she has lied to me." It was entirely possible he knew why I had not heard from her.

The music of the "Mal un muta" seemed to weave among the rising conversations, all eyes glancing again and again at Valentino, the air humming with speculation.

Valentino nodded toward the gentlemen from Urbino—and set them tittering nose to nose like little mice. "Just as before Sinigaglia, every fool has come to scorn my methods and doubt my success. But this new pope will soon submit to my *disegno*. Even now a great enterprise is in progress."

"Your *disegno*." The word alone froze me.

"Yes." I had never observed a soul within Valentino's green eyes, which yielded less than black stone. Now I saw something there, but nothing like one man's soul; rather, this terrible teeming, the writhing of infinitesimal wraiths. "A world where capricious Fortune no longer holds dominion, where each life and each death are redeemed by an inalterable purpose. A *disegno* God never had the imagination to see." He gazed down at Giovanni, whose head remained bowed. "My son will be heir to all of it."

At once Valentino looked up, knowing he had sown new doubts within me. "She lied to you about that as well. She would deprive her own son of what is his by right. The world that I can bequeath him." He shook his head with a sadness that mimicked my own, an image so well crafted that I could believe it entirely. "You have invested all your faith in a terrible Medusa, whose single truth would make hard stone of the blood in your veins, if ever you were to see it." His sorrowing face now conjured a grief so profound, and seemingly real, that it frightened me. "Soon enough, Niccolò, you will have no choice but to look into the face of truth. Or the face of the Devil, however you wish to see it."

He turned away, leaving this prophecy to ring in my ears. But Giovanni, no longer clutching Valentino's hand, remained for a moment, still staring at the majolica floor tiles, as if fascinated with the Borgia crests and emblems intricately painted upon them. At last he looked up.

I could not even silence my gasp. If moments before I had imagined Damiata's embrace, here I saw her *ultramare* gaze so clearly that she seemed to plead with me from within this little boy's desperate eyes.

CHAPTER 27

Often Fortune keeps the good beneath her feet, while she lifts up the wicked.

I exited the Vatican into a dusk that seemed brighter than many recent afternoons; the ever-present rain clouds had briefly vanished and the sky had a faintly luminous, murex tint. I did not return to the inn where I had a room, this in the Borgo that lies between the Vatican and the Tiber, a region of newer buildings. Instead I walked parallel to the Tiber, entering the Via Sancta, a road pilgrims take from the Vatican to the Trastevere. In the same manner that Pope Alexander had previously broadened and repaved the road between St. Peter's and the Tiber, the late pope had also begun to remake the Via Sancta; for perhaps a few hundred *braccia*, the old houses beside the road had been torn down and new flagstones put in place. Then the road narrowed again and the houses crowded in, though behind these ancient brick dwellings, shops, and stables were nothing but orchards and pastures. I smelled the *contado* instead of the city, the odor of wet earth and livestock.

In the little time it took me to reach the Trastevere, the dusk seemed already to have fled into darkness; nevertheless, I was able to rely on a familiar path through the narrow alleys, arriving at the old Santa Maria basilica, which towered over the surrounding tenements. Walking beneath the church's immense portal, I peeked inside, to find vespers in progress, a priest reading the psalm, the words seeming to rattle around the distant altar. Blazing candles burnished the immense marble piers, looted from some ancient Roman temple, to a gold almost as brilliant as the tesserae that framed the giant mosaic figures of Christ and the Saints, the shimmering heavenly host that appeared to hover in the lofty half dome. Had I believed our Lord was in fact present, I would have invoked His assistance.

But in a world God has abandoned to *Fortuna*, I could only think that this goddess now faced an enemy whose implacable will was more than a match for her cruel caprices—and who stood to profit from the very chaos his adversary had sown throughout Italy. Amid the widespread disorder in the wake of his father's death—and the stunningly brief reign of his father's successor—Valentino would have little difficulty playing one faction against another, subverting friendships and sowing suspicion, until he alone could be trusted to lead us forward. The only man who stood in his way was God's new vicar; Pope Julius II had been a lifelong enemy of Rodrigo Borgia, and he had both the experience and the native caution to distrust his predecessor's son. But the new pope was under immense persuasion, by means of both threats and promised rewards, from Borgia allies in the Curia to reappoint Valentino as captain general of the Church. It did not seem he would be able to resist, if he wished to preserve his power—and perhaps even his person.

I lingered at the portal of the Santa Maria church, to consider an offering I might present the new pope: testimony regarding Valentino's crimes. But I quickly lost this faith; I could scarcely begin to prove my case, having at present only my obscure theories—and nothing at all a reasonable man could hold in his hands. The salt mound at Cesenatico, which did not point to any particular man's guilt regardless, had been swept into the Adriatic; the page of a schoolboy's geometry, whatever it might reveal, had vanished along with Damiata—whose unfortunate son still remained hostage in the house of Borgia.

And even were I able to produce a "confession" of some sort, I also had grave doubts that Pope Julius would make use of it. In truth, the new pope could serve his own aims far better by directing attention to Valentino's aggression against the great families of Italy—the Orsini, the Sforza, the Montefeltro of Urbino, and a litany of others—than by attempting to condemn Valentino for crimes against his own family and a few dozen nameless women.

In sum, it no longer mattered what I—or any other man—suspected of Valentino's crimes, or whether he was guilty or not. His political ambitions were brutal enough. And all too soon he would require a *mappa* of the entire world to circumscribe them.

♦

There is a fountain in front the Santa Maria Trastevere, an ancient, eight-sided marble basin; those who credit miracles believe an anointing oil bubbled up here the very day and hour our Sinless Lord was born in the Holy Land. I paused and listened as the gurgling spouts struggled to produce more water than an old man in the latrine. And here I could not help but pause and reflect on the miraculous births in my own household.

As I have written, at the time I returned from the Romagna, Marietta had to be coerced into returning to our house. Nevertheless, we had shared the same roof for only two weeks, when we shared the same bed. I had given my wife neither encouragement nor instruction to do so; she roused me from a sleep in which I had imagined she was someone else. And even when I was certain who she was, I made love to her as if I expected the most extraordinary metamorphosis: that on waking, I would behold Damiata's face.

Well before that dawn, however, I literally leapt from the connubial bed, already pregnant, let us say, with a dreadful understanding of Marietta's motives: If she had been gotten with child by her "cousin" during my time in the Romagna, she could now reasonably claim that I was the father. And she might reasonably expect this *favola* to be found credible, because, of course, she had previously told it.

On that occasion, I got silently dressed and said nothing. Even when Marietta began showing her second pregnancy, I did not betray my suspicions to her. And I had scrupulously maintained that forbearance when I left Florence months later, with Marietta already complaining bitterly about her prenatal confinement, this prescribed by the physician the Corsini had sent to look after her. Instead, I had departed for Rome certain that the new baby's birth date would present a clear resolution to all my questions.

♦

But now another child had set other questions, no less familiar and tormenting, clamoring about in my brain. Was Damiata wasting in a prison somewhere—or already a moldering corpse? Had she been thrown into the sea or arrested as she tried to enter the Vatican? Had her life already ended on a rack in the Castel Sant'Angelo? Or was she somehow hiding here in the Trastevere, still waiting for the opportune moment—or constructing some scheme—to free her son?

Desperately pursuing this last possibility—or miracle, as it were—I left the square in front of the Santa Maria church and ventured far deeper into the Trastevere, down winding alleys seemingly constructed to baffle a compass, the passages sometimes so narrow that my shoulders touched on either side. During my weeks in Rome, I had searched these filthy, trash-strewn warrens an unreasonable number of times—but never before at night. Now the doorsteps and tavern porches that had seemed strangely deserted by day came ominously to life, filled with the click of dice or sudden eruptions of chatter in a dozen incomprehensible tongues and dialects. And the silences that followed were all the more sinister.

Lost among the Trastevere's twists and turns, amid one of the silences I heard a little chiming. The hair at my neck bristled. Unable to distinguish whether the source of this sound was before or behind me, I went forward, within a few steps finding a doorstep where, if unable to hide, I could at least secure my back. The stoop was so shallow that even as I flattened myself against a creaking door, my toes remained in the alley.

All at once, with a sound like a thousand Carnival noisemakers—this din far obscuring the chiming of their bells—a herd of bleating sheep frantically squeezed and stamped through the alley as if fleeing the beast of the bottomless pit. When they had passed I stood there breathless, certain that I had witnessed some omen—and almost as certainly not an auspicious one.

A moment after I watched the gray rumps of the last few sheep recede into the blackness—followed closely by their shrouded shepherd—I saw something that resembled a pale mask, hovering in a doorway the flock had just passed. For a moment I had to assure myself that I had witnessed the Licorn's death. And then I wondered, with far more reason, if Valentino had sent someone to follow me. Perhaps he thought I would lead him to Damiata.

This watcher was a woman, however, evidenced by both her height and the vague contours of her oval face. A stature and a shape so familiar that like a fool who never learns, I ran toward her.

She was probably younger than Damiata, but her face was covered with pustules of the French pox. The words she spit out were unfathomable to me, except that I knew they were an invitation. This oration concluded with a smile, her teeth so black that it seemed she was a creature wrought entirely of darkness, visible only because of her hideous mask.

No sooner had I turned from this woeful countenance than the tenor of her address became angry, the words strangely clicking and screeching. Inside the lining of my mantle, I carried silver coins to offer as gratuities to the myriad Vatican functionaries, without which I could not get from one room to the next. I threw these pieces of silver into the mud behind me, not so much as a kindness, but in the belief that she would busy herself digging them out instead of following me like some evil fate, shouting curses and spells.

I must have run all the way back to the Borgo, because when at last I unlocked the door to my room and sat on my little bed, sweat trickled from my brow even as tears coursed down my cheeks. I did not weep for myself or Italy, and what we had both certainly lost. I wept for my Damiata and the little boy Valentino had snatched away, not only from his mother's loving embrace, but also from the very hands of defeated and envious Fortune.

◆

The sheep were in fact an omen of sorts, because the next day the rains resumed, heavier than before, as if another Deluge were beginning—and a courier knocked on my door with a letter from the

Ten of War, instructing me to conclude my business in Rome and return to Florence. I was only too grateful to comply, the city on the Tiber having become nothing more than a vast sepulcher of my hopes.

I spent the next few days paying calls on various cardinals who had business interests with private Florentine citizens, as well as performing errands for our own Cardinal Soderini, who would not let me get away without some final services on his behalf.

Yet as my departure approached, I slept no better. In part, this was because I had known, for nearly a month, that the question waiting for me in my own house would never be answered. My second child and first son had been born on 9 November, after I had been in Rome less than a fortnight—nine months after Marietta had come to my bed. The doubts I was evidently not alone in entertaining would be assuaged, my colleagues in Florence joyously wrote me, when I saw the *fanciullo*, who was "the image" of me. Marietta herself was among these correspondents, her fawning letter seasoned with sentiments that had never dropped from her lips.

So I could not say how I would feel when I saw this baby boy for the first time. But I knew well enough my feelings for Primerana; I was the father who loved her because he was present the night she was born, whether or not he was present the night she was conceived. In truth, I could have only one certainty regarding the paternity of both my children: If I declared to the world that I had been deceived and sent that adorable little girl, her infant brother, and their mother back to the Corsini, I would do so on the basis of suspicions that could never be proved. And if I were blessed to grow old, I would always wonder if I had exiled my own flesh—my father's flesh and blood—from my beloved father's house.

But it was not my own children who awakened me every hour, it seemed, to hear the rain throbbing on the tiles, my breast aching no less than my bones. In the year since I had last held Damiata, as often as I had lain in her spectral embrace, I had always found her phantom flesh as searing as my memory of her. Now she had become as cold as the marble effigy atop a tomb. And I no longer saw her eyes but instead her little son's, no different than the eyes that haunted me in the Hall of Saints. Pleading with me not to leave him behind in the Devil's house.

I was midway between restless sleep and one such awakening, when I heard a faint knock on my door, nearly lost amid the roar of yet another inundation. I got up with a start, thinking only that Valentino had been reappointed to his office, and I was to be so informed— or perhaps even arrested and jailed, if only to nettle my lords in the Palazzo della Signoria. Or perhaps I would be taken to a quicker end, if Valentino had determined to at once devour Florence.

I dressed before I opened up. The man who waited on the threshold was as dark as a Moor, wearing a workman's cape, soaking wet. Like many residents of the Trastevere, he was clearly a son of the Levant.

He examined me more carefully than I had observed him, then bowed before speaking. "Messer Niccolò. Will you do us the favor of coming? Madonna Damiata has sent me for you."

CHAPTER 28

This would be the true way to go to Paradise: learn the way to Hell.

My guide led me east, toward the Tiber. We walked beneath the massive, baleful stone ramparts of the Castel Sant'Angelo before crossing the bridge of the same name, our ears assaulted by the monstrous roar of the flooded river, which raced hardly a hand's breadth beneath the sturdy stone span. On the other bank, we proceeded downriver, along the Via dei Banchi, which itself resembled a river, the torrent rushing ankle-high over the pavement. Above me in the gloom were the great façades and arched windows of all the palazzi occupied by Vatican officials, German and Florentine bankers, and Rome's most prosperous merchants. In one of these palaces, Damiata had once lived and conducted the business of love.

Shortly we entered the ruins of the ancient Roman Forum, which is little more than a pasture with the great artifacts rising from it—immense arches, fragmented columns, and scattered basilicas that loomed in the darkness like the creations of Titans. When we began to climb the Palatine Hill, the mud became a sopping clay that seemed to have hands, so firmly did it cling to my feet. On the summit were the ruins of the Caesars' palaces, a procession of gaping, hollow cupolas crowned with wild shrubs.

Just before we reached the top, my guide began to disappear into the earth. He had nearly vanished entirely into what seemed a large burrow when he looked up and said, "I will help you."

In the beginning, my descent was no different than climbing down a steep hill, but just when I took a great inhalation—as if I were about to submerge myself in the ocean—and lowered my head entirely beneath the earth, my feet lost purchase on that subterranean slope and could only flail in the void. My guide quickly wrapped his arms around my knees, and by our combined efforts I was able to descend to the floor of what might once have been Caligula's closet.

Having delivered me safely to this dank, foul-smelling little room, my Virgil led me into a tunnel that forced me to crouch, my feet slipping in mud, the odor of damp earth so thick that I could hardly breathe. As best I could judge the distance, we journeyed all the way to the other side of the hill. At the end, we were greeted by another dark-complected man holding a pine torch, who ushered us into a small hemispherical rotunda; with a noise like a swift brook, muddy rainwater streamed through the shattered dome.

My guides began a discussion regarding a rough opening in the pavement, from which the top of a ladder protruded. I knelt beside them, observing a silted floor a good dozen *braccia* below. At the foot of the ladder was a little table constructed of several planks set upon a pair of rough trestles. Atop this rude furnishing, a flickering oil lamp illuminated the wall closest to the table and cast a much fainter light on the wall opposite. The far end of the enormous room faded into a darkness my eyes could not penetrate.

I looked up at my guide. "Is Madonna Damiata down there?"

He turned up his palms and shook his head. But I did not doubt his ignorance; certainly I was dealing with intermediaries.

This time my guide did not intend to precede me. He gestured, with a deference that offered no comfort, that I should go first. And alone.

There are many places we will go to answer a question, where prudence would dictate otherwise. My friend Amerigo Vespucci de Terrenove asked if the Genoese Colombo, who had used our compatriot Toscanelli's maps, had found a way across the sea to China and India, or had discovered a new land entirely; Amerigo risked both life and fortune to obtain the answer. So it should not be difficult to understand why, when the question regards someone who is fully half your own soul, you will sail any sea, or climb down into Hell.

◆

As I descended the creaking ladder, the two men remained on the floor above, looking down at me with wide eyes and half-open mouths. When I reached the bottom my feet settled into cold slime. The silence was broken only by the muted music of trickling water.

I peered into the miasma at the far end of the room. Not one but two faces emerged, quickly becoming more distinct as they approached the lamp. The man was tall, his companion just a boy.

Giovanni still had his hood up but Valentino had drawn his back. His cape was parted in front, allowing the scant light to glimmer on a silver-gray breastplate. He had dressed for trouble.

"*Bene, bene*, I welcome you, Niccolò." I had expected his words to be swallowed up in that vast chamber, but instead they echoed clangorously. "At last you will witness the truth. I will show you my brother's murderer."

The next voice came from behind me. "He is a liar, Niccolò."

Giovanni's eyes sparkled. "Mama! Mama, I am here! I love you, Mama! I love you!"

When I turned, the Aphrodite of my fevered memories was not there. Instead Damiata had become harsh Athena, her dyed dark hair pulled back like a kitchen servant's, her skin entirely without color, her brilliant eyes shadowed.

"I want to go to my mother, Excellency," Giovanni said, quite calmly under the circumstances. I glanced back and saw that Valentino had restrained him, a gloved hand on the boy's slender shoulder.

"Wait a moment, my most precious darling," Damiata said. "Your uncle wants something first."

Damiata had opened her gray wool cape to reveal a black dress, again little better than a servant might wear. She picked her steps carefully, only looking up at me when she reached the crude table. I could see nothing in her shrouded eyes. I could not even distinguish the scent that had always announced her. There was only the reek of burning oil and the rot of a tomb.

"Niccolò, I did not send for you," she said quietly to me. "I would never have put you at such risk. He wants you here."

Fear danced atop my head.

Damiata reached into her cape and withdrew a little packet wrapped in blue fish paper. I knew at once that it contained the sealed page I had last seen at Sinigaglia.

Having known for a year that Damiata intended to trade this item for her son, I could only wonder why she had not been able to bring the late pope to a similar parley. Still less could I understand why Valentino was so eager to obtain this page that he would barter away the boy he claimed as his heir. If it did contain his confession to his brother's murder, the father who might have turned implacably against him upon reading it had been in Hell for months. And as I have said, the new pope was far more concerned with Valentino's threat to Italy's great families.

I was afforded little time to muse on the matter; the exchange took place so quickly that had I blinked I might have missed it. Valentino simply brought the boy forward and snatched the packet, whereupon Damiata and her son embraced fiercely, the boy crying out, "You came back for me, Mama, just as you promised! Oh, dear Mama, how I missed you!" He began to sob and sniffle. "Never go away again, dearest Mama. Never, ever, ever . . ."

"My most precious, precious darling. Mama will always be here. Mama will always, always be with you." Damiata looked at me as she held her son, her eyes suddenly brilliant in the gloom.

Valentino hurriedly unwrapped the blue fish paper. When he spoke, his tone was as mild as if he were merely remarking on the color of the wrapping. "Someone has broken the seal."

I saw Damiata fly off her feet, her son still clinging to her. Some instinct made me leap between her and Valentino, and before I could even reason that he had struck her his gloved hands were at my neck like a pair of falcons, the blackness closing around me so quickly that I could only marvel at how easily a man can be choked to death.

"Mama! Mama!" I could still hear Giovanni screaming. Through the narrowing portal of my vision I saw my murderer's livid face, at last entirely unmasked.

"Your father!" These words seemed to descend from the rotunda far above. But this was Damiata's cry. "Your father unsealed it! Your father saw it! The day before he died!"

"Liar!" Valentino howled this single word as if somehow releasing all the terrified screams imprisoned in the souls of his innocent victims. The strength at once departed his hands.

I fell to my knees, coughing and gasping.

Damiata had not even risen from the muck. Giovanni pulled at her arm. Some rational being that remained within me thought, *If Valentino goes to her now, how can I stop him?*

I got to my feet and with great, rasping breaths stumbled toward the table, thinking that I might make a weapon of one of the planks.

"You murdering, lying whore!"

With her little boy's help, Damiata stood up. "I did not murder your father, Cesare." She addressed Valentino, in both name and tone, as if he were a teenage cardinal. "You did it. You put the knife in your father's heart."

Although my legs were far from steady, I reached the table and snatched up one of the planks. By the time I had armed myself and looked up again, Valentino had become so still that it seemed his Medusa had in fact turned him to stone.

"You should know how long it took me to reach Rome," Damiata told him, almost patiently. "Because your people were looking for me wherever I went. And when I got here I had to move every few days, even in the Trastevere, because they were breaking down doors and searching taverns there, too. For months I lived like that, always running, just as I did six years ago, before my darling boy was born. Then I heard that both you and the pope had become ill. And I knew your people would be distracted with your care and busy securing the papal treasury. So at last I came to the Vatican. It was the day before your father died."

Damiata wiped her muddy hands on her cape, then put them on her son's shoulders and continued. "You don't remember because you were also delirious with fever. But after several days of dreadful suffering, your father had begun to improve. His household was encouraged. I found Burchard"—Burchard was the Vatican's master of ceremonies—"and told him that your father urgently required an accounting on a confidential matter."

Pushing her son behind her, Damiata edged closer to the duke. "In better days I had found Burchard agreeable to my persuasion, and on that day I convinced him that the information I possessed required His Holiness's immediate attention, and indeed might improve his condition. Burchard took the very item you are now holding to your father's sickbed, so that His Holiness could read it. I had left the seal intact, so that he could be certain of its authenticity."

Seeing the road ahead, I steadied myself and tried to grip the plank as if it were a tournament mace. But Damiata had already come close enough to Valentino that she might be dead before I could lift a hand.

"I did not have long to wait. First there was the most terrible cry of pain, more the howl of a demon than anything else, and then His Holiness began to bellow like a bull, so that at once all his people came running. 'Bastard son of a whore! You were never my son! My Juan! My Juan! Where is my beautiful Juan? The Devil's own bastard has taken my son!' Those were the last words I ever heard from your father. When I ran in on the heels of his servants, his face was scarlet and the physicians and everyone else were desperately attending to him. I found the page he had just read beneath the foot of one of the quacks, retrieved it, and left your father in the hands of God, Who took him within a day. If Michelotto hadn't hidden Giovanni along with all the jewels and treasure, I would have gotten my little boy as well, and have done so without all this. All your games and endless delays." Hearing this, I presumed she had negotiated with Valentino for some time after Pope Alexander's death, probably through proxies—and I could only imagine the "games" he had contrived to lure her here. "But now you have what you wanted. And I have my precious son."

Damiata's hands shook and again she gave me a pleading look. I could believe we shared a soul, because at once I understood. Regardless of her own fate, she wanted me to save the boy.

"You presented my father a lie." Valentino's complexion was again as pale as ever, but a slight hoarseness remained in his voice. "In his illness, he could not understand what he was reading. You cheated him, just as you cheated Juan of his life. As you believe you will cheat me. I brought you Giovanni in good faith. But there never was an honest whore, was there?"

"You tried to cheat Fortune." Damiata took a heaving breath, like a woman standing on the scaffold, the black hood already over her head. "You could not wait for your opportunity. Instead it was you who betrayed your father the same day you betrayed my poor, dear Juan. And me."

"The truth about you is here," Valentino said, holding the folded page with one hand and swatting it with the other. As if he were a madman with a violent tic, abruptly he turned to me. "This is the instrument with which she murdered my father—just as with a few carefully placed words to Vitellozzo Vitelli, this serpent killed my brother."

His arm shot out and I believed he would finish wringing my neck. Instead he merely offered me the folded parchment. "She murdered my father with half-truths, which in his reduced state he could not understand." He composed himself and for a moment looked at me as searchingly as he had on the rampart at Sinigaglia. "Read it. You of all men will see the truth."

Damiata clutched her son, her hands still quaking. I placed my plank cudgel back atop the trestles. As carefully as if I were feeding a hunting leopard a scrap of meat, I accepted Valentino's offering.

My own hands trembled as I brought the folded packet closer to the lamplight. I fumbled to open it; the parchment, still partly layered with wax, seemed as stiff as bark. But when I had the page entirely unfolded, I could see that the inner edge had been scored with a knife. The Latin text was in the same copyist's hurried hand as the Euclid's *Elements* Vitellozzo Vitelli had shown me, although the broad margin did not have any geometric shapes drawn in it. Instead this space had been filled with script in good, learned Italian, yet so hastily scrawled that it spilled over onto the original text.

I needed only to read a few lines before I was certain as to the author of these words.

◆

When I had finished reading Valentino's record of his own *traget di capra*—goat ride—I looked up at him. He nodded meaningfully at me, then snatched the page away, his hand darting like a viper.

I turned to Damiata. For a time we stood silent, requiring only our eyes to exchange sad and anxious words. At last I said to her, "You didn't know it would be this."

She shook her head, tears welling in her eyes. "I know you did, Niccolò. But I refused to see it. That is the sad truth. We do not give ourselves to the Devil because we love evil. We love him because he is so beautiful. Without your science, Niccolò, I could not have believed it, even after reading that."

For a moment, the only sound was the hollow rushing of the muddy water far above us. Then Damiata addressed Valentino. "They always say that His Holiness was in league with the Devil, that his last words were to Satan. But the only devil your father knew was the one in his own house. He favored Juan, against all reason, because he knew that if you became the instrument of his ambitions, he would surrender himself to the son he feared more than the Devil. And I better than anyone know why he feared you. Why the entire world should. Because he knew he would come to love the devil in his own house. A love beyond reason. As I once loved you. As we all did. Beyond all reason." Tears clogged her voice. "*Cercar Maria per Ravenna*. When your father sent me to Imola, he knew in his own corrupt soul that I would only find Maria in Ravenna."

Valentino cocked his head at Damiata, with yet another sudden, tic-like motion. "Come here."

I had never seen this brave lady so frightened. But our children make cowards of us. And the Devil knows what we fear most.

"Come here!"

She looked at me, her eyes pleading.

I understood the sacrifice demanded by the beast of this Labyrinth. And I nodded that she should go to him.

"Go to Messer Niccolò," Damiata told her son. "He is our dearest and most trusted friend. Do what he says." Only when the boy had reluctantly shuffled to my side did she take her first step.

I clutched Giovanni's hand tightly.

When Damiata was close enough to Valentino to die at once, she stopped.

Again I saw that strange teeming in Valentino's eyes, as if all the lost souls in Signorelli's *Last Judgment* were trapped within them. "Put up your hood," he said.

She could hardly do it, her fingers were so palsied with fear. Finally, she was able to conceal her dyed, raven-hued hair and settle her hands at her side. And then she offered her former lover a smile so luminous that it almost buckled my knees. In a heartbeat, she had become the same beautiful, spirited courtesan a bitter, forgotten young cardinal had seen those years ago in Ascanio Sforza's garden.

Valentino raised his hand and held it close to her face, trembling. When at last he was able to touch her, it was not even a carnal gesture, only the merest fingertip caress, as if to convince his stunned senses that his goddess stood there in the flesh. He returned her smile with an awkwardness and desire I had never seen among his many masks. Perhaps he imagined she was his sister—as perhaps he had on the day he first saw her. But for the first time, I saw a sincere hope on the face that had so often mirrored the hopes—however false—of so many.

In the blinking of an eye, he threw off this mask. "Take your son. When I look at him I see nothing of me. I see only weak, cowardly Juan. He could never be my son. Take your bastard and the whore's cunt that spit him out. Get away from me before I cut you open and pull out your diseased womb!"

"Climb!" I barked at Giovanni, shoving him toward the ladder, certain that Fortune had given us this one moment and would offer no other. I would never make a more difficult choice, save one, because I had to turn my back on Damiata at her moment of utmost peril. Yet I knew she would never forgive me, in this life or the next, if I sacrificed her son to the false hope that I could save her.

Little Giovanni was no coward, because when he had climbed just a few rungs of that towering ladder, he turned and called out, "Mama, you must come! Mama! I won't leave you!"

Damiata had played her previous role as skillfully as the immortal Roscius, because now her eyes were wide with utter terror. "You must climb up to the top, darling," she told her son, her voice quavering. "Messer Niccolò will follow you." Again her doomed eyes pleaded with me.

I looked at Valentino. You could not say I observed a single transformation, the exchange of one mask for another. His entire face appeared to twitch and convulse, not merely his eyebrows or his lips, but his forehead and even the taut flesh about his jaw, a thousand metamorphoses taking place at once, yet to no resolution. As if this infinitely mutable mask could no longer decide among the many illusions it had always so effortlessly created.

To speak at all was to taunt the Devil—not to mention Fortune. Yet I said to him, "You spared me twice, Excellency." At the same time I reached out, grabbed Damiata, and pulled her to my side. "Once on the *pianura* and then at Sinigaglia. Now you have summoned me here to bear witness yet again. But I do not believe you want me to witness another murder. You must let them go."

He did not seem to understand or even hear, because the remarkable palsy of his face continued without interruption. But I took this opportunity to push Damiata behind me and whisper frantically to her, "If you hope to save your son, climb now."

When the ladder creaked beneath Damiata's weight, I stepped quite deliberately to the plank table, as if it were a rostrum. "You saw something in me," I told Valentino. "Something I could not see myself. You knew that I would become your apostle. I better than anyone could understand that you fear no mortal enemy, that instead you have set your lance against Fortune herself. No man will ever see more clearly than I the Italy you intended to create for us, a perfection greater than any design of God. Excellency, I give you my oath upon the souls of my mother and father. I will go among the nations and tell them the wonders I have seen. The works you alone have wrought."

His twitching face again offered no indication that he had heard. But I intended to wager my life on my conviction that he had. I turned my back on Valentino, knowing that at any moment on my short journey to the ladder he could fly at me and snap my neck before I could even think that I was about to die.

◆

When I put my hands on the first rung, I believed I had already been granted a miracle. I looked up at Damiata and Giovanni, who had scrambled almost to the opening in the lofty ceiling. Like Dante, I armed my soul against a perishing dread, and began to climb from Hell.

The hand that grasped my ankle froze my limbs, instantly poisoning me with a paralysis as deadening as the goat ride. Yet neither did

Valentino struggle against me. Having seized my leg in the vise of his grip, he did not attempt to pull me down.

"Niccolò. You know as well as I that Fortune imposes on us a pace the merely good cannot match. I will not deny to you that there have been necessary evils. But do you imagine your republic would have prospered under the Vitelli? Do you expect the French king's soldiers will honor our women, when all Italy lies stripped and splayed before them?" He paused but did not loosen his grasp. Above me, I could hear only the rattle of water in the rotunda. "I gave you and my engineer general the means to examine your own souls. An opportunity Fortune could not provide you in a hundred lifetimes. To look into my eyes and find the reflection of your own ambitions. Maestro Leonardo, who believed he saw all the things other men could not, was forced to look away."

"I will never look away," I whispered with the fervor of a prayer. "I have given you my oath."

The Devil beneath me issued the most exquisite sigh, as if, far better than God, he understood our human sorrows. "Then go." I truly wondered if this was his command or mine, instructing my frozen limbs to save my life. "Tell all who suffer in slavery and lawlessness that I alone am the way. Tell them what you alone have seen."

I pulled myself up hand over hand. Although it was the last thing I should have done, when I neared the top of the ladder, I could not help but look down.

Valentino still ruled his pit, gazing up, lit by the guttering lamp. I had only a fleeting image of his face. But it was utterly composed. A face with the features of a man, a man of great beauty, yet it seemed as empty and inhuman as the scarred visage of that tortured creature he had loosed upon the Romagna. *Now see the face of Dis*, I thought, citing Dante. *This is the terror that cannot be told.*

Because it is a blank page, upon which we can create whomever and whatever we wish.

CHAPTER 29

Whom we love once, we love always.

I will now reveal what I had read, while still in that pit: a witness of a different sort, written in the margin of a schoolboy's *Elements*. I believe I offer it here correct in every word, having copied it from memory shortly after.

As I have said, the words were Italian, in a well-tutored but hasty hand.

> *Papa, tell me why you accepted Abel's offering and not Cain's. Was not Cain more worthy? Was not Cain a lion of courage? Was not Cain a warrior king? Was it not Cain who took your armies into the field and won victory upon victory after Abel brought you only humiliation and defeat? Was not Cain the savior of Italy condemned to a cardinal's cap—to watch his brother parade his vanity and whores? Was not Cain the learned and gifted pupil and Abel a drunken whoring fool? Yet you my father accepted Abel's offering and rejected Cain's. And now you ask me—you ask—Where is Juan, your brother? I hear you asking me, your eyes never stop asking. Why do you ask me, Papa?—why do you say to me, What have you done? Why do you tell me my brother's blood cries out from the ground? If you know the truth—if you say you know that I led the Vitelli to him that night, if you say you saw me cut his throat to seal with blood my compact with fate—if you know all this, then make me cursed*

of the earth and a fugitive and vagabond. Then mark me and drive
me out into the land of Nod—no more this silent suspicion that fouls
your every glance. Drive me out of your house, but first tell me why
my brother's offering was acceptable to you and mine was not. Tell
me how many victories Abel would have brought to you. Tell me why
God will surrender all his kingdoms to me and you will not accept my
offering.

◆

The brothers of the Levant, having waited in the rotunda, proved agreeable to leading the three of us back the same way I had come. When we emerged from the earth, no stars in their "heavenly chariots" waited for us, as they had for Dante. Instead, the rain had lifted and all Rome lay before us, ash-gray and appearing to smolder in the light mist, the Tiber curling through the city like an enormous snake. In the distance were the great palaces of the Vatican and the massive cylinder of the Castel Sant'Angelo. The ruins of the ancient Roman Forum lay almost at our feet.

Damiata wrapped her arms around me, an embrace that was fierce and of the flesh. "Dearest, dearest Niccolò, I cursed God when I saw how he had brought you there but now I praise the Virgin that we are all safe. I never wanted to go down into that place but I had become so desperate, after waiting so many months, waiting for him to recover his health, to elect his own pope only to see him die . . . I knew that if Pope Julius restored Cesare's office, I might never have another chance, that he could take my Giovanni anywhere . . ." She choked back a sob. "I thought that buried palace would be my tomb. But at least my son would live knowing I came back for him. Instead you saved us, Niccolò." She held me away so that she could look at me. Her eyes were afire. "I have horses waiting for us at the Arch of the Septimii." She took my hand. "We'll say the rest down there."

As the three of us descended the Palatine muck hand in hand, my family and my house on the Via di Piazza became vague and distant memories. Our progress down that muddy hillside, and then among the tumbled stones of the Forum, could have taken a hundred years and I would have savored every moment of it. When, midway through this journey, Damiata glanced at me and smiled, I thought my heart would explode. The life I had left behind in Florence was but a shadow next to the life I saw beyond Fortune's horizon, shared with the woman I so deeply loved.

The Arch of the Septimii rose from the mist, seemingly scaled to a world ruled by giants. Several *bravi* were already on their horses beneath the immense central span; they might have been equestrian statues of the Roman victors in the Parthian wars, the ancient triumph that had been carved in stone all over those thick columns and enormous marble slabs. These men had several extra horses, as if they anticipated traveling far and fast.

"Valentino's people are looking for their master," one of the *bravi* said to Damiata when we arrived. "Most have gone up to the Palatine. But there's one nosing around down here."

Damiata turned to me but we did not embrace. "Niccolò, I could not see why Cesare wanted that page, with his father already dead. It seemed merely part of his game. But as I told you, I was desperate." She bit her lip. "Now I wonder if I have returned him the keys to the Kingdom."

"No." I was not merely comforting her. In truth, I had seen something on that page that even my science had not anticipated. "He is finished. I know that now. But not because of this new pope. It ended for him the day you brought that page to the Vatican."

"Niccolò, I did not intend for Rodrigo Borgia to die. I thought Cesare's confession was all about Capua and that owing to the pope's weakened condition, I would find it easier to ransom this darling boy. I couldn't see what you saw." She smiled wistfully.

"Valentino allows us to will our own blindness," I said, "with a skill no man before him has ever possessed. That is because deception was a craft both born and bred into him. The first man this lost, soulless little creature ever mimicked was the greatest liar in Christendom, a father whose deceit and worldly ambition were exceeded only by the son who observed him so well. The son Rodrigo Borgia soon came to fear, and in his own way cast out. That was what tormented Valentino like nothing else, that his father turned away from his own image, this mask the son had so arduously and devotedly crafted. And that was the truth that killed the pope, to learn that his greed, deceit, and overweening ambition had found a perfect mirror in the son he always feared."

Damiata crossed herself.

"But in the same way," I assured her, "Valentino died with his father. He lost the mirror to which he had always returned, whenever he needed to find himself." This was the Valentino I had witnessed moments before, trying and discarding a thousand masks, desperate to discover who he was. "Yet I believe he always wanted to shatter that glass, because it also reminded him that he was only an image of a man. He had to either steal or destroy the icons of his father's heart, his own sister and brother. And in the end, he had to send his father Juan's amulet. Cain's final offering, after all the victories and conquests had failed to displace his dead brother in his father's heart, was the proof of his fratricide. As much as he needed the pope's power and treasury, Valentino had a greater necessity, perhaps even hidden from himself— to lead his father to Ravenna, as you said, to discover the fatal truth." I cast my eyes over the ghost city that appeared to smolder around me. "And now Valentino has arrived at his own dreadful truth. He could live only as his father's reflection. Without him, he is a shadow."

"He is still a dangerous shadow, Niccolò. He will regret letting Giovanni and me go. He will come after us."

"Yes. I fear so."

"I have prepared for that." Damiata put her hand on my arm, as if to comfort me. "You had to give him something, didn't you, Niccolò? In exchange for sparing Giovanni and me."

"His resurrection. He knows with all his animal instinct that Fortune has dealt him a fatal blow. If he did not know before tonight, he does now. But he believes I will become his apostle. I alone witnessed the *mappa* of his ambition and saw how far it extended." I sighed for the Italy I saw vanishing in smoke, an empire consumed before it ever existed. "And I do believe. Not in him, but in the Italy he created for me. My own empire of hope. In time, I believe I will find the wisdom and courage to describe it. To write those words on the blank parchment he presented me tonight."

Damiata clutched little Giovanni closer to her before she looked up, her eyes as brilliant as flashes of lightning on the horizon. "More than anything, the Devil requires that we believe in him. But that ensures your family will be safe. Regardless of what you decide."

I knew at once the choice she meant. I could see only her eyes, yet never had she been so naked before me, not even in the bed we had shared.

Her question was similarly unadorned and guileless: "Will you come with us?"

As often as I had dreamt it, I could not have imagined what it was like to truly hear those words. For the first time I was certain beyond any doubt that Damiata loved me as entirely as I loved her.

And I finally understood this: the only reason I had been unable to see the truth within my own soul was because I had not, until that moment, been able to see the truth in hers. At last, I knew myself. And I knew the answer I would give her.

As did she. She put her finger to my lips. "I know, Niccolò, I know. My darling, I have been places in your soul even you do not yet know. I have seen the man you will be, your profound kindness and deep intellect, your unending courage, the things you will do with your science of men . . . I have always known what your answer would be. But neither of us would ever know peace unless I had asked."

"I will never have peace," I said, hardly able to breathe, already adrift on an endless ocean of regret. "I can only hope that the children of Florence will know peace."

Damiata's eyes filled with tears, the perfect mirror of my own. She took my hands but did not embrace me. Yet somehow this clasp was more searing and intimate than our embrace on the hill above.

"My love, I once promised you I would see you again, and Fortune allowed me to keep that trust." She could not blink quickly enough to keep up with her tears. "But now I must promise you that I will never see you again, not in this life. I must live for my Giovanni, and you for your family and your republic. It is only our souls, which searched for each other all these years, that will never again be parted."

Here she heaved with a sob and I took her in my arms, although I knew I had also pushed the fatal spear through my heart. I drew in the scent of her hair as if I would never take another breath.

She clung to me as desperately as I clutched her. "Now you must go home, companion of my soul. Be happy with your life and remember your promise to me." Then she whispered the last words of a life that had to end. Yet through some numbness of the senses and the soul, I did not believe—or refused to believe—that I had heard them.

◆

Nothing in this life of mine has been more painful than standing beneath that ancient arch and letting Damiata go—not even hanging from a rope in the Stinche. When you are tortured, there is eventually a merciful numbness. You welcome your separation from the life you inhabit. At this parting, the very separation from that life—the life I so dearly wished to inhabit forever—was so excruciating I could not hope to survive it.

Yet Damiata herself left me the only possible remedy for my torment. Without looking back, she helped Giovanni onto the saddle in front of one of the riders, then mounted her own horse. The entire party slowly vanished into the mist, as if disappearing into time itself, the fading beat of hooves an echo of a lost empire, a memento of how, inevitably, everything human is reduced to dust and ruins.

Just when it seemed I would lose sight of her entirely, she turned. That was when I heard her final words, whispered within a mind that had mercifully spared them until that moment.

Remember me, my love, even when you reach the far bank of Lethe, even when I am once again only a vague presentiment in your soul. Because I promise you, my dearest, most darling Niccolò, I will find you in the next life.

CHAPTER 30

It is and always was and always will be, that evil follows good, good evil, and the one ever the cause of the other.

History will record that Julius II never appointed Duke Valentino his captain general; instead this warrior pope armored himself with steel rather than faith and led his own armies into the field. With a series of clever lies, Pope Julius contrived to have Valentino imprisoned, taking the maestro of deception entirely unawares. Like the *condottieri* whom he had outfoxed at Sinigaglia, Valentino could not believe that he would find another man's word as worthless as his own—particularly as the new pope was well-regarded for his honest dealing. But I believe that Pope Julius, having suffered so much from the sins of the father, understood Rodrigo Borgia's son as have few other men—and was wise enough not to allow him another opportunity to mirror all Italy's hopes.

Nevertheless, Valentino continued to battle Fortune for the rest of his life, making desperate attempts to escape his confinement and return to power. At last exiled to Spain, he reached the border fate had set for him three days before the Ides of March, *anno Domini* 1507, while employed on some minor errand for the King of Navarre. Although he was riding alone, Valentino attacked a party of three armored knights and their many footmen, taking dozens of wounds before he finally gave up his race against time and Fortune.

When considering Valentino's efforts to conquer *Fortuna*, one cannot but observe that the very defect of his soul offered him considerable advantage. To kill without hesitation or remorse, to deceive with a skill and ease born of a lifetime of practice, to observe humanity's hopes and fears with an unnatural keenness—these traits are marvelously suited to a man ambitious for high office and great power. Yet no matter how lofty this rare man's ascent, he remains enslaved by his own nature. Valentino possessed an intellect far superior to Nero, yet just as the latter was compelled to put on a wig and leave his Golden Palace at night, to risk his own life murdering and robbing his subjects like a gutter-dwelling cutthroat, Valentino condemned himself to live in a foul Labyrinth of deception and cruelty, which he could never escape.

Here it is fair to ask why, knowing Valentino's true nature as I did, I wrote in *The Prince*, "I do not see what better instruction I can give a new prince than the example of Duke Valentino's actions." I will not apologize for this judgment, but I will defend it, first noting that I composed my little pamphlet after we Florentines had lost our republic and our *libertas*, and, in fact, all Italy had become much as it remains today, prostrate before foreign monarchs and their armies—as Valentino himself warned. And because principalities and other petty fiefdoms now far outnumber republics in this Italy of ours, my intention was to write a short work on principalities only, without considering that a republic can secure the common good to much better effect than any prince or monarch, however accomplished; this I take up at much greater length in my *Discourses on the First Decade of Titus Livy*.

My object in *The Prince* was to show defeated Italy a model of her savior, a man as perfect in the bold acquisition of power as Michelangelo Buonarroti's great marble *David* is a perfect illustration of the human form and divine spirit. Just as Michelangelo did not portray David the murderer and adulterer, I did not represent the entirety of the man I took as my model. Instead, upon the blank page that Valentino presented all of us, I invented my own rare man: a leader of prodigious gifts, unerring judgment, fearless ambition, and profound insight into the ways of men. This Duke Valentino became my own artfully crafted deception, toward a good end: the salvation of Italy.

I am certain that Valentino himself foresaw this, when he made me his witness. He knew that I would hold my own mirror to his face, and transform him into a hero whose example would live long after his corrupt flesh and evil designs had gone to the Devil. In truth, over the years, I have come to believe that Valentino intended me to read his confession to the Duke of Gandia's murder, and it was for this reason that he summoned me to the pit. That page torn from a schoolboy's geometry, however fatal to his own ambitions, was for him a sacred scripture, his book of Genesis. In the beginning, he had not waited on either Fortune or his father, but alone had plotted the *mappa* of his fate.

Nevertheless I would be a hypocrite not to anticipate that the good intentions I brought to *The Prince* will also be the root of some other man's evil, if only because the way to the house of the Devil is the same for the good man and the bad—and the journey just as necessary for them both. The times change, but the nature of men does not. Such men as Valentino will only find our new age more favorable, and they will tell us that their evils are only necessities of the times. But they will linger in the house of the Devil, savor his vintage, and acquire a taste for it.

◆

Just before I left Rome, I received a large package from the Fugger Bank, containing the pages bundled here but no other word. I did not read them until I returned home, to sit in the library I had inherited from my father, that tiny room on the second floor of my house being the sanctuary most sacred to me. I can only say that my tears, like Damiata's, are still to be found on those pages. Her words revealed to my intellect what my soul already knew: she had been false only when the fate of her son was at stake. In all other matters, both of the heart and the mind, she had been entirely faithful to me.

In the same manner, Damiata kept her final promise; thereafter, I never saw or heard from her again. Even so, for years she stood at every street corner, glided across every *sala grande*, peered from windows in every city and town. I was certain I saw her at a performance of my *Mandrake* in Florence several years ago—although in my mind she has not aged as I have. Yet her Giovanni would now be—now is, I pray—nearly the same age I was when I fell in love with her.

But fleet time obscures nothing, only sharpening my memories. I keep my promise to Damiata every day, not just the one afternoon she was content to claim. Soon enough, I will look for her in the next life.

And in truth, she has never left me. Without her abiding presence in my soul, I might have become the Machiavelli of *The Prince*—I needed only Valentino to take me there—but never the Machiavelli of the *Discourses*, and certainly not the Niccolò of the *Mandrake* and the *Clizia*. Without her love, I never would have learned how to love Marietta. Damiata led me to the higher spheres, the brighter light, and showed me the great power of love over all else in this sad world—although I know that you and all my gossip-bench gang are weary of hearing that *canzone*.

So here I finish my account of those beautiful and terrifying deceptions that inspired—and became—*The Prince*. And I leave you with this one truth, which governs all the affairs of mankind: Although Valentino believed otherwise, there is no grand design that can defeat Fortune's eternal caprice. Only *Amor* can defeat *Fortuna*.

Only great love, as I was told in a lifetime so long ago, can journey beyond the shores of fate.

AUTHOR'S NOTE

Research for *The Malice of Fortune* began with the eight volumes of Niccolò Machiavelli's *Tutte le Opere*, or Complete Works (including fifty-two diplomatic dispatches from his mission to Duke Valentino), as well as hundreds of personal letters, a number of these referring in detail to his time in the Romagna and the dramatic denouement at Sinigaglia (now Senigallia). All of the major events in *The Malice of Fortune* are described in these letters and dispatches, which also offer considerable insight into the Florentine secretary's admiring but wary relationship with Valentino, his frustration with his own government, and his troubled marriage—as well as his repeated requests to colleagues in Florence for a copy of Plutarch's *Parallel Lives*.

Machiavelli's personal correspondence reveals a lifelong fascination with courtesans and actresses, and his sole vice seems to have been a succession of transporting love affairs he confessed to his friends with florid enthusiasm. His kindness to an abused mule is derived from one of the last letters he wrote, shortly before his death in 1527, when he advises his son Guido to treat a young mule that has "gone mad" from overwork by removing its bridle and halter and letting it go "wherever it wants in order to regain its own way of life."

The notion of Machiavelli as history's first forensic profiler is based on his unique approach to analyzing events and the men who shaped them, a method unprecedented in its psychological emphasis and penetration. Machiavelli described his technique for "querying" historical figures in a 1513 letter: "I enter the courts of the ancients where ... I am unashamed to converse with them and ask them the reasons for their actions, and they in their humanity answer me . . . I transport myself into them entirely."

Leonardo da Vinci left a similarly voluminous if considerably less organized record of his life, comprising thousands of notebook pages that were arbitrarily compiled into "codices" after his death. The eclectic clutter of his studio is attested by his own inventories; his *mappa* of Imola is presently in the collection of the Royal Library at Windsor Castle; and in the summer of 1502 he remarks in one of his notebooks that Vitellozzo Vitelli has promised him a treatise by Archimedes. Both Gian Giacomo Caprotti and Tommaso di Giovanni Masini are well-documented members of his household. All of the details of Leonardo's anatomical and scientific work, as well as his concepts and terminology, are derived directly from his notebooks. I have also made an original addition to Leonardo's biography, surmising that his dreadful fascination with vortexes began as a four-year-old, when he witnessed a two-mile-wide tornado that devastated a large area of his native Tuscany in August 1456. And, of course, I offer an explanation for one of the great mysteries of Leonardo's life: After decades of seeking a patron capable of realizing his visions, why did Leonardo abruptly leave Valentino's court at the pinnacle of the latter's ambition and power?

Damiata is mentioned in contemporary accounts as the mistress whom Juan Borgia, Duke of Gandia, set out to visit on the night he was murdered. "Madonna Damiata" was investigated as a suspect in the crime, but faded into obscurity as the pope's inquiries into his beloved son's assassination mysteriously came to an abrupt yet indeterminate conclusion. Her lively, erudite character is based on such famously learned courtesans as Veronica Franco and Tullia d'Aragona, as well as Pietro Aretino's *Dialogues*, a saucy skewering of Rome's early sixteenth-century courtesan culture.

Zeja Caterina is based on a Romagnole witch and healer named Diamantina, who was interrogated at great length by the Inquisition in 1603. Many of the details of Romagnole witchcraft or *stregoneria*, including the *Gevol int la carafa* and the use of a textbook as a "book of spells" to impress illiterate clients, are derived from the transcripts of this and other contemporaneous witch trials in the Romagna. The use of narcotic ointments to induce the witches' "night flight" or "goat ride" is referred to in numerous Renaissance-era sources—among them Giovanni Battista Porta's *Natural Magic*—along with specific formulas and detailed descriptions of the resulting hallucinations and motor impairment.

Valentino's character remains as enigmatic and challenging for the novelist as it was for his contemporaries, who had great difficulty reconciling his messianic leadership qualities with the sinister rumors of his private life. Crimes against women or lower-status men were seldom remarked upon by sixteenth-century observers, so we are mostly informed of Valentino's prominent male victims. Beginning with the death of his brother in 1497, he embarked on a personal killing spree that included at least a half-dozen other high-profile victims whose elaborately plotted murders far exceeded any practical necessity or political utility. Valentino enjoyed playing cat and mouse with his victims, sometimes sending them on carefully contrived errands or seeing that they were warned that their arrest was imminent, then waiting weeks or months before finally springing his trap. From the accounts we have of various executions, he preferred to visit the condemned for a valedictory interrogation, then withdraw to a concealed place and watch while Michelotto administered the garrote.

But in Valentino's case, female victims were also noted. He was widely believed to have kidnapped and raped two women of high social standing, crimes of which he was almost certainly guilty. The story that forty young women captured at Capua (where six thousand men, women, and children were massacred by Valentino's troops) were sent to Rome for his "pleasure" circulated throughout Europe; most subsequent historians have accepted these reports as at least plausible. The murders of the *streghe* in the Romagna are hardly the type of offense history would remember, but they are composited from characteristics of Cesare Borgia's documented crimes: a predilection for voyeurism, torture, dismemberment, sexual sadism, riddles, and geographic game-playing.

So, was the model for Machiavelli's *The Prince* a real-life, Renaissance-era Hannibal Lecter—an unusually high-functioning psychopathic serial killer? We will never have a definitive diagnosis of a man who died centuries before such terms entered clinical practice, forensic science, and the culture at large. But the traits that were most noticeable to Valentino's contemporaries are remarkably consistent with psychopathy as it is broadly understood today: an exceptionally persuasive and manipulative personality that masked an extreme emotional coldness; an absence of empathy and remorse; narcissism; inexplicable risk-taking; grandiose self-importance; a gift for mimicry; a sense of having been slighted in childhood; and in the end, a propensity to blame everyone else.

As today's mental health professionals continue to debate the symptoms, causes, and even nomenclature of psychopathy (the prosaic "antisocial personality disorder" is often favored by clinicians), the case of the recidivist criminal Jacopo—taken word for word from the renowned Florentine physician Antonio Benivieni's *The Hidden Causes of Disease*—offers an interesting historical footnote. Benivieni's belief that Jacopo's incorrigibility could be explained by a defective region of the brain he called "the seat of memory" is eerily echoed by recent research: psychopathy has been linked to deficiencies in an almond-size neural bundle known as the amygdala, which plays a key role in both fear responses and our memory of emotional events.

Regardless of Valentino's clinical condition, the most trenchant insight into his character is provided by the two men with whom he is inextricably linked in history: his father and patron, Pope Alexander VI, and the author of his immortality, Niccolò Machiavelli—both of whom regarded him with extraordinary wariness. Few decisions in history are more baffling than Pope Alexander's choice of Valentino's younger brother, the hapless Juan of Gandia, as the instrument of his prodigious worldly ambitions, while keeping one of history's most gifted and capable natural leaders sidelined as an inconsequential cardinal. Pope Alexander was far too shrewd a judge of men to have overlooked Valentino's exceptional abilities, without some profound fear—as was rumored among his contemporaries—of his eldest son's true nature.

Equally unaccountable, for generations of scholars, has been Machiavelli's marked ambivalence regarding Valentino, extolling him in *The Prince* but in other works excoriating him in the most damning terms. However, Valentino did not begin his transformation from Italy's savior into a proverbial villain until Machiavelli's close friend and correspondent, Francesco Guicciardini, began writing his classic *History of Italy* in 1537, ten years after Machiavelli's death. Guicciardini's denunciation of Duke Valentino is scathing, and he breaks with earlier chroniclers when he insists that Valentino murdered his brother. Subsequent historians followed Guicciardini's lead, and Valentino's deadly flaws have long colored interpretations of Machiavelli's intent in making him the exemplar of *The Prince*. "Machiavellian" came to describe and justify values and behavior that Niccolò spent his life fighting against—and today is arguably the most misunderstood and dangerously misused adjective in the popular lexicon.

If Machiavelli had not made Valentino the model for *The Prince*, however, it is unlikely he would have achieved his own immortality. Machiavelli's magnum opus, *Discourses on the First Decade of Titus Livy*, represented his true political philosophy: An ardent champion of the Florentine republic, Machiavelli preferred the imperfect wisdom of the people to the will of princes and passionately advocated representative government—a radical egalitarianism that would not become a potent political force until the American and French revolutions more than 250 years later. *The Prince* was, in effect, merely Machiavelli's plan B: what to do when political prudence has long been disregarded, chaos reigns, and the only choice is between effective or ineffective despotism.

But Machiavelli's Duke Valentino, with his deft propaganda, narcissistic personal cult, blitzkrieg-like military tactics, and administrative efficiency, wasn't simply the ideal prince for a sixteenth-century Italy that had spiraled into catastrophe. Valentino was the first modern leader, his conscience-free, lethal expedience providing a remarkably effective and enduring template for sociopaths seeking power in any time, place, or organization; the same amoral realpolitik that has guided mass-murdering dictators is now studied by corporate CEOs and marketed as career advice for middle-management schemers.

Fortune's final irony is that the uncertain world she still rules continues to struggle between Machiavelli's two competing visions. The democratic idealism of the *Discourses*, however, is remembered only by scholars, while *The Prince*, its harsh remedies penned on the eve of destruction—and a terrifying secret buried between its lines—has become both a literary icon and a perennial fixture of popular culture.

CITATIONS FOR CHAPTER EPIGRAPHS, PARTS TWO, THREE, AND FOUR

Chapters 1, 4, 9: Niccolò Machiavelli, *The Art of War*; chapter 2: Niccolò Machiavelli, *Tercets on Ingratitude*; chapters 3, 29: Niccolò Machiavelli, *History of Florence*; chapters 5, 7, 8, 10, 11, 13, 14, 16, 18, 26: Niccolò Machiavelli, *Discourses on the First Decade of Titus Livy*; chapters 6, 12: Niccolò Machiavelli, *The Mandrake*; chapter 15: Niccolò Machiavelli, Carnival song "By the Hermits"; chapters 17, 21, 23: Niccolò Machiavelli, *The Prince*; chapters 19, 27: Niccolò Machiavelli, *Tercets on Fortune*; chapters 20, 22, 30: Niccolò Machiavelli, *The (Golden) Ass*; chapter 24: Romagnole folk saying; chapter 25: Matthew 4:8; chapter 28: Niccolò Machiavelli, personal correspondence.

The following texts were consulted for the English translation of Machiavelli's writings and letters, for which the author alone assumes responsibility: *Machiavelli: The Chief Works and Others*, translated by Allan Gilbert, Durham and London, Duke University Press, 1989; *Machiavelli and His Friends: Their Personal Correspondence*, translated and edited by James B. Atkinson and David Sices, De Kalb, Northern Illinois University Press, 1996.